Béjart's Caravan

Béjart's Caravan

BONNIE STANARD

Cuidono • Brooklyn

ISBN: 978-1-944453-18-3
eISBN: 978-1-944453-19-0

Cover image: Sara Nalle

Cuidono Press
Brooklyn NY
www.cuidono.com

For

Cindy, Noemi, and Ellen

*I prefer an easy vice
to a tiresome virtue.*

— Molière. *Amphitryon,* Act I

☙ Scene 1 ❧
a religious experience

Argon strolled across the stage's creaking boards, strummed an interlude, and hacked up ill humors from his gullet. Gone, and he knew not why, was his rousing voice. Gone were the days when he bounded about the stage and sang jubilantly. He longed to recover the shouts of "bravissimo!" He bobbed and pranced with rhythm and gusto and attempted a ditty, but his gutless voice betrayed him and he plucked the lute.

Several actors had offered suggestions about how to improve his voice. Leon proposed that virginity was at the root of his problem. "Get your pincel out and put it to God's use with some wench. That will clear more than your voice." Leon's philandering was no more nor less than that of most people. However, the Church excommunicated actors, not because they were more promiscuous but they did not conceal it under a mantle of propriety.

Argon's bodily changes were bringing on hesitations. Unfamiliar urges came astride him in the dark of night. His thoughts veered into unknown territory. Nighttime moans from one or another caravan took on meaning. He became suspicious of his father's ill-defined absences. Because Argon had entered a period in which certitude had lost sway, Leon's advice gained leverage.

From the rabble of sheep herders, mongers, smiths, wrights, and servants in the courtyard came "Bravo!" "Salut!" Argon swallowed what felt like a wad of wool and attempted a verse of "Mary Mack."

Bickering voices arose from back of the crowd. "Imbécile!" A scuffle. Argon's voice fluttered. He thrummed his lute loudly. His mastery on the lute and costume trimmed in jewels and gold threads saved him from a hailstorm of rotten cabbages.

Behind a sheepskin screen, Béjart, primary shareholder of the Augusto Troupe, stood and brooded over the change in his son's performance. The principal roles were reserved for Béjart, but his authority did not derive from his appearance, which improved with rouge and powdered chalk, though his nose was still his nose. It was evident that Argon would surpass Béjart in appearance.

To wrest attention from the scuffle in the audience, Béjart sent to the stage the juggler. "Start with the knives," he said. Swiftly flying knives spun up in the air as the Troupe's musicians hammered the tabors. Gasps replaced grumbles.

Béjart gathered the musicians. "Heigh! Step lively!" He led them on to the stage. One player followed in the footsteps of the other, pounding out music with cymbals, lute, psaltery. The boisterous parade trailed off the stage and disbanded behind the sheepskins used as a curtain.

Because the final act foretold future attendance, Béjart motioned Isabelle to the stage. "Ducky, make the sap rise."

Isabelle, who was born with a need to make the sap rise, stepped forward wearing a white wig the size of a firkin and flourishing a plume of feathers. Her scarlet silk costume's tight square-necked bodice exalted her bosom.

Even disapproving Catholics paused in the courtyard to view her décolletage. The button maker swallowed his adam's apple. A wet nurse flaunted competing cleavage. Constant speculation about Isabelle's endowments, which she covertly encouraged, had circulated among the actors.

As she inhaled, her bosom swelled. She swallowed for control and with a virginal voice delivered lines of a bygone rhyme:

> *Oh, Johnny be fine and fair and wants me for to wed.*
> *And I would marry him but me father said…*

With contralto authority, she said:

> *I'm sorry to tell you daughter what your mother never knew,*
> *but Johnny is a son of mine and so is kin to you.*

Shouts of "Hist!" "Ifsoever!" "Marry!" drowned her voice. She stepped closer to the audience and the clamor died down. In a motherly tone, she said:

O daughter, your father sowed his wild oats,
but you need not fret.
Your father may be father to the lad but still,
he didn't sire you, so marry if you will.

Roars of laughter. "All hail! A verse for good King Louis!" Thunderous clapping. Coins pelted the stage — sous, groats, pfennigs. Béjart jumped on stage and joined Isabelle. They bowed to all sides.

Shouts rang out. "Heigh!" "Our king sires a kingdom!" "Huzzah! To the King's cock!"

King Louis's throng of legitimate and illegitimate offspring was becoming legendary. The Queen had just birthed a son. "A kingdom of heirs!" the villagers cried.

Two of the King's favorite mistresses had added five illegitimate progeny in the previous six years. "May his sons marry his daughters!" shouted paysans, who didn't care about the King's mistresses, though the name Louise de La Vallière was well known at Court. She gave the King a son in 1667 after a daughter in 1666. Another envy of many a courtesan was Madame de Montespan, who had birthed two illegitimate sons, one in 1669 and one in 1670.

"God bless the King's prick!"

"Boooo." Somebody bellowed. Somebody hissed and spat. "A pox on your oaths!" "Prithee, pity for the Queen!" The King and Queen Maria Theresa had just lost a five year-old daughter, known as La Petite Madame. This, following the death of their three-year-old son the previous July of a chest infection.

Ridicule was met with rebuke. A yell. A bawl. Loud voices wrangled in the courtyard with derision for the King, with adoration for the King. A scuffle broke out.

The actors sneaked away and returned to their caravans.

✳

Throughout the French provinces, acting companies such as the Augusto Troupe traveled from village to village in their colorful caravans and set up portable stages. Centuries earlier the Church introduced outdoor plays, intended to fan the flames of faith, but the flames had gone astray. Braggarts, liars, fools, and lovers became actors and joined to form companies. Some of these traveling thespians were so successful they made their way to the court of Louis XIV and royal patronage.

Béjart hoped their courtyard performances might impress some passing nobleman. He wrote scripts, groomed the Troupe and, as they traveled from village to village, perfected their shows. Molière had done much the same and look at him — now performing at the Palais Royal and paid a pension of 7000 livres by the King. It was a future Béjart dreamed of.

The following afternoon the actors staged a parade of musical mayhem: acrobatics, saucy skits, juggling feats. Argon's voice rallied, and as he strolled front stage singing "Make no mistake she's the one I'm going to take," his glance settled on a stranger in rough wool breeches and wearing a floppy hat with owl feathers. Argon had seen him in a previous audience in a previous town. The man affected a look of superior disinterest.

Among the rabble, the stranger's foothold was secure, though the boisterous peasants would not have guessed his noble lineage nor that the younger man at his side was his page. On this particular day, the stranger, who took pleasure in disguises, wore the clothes of his gamekeeper. The feathered hat was for notice, but not Argon's. He was trained to indifference as a way of life, but he was anything but disinterested. He awaited Isabelle.

Isabelle appeared center stage and intoned a verse about Tom: "My wits were lost when him I crossed." The onlooker with feathered hat caught her eye, and she flaunted her assets with more daring.

Rustics bellowed, "Hey nonny nonny!" From the audience a paper rose flitted to her feet. She bowed ever so low to pick it up. "Diddle li dil," somebody shouted. Those with a view of her intimate attributes sputtered, "Some plumpers! Heigh! Oyez!"

Isabelle planted the rose in her décolletage and sauntered off stage. Béjart leapt forward and loudly declaimed lines about a lusty blacksmith and a damsel in need of his iron or his hammer or both, a fabliau that risked excommunication if uttered in Paris. However, in the provinces where regulations varied locally the actors did not shy from obscenity if they could draw a laugh.

Upon his exit, Béjart crouched out of sight behind a rail of sheepskins where he watched the interludes. He twirled a stick between his fingers. When an actor spoke words he had written, he mouthed them at the same time. His words... he never tired of hearing them. There had been intoxicating moments when his body became spirit in words. It was then that his art became his god, that his belief in himself absolute.

When the final song ended, shouts rang out. The joyful roars of onlookers fed the knot of ambition in his belly.

The following afternoon the Troupe readied to perform *Les Propheties de Mirabelle*, Béjart's crowning achievement. It mattered little if Isabelle or Argon muddled the lines of a well-known satire or blundered the lyrics of a ballad as long as they amused the audience. Performances of burlesque had been known to deteriorate into mayhem, especially if fumes of wine befuddled their heads. However, exactitude and superior execution were required for *Mirabelle*.

Béjart drained a flagon of ale and sent Etienne, of uncertain age but the youngest of the Troupe, to the tavern for another. He was sweating under a wig worthy of the King. The church bell had just rung the hour and Leon, who played the part of a deceitful courtier who flattered Mirabelle, had not returned. Villagers, along with dogs, pigs, and goats, milled about the temporary stage in the square.

The actors were unrecognizable under their face paint, wigs, and costumes of brilliant colors. They waited behind the canvas screen, wordless. Béjart gulped ale, swore under his breath, and said, "Argon, search the caravans."

Leon had taken leave for the night. His extended absence strained Béjart's liberality, for members of the Troupe were allowed to come and go as long as they appeared for rehearsals and performances. Into the square hurried Leon, wearing a mask and wig and carrying a bottle of wine, which he gave to Béjart.

Béjart had begun writing *Mirabelle* as a farcical interlude in which a knave courted a vain countess too stupid to realize a hat made of a bird's nest made her look absurd. He added skits, the countess became Mirabelle, the skits became scenes, the scenes became a play.

Béjart bounded on stage and announced to the meandering villagers, "Here, now! A comedie worthy of the Court!" Musicians played dramatically. Isabelle strolled full front as Mirabelle, a snout affixed to her nose. Her chin, owing to thick wax, came to a point. Her face couldn't launch a barge. Nevertheless, Mirabelle thought men fell in love with her because of her beauty. The villagers laughed at Isabelle's bird-nest hairpiece. Hooted cheerfully when she exited.

The two courtiers, Argon and Leon, swept from stage left to right and recited their amour for Mirabelle while vying for her money. A dog hurtled through the crowd, growling. It charged on stage, lunged and nipped at the actors. Argon's high kicking dance merely intensified its onslaught. The mongrel chomped into his boot. There was no shaking it off. Leon pushed aside his trunk hose, pulled out his prick, and with the accuracy of King Louis's best archer, pissed on the dog, which exited the scene.

"Sacré Dieu!" said Béjart from behind the backdrop. Should he get Leon off the stage? He gazed anxiously about the villagers, pumping their arms like bellows and shouting, "What a wonder!" "Begad!" Which was met with hisses of "Ugsome!" "Brassy!" A couple of eggs landed on the stage.

Béjart said to Etienne, who could be spared since he was not yet an actor, "Go to the church and wait there until we fetch you. If some taleteller clambers up to the door, hasten and let me know." If the priest charged them with sacrilege, retreat to the next town was the only safe recourse. In the meantime, Isabelle stepped on stage, her hips and shoulders swaying.

Isabelle played Mirabelle with clever whimsy and haughty ignorance. Heights of pathetic lust. Flashes of duplicity. Even so Béjart struggled with the worm of resentment, for she dominated not just his stage but his script. She twisted to her own purpose words he had selected with great care. The script had endured alterations from the stage. If crowds whooped heartily, Béjart bowed to the will of the audience and re-wrote lines to incorporate what Isabelle improvised. Only to discover she changed them again. Or ignored the change.

The audience settled down. Leon, when he returned to the stage to play his part, was not met with potato peels or fish heads.

At the conclusion of the performance, Isabelle and Béjart bowed in every direction, and before they stepped off the platform the juggler, dressed in red and orange stripes, bumbled onstage and tottered down center. He walked on his hands and jiggled his toe bells as the musicians played *'Twas You Sir*. Laughter and shouts of "All hail!" "Yah!" when he bounded off stage. Since the youngest of the Troupe was watching the church, the actors circulated in the crowd with beakers, collecting coins.

As the peasants stirred and spread about, a captain smartly dressed in a uniform, a rondel at his waist, mounted the stage, followed by a soldier bearing the flag of the local chevalier. "Hear ye! Hear ye! Good people." His commanding voice dissipated into the noisy crowd. The soldier pounded a pike on the stage until the villagers paid attention. The captain said, "I bring you greetings from our noble lord, presently with the King in the low lands of Holland. Fighting to free us from the Dutch scourge."

Béjart grabbed Argon and gathered the other actors as the captain thundered: "They tax our traders and vex our farmers."

"Get thee from this menace and preserve yourself." Béjart knew the risk of a captain who had yet to muster the soldiers required by his knight. When he was but a youngster, he hid in a wagon of hay for two days to avoid being forcibly conscripted.

Mostly scrags, churls, and waifs paid attention as the captain offered money, wine with every meal, and women to warm their beds.

Etienne, relieved of church duty, hid behind a basket of barrel staves outside the cooper's shop and listened, twitching with ambition to get his hands on the advanced flintlock musket the captain displayed. Most of the actors slipped into a tavern and sat in a corner.

Béjart returned to the caravans where he found Isabelle. Leon's drunken display had been followed by her brazen mutilation of Mirabelle's lines. Leon could be required to pay a penalty for being drunk, but there was no penalty for scraping the lines. "A hell bound performance of paltry merit!"

"You mete out insults on what account?" she said.

"Name a scene! Name *one* in which you followed the lines as scripted!"

"Every word is not so precious as the sense." Isabelle spoke like a scholar coaching the tutor.

"The *sense* does not pass the cues to other actors on the stage!" Béjart said.

"What am I to do with a stale line like 'Who knows the difference between substance and shadow'?"

"*Stale* is an amateur's understanding of the line!"

"I followed my part until somebody threw a horse turd at me." She flicked the stiff silk of her billowing sleeve as if to loosen and dispatch some such residue.

"That was Argon. I told him to throw turds when you misspoke your lines."

Béjart had found dried turds effective in alerting onstage players to missed cues. It was usually Isabelle who trailed off script. Argon had apologized to his mother more than once.

"Did not the gallery approve? Did they not laugh and frolic?" Isabelle said.

"You are not the only actor on the stage!" Béjart bellowed.

"I am the only actor to save this comedy from becoming a tragedy!" And with that she demanded that he expand her role. Her willfulness submitted to no argument, except Béjart's reminder that he owned the major share of the Troupe and that her share was contingent on his.

The currents of anger drifted from them to nearby pigs, rousing them with ear-splitting squeals from their pits of filth.

Argon made busy feeding the horses and stayed as far removed from his parents as possible. This did not save him from his mother. She always found him afterward, wounded by his complicity in the horse turds, or whatever Béjart had done that caused her grief.

"I deserve so much more, least of all your regard," she said.

Had Argon not been accustomed to her many disguises he would have been distracted by the glaring rouge of her lips. "Béjart does his best to bring our show to a good end."

"Ha! Béjart couples his vice with many virtues to procure a good end for Béjart."

Argon was never sure where Isabelle's acting began and ended. "Where would Augusto Troupe be without him?" he said.

They both knew Béjart was the heart of the troupe. He organized their divertissements, recruited costumes from deceased lords, and secured venues. Because he knew which duke, count, or marquess controlled what territory, he gained permission from them for the Troupe to perform in the villages. At times, he inveigled invitations to entertain at chateaux.

"Do you not see?" she said. "He puts me nethermost to celebrate himself." The pearl finish in the white paint on her face radiated in the dying sun, but her kohl-colored eyes were shining even brighter. As a youngster Argon had asked why she turned her face into that of a stranger. She had replied, "I want to be a master of illusion."

Argon said, "I am only another member of Béjart's troupe withal. What can I say when the order is given?" It was not lack of courage that hindered his defending Isabelle, rather it was a sense of ambivalence toward her, which made him reticent, for she played the role of mother with less clarity than the roles she delivered on stage.

At this, the hair on her wig trembled. "I will not be treated like a bleating cheat! Not by you nor any of this piddling company." She grabbed him by the shoulders and gazed into his eyes. "You are my son. Give me due respect." Her bosom heaved so to test the fabric of her bodice.

With the touch of her hands Argon was befuddled by emotions he could not identify much less understand. Her aggressive vengeance repulsed him but he wanted to hug her, an embarrassing desire for a person of his age. His unrequited desire for her affection swept over him like a fault.

"I am sorry," he muttered, instinctively reaching for some tenderness from her.

※

As the actors supped on spitted fowl at the tavern, the torches gasped. A sudden flash of lightning. Thunder cracked like the whip of an angry god. Customers near the window slammed shut the shutters barely ahead of rain.

The rain poured down. They drank beer and played knuckle-bones with the paysans. Argon rubbed the shadowy hairs on his upper lip, a source of ridicule from fellow actors, and eyed a maiden who had entered when the rain started. Because the chairs were taken, she crowded together with others at the door. Her breasts throbbed, or perhaps it was his vision.

When the rain ceased, one after another actor asked about a bed for the night only to be taken aback by the fee. The innkeeper, crafty enough to benefit from the carnival atmosphere, overcharged for everything, including accommodations. The actors, most of whom could not afford the fare, were left to beseech a cot from the townspeople or withdraw to the caravans.

Isabelle and several of the actors left for the caravans. Béjart departed in the wake of a damsel flattered by his attentions.

No longer was Argon stalled in guesswork about his father's wenching inclination. He too was of an age to charm a female, though he was unsure of where it would lead. An urgent agitation propelled him to the maiden's side. She allowed him to look at her cleavage. He bought her ale. He touched her. By promising to mention her name in a ballad, he won lodgings at her house for the night. Florance was her name.

They started out the door. The flambeau he bought from the tavern keeper illuminated her prominent eyes and broken tooth, which moderated his enthusiasm for her plump bosoms.

Church bells tolled the ten o'clock hour. Their singular flame lit the slippery road. When the pavings gave way, they walked near doorways to avoid a filthy stream of detritus. Despite that, Argon's boots picked up muddy manure where pigs had wallowed. They passed cottages with hay dripping from attic bays. As they travelled further from the village center, the cottages became half timbered with cracked plaster walls and crooked chimneys. A dog growled in the shadows. Argon tensed, ready to use the flambeau as a weapon, but the dog merely growled.

The one-room cottage was basic even for Argon, but at least it had a roof and a promise of a mattress. The door slammed shut and he faced Florance's mother, who was bent to a spinning wheel. The pedal creaked. The wheel whirred. The spinster murmured mindlessly.

He outened his flambeau, which gave off a whorl of black smoke that dispelled the stench of moldy grain. In the shadowy candlelight, the room looked cozier, less forlorn.

Florance ignored her mother and lingered in the candlelight with Argon, gazing at him with a sensual look. A deep breath.

Argon, regretful of what he had gotten himself into, strolled to the corner of the room and a pile of straw. "Gramercy, this will make a fine bed."

Florance smiled mysteriously and touched his shoulder, stroked his arm. "A finer bed in the loft with me."

"Nay. My supper gnaws at my bowels." Argon sat on the straw. "Mayhap bad ale." He did not want to be in the room with her, much less in the loft. His manhood wilted at the thought of kissing a mouth with such teeth.

"I may be of service withal." She leaned to him and ran her fingers through his long hair.

That was not so repulsive, but he did not follow as she climbed a ladder to a sleeping quarter in the loft. "Give you good night," she said.

Argon dozed uneasily on the peaty hay. His legs itched with crawly creatures. By the light of the candle, the mother continued work at the spinning wheel. Her toneless voice, as she mumbled to herself, rustled peacefully like wind moving back and forth a leafy willow.

Little did Argon realize she was accounting to him the talents of her daughter, the main one being that the girl had the grip of a ropemaker and could squeeze the life from a cat. In the same toneless manner that put Argon to sleep, she said the girl scorned spinning, refused to tote water, and ate like an ox. The mother credited the girl with the talent to be the perfect leman for Argon. She would gladly give her to him.

Late in the night the mother took the candle and went to the loft. Darkness made bold a noisy mouse. The scratching of its claws turned to scurrying as something much heavier scuffled on the floor. A warm body nudged close to him. The savor of sweat accompanied the presence and persisted in his nose. In the bleary drift of lingering sleep, Argon felt a hand reach into his chausses and fondle his prick. Or was he dreaming? Whatever it was, whether a witch or a hobgoblin or demon, his crotch quickened at the touch.

The kneading fingers took control of his thoughts, his senses, his will, his ability to move. His blood rushed to the invading hands. Even the smell became desirable.

"Ohhh." The witch's magic channeled him toward heights he had never known. "Argh." An opening took him inside. Shook him bodily. Ousted the hay, the room, the cottage. He knew mastery, blind beauty, fleeting breath. He shuddered. He was in the presence of God. The power of the moment collapsed. Breath departed. The glory departed. He became what was left, depleted, soppy with sacred experience. A changed person. Melded with the saints. Sleepy.

He awoke, disembodied by darkness but aware of a smell. Arms and legs covered him. Hay in his clothes itched. The floor hatched splinters. A snort of old fish blew into his face. The dark that had sanctified his every compartment now had a stink. It scratched. It snored. It violated his memory of a divine happening. Had it happened? Or had he drunk too much ale? The paradise as he had experienced it defied explanation. He did not want the angel to have a broken tooth.

He untangled himself, groped himself to the door, slipped out of the room, and stealthily negotiated the street back to the caravans.

☙ Scene 2 ❧

deceived on all sides

For several days the Troupe performed in the village square. When witty ballads failed to draw jubilant noise, the players switched to bawdy ones. A hushed audience gave rise to more exaggerated efforts. Acrobatics with flaming batons. Backward somersaults. Knives. Frenzied dancing. Béjart judged the crowd's favor before chancing a farce—a cuckolded viscount or obnoxious baroness—or recitations about drunken maidens or gypsy lovers.

Interludes were opportunities for musical burlesque, though Béjart had suspended songs once played so beautifully by a violin player who had been dismissed for performing drunk and failing to pay the fines required by the Troupe's shareholders.

Of late, Béjart informed Argon that he was not to sing alone, but with another player. At a moment when Argon expected to grow in theatrical ability, his voice betrayed him despite vocal exercises.

Argon choked back memories of his younger voice, which had inspired a riot of adulation from audiences. His performances had brought in the greatest shower of coins of any in the Troupe. He clung to the expectation that one day he, like his father, would have the vocal authority to command attention from passersby and obedience from children. He approached his father in size, but his erratic voice waylaid the possibility of his taking important roles.

It was apparent to Béjart that Argon was no longer a child. His shoulders and physique were becoming manlike. His eyes, vivid brown and buoyed in exceptional white, communicated measured innocence and curiosity and attracted females of all ages. Should his voice regain its quality, Argon would soon be of an age to warrant a share in the Augusto company.

Notwithstanding a smaller audience for *Mirabelle*, Béjart demanded that his superior script be expertly performed on the chance that an aristocrat appear in the crowd. With the favor of a duke, even the Hôtel de Bourgogne was within his reach.

Béjart had no concerns about Isabelle's maquillage and costumes, but he carefully assessed that of the others. If anything was amiss, he either made or found whatever was needed — elevated boots, jewelry, crowns or cloaks, fake beards, wax adams apples, and warts. He was seldom satisfied until the actors were unrecognizable. "Illusions must not be spoiled!"

✳

"Your ladylove was dallying about at midday, looking for you." The meddlesome actor, name of Agnes, teased Argon as if he were a youngster.

When Agnes became the sixth shareholder in the company the

previous spring, her opinion of herself soared. Not all actors owned shares. Some contributed to the company for meals and a cot to sleep on.

"A beggar beseeching a sou," Argon said dismissively, but he had not forgotten Florance. Since he had not seen the creature who had, in the dark of the cottage, taken the spirit from his body and given him a piece of heaven, he convinced himself that he had been visited by an angel.

"She said she had a present for you. I showed her your wagon."

"My wagon! You would lead a thief to my gold purse?" He winced.

"You mean your silken purse tinted gold?"

"Fie! May pigs shit on your shoes!" Argon's words abused his delicate lips.

"Have ye now a treacherous tongue?" Agnes simpered even when imperious.

Argon took in a wisp of reason with a breath. "What of her aspect? Did she have curls?"

"You needs speak with a civil tongue to me." Agnes made busy picking nits from a wig spread across her lap.

Argon, who had learned from Béjart to feign subservience, said "I repent my words of haste. In truth, a strumpet troubles me with her attentions."

"She was exceedingly common in appearance, flat lips and poppy eyes. No Queen of Beauty. But not an evil wench." Agnes, who believed a person's soul resided in the black of their eyes, convinced herself that she could tell evil souls from good ones by looking deep into their eyes.

Argon had no doubt — his visitor was Florance. He told himself she was not the angel of his night. However, a worm of worry persisted. Was she going to make unwarranted claims of him?

"She said she will come until you pay her what you promised." Agnes sensed Argon's distress and covered a smile with her sleeve.

He gulped. What chance had his word against that of a village daughter? He shuddered. He would be married off to her posthaste.

That evening as the players ate supper at the tavern Argon approached Leon, who had retained a bed in an upper room. "I vow I promised her nothing." He pleaded with the actor to share his bed.

"Like any woman, she is a venomous serpent desirous of man's blood," said Leon, whose experience with his sister-in-law had given him reason for acrimony. He ate beef and marrow pie, which Argon envied as he took another bite of frumenty.

Though Argon nodded as if he agreed, a shot of guilt ached in his temples. He thought of his mother Isabelle. She was inscrutable and maybe she wanted Béjart's blood, but she was not a venomous serpent.

"And if you partake of her fruit, you will choose between a harness or hanging from a tree at the village gate while crows peck your pillicock." Leon handled a spoon and knife exceptionally well.

Argon put down his wedge of bread and picked up a spoon to dip his porridge. "She is but a spinster's daughter."

"Maidens hear not what you say but what they want to hear." Leon took pity on Argon and allowed him half his bed.

After supper, Argon followed the light of his candle as he climbed the tavern stairs with his blanket. At the proper room, he opened the door on five beds, most of them occupied but none by his fellow actors. He lay down on a nearby empty bed.

A nearby voice spoke above the guffaws coming from the tavern below.

"What's to do?" said Argon who thought the man spoke a foreign language.

After the words were repeated, Argon made out, "That be the heathen's bed."

He moved to the only other unoccupied bed. With a wood floor beneath his feet, protective walls, and a straw mattress, he felt safe and fell asleep despite the roaring downstairs and the galloping snore of one of his roommates. He was awakened by stumbling curses. "God's Wounds!" Somebody entered, followed by a smell more foul than a dead rat.

"Tell me again about the red men," said a voice from another bed.

"Leave him be," said another.

"They be barbarians. They put their dead peoples up on a sky hammock for the buzzards to pick at them."

"Shut up and go to sleep."

"Live in tents they call wigwams. Made out of bear skins and sticks."

"Just think of that. There be a land on the other side of the world."

"By cock, shut up!"

"Them red men hide in trees and be a white person pass, they jump down and chop open their head with a hatchet."

"By hell fire, if you don't shut up, I'm going to shut you up."

"You do not know hell fire till you been in country where there be nothing but woods crawling with red-skinned varmints."

A scuffle broke out. Somebody fell on Argon, who pushed him on the floor. The door hinges squeaked loudly followed by a whoosh. A scuttle of feet. Beds bumped the floor. Bodies thumped the walls. "Argh!" "Dunderhead!"

Candlelight appeared in the hallway outside the open door. A flurry of feet. The bustling quickly stilled as a taper lit the doorway. A bear of a man carried the candle in one hand and a mace in the other. All was quiet. Every person in a bed.

"By Saint George's pecker! What perturbs here?" The attender slammed the mace against the wall. His candle flame went wild. Not a sound from the beds. Flushing choleric humors with choice words, he shouted, "Another peep, and there be a hill of flesh out the window." He turned and left.

In the quiet that followed, a voice whispered, "You be as much a heathen as the red man."

"Words dropped like turds from a horse's arse."

"God's pity." "Go to sleep." "Quiet." "Bedded with …"

In the middle of night Argon was awakened by his bedmate Leon, who had, unbeknownst to Argon, come to bed. Leon twitched and choked out, "Ougg. Hell. Hummph. Be done."

Argon reached over and shook his shoulder. "Wake up. It is a nightmare. Wake!"

"Huh? Lo, she found me." Leon rolled to his back, pulled off one of his boots, and scratched the bottom of his foot.

"Who found you?" Argon lay against the wall, which kept him from falling to the floor.

"The giglot." He rubbed his foot. "She … she … gets in your … toes …"

"Put your shoe back on or another foot will be wearing it tomorrow," grumbled Argon.

"Made … a churl … of me." He moaned.

As Argon lay back and turned to his side, he measured the risk of losing Leon's shoe to the inconvenience of his putting it back on his foot. Thinking along those lines, he fell asleep.

Argon returned to the caravans the following morning and removed costumes from his trunk in case he needed a hiding place if Florance returned. "It is winded about that the priest said at morning mass, 'To give to actors is to sacrifice to demons,'" he said to Béjart. He did not admit to hiding outside the north door of the church and listening to the sermon.

"The priest has an unexhausted faculty of railing and slandering," said Béjart.

"Wherefore do priests get God on their side?" Argon had not questioned God before his encounter with an angel. The occasion of sex had had a dark and unraveling effect on him. He was becoming aware of the fictions in truth, the otherness in people, the limits of human experience.

"The Church says so. And God worked poor serfs to death to build churches where priests can turn wine into blood."

"Have you ever been in a church?"

"Nay. Actors are not allowed."

"What about the King's actors?"

"No. Not even Molière," said Béjart.

"But the King protects him," said Argon.

"The King could only save him from expulsion when the Archbishop called him 'a demon in human flesh.'" Béjart knew but didn't say that the Archbishop had forbade on pain of excommunication any performance of Moliere's *Tartuffe*.

"Did your father go to church?"

"My father was a gleeman."

From that, Argon understood that even his grandfather had not been inside a church.

"And your mother too?"

"My mother died in childbirth," Béjart said. "Guard my words well. Stay away from churches. Not a year agone, an actor near Sainte-Marie village showed himself in the churchyard during Sunday mass. They accused him of setting fire to the church's oak tree and held his bare legs over flames."

Because it was Sunday, the Troupe removed its stage props from the courtyard and suspended performances.

They stayed another three days in the village, during which Argon painted his face with thick maquillage and pasted on bushy eyebrows and a beard for fear of recognition by Florance. He chose the biggest hats. When she appeared in the audience, his voice took on a Spanish accent in a treble-tone. Double-treble if she stood near the stage.

At the end of the run, as the company packed their floorboards, frames, and canvases, Florance and her mother approached the caravans with the village priest. Argon, as luck would have it, was behind a nearby soap-boiler's shed taking a piss.

"A youth with lengthy dark hair, you say? An aquiline nose… cleft chin? Ave. There was such a one with our Troupe," Béjart said, recognizing a description of Argon.

"He seduced this fair maiden with promise of wedlock," said the priest, a slavishly obedient Catholic. Florance's lower lip rolled out.

"He was a worthless clod," murmured a nearby actor for benefit of the priest. Another hummed agreement, as if they condemned their fellow actor.

The mother said, "My poor Florance. She is too trusting."

"Wellaway, I doubt not your claim, but the young man you seek abandoned our Troupe yester night," said Béjart, who was taking measure of his son in light of this development. That the girl wore a rough linen smock and thick leather clogs bothered him more than her accusation.

The priest, who believed not a word Béjart said, turned to the girl. "Look about. Do you see him?"

She sniffled and gazed at each actor in turn, more desperate than her mother knew, for she had become aware of her gravidation, consequent to a passionate encounter with a passing peddler who left his seed and took the broach he had given her.

"Your actor opened his mouth and thrust out words to this poor maiden's misfortune." The priest put his arm on the girl's shoulder, for she had confessed her condition to him. "Look carefully."

Argon halted behind a caravan upon hearing the priest and ducked into Isabelle's wagon. His throat was constricted with guilt. Beyond the denials, he had to believe either that his angel had been Florance or that God had sent an angel to him in the darkness. He wanted to believe God had awakened him to the beauty of the power within his own body. But here was Florance. She looked bereft.

Had it been her? Had he mumbled a promise to her in his rapture? Poor Florance … was her situation his fault? He hardly believed his night in her house had produced such confusion for himself and consequences for her. Even if she had been his angel, there had to be some solution other than his living in Bourges with her the rest of his life.

Florance and her mother studied the face of one actor and then another, testing mustaches for roots.

"This is the disastrous effect of these entertainments," the priest said loudly enough to be heard by chance villagers, a charge of resentment in his voice. The priest had protested granting a license for Augusto Troupe to perform, but the town consuls had granted permission anyway.

Florance paused at Leon and smiled, brushed her hand to his white cheek and brought away white fingers. He recoiled and mended the track marks of her touch.

She grabbed his arm proper. "You reduce me to despair with your promise of love." She forced tears into her eyes which, as she thought of her predicament, turned to real tears.

The actor stepped back and bowed to the girl. "Your eyes deceive you, Mademoiselle. I seldom give myself to common embraces."

Argon's pangs of conscience lessened upon hearing Florance name Leon, who in this instance was guiltless. This cast a different light on her, for Florance was either blind or lying.

Others of the Augusto Troupe gathered nearer in sympathy for Leon. "He seeks uncommon favors," one whispered. Another whooped. "From uncommon maidens."

The priest, disgusted by the bullish asides, refused to be diverted from his goal, which was to save his congregation the embarrassment of another bastard birth. "Wherefore would this guileless maiden shame herself with a false claim?"

"My Lord, you well know this is no guileless maiden." Leon's words took on a tone of authority.

Though Argon had been moved by Florance's plight, he now came to the same conclusion as Leon.

The priest cleared his throat, giving himself time to think, for the girl was not of a favored family. At the same time, he did not see fit to allow the actor's suggestion go unchallenged, as if a Bourges demoiselle were not good enough for a mere actor. "I assure you, this maiden is present at Holy Mass every Sunday. Her prayers are heard. Her sins forgiven. It is her misfortune that the vice of an actor has lured her from a life of virtue."

The actors kept silent as the priest's accusation impugned all of them. Their popularity with audiences had earned them no favor from the Church.

Béjart came alongside them. "Seigneur, we are sinners all, are we not?" He dared not say that even the priest was capable of sin. "The Augusto Troupe praises God with our frolics and buffoonery. It is not our intent to lure good village folk to wrongdoing."

The priest hardly heard him. His thought was a prayer to Jesus, a plea for help to overcome the tremble in his voice, which he attributed to the presence of Satan.

Leon shifted his feet, more to form a physical bulwark. He was becoming the scapegoat. "Whether or not there be sin in theatrics, the villager is accountable for the sin they commit."

Florance's tear-stained eyes cast a pleading look on Leon, for she preferred him to Argon. Her mother, who knew this was not the young man they sought, did not intervene. Her hope was that her daughter might succeed in attaching herself to some man who would take her off her hands.

The priest, knowing his support from devout Catholics in the village, summoned his lung's capacity. "We will not have our purity poisoned by heretics." The threat he usually employed, of trial at the seigniorial court, was ill advised since actors disappeared as quickly as they appeared. Without the bailiff he could not hold the man prisoner. However, he had the power to brand the Troupe as dishonorable, a mark capable of ending permissions by village counsels throughout the domain.

"Prithee, my Lord, a moment for a prayer with me." Leon approached and brushed the priest's shoulder to motion him toward more privacy.

The priest, who did not countenance familiarity, pulled away. But as Leon strolled away from the group, the priest followed.

Leon leaned forward and looked at the ground, saying with a low voice, "The Church is no doubt aware of the good deeds of Duke Théodore of Bellay." He glanced up and into the watery gray eyes of the priest. "Before you file a complaint against me, inquire of the Duke his relation to Leonardo of Bellay."

"To what end?" The priest saw the steadfast depth of the actor's eyes and knew he was in the presence of a man of substance, an acquaintance of a duke, no less. Given this insight, he decided the girl likely had sought sexual favors of this person of means and was using the Church to seek financial advantage.

"To your own benefit." Leon swallowed and looked with an imperturbable manner back at the group of actors. He needed the priest's good favor, for he did not want his name or connections winded about.

The priest turned and paused a moment before going ahead of Leon to return to the group.

There was no satisfaction for Florance, her mother, or the priest, all of whom retreated to the church. Florance prayed for an onset of menses, the mother for a man to marry her daughter, and the priest for forceful homilies that would turn wenches from their tawdry ways.

☙ Scene 3 ❧
a story about a fart

Aside from the dray horses that pulled the caravans, there were three other horses. Two of them were communal property of the Troupe, the third was Leon's, who personally owned a stallion worthy of a nobleman.

One of the Troupe's horses was reserved to Béjart. Argon often rode the other because he was best at sitting the old saddle, which was frayed in more places than the cinch. However, on this occasion the juggler rode the horse, balanced on the saddle. When the horse went off its rocking-chair gait, he swayed, the saddle slipped, and the juggler landed on the ground. In the meantime, Argon hid in Béjart's caravan until they were well into the countryside.

They left behind the village of Bourges, which had rewarded them with bellowing roars and liberal coins. It was the time of year when the country was plentiful and full of fruits—grapes, figs, apples. The actors availed themselves of whatever bounty appeared in roadside fields. The wagons crunched into dirt, one trailing the other like lethargic ants. Theirs was a life of wandering not unlike that of gypsies, though villagers, limited as they were to occasional troubadours, credited actors with a measure of respect for bringing entertainment, something other than hangings, bear baiting, and brothels.

They approached a crossroad with no sign to tell them the direction to the village of Nevers, which was smaller than Bourges. Béjart consulted a map he'd bought from a scrivener, but it showed no crossroad at all. They stopped and rested the horses. A glorious sun was spun by the wind, which tittered in nearby alder trees. Even the flies were lazy.

A friar of long legs and buoyant step appeared, humming as he walked.

Béjart greeted him and pointed straight ahead. "My lord, does this road go to Nevers?"

"Ah, no, my good man. Take that road." His broken finger pointed to the ground but his arm stretched toward an opposing branch.

The actors stretched from blankets on the ground, returned to the wagons, and resumed their journey.

By midday they came upon a sign for the hamlet of Montrond. "Montrond!" said Béjart. "Crooked-nosed friar!"

Leon rode his horse up to Béjart. "We're headed south, away from Nevers," he said.

"Oui. I know."

Upon reaching a winter field, they began to turn the caravans around. Isabelle's, being the heaviest, bogged down in the soft embankment. Argon pulled on the horse's reins while the others tugged at the spokes of the wheels. "Heave ho!" They turned the wheels. "Gad!" They groaned, the horse snorted. The caravan bumped and rolled back into the road.

They retraced the route back to the crossroads. As the angle of shadows admitted to an eastward journey, it suggested they were headed in the right direction. Upon nearing a bridge, they departed the roadway and diverted onto a wagon path used to approach a brook, where they watered the horses.

Argon stooped on the bank and swirled his hand in water, soft like cold ashes. The current around his fingers pulsed in a rhythm he felt in his blood. He was hardly aware of a sense that his self-hood was one with the water, that it was abundant and full of life. Without effort, his hand swayed back and forth.

Eugene, known for his mysterious need of privacy, dipped a firkin into the stream and watched it fill with water. "By the rood! We wasted a morning on the wrong road."

"Another man of the Church. Sent to curse us." Isabelle, dabbed her neck with a wet cloth.

"Not a finger-width of truth in the cross he wore," said the juggler, who lay on his belly and gulped water, which settled the effects of too much wine taken the previous night.

"Might as well ask a frog for directions." The actor with swollen feet, name of Hubert, removed his boots with effort and waded in the stream. He hunched forward and drank from his cupped hand. What looked like a snuffbox floated by. "For God's pity!" He splashed backward barely avoiding a dunking.

Leon plowed into the creek after it. Argon sloshed faster and was able to reclaim it from the current. The box, with a locked lid, fit into the palm of his hand. He tugged the top but could not open it. Leon removed the dagger from his belt and cracked the seal. "For you." He offered the open box to Agnes, who took from it a lock of dark curls tied in a knot.

"By my faith, a remembrance of a death. Some ill spirit is afoot belike," said the actor with swollen feet.

Agnes shrieked and dropped the hair. It was taken by the current.

"Quick. Pick it up and put it back! The spirit of the dead will curse us." The actor with swollen feet reached for it but was too late.

"Nay, it is a relic. Mayhap a lock of Saint Genesius's hair, or that of a more godly saint," said Leon. The relics that he sold, bone fragments found in places as holy as a butcher's lane, gave evidence that he could be trusted to fabricate tales.

Isabelle said, "'Tis a dark knot. It means Agnes will be tied in a dark knot."

"Leon touched it first! Leon will be tied in a knot." Agnes's heart-shaped face was losing its color.

Leon laughed and said to Agnes, "I have a wood cross blessed by Saint Genesius. It will keep you safe from a spell, or my tongue be leaden."

"'Tis the last memory of one who died." The actor with swollen feet pulled forcibly getting his foot into his boot.

Béjart strolled back toward the wagons. "Let us be gone."

Everybody dismissed Leon's jest and forgot about it except Agnes, who bought one of his carved wood crosses.

Béjart rode ahead, leading the train of wagons. As the major owner among them, he tallied the money they took in at shows and divided it according to the shares. If money was needed for repairs or supplies, it was the responsibility of the owners to find it. One summer when they were in Flanders at a time when the King's soldiers invaded the Spanish Netherlands, a French regiment confiscated two of their horses. The Augusto owners had been forced to pawn their costumes to replace them.

Eventually fields of oats or barley turned to grape vineyards. Local lords had discovered wine to be more profitable than bread. The road was flinty and they went slowly and guarded against a lurch that might crack a wheel or lame a horse.

A mist lured day into evening and turned to drizzle. Rain spit in their eyes. Water trickled from their hoods onto their nose. The horses' hoofs squished in puddles. The road passed from forest land to field where oats dripped with pods ready for harvest. Béjart leaned from his horse and called to Isabelle, who was driving their caravan, "When we get to the field, pull aside."

Between the woods and field was a shrine the height of a peasant and as wide as a dovecote. Stone-built with an iron cross on the roof, the shrine sheltered a wood carving of a saint. Isabelle gave it wide berth as she urged the horse and caravan into the side of the field, as did the drivers following her.

They drew the wagons close together, parked, and tethered the horses to trees. One after another, the actors visited the shrine. In an ancient style, words were carved above the small arched opening. Such was the gloom, they conjectured one to another about the words until they figured them out. "Stand ye in a haunted place."

They clutched their hooded cloaks and scampered back to Béjart.

"Let us move from the shrine," said Agnes.

"What a mischance." "Hapless." Several actors mumbled.

Béjart said, "I have seen this before. 'Tis but an incantation against gypsies. Get yourselves in your caravans and out of this infernal weather."

Confined to their caravans, they ate bread and drank wine, and climbed into their cots. Sleep did not come easily. The horses were restless and snorted as if spirits were in the dark. Béjart turned over and instead of going outside to investigate, climbed into the cot with Isabelle. Warmed himself. Very warm.

Agnes squealed. "Ave! A demon! I am beset by a demon!"

Béjart threw on his cape and boots and charged outside. "What goes there?" In the thick, wet darkness Agnes plowed into him.

"Get into my caravan." Béjart's steps, slowed by mud-flagged boots, proceeded cautiously in the darkness toward Agnes's caravan. "This cursed weather…"

He bumped into Leon, who said, "Damnation! Has Agnes gone daff?"

Béjart pounded on the side of Argon's wagon. "Strike a light and open your gate." The flickering candle Argon held to his open gate threaded light through beads of drizzle, illuminating a tall, dark shadow.

"Pray, have mercy!" came an unknown voice.

Candles flickered to life inside other wagons.

"Who goes there?" said Béjart.

"Have pity on me, for God's sake!" said a voice in accented French.

"God rot it, man! What are you doing?" said Béjart.

"Be quick or your belly will feed the buzzards." Leon raised his broadsword.

"For God's sake. I am but a want-wit with no home. A wretch in the eyes of God and man."

"Who comes with you?" said Béjart.

"Pray, good sir, I am alone. Holy Mary is my only companion." His French blundered occasionally into Dutch.

"What do you want here?" Leon advanced on the creature, which withdrew beyond the cast of light.

His voice spoke with the heft of darkness. "In God's name, shelter for my sore body. A dry place to sit and rest."

"It is a ploy. Highwaymen will follow," Leon said to Béjart.

"Yea. He is a spotter," said Béjart.

The stranger's eyes gleamed in the shadows. "Nay, nay. What highwaymen will have designs in this plight?" He emerged into the light, a bearded face shrouded in a hood. His arms clutched his canvas to himself.

In the end, the actors took pity on the stranger and let him stay, but nobody agreed to his staying in their caravan. He borrowed a sheep canvas and made a bed under Béjart's wagon. Béjart settled back in his cot but slept lightly, conscious of the presence on the ground under him.

The sun arose through clear air and shone on bright, clean oat panicles, leafy beeches, and twining byrony. The Troupe built a desultory fire of wettish wood and boiled a pot of wheat porridge spiced with raisins Leon had won in a card game.

"I ask no charity." The stranger, wearing a hooded cape, rounded up porridge in his thin fingers. "My stories will captivate village folk."

"They needs draw a bucket of coins so much do you eat," said the juggler, who wasn't the only one to notice the stranger's appetite.

"Have you not noticed the rain has stopped?" said Isabelle, who wanted a better look at the stranger.

"When ye have no roof, a hood is a habit." The stranger pushed back the hood to reveal a head that would have looked natural had it been completely bald. But hair grew in patches where there were no scars.

"We have no need for a storyteller." Béjart stood and washed his bowl in a nearby pail and put it into the casket.

"Your voice is powerful enough but your words are strangled in too many languages," said Isabelle.

"Tell us a story," said Argon.

The stranger's severe gaze brightened. He shed his cloak. "I'll tell you about two girls by the name of Juliette and Ursula. They dwelt in Brilly, some people considered them silly, but they craved to go dancing."

He stood, tied his loose fitting chausses, and danced a jig about the grass, his wet shoes spraying those nearby.

He paused close to their faces. "They made much effort getting prettified. 'I have a powder,' said Juliette, 'that gives a lovely blush.'" He angled to Isabelle and tweaked her cheek. "It cost me three sou but wait till you see what it can do."

He reared back and clapped his hands, an amorous look to his face. "They set about preparing their toilette. With the powder in a plate, Juliette said, 'Now you see, you have to wet it. You need to piss on it to make a mixture.'"

An actor snickered. Another whooped. One hissed.

The stranger strutted. "'I will hold and aim the plate while you urinate.' Juliette held it neath Ursula who squatted ever so close and tried her most." He squatted as he spoke. "She went at it with might and main till from the strain she let out an enormous…" He let out a fart while in a squat. "Which scattered the powder away. Juliette cried, 'You blew my powder through and through. And this cost me three sou. Give it to me.'"

His voice, which had hit a falsetto, descended. "Of course Ursula didn't agree. 'You didn't hold the plate properly and it's your fault it's lost.'"

His voice changed as each girl spoke. "Juliette said, 'If you had said a fart was on the way, I'd have pulled the plate away. So the loss is your fault.'"

By this time, the stranger's enthusiasm and delivery had made the occasional foreign pronunciations hardly noticeable. He gripped his cinched waist, turned from one actor to another, and spoke as a lawyer might to a judge. "So speak your mind and say who should pay. The one who held the plate? Or the one who gave a fart? What do you say?"

Despite the applause, Béjart said, "Storytelling has gone out of date. People want hustle and bustle. Music, comedie."

"You are miserably behind-hand," said Isabelle.

"I can act as well. Try me. Just for one show." The stranger bowed to Béjart.

"Can you read?" said Isabelle.

"I have the memory of an elephant. Only read me a line and I can recite it," said the stranger.

"Wellaway, that tolls a dirge for an actor." Agnes didn't like the man's burn wounds. They reminded her of the fire that turned her mother into scorched meat. His smell bedeviled her with the memory of the stink of her mother's sick bed.

"I can perform a knack best as any juggler. Villagers are amazed when I cut a man's head off and mend it. I can do it. With a table and two men. And sheep's blood, lots …"

"You are a worthy man with a talent, but one we have no need for," said Béjart.

"He could sleep where Suzanne slept," Argon said, bringing up a name everybody wanted to forget, in particular Isabelle. The Troupe had at times added a giglot because of Béjart's infatuation, but none had been so ill prepared for the stage as Suzanne.

"Forbear your decision. Let me perform for one show. I will make a coin disappear. People will be amazed." He took a Spanish pistole and held it to the actors. "See this coin. I will make it disappear. I need but a bit of sticky wax."

"I have seen that before. Only a dimwit is fooled," said the juggler, who had done the trick himself. Just a matter of twisting the fist and sticking the coin on the back of the hand.

"Give him a chance," said Argon.

"Such as we gave Remy?" said Béjart.

The actors behaved as if they hadn't heard Béjart, for the memory of Remy was distressing. They ignored the stranger and washed their bowls, cleaned the pot, and put out the fire. Remy had a talent rarely found outside a papal choir. His high piercing voice had brought astonishment and tears. But he was a castrati, and rogues had menaced the Troupe and hounded him. Somebody threw him into a well where he died a slow death before they found him.

Béjart led the caravan back on to the road. When he discovered the storyteller walking behind them, he kicked his horse to a trot. The wagons quickened their pace. At noontide, the storyteller was no longer in sight. They stopped at a farmhouse, but only long enough to water the horses.

"The poor man has nowhere to go," Argon said to Béjart.

"We cannot take on every person who has no home." Without his long curly wig and wearing a baldur, Béjart's thick black eyebrows stood out menacingly.

"He is not every person. He is one person who needs help."

"There are many a person without a home. What about the beggars in the villages? Should we give them homes?"

"At least they can sleep in a stable. The man may die in the woods with no cover." Argon spoke quietly. He knew better than to openly challenge Béjart's decisions.

"Your mother had no home before I met her. She went to a nunnery. Let the man go to the church. What is it for if not to help?"

"Isabelle in a nunnery?" Argon found it hard to believe. "She hates priests."

"When you're at the mercy of somebody else, it is easier to hate them than to hate yourself for your miserable situation."

In the afternoon sun, the wagon wheels clicked and scraped in rhythm as the drivers nodded. One horse and then another gave off an occasional fluttering sigh. They passed a field of oats where reapers would have been working except for the recent rain. Like the farmers, the actors were at the mercy of the weather.

They stopped at another farmhouse. "You may water your animals, but I'll not accord you lodgings for the night. I have no place for such as you," said the farmer, though the moon had appeared in the sky.

The Troupe paused aside a pasture, thinking to stop for the night, but the sheep bleated long and loud. It was quieter further on at a field spotted with several sheaves of wheat the farmer had failed to gather before bad weather. They parked their wagons where the field met the forest.

The actors ate bread and cheese and apples they had taken from a roadside orchard and took to their cots. Hardly had they fallen asleep when a voice sprang from the forest. "Hail! Good fellows. By Saint Denis, the leaves and trees are black. A screeching owl is poised to pluck out my eyes. By all that you love best, might I make a bed on the ground under a wagon?"

Béjart awoke from a dream in which his father put fish into a pot on an open fire. He had not thought of his father in a long time. His father had been fishing with his grandfather. It was no dream that the youngster Béjart and his father had eaten fish his grandfather had caught. The dreamy presence of his father, so close in his sleep, disappeared in his wakefulness.

"Get thee hence!" Béjart called to the woods as he descended his steps. He walked around the caravans in utter darkness.

Agnes's voice quivered. "He is a sorcerer."

"By the saints! This is no sorcerer," said Béjart.

"Even the devils in Hell find lodgings. I am but an unlessoned actor. I would be your prentice," the storyteller called.

"By Saint Martin's maw, let us be in peace!" came Leon's voice from another caravan.

"Why treat me with ill will? What cost to you the ground under a wagon?" said the storyteller. As much as a safe place to sleep, he needed food and water, which he dared not mention.

"Crafty you be. You bring mean season to peaceful people." Béjart answered the storyteller. He stumbled into Leon in the dark. "We will never find him in the dark," he mumbled.

The stoyteller said, "You anoint my cup with a bitter taste." An owl's screech provoked a rustle amid low growing bushes.

"What ho!" said Argon, forewarning his presence. "He is but a lonely vagabond. He can sleep under my wagon."

"Fie! He will find me and petrify my tongue and steal my soul." Agnes was upon them. "I dare not go back to my cot." Her terror arose from a deep-seated fear that she owed the devil her soul for the way she had deserted her infirm mother.

"Your tongue would do well with less exercise," Argon said to Agnes.

"I need safekeeping!" Her voice climbed the scales toward hysteria.

"Calm yourself." Béjart had no need of two problems in one night.

"What is the harm of allowing him the benefit of our protection?" said Argon.

The voice descended on them from the woods. "My fate will be yours. You will find your unknown future in my bones."

"That is the curse of a demon!" squeaked Agnes. She grabbed Béjart arm.

Béjart, with Leon's agreement, said, "Leon will rest in your caravan the night." Because Agnes was less afraid of Leon than the devil, she was satisfied.

"Abed! We must be up and on our way at daybreak," said Béjart. The actors returned to their cots and pulled up their bed cloths.

The storyteller spoke in the darkness. "I will tell you something amazing. You've never heard the like of this."

A yip came from one of the caravans. Somebody coughed.

Béjart roused from a coddling languor. His breath turned shallow.

Argon whispered, "The storyteller is a desperate soul."

"I will disappear from here. From there. From ... But so will you." The storyteller's lonely voice, thick with sorrow, nasal and gruff, spread like a spirit among the wagons.

"Logger-headed clod!" The actors moaned. "Button-arse." They tossed and turned.

Agnes squealed. "I feel his breath on the canvas!"

"A pox upon thee! I am leaving forthwith!" Leon, in the other cot, searched for his boots in the dark.

Agnes snuffled a cry. "Have pity on me! My lips are wax-sealed! Never will you hear a whisper from me." She pleaded with him to stay in her caravan.

Leon fell back into the cot but kept his boots on. It was a night of unsound slumber. Only the juggler, who drank himself senseless, got any sleep. Least of all did the storyteller, who cowered under a bush and talked continually to calm his fear of the owl. Overcome by weariness and fatigue, he slept as peacefully as the angels before the sun rose.

When morning came, the actors hitched the horses and returned to the road. They stopped to break the fast of the night and ate rye bread. Otherwise they only paused to rest the horses. By sundown, they drew within sight of a city wall. Béjart blew his horn. Horses panted, lowered their heads, and plodded their hoofs. With night-fall upon them, they encamped outside Nevers and built a fire. After a supper of spitted squirrel, they took to their cots uneasily and lay abed expecting the voice of the storyteller, which did not come.

Argon knocked on the door of Béjart's caravan. "Mayhap the storyteller has met ill fortune."

"I must worry about getting through Nevers' gates and to the town center. I have no time to worry about a storyteller!" Béjart paused. He realized in Argon's innocent eyes a deep concern and pulled his son into the caravan. "What, prithee, would you do?"

"Let us search for him."

"All the way back to camp of yesternight?"

"What if a boar attacked him? What if he fell over a dead tree? What if robbers set upon him?"

"He knew the danger when he set out alone."

"Mayhap he had no choice."

"You do not know that. Take care that you do not endanger yourself looking to the safety of somebody else."

Argon returned to his caravan and lay abed, warm under woolen cloths. Such comfort was his while the storyteller trembled at some tree. Alone and vulnerable to danger. What was Argon's inconvenience to the value of another man's life? He roused himself and sat on the side of the cot.

Eugene, the actor who shared his caravan, spoke softly from the opposing cot, "What troubles you?"

"Go with me," said Argon.

"Where to?" The actor, four years older than Argon, was treated with partiality by Béjart.

"To find the storyteller."

"The time to find him has passed."

"What if he dies because we left him?" Argon put on his boots.

Eugene reached across the darkness, found Argon's knee, and patted it. "His life is not ours to give or take."

"I am going to search for him. I cannot sleep if he be dying."

"And where will you be the morrow? Dead? Your life lost to a vain effort?"

"No person should die alone in the woods."

"Aye. No person. Not even you." Eugene's cot rustled as he settled in.

Argon put on his boots and knocked at Isabelle's caravan door, the only door as such in the company.

Isabelle disliked knocks on her door. Especially when she was abed.

"Can you convince Béjart to look for the storyteller?" said Argon.

"Wherefore? The storyteller sleeps in some farmer's barn belike."

Argon paused. A knot loosened in his head. They had passed

fields. Which meant farmers. Which meant there were abodes, though they had not seen one.

A relief swept over him. He returned to his caravan and cot. But the darkness crawled with worms of discontent. He lay awake. There had been no farm house on the road. The storyteller's plea came late of night. Where was he to find shelter at that hour?

Argon's breath halted, slipped. It was giving him the message that the storyteller was dying. He had not spoken up against Béjart. He had not insisted they take the stranger with them. His cowardice was costing a man his life. His eyes stung. He swallowed. He prayed to God that the storyteller would forgive him.

☙ Scene 4 ❧
entering Nevers

Béjart rode through Nevers' massive wood gates at early light wearing the costume of a wealthy trader, a suit with doublet of maroon satin and velvet hose. No gold threaded cape or jeweled belt, nothing to suggest a thespian. Village consuls, who gave or denied licenses, answered to the local bishop on matters of morals. What bishops thought of the morals of actors was common knowledge.

He stood in a chamber above the printer's shop facing three serious men, tradesmen prominent in the village, and made promises — no vulgarity, no unsheathed swords or untrussed paps, no campfires, no fortune telling. He had bargained from village to parish to lord for whatever became his welfare as well as that of the Troupe and found it necessary to make boot-licking an art.

With the license in hand, he and the Troupe entered the village in a carelessly orchestrated parade, bordering on mayhem. The juggler, name of Samuel, dashed ahead alongside Etienne, and shouted, "Minstrels! Mirth! Music! Song!" Children screamed and pointed at their gold and red outfits. Leather workers, lively with the odoriferous smell of their trade, looked up from their vats. Wool merchants gaped at the lead caravan's red roof with varnished yellow lettering — "Augusto Troupe."

The juggler somersaulted from one stall to another. Juggled pebbles and stones and kissed a pig, was scolded by the pig. The youth performed wobbly cartwheels and chased urchins with a piercing chant.

The wagons squeaked in their hinges and joints. Dogs barked and leaped at the wheels. A sickly sheep stumbled into the cess trough in the road and a wagon rolled over it. Villagers dashed alongside and grabbed handbills. Children and chickens scattered, making way for the carnival of players who waved flags, beat the tabor, and trilled pipes.

"Gleemen! Come see!" Children streaked into and out of the alleys.

Idlers and workers congregated in doorways. "Ho! Music! Dancing!" Béjart shouted from horseback and threw a carved cross to onlookers. "Come see! Mystery! Thrills!"

They rumbled past wattle and daub huts, past thatched roofs where pigeons roosted; past dwellings of timber dried hard as stone, shutters askew, chimneys expelling a haze of smoke; past shops and cottages. Past the very steps of the church.

The entire village turned out, save local priests who did what they could to rescue parishioners led astray by actors. There had been a day when miracle plays glorified the church and swelled the hearts and souls of God-fearing people. But those days were gone, replaced by gaudy theatrics the church considered not just poor taste but sinful. Despite sermons denouncing them, itinerant shows continually increased in number. Some two hundred acting companies, among them the Augusto Troupe, were touring the provinces by the time the King was on his fifteenth mistress and siring a brood of illegitimate children.

At the town center the caravans halted. Béjart shouted, "Good people! Dazzling divertissements! Stunning acrobatics! Tomorrow. Here, in the square!" They posted handbills on the tavern, apothecary, fishmonger, everywhere. They tied pendent notices on dogs, pigs, and trees.

With permission of the consuls, they herded their wagons

together inside the wall near wood shelters where the sheep shearer and horseleech did business. Béjart hired an ostler to tend their animals and protect them from thieves.

It was late in the day and the Troupe gathered to descend on the tavern for a meal. Eugene, more guarded in his privacy than the others, was not to be found.

"He is in my caravan," said Béjart, who was aware of the actor's physical disorder and protected him.

"Why does he hide behind a lock?" said Agnes, living up to her reputation for being meddlesome.

"He is feeling a chill." Béjart stepped aside to avoid putrefied swill in the cobblestone street.

The group, noticeable in their brilliant costumes, passed gray, thatched houses, some of them surrounded by a ditch to keep in the family's animals, an ox or sheep.

"Will you make a wood door for my caravan?" said Agnes, who would have more than a gate. She followed Béjart, stepping around a pig rooting a moldy cat carcass.

"Wherefore do you need one?" said Béjart.

"Wherefore anybody?" Agnes scrambled to remain within earshot of Béjart.

"She needs privacy to rid her armpits of stench and hairs," Argon said to the other actors.

"Yes, 'tis a secret, the way Agnes primps her face," said Georgette, who shared a caravan with Hubert.

"No amount of tin glass can give her a chin," said Isabelle.

"Wind suckers! Jealous of comeliness that is not yours!" Agnes began to tell them of a lover who had adored the way her chin peaked with gentility, but they hastened to the tavern, blathering about ragout or swan pie, as if they could afford it. Her lover, that was the way she thought of him, had married the bishop's daughter. He disappeared from her life but his words remained with her. "So petite and perfect are your lips." These words came to her when she painted her lips.

At the tavern's ale-scented tables, they slurped greedily on mutton marrow bones, their first meal of the day. Raucous patrons squeezed together on benches, and when they could not find seats, sat on the cold hearth and grew noisy in their cups.

The owner approached Béjart's table. "Good man, I am well willing to pay for a rhyme to pacify the carousers."

Béjart pounced on the offer. He stood on a stool. "Kind sirs! Fate shines on you!" The actors clanged their tankards loudly. The rabble quieted. "This night we have here, in our very presence, an actor who defies expectation; she is the envy of Paris and London. I present to you the Grand Dame Isabelle!"

Isabelle, wearing her daytime wig (only colored glass jewels, no feathers) sashayed to the hearth twirling a lace ruffle, turned, and struck a pose. "Once a count called me *Mother Nobs*." She exploited her décolletage. The men gawked and hooted. She cut her eyes and perked up her nose. "I shall recite 'My Thing Is My Own.'"

> *A Master of Musick came with an intent,*
> *To give me a lesson on my instrument,*
> *I thank'd him for nothing, but bid him be gone,*
> *For my little fiddle will not be played on.*

The locals hurrayed and laughed as she delivered with innocent amusement more scurvy rhymes. She ended with lines common to troubadours.

> *God save thee, fair barley so good ale may flow*
> *We raise up our tankards and down it will go…*

"Fare-thee-anon." she smiled, bowing to the crowd. The applause was what Isabelle lived for. The noise carried to the nearby rectory where the village priest sat at table and gulped wine, the better to swallow his steak pie.

✳

The actors lingered at the tables in the noisy room where the smell of sweat overtook that of ale. A drizzle turned to mist, which scattered as fog, which became heavy and dripped, sprinkled, and for a moment swelled to a downpour. Several of them started a game of brelan. Locals joined the game, but none gambled to match Leon. Isabelle and the females retreated to an upstairs room, gossiped, and napped.

With a portion of the takings from Bourges, Béjart retrieved his horse and sloshed through muck to the saddler's shop. Even Argon, who sat best their worn saddle, had fallen from it when the cinch strap gave way.

The smell of the shop carried none of leather's history in solutions of urine and dung. Its scent, like tree bark, conveyed dignity whether or not the shopkeeper had any. Béjart hardly realized his affection for the smell, which was due to a memory of taking shelter with his father in a room of leather goods. It had been a cold room and they had huddled under stiff hides.

Béjart stepped around curls of leather strewn on the floor. Six new saddles and two used ones bestrode a rustic wood timber. He examined the leather, pinched the padding—wool in some, horse hair in others.

"Divers saddles for sale," said Béjart. In fact, so many he only inspected the new ones. He did not want to buy a stolen one.

"Aye, these ones for the cavalry." The saddler pointed to two of the better saddles.

"Mayhap I buy one of them."

"This is finest leather." He patted the polished cantle of a third saddle. "You shall have it good and cheap." His guttural French, difficult to understand, was caused more by teeth that stood somewhat out of their ranks rather than by the German language he had spoken as a child.

Béjart stroked the leather, but turned away from uneven stitches at the saddle-tree. Nearby was a saddle that turned out to be black under a layer of dust. Its pommel and channel were made of a single length of leather.

"Sire, how much this saddle?"

"Eight écus and two livres, so little for such a good saddle." He cupped his palm on the horn. "Made with finest cowhide from Holland."

"So much money. Not the best saddle," said Béjart, though he was thinking the opposite.

"Just two weeks agone a soldier offered twice that."

"Seven écus is a good price, that you know well!" said Béjart. It had a goodly fender, longer than most.

"Thick leather. It is well fitted. Here, look!" He rubbed his brown-stained finger across the seat. "I will abate nothing."

Béjart said the gullet was goat leather, not worth five. "Goat leather!" The saddle's lips sputtered. "Worth nine, or you take money from my purse." Béjart said the cantle wobbled, not worth eight. The saddler wiped brown spit from his lip. "Just look." He shook the cantle. "Worth eight."

"Seven écus and two livres and I give you my saddle. Neatly served and sound."

The saddler said, "That is evil-boden," but he accepted the offer.

When Béjart returned his horse to the village ostler, he dared not leave the fine new saddle with the ostler. He locked it in his caravan along with the others.

At the tavern, a fire had been started in the fireplace. Béjart sat near it and drank ale until his clothes felt warm, if not dry. The barmaid recognized in him a need for admiration. Her compliments warmed him while his ale warmed her. Their conceits enhanced their opinions, each of the other. In due time their mutual admiration led to the back stairway and a gangway to the adjacent building.

⑨ **Scene 5** ⑨

sweet bitterness

The following day, clouds remained, and the cobblestones of the village square were pitted with puddles. Nonetheless, the players unloaded hewn boards and rolls of backdrop canvas from their wagon. They hammered boards, raised a frame, and covered it with the canvas they had painted to look like the interior of a room, complete with a black chair, red fireplace, and blue mantel. Peasants, maids, and mongers came and went through the square. Some stopped and looked on while the actors laid boards for the stage floor.

A number of villagers stayed and others arrived for the afternoon performance despite the threat of rain. During the following two days of middling weather the Troupe turned ballads into skits and essayed songs Argon had stolen from other troupes. On Saturday the sun came out in such splendor that Béjart bought wine to celebrate. Isabelle took her cup to her caravan.

To prepare for their afternoon performance, she surveyed her chest of potions, pomatums, creams, vitriol oil, numerous paints, and mouches. She stared into her mirror. What she saw was a realization that her time for theatrics and beautifying by a mirror would not last forever. Her love of an audience's adulation was one thing, but she had begun to envy a life of greater comfort. Her musings were upset when Agnes plowed into the caravan.

Agnes glimpsed Isabelle's array of cosmetics. It was rumored that Isabelle's power to captivate audiences was owing to magic. "I need my feathers…"

"I'm preparing my maquillage!" Isabelle cried out in a voice that could be heard in nearby wagons. Members of the troupe had little privacy, except for the quiet actor and Isabelle, whose celebrity accorded her privileges.

"You have the feathers for my periwig," Agnes said as she looked at the open pot of glistening white paint and the swath of it on Isabelle's chin.

"That is the foulest lie. And it be told with paltry acting talent." Isabelle rarely borrowed anything from Agnes, certainly not her feathers.

"Where did you get your paint?" Agnes stuck her finger into the pot with a concoction of ceruse.

Isabelle slapped her hand. "Paint will not improve your performance." She had no intention of divulging the name of the hag who had made the potion for her. Isabelle believed the product had remarkable powers, though she would not admit this even to herself. In a day when magic was denounced by the church and witches were hanged, rumors could endanger a person's life.

"I have saved écus. I can pay," said Agnes, whose manner of acting attempted an imitation of Isabelle but fell so far short only she herself knew of her effort.

"I am no governess for the dullard. And your pretenses are tiresome. Be gone!"

"I seek to better my sophistication. My theater skills. Will you not give me some consolation?" Agnes whined and lowered her face.

"You have lofty ideas — expecting consolation for your insolence!" said Isabelle.

"You grieve me needlessly!" Agnes pouted dramatically and departed.

Isabelle returned to her task, and though she had the powdery complexion of her English mother, she slathered on white paste, producing an iridescent sheen. The makeup hid a pustule on her cheek but she applied a small mouche over it anyway. Dragon's blood gave flush to her cheeks and lips. Despite fashion's fervor for small, well-defined lips, she applied color to the full extent of hers. When she opened her mouth, she expected people to see as well as hear her. She attached greater importance to her maquillage of late because of a particular follower.

She knew it was no coincidence that the vain man of noble demeanor had appeared in more than one audience. He had worn ordinary clothes, uncommonly clean and without wear. Her intuition, that he was a man of status, had been proven true.

Before the age of twelve, she had learned that a woman's ambitions were conditional upon the passions of men. It was through this means she had managed to escape a convent and find a place in the traveling troupe.

The passions of men were extreme and two-sided like a coin. Either heaven or hell. The flip of the coin couldn't be controlled, but to do well, a woman had to. And how to accomplish that but by deceit? Deceit artfully and secretly employed.

She became aware of the danger inherent in men's passion when a fellow actor had been forced to leave France and change her name because of a rejected suitor's vengeance. The lesson therein, and one of the most important, was to restrain courtship to suggestive gestures ambiguous enough to give no grounds for provocation.

Even after years with Béjart, she did not take their relationship for granted. His infatuation for her had opened the door to the Troupe and her success on the stage kept his interest. She was unaware of it, but as her reputation spread and the Troupe prospered, Béjart was loath to see his popularity undermined by hers. He grew irritable toward her, in large measure because the Troupe needed her almost as much as him.

Isabelle adjusted a mouche on her cheek, attached another above her eyebrow, and applied eyeshadow. With a pointed brush, she painted a faint blue vein on her forehead. Pearl powder gave her breasts a metallic shine.

From a box inlaid with ivory she withdrew a letter and read it, as she had done numerous times. Her breath didn't quicken nor did her heartbeat thunder, but her imagination soared, for within her purview were the stages of Paris if not the splendor of the Court. Lord Dubois's lines exhilarated her: *The sight of you gives me transports of elation which I cannot control. You alone can captivate my heart, and I would that my actions assure you of this.*

Her reply had been written and re-written. Rather than tear the latest version into pieces as she had done with others, she folded it into her tightly strapped bodice.

The sunlight was never so bright as the glittering actors preparing for the show. When the church bells gonged the hour, excitement grew. Today was to be a performance of *Mirabelle*, which Béjart had described as "endless merriment worthy of the King." Sheep herders and plowmen shambled from fields into the square and jostled with villagers for position near the stage.

Throughout the summer the actors had polished their

performance of *Mirabelle* from one village to the next. Béjart had changed the script depending on how audiences responded. He adjusted scenes, lines, and actors, refining the comedie for a wealthier, more knowledgeable audience.

Isabelle had grown to resent her role as the unsightly countess, even though it was the major role in the play. An enormous nose and wax wattle at her neck limited her appeal. She played arrogance well, but the hideous appearance chafed.

She stepped on the stage and spoke her lines rapturously as she gazed about the spectators, looking for Lord Dubois. Many floppy hats and baldurs, but not one with the feathers she wanted to see.

Argon, playing a courtier infatuated with the countess's maid, bound on stage, swirling his brilliant gold cape. He glided from one side to the other, declaring his intention to challenge her other suitor to a duel. From practicing elocution, his voice had improved. He was on the verge of asking his father for a more prominent role.

He wore maroon pantaloons Hubert had fashioned from a cloak Leon had filched from a viscount while at a card game. As a rule, traveling actors were assumed to be of questionable moral rectitude, and the Augusto Troupe lived up to that presumption. Hubert's tailoring expertise managed to transform stolen cloaks into breeches, skirts into bodices, shawls into skirts. In such manner, the actors had managed to evade accusations of thievery and preserve a tolerable reputation.

Argon, the courtier, declaimed to the countess in a strained voice, "Earwitness! He will feel the prick of my sword!" Without warning, his lines came out throaty and hoarse.

"Such ill-brewed words, my lord," Isabelle, as the countess, replied. "The season of anger does you no goodwill. Be steady in bitter pains, even with the loss of love. Best to remember that we all have an ambition, a longing to see our heads filled with dew."

Isabelle had gone off-script, and Argon swirled back from front stage. Her speech made his lines seem idiotic, but he said them anyway. "No grave is too deep for his devious pursuit of my lady's love." His head itched under his wig.

"Mayhap you will live long enough to forgive me, for I weep for the sins I cannot resist."

Argon looked at Isabelle for a sign of what she was doing—of where her lines came from and where she was going. He was surprised to see tears in her eyes. He was speechless.

She took his hand. "The thing may be unseemly to you, but do allow that your lady's mind is bent to commit herself to greater skill and purpose." Isabelle's emotional distress quivered in her voice.

Argon stepped to the side of the stage and called loudly enough that the actors behind the canvas backdrop heard him. "Ah, my lady! What sweet bitterness is the remembrance of music," a line the actors used to signal the need for a rescue when the play had gone astray.

Béjart grabbed his lute and, playing a vigorous dance tune, bounded on stage. As he launched into a second song, Isabelle's voice pierced the notes with "Withal, noble sir, play yonder for the duke with a plumed hat!" The lines forced an exit upon Béjart, after which she resumed the expected script, saying lines Argon recognized.

After the show, Argon said to Isabelle, "You made me out a fool!"

"Nay, my son. 'Twere pity we could not have writ the words ourselves."

"Béjart saved us from an onslaught of cabbages and rotted onions."

She smiled, but her eyes were sad. "Mayhap you will remember my lines. Mayhap you will find them useful when passages be confusing."

"You have a choleric humour today," said Argon. Her explanation had him as confused as her improvised lines.

Béjart was less kind in his denunciation of Isabelle's performance, but plentiful drink had moderated his harshness. Fortunately for her, the tavern keeper had arrived early with a flagon of ale in appreciation for the Augusto Troupe's visit.

The players invaded the tavern for more drink than food as a farewell to Nevers. Béjart gained the attentions of a beautiful maiden, to the envy of every other yeoman. As long as he did not inspire a duel with the older man accompanying her, the actors paid them no heed. However, Isabelle and Argon both noticed Béjart's avidity for the young maiden. The truancy of the maiden did not accidentally coincide with that of Béjart. His philandering was no secret, but it was usually more discreet.

Men of substance had mistresses, so a wife such as Isabelle could hardly begrudge Béjart's affairs. She sipped wine, and with the gaiety of a skillful actor entertained several men who paid for her drinks and vittles. There had been moments when she considered adding poison to her husband's bowl of porridge, but her resentment had eased since her encounter with Lord Dubois. Following the show, his page had appeared and taken her letter.

Without title or peerage Isabelle could only challenge fate with her wiles, to which end she gauged how next to proceed in a way that promised the stars without evoking the deep and surrounding darkness.

Béjart took his pleasure with the maiden in his caravan on Isabelle's mattress. It was made of feathers, a concession he had made to please her after he had impregnated one of the players, who had been dismissed. That he vouchsafed his wife the luxury of a feather bed was a source of pride. The comfort it afforded was his as long as Isabelle was not about.

Béjart's love for Isabelle was pitted with envy of her ability to seduce an audience. The longer she played the role of Mirabelle, the more Béjart began to see in Isabelle traits of Mirabelle. Saw her as vain, arrogant, pretentious. He saw the ugly beak even after Isabelle removed it. She became less a temptress and more of a harpy. As their coupling became less frequent, his interest gravitated to other, more demure women, and on this particular night, the other woman had made him aware of what he missed in his wife.

❧ Scene 6 ❧
obvious hostility

The following morning, Béjart introduced the Nevers maiden as a new member of the Troupe. "Louise will cook and prompt and participate in ensembles until she is more practiced on the stage."

"The height of the season has passed," Isabelle said. "Why engage another actor now?"

Louise, who stood beside Béjart, did not smile, nor did she invite social exchange.

"The crowds get thin as the weather gets colder," said Agnes.

"Fewer coins in the pot," said Georgette, mother of the youngster Etienne.

"And we must divide less money more ways?" said the juggler.

"What? Shareholder? Are you proposing a vote to make her a shareholder?" said Leon.

"Nay. You misconstrue. She will attach as a nethermost member," said Béjart. "Withal, Louise has a spark of cheer to attract lecherous old farts when we're installed in a chateau."

Isabelle felt the sting of insult. "Do I not add a spark of cheer?"

"Two sparks are better than one," said Leon, not that he liked Louise, but he had good business intuition.

"Agnes, she will share your wagon," Béjart said with a tone of finality.

"Wheresoever will I sleep?" said Etienne, who had been sleeping in Agnes's caravan since the storyteller's visitation.

"We will find a place for you," said Béjart.

The men readily acceded. The women sniveled under their breath. "Faugh." "Putain." Isabelle could be heard clearly, "No thanks for short courtesy. What Béjart needs the Troupe needs."

The Troupe took counsel from past experience. Such as Louise usually lasted as long as Béjart's interest.

Louise accepted the obvious hostility. Her gratitude to Béjart was unlimited. He was her chance to change her life, the promise of better times. The stage was a frightening prospect, but she was eager to learn and prove her ability.

While the actors packed the caravans, Béjart made ready to travel ahead to the village of Auxerre where he expected to secure permission for the Troupe to perform.

"How long will you be gone?" Louise spoke evenly as if no wounds had been made by the attitude of the Troupe toward her.

Béjart, well aware of the animosity toward Louise, said, "Do not be discouraged. Actors have big heads and little hearts." He belted on the new saddle. The gullet fit well on the withers, not too wide nor too narrow. "Do whatever Hubert asks and ignore the rest." Into one of the panniers attached behind the saddle he put his periwig of thickly curled black hair. Into the other he placed his waistcoat of red velvet and a lace collar with a tasseled closing. Quality clothes, the better to influence members of town council.

Argon approached. "Perchance I can go with you?" He had attained the height of a man but did not yet command respect as an adult. Louise stood apart and awaited Béjart's departure with trepidation, unsure of the situation she would face once alone with the actors.

"You needs be here with Hubert. Learn from him. It will not be long until you will take his place and be in charge when I am away."

"Am I not old enough to learn ways to win the favor of village councilors?" said Argon.

"More important now is that you look to the security of the actors and our equipment."

Béjart glanced from Argon to Louise. He did not advise his son to safeguard Louise, for Argon was closer in age to Louise than he. He hesitated with a thought of taking Argon with him but the thought passed. "It is hard enough for a person of my countenance to get the ear of authority. When you have the voice of a man, I will listen to what you have to say."

"I might ride with you and, like a shadow, witness the council chambers."

"Young gallants have no place in village councils."

"Staying here, I have nothing to do."

"You will lend authority to Hubert. He is of an age to benefit from your help."

Argon knew further arguments were futile but couldn't help feeling rejected. He turned and walked away, his shoulders slumped. "Authority, what authority?"

Béjart gazed at his departing son. Louise approached and nuzzled into his arms. He embraced her and gave her a kiss that erased concern for Argon. Her spirited body and gentle sigh heightened his regret at leaving. At the same time, he had timed this well. If she was still there when he returned, she had the mettle to survive Isabelle.

Béjart set off, secure in the new saddle and animated by his new paramour. The stone road wound through glade and field. Occasional peasants enlivened the route, affording an opportunity for banter or questions.

Though some town officials eagerly granted permission to the Troupe, others had to be cajoled. He knew not what to expect at Auxerre, whether he would be denied audience or put off or interrogated or required to sign documents. On occasion, it had been necessary to promise that the actors would avoid scandal. He had been "encouraged" to donate to the local church. For official benefit, he carried with him a list of plays to be performed, giving a proper title to each burlesque and comicality.

Auxerre was his immediate destination, but with winter coming on, he also needed to seek out and solicit the favor of a wealthy patron to provide the Troupe with lodgings and fare. Some traveling troupes were forced to disband when the weather grew cold and the outdoor season ended. The more successful ones, such as the Augusto Troupe, became personal entertainers of noblemen in exchange for winter quarters.

Just as important to Béjart as their winter lodgings in a chateau was the opportunity to perform before a cultured audience. Aristocrats and their guests had connections to Paris and by extension, the Palais Royale or Hôtel de Bourgogne. More than village peasants, they had the refinement to recognize in *Mirabelle* the intrigue, betrayal, and lust of a plot as spellbinding as those of Molière. The vain countess, her avaricious protégée, and diabolical lovers were characters just as exciting as any presented to the King.

After Béjart left on horseback for Auxerre, the train of caravans trailed over the stone-paved road. Though the night had been a cold reminder that the season was changing, it became a memory in the bright morning sun. The Troupe passed fields with sheaves of wheat waiting to be hauled to storage. Carts pulled by oxen and loaded with grain clattered by. Like a rolling sea were the hills, sometimes bare, more often wearing a crown of trees. On long rising slopes, the wagon hinges could be heard grating, the horses blowing.

Isabelle sat beside Eugene, who was driving her caravan. He could play the lute with such emotion it cast a wistfulness upon even the simplest of tunes.

Eugene had refused to drive but Isabelle cajoled and threatened and said, "Truly, you will have privacy as you like. If need be, you can rest in the caravan and I will drive." So he relented.

According to the priest who had been his guardian, Eugene had nothing to fear from the visitations. The spirit that shook him was the Angel of Imperfections, sent by God. Eugene had been chosen by God to be an example to others. He must be brave. Treat others with kindness. Make music to cheer the heart.

A wheel suddenly sank into a crater. Isabelle said, "Mon Dieu! Prithee, do not break my vials and dislodge my mattress!"

Eugene apologized and slapped the lines on the horse's rump. Though aware of her annoyance, he did not know the reason and blamed himself.

Isabelle paid little attention to him as she simmered with resentment. She had asked Argon to drive her wagon, only to discover he had already agreed to drive for Louise.

"Where is your mother?" Isabelle said to Eugene.

"I do not have a mother." Eugene did not volunteer the memory that came to him of a friar saying a prayer over a hemp cloth. He remembered his mother as the cloth but could not remember the face covered by it.

He had found a way to perform without being on stage. He crouched behind the sheepskin screen and accompanied the other musicians. When he played the shawm or lute, audiences applauded the actors on stage, but both he and the actors knew the acclaim was as much for his ability as theirs.

"Did she abandon you?"

Eugene shifted on the wagon's wood bench. "No."

"A mother might have reasons to quit a family." She looked at him for a sign he had accepted what she had put forward. Though she had no idea where her communications with Lord Dubois would lead, his latest letter had suggested that his carriage meet her after a show in Auxerre. At last Paris was within her reach if she gained favor with Lord Dubois. But to get to Paris she would have to leave the Troupe and most distressingly, Argon.

☙ Scene 7 ❧
three drops in a glass of wine

The caravans encamped for the night in a meadow where fresh cut grain perfumed the air. Isabelle, setting in motion a plan to captivate the ardor of Lord Dubois, feigned stomach pains. As the actors sat around a fire kindled by straw from a haycock, she complained aloud of feelings of suffocation, commonly known to indicate a roaming womb. "There is a wise woman hereabouts known for her powerful elixirs," said Isabelle by way of announcing her intention to seek the woman.

In the early morning, she enrolled Argon to hitch a horse to the canvas-covered caravan rather than her own, which was wood-covered and slower.

Hubert, who limped from swollen feet, drew near Argon and asked with acidic precision, "What business is this, hitching up the horse?"

"Isabelle is going to visit a healer for her stomach." Argon buckled the headpiece on the horse.

"Then she should take the wagon instead of one of the caravans."

Isabelle approached them, skirts sweeping the ground. "The healer's cottage is twenty leagues distant."

"Then you should betake yourself to the apothecary at Moneteau."

Her posture stiffened. "A stranger of no known ability? In troth, I will be attended by a healer of my own choosing."

"Madame, are you saying that you, rather than myself, are in charge of this company in the absence of Béjart?" Hubert elevated his voice to match that of Isabelle.

"Are you suggesting that you have authority over the care and healing of my body?" Isabelle looked at Argon. "Argon, would Béjart turn a deaf ear to what I require?"

Argon pulled the lines through a ring on the head piece and spat on the ground as if the question gave him a bad taste. It was unlikely that Béjart would easily acquiesce to Isabelle's demand, but on the other hand, Isabelle was likely to prevail. "Might as well let her go, Hubert."

Isabelle required a fellow traveler to protect her from thugs and thieves. Hubert, because of his maturity, was best suited for the role, but for obvious reasons he was not considered. Leon was a hardy garçon, but he laughed at abusive jokes and repeated them as though they were not insulting to Isabelle. He had a darkness she didn't trust. Etienne was out of the question, too young. She didn't want Argon to know of her undertaking. The juggler was of such slender physique he needed protection himself. She wrangled to get Eugene to accompany her.

They left in traces of morning light and reached the hut of the old woman by early afternoon. Eugene stayed with the caravan while Isabelle approached the door and called out "Madame Maud Fras." When nobody answered, she slid inside the sod and timbers building. The ceiling was so low she stooped to keep her hair out of the thatch. The sound of Eugene testing the strings of his lute drifted away as she entered. Light from the fireplace hardly reached the door, and Isabelle stumbled into a table, quickly catching a vial of sticky red liquid before it fell.

The healer, sitting near the fire, looked up. A scornful look turned to radiance as she said, "Ma chère dame, I was expecting you." The distant tones of the lute accompanying Isabelle into the room was reason enough to assume the guest had the fortune to engage a personal musician.

From the greeting, Isabelle took it that Madame Maud Fras had foreseen her mission. Something brushed her face. Hanging from the roof timbers were sprigs of dried plants. Isabelle had never seen a white bird with such black eyes as gazed at her from its perch. Even though it was in a cage with wood-carved roses, it was still in a cage.

No apothecary had such varied vials as the shelves on the far wall. A moment of envy passed. Odd shaped bottles contained demonic colored solutions. Perhaps Italian or Spanish. Above the fireplace beakers on a shelf were emitting a fine trail of vapor. She did not know it, but these were filled with cloudy white wine and had been steeping for weeks with cinnamon sticks, rhubarb root, vanilla pods, and mandrake root.

At Madame's invitation, Isabelle sat on a stool near the fire and took the offered wine, not knowing that a pinch of black mandrake had been added. Its easeful influence never failed to give those who drank it a veneration for the provider. From outside Eugene played various melodies on the lute, perfecting folk ditties.

Madame Maud Fras's eyes sparkled. She pulled a scarf with gold threads over her shoulders. Though her skin was wrinkled, the fine cheekbones and a delicate chin attested to a once beautiful face.

Isabelle described Lord Dubois and his interest in her as a

paramour and her interest in enhancing his interest. Madame nodded and made soft murmurs like the sounding of a dove at sundown. The white bird in the cage chirped. It shrieked, bubbled, screeched. Isabelle realized the bird was speaking to her. Something about a cage. Its cage. Her cage. A bitter cage.

"Do you require an oil to pleasure the skin or a potion for his wine?" Madame said.

"Something to add pleasure to the tongue," Isabelle said, feeling pleasure in her tongue. The dark room flickered with flames playing in the fireplace. A wisp of white smoke curled out of the fire and filled the room with an exotic scent that overwhelmed her.

Maud Fras took a jar in hand, uncorked it, and sniffed. It contained a mandrake concoction condensed from the wine-filled beakers. As she was measuring the thick liquid into a vial, she paused and listened and could hardly believe she heard "The Cambric Shirt."

Eugene's nimble fingers played the tune with expert skill. The melody brought to Maud Fras's mind a duke who had loved her with more than passion. He had been killed by thieves on his way to her door. Thieves, so it had been said. But she knew he had been set upon by thugs hired by his wife. She added creamy mandrake to the vial.

The song made the presence of her lost lover so real she sniffed a small pouch of amber powder to regain spiritual balance. With unsteady hands, she added another portion of mandrake without realizing she had already added the proper amount. Stirred in a bit of St. John's wort, a tipple of bat's blood.

Eugene, who had gone from practicing well-known ballads to inventing new ones, grew restless. He knocked at the door. He was hungry and there remained no more bread.

Madame Maud Fras picked up a loaf and a flacon of wine and opened the door. "Ave, jeune homme. You must be hungry."

"Well met, mistress. Pray, fetch my lady," he said, eagerly accepting the bread and wine. He looked past her into the room but it was so dark he did not see Isabelle.

"Yea. Make ready, for she will leave forthwith." She closed the door and roused Isabelle, who, under the influence of enhanced wine, was dreamily watching the caged bird.

She handed the vial to Isabelle. "Only two or three drops in a glass of wine, ma chère dame." She wiped her hands on her apron. "Love is a treacherous business, capable of as much danger as delight. Be wary of a man you have left unsatisfied."

"I know of men and their dissatisfactions," said Isabelle.

She departed the hut with the small vial safely tucked into her girdle. Its presence in her clothing imparted a sense of conquest. She was confident of having sway over Lord Dubois. An enigmatic smile took hold of her lips.

On joining Eugene at the caravan, she realized a great affection for the young man. He clicked his tongue and woke up the horse. "It will be dark ere we get back to the Troupe," he said. Night heightened danger, not just from highwaymen and wild animals. Unpredictable craters had lamed many a horse and broken wheels.

Isabelle retrieved a torch from the rear and lit it at Madame Maud Fras's fire. Eugene guided the horse into ruts leading back to the public road. A cold wind from the east rattled the canvas cover. Eugene said naught, but he wished for a hostelry with a good meal and a big fire. He slowed as they neared a monastery, a place where many a traveler found a night's rest.

Isabelle hated priests and by extension, monasteries. She was unable to erase a memory from her childhood of a priest who wore no garments under his tunic. She had been naive, had rubbed his wand with magic oil. He said it was the "milk of kindness."

"A pox upon them!" she said as they passed the turn-off from the public road to the monastery gate. "Be quick. We are within reach of gallous priests."

Eugene stood in the caravan, slapped the lines on the horse's haunches, and clucked loudly, for light was draining from the sky. The horse stepped lively and hastened forward. At times the road was rocky. At times pitted with stones. The sun was setting behind fields divided into long strips alternating sprouts of a fall crop with nub reminders of harvested grain.

When night descended, Eugene tightened the lines and pulled the horse to a stop. "I will ride atop the horse and hold the torch."

"That's unseemlie. Faith! The horse is not so blind!" said Isabelle, but Eugene was already climbing over the horse's flank.

"Hand me the torch," he said.

The two of them found the Troupe had moved ahead and camped in a layby near a stream. There was hardly a morsel left from a supper the actors had cooked over an open fire. Isabelle shared with Eugene her flagon of wine, a nostrum which made it easier to sleep despite a clawing hunger. The following day the Augusto Troupe continued their journey, passing with care the forest signposted "We firebrand poachers."

For the benefit of others more than Leon, the experienced hunter, Hubert said, "Dare not nab a rabbit hereabouts."

"Some grandee curdled with fat would starve the rest of us," said Agnes.

꩜ Scene 8 ꩜
smell-tainted room

Béjart regretted not stopping at a farmer's maison as the road grew long and his leather waterskin empty. By the time he reached a stream, the moon was high in the sky. He slept nearby couched in sheepskin and soothed by the trickle and glide of water current going downstream.

The village of Auxerre was populated by former villeins attached to the chateau of a lord who retained Huguenot sympathies. He had a major influence in the village's affairs, to the Church's disadvantage. Béjart easily gained the jurat's approval for the Troupe to perform.

At the printer's shop, he hired the apprentice to draw a local map from which he ascertained the chateaux thereabouts. He set out, hoping to find one receptive to housing winter entertainers.

Wearing his shoulder length wig made of curled hair and a waistcoat trimmed in fur, he gained entrance at Chateau Durckheim, owned by the Marquess de Birague. The chambermaid led him into the antechamber where Lady Birague received him. A sweet smell assaulted him from vases of cut roses which sat on tables as well as the étagère and chimney piece. Lady Birague sat on a stool concealed by a brocade skirt spread out to the size of a cupola.

"Make me laugh," she said, her face gloomy as sunlight poured through windows behind her.

Béjart recited a ribald poem that began with, "There was a man from Dijon who loved a game with dice..." And after he lost his house, his horse, and his hair, the ditty ended with "... he encountered a strumpet with the ticktock and now he's lost his pilicock."

A painting the height of a woman was hanging on the nearby wall, a likeness of Lady Birague. Framed with discriminating taste, with gadrooned detail. But a wide patch of bare canvas lowered into the frame at the bottom. An unfinished painting. Béjart was unsettled. It was a dream of his to have his portrait painted. Had he a wall, it was the first thing he would spend his money on.

A vague sense of distress crossed her face. The rose scent merged with that of a privy and smelled worse than rotting flesh, but Béjart refused to be discouraged. He ignored her apparent discomfort as well as the smell.

"Make me happy," she said.

Béjart crooned a ditty about Risselty-Rossilty, hey bom-bossety nickety-nackety, and rhymes that added up more verses, ending with, "If you want any more, you can sing it yourself. Risselty-rossilty, hey bom-bossety nickety-nackety, retrical quality willaby-wallaby, now now now."

She sighed. "Dispel the bad spirits that haunt me," she said.

Béjart realized her unhappiness, but the smell in the room emptied him of sympathy for her. He would have asked about the unfinished portrait, but she motioned his dismissal. He knelt at the hem of her dress and offered himself to her service, whatever that might be.

To her chambermaid who saw him out, he said, "Why is the portrait unfinished?"

She bowed as if she might lose stuffing and, without a word, motioned him toward the passageway.

He slept soundly in the guest chamber, gratified that Lady Birague's smell had not tainted his room. The woman's condition diminished his enthusiasm for spending the winter there.

The following morning as he ate at the table with the servants, the chamberlain delivered a letter from the Marquess with an invitation to conduct divertissements over winter at Chateau Durckheim. The Troupe's secure lodgings and performances in the chateau's Great Hall overshadowed Béjart's reservations about Lady Birague.

Béjart returned to the Troupe with the good news that they had permission to perform in Auxerre and winter quarters at Chateau Durckheim.

With a sense of accomplishment, he watched the other actors around the fire Hubert had made. Argon helped Agnes learn lines to a new satire he had written with Eugene. The juggler Samuel practiced a contortion, his head downward so as to look through his legs backward. Eugene strummed the lute and sang softly. Béjart motioned Louise toward her caravan.

In the dim light, he disrobed and shivered into the cot with Louise, her body releasing a warmth not far removed from happiness.

Béjart would have preferred Isabelle's feather mattress, but he had no heart for the physical demands she made of him. He had been mistaken when he assumed she would take Leon for a lover and thereby vent some of her boudoir fervor.

In contrast, Louise was pliable and accommodating. That her

position in the Troupe was entirely dependent on Béjart's favor hadn't discouraged him from assuming she was enamored of him.

"You are cold." Her voice softened the cold and drafty quarter.

"And in need of your liberality." His hand swept under her shirt and gathered pleasure from her skin.

Unlike Isabelle, Louise allowed their swiving to proceed at his pace. She rolled on top of him and reached into the basket of ointments. "Oil for your dagger." she said, opening a pot containing a magical unguent with herbs to enhance love.

She massaged Béjart's saddle-sore groin. Since he had not yet given her a wool pad instilled with ingredients for a pessary, he used her by the rear. She did not object and in fact appreciated his concern for protecting her from being brought to bed of a babe. She responded with greater affection for him.

Her humours were clogged with black bile from the past. Though she had not avoided accouchement, she had escaped motherhood the only way she could. But that escape haunted her.

Béjart's former lover had been careless about using the pessary. When her menses ceased, she had refused to take the dose of alpine snakeroot he bought from a midwife. His anger over her simpering protestations had prevailed over his good judgment, and instead of forcing her to swallow the abortifacient, he had forced her to leave.

Louise's hands stroked Béjart perfunctorily. It was necessary to accommodate him to retain a place to sleep, but she did not see this as unfair treatment. Not like her father who had forced her more than once into some man's bed to pay his gambling debts. She appreciated things about Béjart. He did not bite her nipples nor push her on the floor when he was finished. He did not stink of undigested cabbage nor drag horse manure into bed. He did not slobber drunkenly nor curse her.

Louise knew she was a comely maid, but because this asset had only brought her misfortune, she reserved her words and withheld smiles. At the same time, she wanted a congenial relationship with the actors. She was clever enough to realize that her future in the Troupe depended on not only Béjart, but Isabelle as well. If Béjart was the Troupe's right hand, Isabelle was the left, though Béjart would never admit it.

When they emerged from the caravan, low clouds began to drizzle. It put out the fire. Though their potage of barley and onions was only partially cooked, the actors filled their bowls and sat in the wagons and ate, some with less appetite than others.

❧ Scene 9 ❧
a storm in fair weather

The following morning the sun appeared and produced a day warmer than any in a fortnight. Béjart's clipped commands signaled a storm approaching despite the fair weather. The sun lasted until they stopped at a farm to water the animals.

As Eugene and Argon played and sang songs to show their appreciation to the owner, Béjart sought out Isabelle. He put his hand on her forehead. "I'm distressed that you were ill while I was away at Auxerre," he said, though the tone of his voice betrayed no sympathy.

Isabelle did not ask nor did she want to know where Béjart spent his time when he disappeared from the group. "I was much afflicted by your absence. Such heaviness waxed in me bodily and brought on sickness."

"So waxed, did it? That you recovered in a day?"

"A day, forsooth! Even with physic I durst not leave my bed for two days."

Béjart became enraged, for he knew from Hubert that this was untrue. He accused her of faking illness, of a clandestine affair, of seeking a sorcerer, of disputing his order, of insulting Hubert, of using the company's horse and caravan without permission, and of despoiling Eugene's good nature.

"You were not here to see my misery!" Isabelle railed back at him. "Bitter pains came upon me, and where were you? At some place of avoidance. When have you wiped my fevered brow or brought a cup of broth to my sick bed?"

So loud was the noise the farmer came out of his maison and told them to leave. Grumbles emerged from the actors as they drove the caravans in the ruts leading to the high road. As if the weather played a part in their drama, clouds thundered in the distance.

"Can you not settle your disagreements with less malice?" Argon, driving Isabelle's caravan, jostled the leather lines to the horse, urging quicker steps. Before them the road veered into a mist.

Isabelle twisted against the hard seat. "Malice? Perchance malice is the mate to love. No matter my regard for Béjart, I will not be pushed aside."

"How can love and malice live together? One will destroy the other." Argon did not say that he feared his parents were destroying their love for each other.

"You will find there is no purity in love. It has dishonored many a woman. It has disgraced men." Isabelle was wary not just of Argon's questions but of love itself. She climbed into the back of the caravan and brought forward their canvas capes, just as the haze turned to a drizzle.

"Béjart will not be a whole man if he is without you," Argon said, attempting to determine if Isabelle could be trusted to leave things as they were. Since he had come to realize that mutual agreement rather than marriage governed unions in the Troupe, their disputes put into question their union.

"Whether or not he is a *whole* man, as you say, is up to him. That is not in my power to sway."

Argon wanted to plead with her for his own sake, for he could not imagine a day without her. "You underestimate the strength you give him."

She breathed a huff and looked at him. "He does not need my strength and that's to his credit. You will find that your well-being rests on yourself alone."

Argon was not the only actor who resented plodding through soggy weather. They could have stayed in the farmer's dry barn had it not been for the scene Béjart and Isabelle created.

After protests from the actors, Béjart signaled the lead caravan to divert off the high road to a forest clearing where noblemen on a hunt would take respite. There they encamped for the night. There was no fire. There was no barley for porridge. The coffee tin was empty.

The following morning they set out without sun but also without rain. Argon's voice was raspy. The exercises Béjart advised hadn't worked. Spending his last sou, he had bought a potion of fleawort boiled with oil of lilies. The village apothecary had said, "Gargle with this. It will give your voice strength."

To Argon's relief, the greasy unguent made an improvement on a Friday, but his voice grated on a Monday. He gargled more often. By Thursday, he spoke in a whisper.

Eugene, who sat beside him, said, "A friar, name of Nicholas Vallans, cured me of pustules the size of an egg."

"And he is apt to cure my voice?" Argon gazed mindlessly at the road and Eugene drove.

"He learned from the famous healer Nostradamus," said Eugene. "I vow, he is a man of merit. I was but an urchin, doomed to die, and he treated me with a potion. Made of bat droppings and hellbroth." The pustules healed, but he did not mention that in spite of the friar's potions, the spells that came upon him did not go away.

"Does he live hereabouts?"

"I know not what has become of him."

As the Troupe continued by way of a stone-paved road, they came upon a farmer's maison where they stopped to water the animals. Argon sneaked about the storage buildings until he found a silo with hogsheads of turnips and piles of barley. When he returned to the caravans, the pockets of his cloak bulged with edible loot. As soon as they were back on the road, they discovered that Leon had liberated a rabbit from the farmer's warren and had it in a sack.

On encountering fellow travelers, Eugene slowed down and, with a congenial, "How now?" asked about Brother Vallans. Most of them glanced at the train of caravans painted with images—a griffin, monster hawk, faux heraldry—and said, "Alas, but nay my good man, no Vallans in these parts," and tipped a hat by way of saying "fare-thee-well."

Their journey took them on a back road with few fields. Their hope of a tavern and a meal and warm bed sank with the sun. They watched for a glade where they might encamp but had to settle for a thickly grown side road that led through the woods to a pasture. With the caravans stationed near the encroaching brushwood, they unhitched and tethered the horses.

A stew made of the filched turnips, barley, and rabbit bubbled in a pot over an open fire. Georgette, understood to be Hubert's wife, coached Louise in how to play her part, a signal that Béjart intended to make her a permanent member of the company. "Never turn your back on the best dressed man in the audience," Georgette said. "And when you must turn about, swish your dress and show your legs."

Isabelle, curious about Maud Fras's elixir, placed a drop into her noggin and sat on a stool and gazed into the fire.

Leon on the pipe and Argon and Eugene on the lute played ditties, mumbling well known lyrics and changing them until they became coarse, then erotic, then disgusting, at which time they belted them out. The woods echoed their lust.

Isabelle's enhanced wine coursed in her veins like a flame from the fire. She blushed from her neck to her crotch. As she looked in turn at the actors, affection welled up in her chest, causing it to thump an itchy rhythm. She sighed. In the surrounding trees and bushes she saw shadows with devious beauty and depth. She loved shadows. Skeletal trees bared their bark. She loved the trees. She loved the way they pricked the sky.

"Leon, sing the ballad about the squirrel," she said as the musicians drifted from note to note, rather lost to song.

"What squirrel ballad?" Samuel was confused.

"At the risk of leading Etienne astray?" said Leon.

"We must not speak the word by whiches ... we call that thing in a man's britches," recited Isabelle. She stood and turned to Béjart. "Is this wine spoilt?" She offered him her noggin, curious to see its effect on him.

He sipped. "It has a strange taste, but not of mold." He handed it back to her.

"Taste once more. Would it be tainted with venom?"

Leon sang about a young girl so cautioned by her mother to beware of what men had in their britches that she was seduced by a con man who referred to his own genitalia as a squirrel with two eggs in its nest.

"I have to talk to you," Isabelle said to Béjart, conniving to discover the elixir's effects. "Come…" She took a candle and headed to their caravan and motioned him to follow. Inside, she handed him the remainder of wine while she removed her bodice, revealing breasts barely contained by her chemise.

Béjart sat on his cot. "Give out whatsoever comes to mind."

Isabelle removed the leather band tied round Béjart's head and sat beside him. Her throat ached. "Leon paid Hubert five sou to make another mask." A tremble traveled up her backbone. She could not judge the distance to Béjart and was breathing into his lips.

She removed her chemise. Her nipples yearned to be touched. He removed his doublet, his shirt, boots, hose. He took her in ways of desperation. Of anger. Of need. Of thrill. In their violent and rude coming together, their bodies struggled to become one. The sideboard of the cot broke. They tumbled on the caravan floor, lashed at each other until fully spent.

They climbed into Isabelle's cot. Her chest ached. She took deep breaths.

"Is this what you wanted me to know?" said Béjart, whose body had performed so vigorously as to amaze him.

They cuddled. Isabelle nuzzled his face. The stubble of a late-day growth engrossed her.

"Or are we talking about Leon?" said Béjart, his breath seeking reinforcement.

"Is it not strange that he sometimes wears a mask when it's merely us?" Isabelle felt hairs inside her throat.

"Every actor is strange in his own way."

"He hides his face, and for what reason?"

"Actors hide more than their faces." Béjart recognized a familiar feeling which brought to mind a certain tonic. "Where did you get that wine?"

"It was a present." Isabelle, despite the lull in her head, was aware of Béjart's suspicion.

"Who gave you a present?"

"Oh, not for me. An admirer gave it to Louise. I asked her to share it."

"Louise?" Béjart's spirit was too peaceful to admit jealousy. Or suspicion.

As the candle burned down, the cot became too small for the two of them. Béjart slept on the straw mattress on the floor.

By this time, the actors had crowded together in their caravans. Because the night was cold, Argon and Eugene pushed their cots together and cuddled under their combined sheep skins. Louise lay in her cot alone. Not until she arose and put on her cloak and shoes was she warm enough to rest.

The following day a traveler, upon Argon's query about a Brother Vallans, said in passing that the man had died of late from a frog disease.

Eugene sank into doleful silence and let the lines droop to his boots.

Argon took over driving the wagon. "There must be more than one Brother Vallans."

Eugene could not put words to his thoughts. Brother Vallans had been the gift from God that saved his life. There was only one of him. If he were dead, Eugene had lost his connection to God.

The wagon before them had pulled ahead some distance.

"Withal, that traveler stowed treachery in his princely mantle." Argon whistled to rouse the horse to a quicker step.

"For what reason would a stranger lie?" Eugene spoke distinctly like an actor.

"For what reason bear the truth to such as we?"

"Have ye newly come to be a seer?" said Eugene.

"With open eyes, anybody can be such a seer."

Eugene had not revealed to his companions how much he owed the mystical friar, who had given Eugene's mother a Christian burial and taken charge of him when he had no protector.

✐ Scene 10 ✐
a grand mishap

A stone wall with crumbling mortar and weeds sprouting in cracks surrounded the city of Auxerre. At the narrow gate, a putrefying smell assaulted the actors, who grabbed for something to cover their noses, a kerchief or shawl. Accompanying the smell was the sight of a corpse, perhaps a week past life, hanging from a gibbet. Buzzards perched on the wooden transverse and tore at what flesh was left.

The wagons rolled inside. Beggars wrapped in dirt-daubed cloaks appeared out of covert passages, hands outstretched. The earthen road widened. They passed tanners and leather workers. Passed wood cutters and a crowkeeper. Passed family homes, made of mud and timbers with thatched roofs and attached stables. A rut of effluvium straggled down the side of the street, fed by slime and waste.

As they paraded through Auxerre, the colored caravans lost brilliance in the gathering fog. The painted flags, shields, griffin, and hawk, dazzling in sunlight, dulled in the mist. Leon drummed loudly on his tabor. Samuel blared on a sheephorn.

Villagers unbolted shutters and craned out windows to see. Doors squeaked open. Onlookers crowded sheltered doorways at storefronts housing the baker, apothecary, fishmonger and other merchants.

As the Troupe came to a halt in the town square where they expected to raise their stage, curious onlookers lolled nearer. Béjart jumped from his wagon and led several actors in a riotous interpretation of "Wine Does Wonders." The scattered audience, dressed in coats and oilskins, guffawed and wagged ever closer. "Come back for daring feats! Wild comedie!" Béjart shouted.

The wagon with staging equipment remained in the square and became Argon's responsibility while the others pulled away. They parked inside the city wall near decrepit stalls of peddlers known more for begging than selling. Once the animals were at livery, the actors returned to the town center where they had left Argon.

"Who is to stay in the square with the stage properties this night?" Béjart asked as they ate supper at the tavern. His question was directed at the men, for women did not have the authority to deal with such things as hooligans or bandits. Or tricksters who might splinter the wheels. Or Catholics who might rip the canvas.

However, the actors' attention was taken by a smoking competition across the room and loud brawlers making bets. Three men fiercely puffed on pipes, each trying to be the first to finish a pipe full of tobacco in the shortest time.

Béjart pounded the table for attention. "Faugh! Let us get this thing decided."

"I propose a game of brelan. The loser stays with the property," said Leon, known as a formidable opponent at cards.

Hubert objected. So did Samuel, also not good at gambling. "By arm wrestling," he said.

"Knucklebones," said Argon.

"By our craft," said Hubert. "The last one to get a smile from the tavern wench." He nodded toward a woman of grand bosom sloshing tankards of ale on a table.

They agreed and moved to sit together at one table. Leon hailed the wench, who bobbed from one unruly rogue to another getting to them. "My-lady, a sou for a smile," he said.

"'Tis foul!" exclaimed the others.

"Pray, sire, what shall you have?" She didn't smile.

"You sprite spirit!" Hubert, with a twinkle in his eye, touched her arm. "What doth it take to enjoy your favors?"

"Sire, more than your pleasant manner." Though her cheeks were pitted by the pox, she had a playful gleam in her eyes. As she departed, Hubert claimed she had smiled. Leon disagreed, but the group sided with Hubert.

Samuel and Eugene tricked her into a smile with a caricature of the smokers. The game dwindled to Argon and Leon. Upon the appearance of a smirk, each of them claimed she had smiled for him, but nobody was convinced. Béjart settled the dispute by having both of them guard the caravan.

They took turns. Argon stayed with the wagon while Leon sat in the tavern and then they switched places. As the actors drank with locals and fabricated stories about performing at the Sun King's court, the beef tallow candles burned to a nub. The church bell tolled the matins. The tavern keeper blew a shepherd's horn.

The town of Auxerre was of a size to offer a choice of several taverns and inns. The actors who wanted sleeping quarters found ones they could afford and slept two or three to a bed in one or another hostelry.

Argon and Leon hollowed out a space under the canvas and slept in the wagon. Béjart remained with the other caravans and guarded them as well as Isabelle, who preferred her feather mattress to a straw bed in a room with numerous, often foul-smelling, inebriated occupants.

Clouds obscured sunrise. The morning mist was so continuous that pearls of water appeared inside the waxed covers of the caravans.

✳

During two rainy days the props remained in the wagon. Béjart visited the printer for playbills. Eugene, having discovered silver wound strings, replaced the sheep gut strings on his lute. Hubert, with a replenished supply of ink, wrote copies of a script. Argon spent much of that time in the nearby alehouse determining his tolerance for strong drink at the prodding of Leon.

When the sun came out, they unloaded the stage floor in the square near a corner where the backdrop occluded less frequented shops such as the woolmonger and mason. The stage was easily accessed from the alehouse, tavern, baker and cloth shop where paysans congregated. They assembled the stage floor, raised a frame, and attached the painted canvas that provided a backdrop.

Argon jostled along the meandering cobblestone streets and pressed playbills on peddlers, merchants, and yeomen. At his side, Etienne beat a tabor and chirruped "Hoy! All Hail! Harken!"

While Etienne rang bells and blew on the sheep horn, the actors, wearing woolens stockings, leapt on stage and strolled back and forth, dancing and singing in company. Others drifted on and off stage, but Argon and Béjart remained, bringing forth music by plucking their lutes and singing, "Here's good luck to the pint pot, Good luck to the Barley Mow..." The lyrics easily escaped Argon's throat, once more unblemished by crustiness.

When Béjart strolled left, Argon went right. His fingers boldly commanded the strings of his lute. Smoke arising from a tavern chimney curled into their path. Dark cinders bespeckled Argon's red satin cloak, a sign of sorcery that distracted him as he shook them off. He fingered his lute off-key.

Béjart eyed his son a question, what's wrong? and strolled forward on the stage, singing louder until Argon recovered.

The rabble of alewives, ostlers, and artisans grew in size and loud in noise. In the audience stood a man wearing a broad brim hat bordered with braid and flaunting a jeweled clasp, which Argon little noticed. But he did notice the toad-like eyes and waxed mustache.

Argon danced off as Samuel triple-somersaulted on stage and juggled balls with hands and mouth.

The actors returned with a comedie about a marquess who pursued a milkmaid thinking she was the daughter of a wealthy cloth merchant. Argon had stolen the script from a rival troupe.

His good memory for dialogue was the reason Béjart occasionally sent him to spy on other troupes.

Isabelle had borrowed, by way of Agnes, the maid's plain apron to wear. Though she was obviously mature for a milkmaid, Isabelle laced tightly in a breath-defying truss and played the part. She had turned her raven hair to red-gold with a concoction made of urine. Youth was elusive, but false locks pinned about Isabelle's face convinced her it was attainable.

While declaring her lines on stage, she furtively searched the audience for Lord Dubois, whose latest communication had raised the hairs on her skin. *I am going to try to make you love me,* he had written. He wanted *the full satisfaction of his desires.*

Among the onlookers, Isabelle caught sight of a unique hat, that of Lord Dubois himself. Beside him was his servant, who had delivered his letters. Her voice took on brilliant authority. Her bustling gestures became elegant. She excelled at coquetry and, on exiting, made a languid departure.

From behind the sheepskin drape, with dark cinders swirling above their heads, Argon and Leon peeked at the crowd. Argon pointed to the man and whispered. "Old Nick himself, come to beguile us."

"Perchance a versifier of another troupe spying on us," whispered Leon. He did not say *like we have spied on other troupes,* as that was understood by both of them.

"A cheat would not stand so boldly." Argon peeked again through the hanging sheepskins.

Isabelle dared not say a word. She knew the stranger to be a cheat by their reckoning, but a nobleman was never considered a cheat, regardless of what they did.

Louise stood nearby, ready to prompt either Béjart or Georgette should they forget their lines. She looked from the script she was holding and turned to listen to Leon.

"Perchance from Paris ... a nobleman on a quest for actors for the Palais Royal." Leon took over the peek hole.

Louise squeezed near them to get a look. Argon was distracted by her bosom. Her warm breath. The sight of her somber lips had more than once shot his body through with desire.

"Molière's man. He might be Molière's man," whispered Leon.

For Isabelle, it was almost too much to hope for, that Lord Dubois might be known to Molière.

Argon pulled him backward to get another look. The prospect of the Palais Royal intoxicated him.

"Let me see," whispered Louise. A gold threaded scarf tied into her hair was scented of thyme. As Argon backed away and allowed her in front of them, he touched her shoulder.

Béjart was coughing from the stage. Louise, late to recognize his signal, hurried back to her station and scrambled to the page in the script. Before she found the lines Béjart had forgotten, he stormed off stage with the words, "What sweet bitterness is the remembrance of music." Georgette, playing the merchant's wife, found herself alone on the stage.

Argon strutted on stage, singing and playing his lute as Leon fumbled after him with his pipe. Lusty with the ambition to impress a possible emissary of Molière, Argon sang, "Good friends and companions, come join me in rhyme; Come lift up your voices in chorus with mine…" The lyrics emerged with gusto, and as he was overtaken by his song, his voice trembled.

Georgette joined the singing and Leon danced off stage. The restless audience quieted to Argon and Georgette's music, but Béjart didn't notice. He confronted Louise. "My dear, did you enjoy your favors while I coughed up my belly waiting for a prompt?"

She looked at the script and whispered, "I assure you, I would rather eat a cartload of hay and die than suffer your displeasure."

"Why be here if not to render profitable service?" He cocked his head to one side.

The threat of being dismissed frightened her into silence. The script twisted in her fist.

Leon reached for the script. "Louise renders profitable service." He looked at her, "Do you not?"

"Damnation! Do you mete out insult?" Béjart muttered, his black eyebrows furrowed. His black Italian eyes challenged Leon.

Leon shrugged his shoulders. "Louise can read your scrawl. She speaks no scurvy language. Would you put pins in dolls?" He whispered with irreverent provocation.

Because the Augusto Troupe owed Leon money, Béjart ignored his mischief. When he strolled back on stage, the stillness of the onlookers momentarily perplexed him.

Louise whispered from behind the canvas, "I assure you, I would rather eat a cartload of hay and die than suffer like this."

Béjart picked up the line and the show continued.

To conclude the comedie's final scene, Béjart and Isabelle danced on stage while the musicians played a rousing tune. Etienne threaded through the crowd more vigorously than previous times. "Please the lord, a sou for the pot!" He shook the coins. "Come now!" He bowed when a coin was dropped in the pot.

As Isabelle dallied near the stage amid brawlers, she drank a potion from her vial to calm herself. Lord Dubois's servant appeared in their midst. As a precaution, she turned away from him as if she did not know him, and it was only with some effort that he approached and kissed her hand, leaving a note in her palm.

The performance had ended only to be followed by a scene worthy of Racine's *Andromache* when Béjart found Isabelle. He ushered her behind an apple shed. "A grand mishap! And it's no wonder. A maid is not domineering!"

"A maid does not have to be a toad-eater," said Isabelle. Thunder rolled nearer, punctuating her words.

"You played her like a pushy whore hounding the marquess."

"It takes more than fluttering heartbeats for a maid to attract a marquess."

"Your lines arose as if wrung from your bowels, not your bosoms." Béjart poked her in the belly.

Isabelle slapped him. "Did the paysans not pitch coins into the cup?"

The sky opened and rain pelted down. Brought on by the storm in their camp, according to the actors, who hurried to take down the backdrop and secure it in a caravan.

In the cold drizzle that followed, Isabelle, furious with Béjart, sloshed through the mud to Les Trois Lunes, a tavern where Lord Dubois awaited. Her cloak dripping, she entered the dark room lit by a wood fire. He sat at a table in a corner near the fireplace, a wine bottle before him.

Isabelle walked with artful confidence to his table and waited for his invitation to sit. Eventually he nodded her toward the chair across the table. That he made her wait confused her. Instead of speaking to her, he called the tavern maid to the table. "Do you not notice my dry wine glass?"

His brusque manner was met with apologies. The maid picked up the empty bottle and said, "Prithee, I will fetch wine to you anon."

"Fie and such gaucherie! Ale-louse!"

The woman scurried away, for enraged men could destroy an alewife's fate.

Isabelle wiped the smile from her lips and took account of his offensive behavior. By speaking calmly, she calmed herself. "My lord, your long absence causes me sorrowful remembrance."

"You have as lively towardness as a man could wish," he said.

Her thoughts were racing to make sense of what he said. "It is apt that we meet and bring our purpose to a good end."

"Ah, the vices we see nowadays."

"Though I never refuse exhortations that are meet to correct my faults."

The tavern maid brought red wine and poured a glass for Lord Dubois and one for Isabelle. She took a deep draft and looked at the flames of the fire.

Lord Dubois motioned over his servant and whispered in his ear, after which the boy left the room. "In my ripe age, I expect no less than soul and body together. But truly, the horse of Troy never deceived with such utter mindlessness."

"My lord, I am here with no ill purpose."

"Mayhap your wanton trade of living leads you every way by right or by wrong. Would you make me a laughing stock?"

Isabelle's breath came shallow. His displeasure threatened not just her standing but that of the Troupe. "My lord, this is no small pain. Prithee, inform me frankly the means of your disfavor with me."

"Outwardly you declare an unsurpassed beauty, but inwardly you are full of towe and rags. Your pleasant manner cloaks an ill end … to boldly lay hand upon my possessions and reputation." With that, he stood and walked to the door where his page had reappeared.

He left, carrying himself with greater regal bearing than usual, for Isabelle's letter had humiliated him. He was unaccustomed to a woman's demands. People who knew him would have known that he was quick to take offense and quick to seek revenge.

As Isabelle gulped wine she noticed on the table a letter. Though the light was dim, she was able to discern it was addressed to Lord Dubois. The signature was her name—a letter she had never seen before, much less written. She picked it up and turned it to the light to read. She held wine in her mouth to keep from screaming.

The writer, signed as Isabelle, wrote of the beauty and ability she had to enchant men. *So many men burn for love of me as you know.* She had passion beyond reason, which came to light in sumptuous surroundings. She required *chambers of very riche cloth of golde, of silke.*

Isabelle's absence from breakfast was explained as an excess of humors, an excess that had jolted the sleepy Argon into wide-eyed morning when he had attempted to fetch her. He knew to approach her with caution, for, whatever he said, she was as apt to lather him with kisses as twist off his ear. Others in the Troupe blamed her flashes of hot and cold temperament on her English blood.

Isabelle lay abed and took liberally of a tonic. The question of whose hand had written the false letter to Lord Dubois had given her a fever.

She could only speculate. If Béjart had written the letter after discovering her pursuit of Lord Dubois, her worries were just beginning. Her husband had the authority and the temperament to throw her out of the Troupe. Should that happen, it would not be the first time she found herself without a home. Her fever grew worse at the option of having to take refuge in either a nunnery or a stable.

Béjart, unaware of the letter or of Isabelle's torment, found her sitting on her feather bed among writing papers. "What manner of ill troubles you?"

"Colic of the stomach," she mumbled. Stomach colic was a way of describing what a medecin would call menstrual retention.

ꙮ Scene 11 ꙮ
nothing but base flattery, self-interest, deceit and roguery

Argon clambered onto a caravan and urged its horse along the stone paved road that led out of the square and in a north-ward direction toward the chateau of the Marquess de Birague. The town of Troyes, being on the way, was a planned stop over for several days to perform at the Fair of Saint Remi. It was attended by merchants who came from as far away as Italy to sell cloth, leather, spices, metalwork, and other goods. Bankers came to exchange moneys.

Loaded down with trunks, canvases, and timbers, the wagon creaked in its wood joints. Argon's mood was lighthearted, elevated by a sense of freedom in leaving behind the village of Auxerre. He was grateful that he was not a tradesman or farmer who lived and died within leagues of where they were born, as rooted to the ground as a tree. It was in his blood to be about the country. After a spell in a given location, the unknown became commonplace and his senses dulled. The longer the stay, the lower his spirits, the duller his thinking.

Upon discovering he had gone so far ahead as to lose the others, he pulled up in the road and waited for the wagons to catch up.

When the caravans approached, he took his place at the head, while Béjart rode at the rear. They trailed along at a steady pace, halting when the horses needed rest. Gusts of wind cut capers in the woodlands. Beech trees, signaling the end of summer, inclined to russet, the oaks to gold. The acorn's scaly cups fattened with brown nuts.

At a rich peasant farmer's manor house they begged permission to water the stock and were allowed into a stone-paved courtyard surrounded by numerous buildings: a silo, storage sheds, shelters for livestock, barns for threshing grain, and stalls for milking cows.

They had traveled only five leagues, but the sunlight was departing and chilly ghosts of evening were arriving. The surrounding walls safeguarded them from what had become a bracing wind. Though Béjart's silver tongue was unable to persuade the owner to allow them to stay overnight in the courtyard, his silver coin did.

Eugene and Samuel discovered a storage shed with carrots and turnips and helped themselves to a handful. Etienne built a fire and his mother Georgette prepared the vegetables and put them into a cook pot. The actors took bets on whether Samuel or Argon could get the most milk from a cow in the least time. When the contest ended, Samuel's pot was declared the fullest. The actors gathered close to the open fire, warmed their hands and feet, and drank wine while the potage cooked.

After supper Leon blew a note on the pipe to begin a gypsy song, and the others joined in, singing and playing their instruments. From various buildings came the farm laborers — the ostler and goatherd, along with wives and children, who remained in the shadows listening to the music. Wood to stoke the fire appeared from the darkness, carried in by first one and then another.

Isabelle gazed into the flames. Even if she had the ability to deliver a letter to Lord Dubois, she had little inclination to write one that begged forgiveness for demands she hadn't made. However, her every minute was directed toward devising a scene in which she reclaimed his respect. The theater of her mind searched for an actor to take the role of an intermediary to plead her innocence, somebody of noble birth and considerable influence. The Marquess de Birague came to mind.

The Marquess, being of peerage, knew others of his station, and if he didn't know Lord Dubois personally, Isabelle assumed he knew him by reputation. Her task was to use her wiles, with covert gentility, to earn an audience with either the Marquess or his wife and persuade one of them to her cause.

The fire dwindled eventually and the audience of farm workers faded away. Darkness closed in. The women lit candles and ambled to the sheep skins in the wagons. Agnes, who hadn't endured a winter with the Troupe, complained that unseasonable weather was a harbinger of misfortune.

The men dozed with their feet to the embers until waking in the night chilled to the bone. It was the night moreso than the day that told of the changing season. Argon slept in the cot with Eugene. Hubert and Georgette gratefully squeezed together. Though Béjart's restlessness and noisy breathing kept Isabelle from sound sleep, she appreciated his warmth. They cuddled like new-found lovers. Etienne and Samuel climbed into the barn loft and took cover under hay.

The following morning as they harnessed the horses to the wagons in preparation to leave, Argon discovered the canvas used as a back-drop was missing from the wagon. They searched every caravan and inquired of the farm laborers without so much as a clue about its disappearance. Béjart knocked on the manor door while Argon saddled the riding horses.

"Ave, Monsieur," he said and after a pleasant response from the farmer, "We take leave, but without our canvas that came amiss in the night. If you should come upon it, prithee send word to me at Chateau Durckheim or to the Marquess de Birague."

"Sirrah, such canvas is worth not so much. But perchance

enough to repay me for the milk you took from my cows, the carrots from my granary, and hay from my barns."

Béjart controlled his ire. "Ah, Monsieur, such is cheap fare for our canvas, painted with likeness of chairs, mirror, and such. I say certainly its value is far more than a soupçon of carrots or hay."

"There is an expense in causing my lady an irksome night. Such cost is dear, for her sleep is not untroubled even in the most wholesome night."

Béjart was drunk with wrath. "Sir, its worth to you is but a fraction of the worth to our company."

"For an écu, you must me win," said the farmer.

Faced with the man's unreasonable demand, Béjart turned to leave and mumbled, "On my life, may the best of devils break your neck." Though incensed, he was not surprised, for he had encountered the parsimony of the bourgeoisie before, especially those of recent wealth.

He marched to his horse, swung himself into the saddle, and waved Eugene, first in the line of wagons, to proceed forward. The caravans trailed out of the courtyard and took the wagon path to the high road. As Béjart rode at the rear of the caravans, Argon, sitting astride the other riding horse, slowed his pace and pulled up beside Béjart.

"We go to the fair without the backdrop?" said Argon.

"We travel until we find a solution. The cost of a new canvas is not so much as an écu."

"But the cost of paint. Where will we find paint hereabouts?"

"We needs recover our backdrop from the farmer," said Béjart.

"I will return in the dark and steal it," said Argon.

"Perchance it be rolled under his bed. What then?" said Béjart.

"Pay the ostler or goatherd half a sou to steal it for us."

A briskness echoed in the rattle of the wagon wheels as Béjart considered this possibility.

The caravans unaccountably slowed down to a sloth's pace and Béjart rode to the front of the line. They were behind a sheepherder wrapped in a cape from his nose to his shins and driving a small herd of wooly sheep in the middle of the road. Trees grew forest-thick on each side. Eventually a field opened up on one side, but the herder and his sheep remained in the ruts, obstructing their way.

"Goodman, pray take your sheep to the field so we can pass," said Béjart.

The sheepherder merely plodded along, his sheep bleating and trotting in the road.

"My good man! Pray!" Béjart shouted.

Eugene shook the reins loudly clinking the metal, but there was no change in the sheepherder.

The dog's barking at the Troupe finally caused the sheepherder to turn.

Béjart said to Argon, "Take a sheep if you see good odds." He urged his horse in advance of the herd, turned, faced the man and his sheep, and whistled. "My good man, if you please, guide your sheep to the field so we may pass." He shouted loudly and waved toward the caravans. The sheep began to disperse.

Argon grabbed a sheep that wandered to his advantage and shoved it into a wagon.

The sheepherder stumbled forward with his staff and commanded his dog with the voice of a barn owl. His dog cut circles around the sheep, kept them within range, and herded them into the field.

With the road cleared, Béjart nodded in thanks to the sheepherder and the caravan moved ahead. Béjart rejoined Argon at the rear. "The man is as deaf as a cook pot," he said.

They sold the sheep to a peddler of ointments they met on the road. With the money, Béjart returned to the farmer and bought back their canvas backdrop. It was well dark by the time he returned to the Troupe, which had camped at a wayside shrine to the Virgin Mary.

Georgette made a hearty stew of squirrels Leon had killed. Louise, though the official cook, was less talented with the spoon than Georgette. Satiated with chunks of meat spiced with pepper, cumin, and garlic, the actors belched and farted contentedly throughout the night.

When they arrived at the Fair of Saint Remi, they were allowed to set their stage on a tennis court. The actors opened their trunks containing wigs, skin patches, pots of oils, toners, white paint. Depending on Béjart's choice of divertissements, they plundered one another's makeup. Louise and Georgette tried plaster noses and wool eyebrows. Samuel wrapped his belly in padding. Leon put on his eye patch.

Louise wanted to perform a mime, which Béjart rejected as too subtle for the bustle of tradesmen. Isabelle had a beguiling effect on the groundlings, who dropped ever more coins in Etienne's cup when she tossed paper roses to them. The musicians sang Argon's new ballad for interludes between diversions.

Eugene, who provided musical accompaniment from behind the backdrop, watched over instruments and costumes not being used if all actors happened to be on stage. While the Troupe was performing a musical burlesque, Béjart noticed with concern as a boy approached behind the stage. He discretely danced off stage and found Eugene lying on the ground, his eyes rolling. This did not alarm Béjart, for he had seen such instances before. He covered Eugene with a piece of woolen cloth. Agnes and Samuel came from the stage.

"Why is Eugene under a cloth?" said Agnes.

"Is he dead?" said Samuel.

Argon and Georgette arrived.

"No. The light affects his eyes uncommonly. He ate chewet and it's made him sick.

Eugene made a gurgling noise.

"I gave him bryony." Béjart turned the covered body on its side. "He will be in fine fettle momently."

"Wellaway," Georgette said and turned to Argon. "Are you going to stay here while Leon sings your song?" Argon hurried back on stage.

"He's cold. Get another cover." Samuel noticed the cloth shivering.

As Leon came from the stage, Eugene sat up and rubbed his eyes. "Been to the alehouse?" said Leon.

"He can't tolerate chewet," said Agnes, readying to go on stage for the sixth diversion. Béjart's schedule listed sixteen spectacles, not counting interludes. The Troupe performed even numbers one afternoon and odd the next, alternating the two.

"Leon, see that Eugene doesn't eat any more chewet." Béjart said, suggesting that Eugene might need attention. He stood and prepared to go on stage ahead of Agnes.

"Where's my psaltery?" Georgette looked in the trunk and under the sheep skins. "I'll not go out there and sing "cambric shirt" without it."

Louise looked for it. Leon. Samuel. It was no where to be found.

Béjart bounded off stage. "Georgette, you're next!"

"My psaltery is gone," said Georgette.

"What? Samuel, take the next spot."

Samuel went on. The ensemble concluded the performances without Georgette. Etienne plied the crowd, cup in hand, until the onlookers complained. "What? Again?" "Go otherwhere!"

The Troupe retreated to the caravans and built a fire. They shared what they had bought from vendors at the fair — bread, cheese, and salted olives. Georgette and Louise made barley soup. "A boy stole Georgette's psaltery." Béjart realized this was the only explanation. "When Eugene was ill, a knave, mayhap of Etienne's age, was behind the stage."

"Where am I going to get another one?" said Georgette.

"Troyes is of a size to have a seller of instruments," said Leon.

"I should not have to buy one." Georgette spooned soup into the actors' cups. "It's not my fault it's gone."

"I'm not going to buy it for you," said Agnes, eating more than her share of olives.

"The Troupe should pay for another one," said Hubert.

"The Troupe didn't pay for my pipe," said Leon.

"Instruments belong to their owners, not the Troupe," said Béjart.

"I'm sorry. I'll pay for it." Eugene, though pale and wan, took the soup Louise offered.

"That's fair. It was Eugene's fault," said Agnes.

"Wherefore? He was taken ill," said Argon.

"First, we will try to find the thief and take it back." Béjart drank from a bottle of wine a merchant had given them as a sample.

"Troyes is a big town," said Leon.

"The morrow, we'll search the streets." Béjart described the villain and his clothes. In particular, they were to look for a felt hat in the color of goose turd.

Except for Eugene and Isabelle, the entire Troupe scoured the streets. Samuel spotted the hat. The churlish boy wearing it was winding up a bucket of water at the town well. A housewife arrived and argued with him.

"Nay, I'll not pay. Ugsome grig!" She shoved him to the cobblestones and poured into her bucket the water the boy had drawn.

When she was gone, the boy drew up another bucket of water. A beldame arrived and instead of shoving the boy down, gave him a denier. He poured the water into her bucket.

Béjart's directions were to follow the rogue until they found his abode, but he wasn't going anywhere. Samuel was unsure of whether he should wait and watch or fetch one of the Troupe.

Eventually Argon showed up at the well. "Béjart is at the cathedral square, in the undercroft alehouse. Fetch him and I will watch the boy," said Argon.

A butcher's apprentice lumbered to the well. "You again? Scrounger! Charging for water! Stealing from the dull-witted." He kicked the boy, who lurched to his feet and ran from the well. "By my troth, I'll cut off your ears and feed them to the pigs!" shouted the apprentice.

Argon stealthily hurried after the boy who cut and dived around a wagon, costermonger, and a pack of dogs.

By the time Béjart and Samuel returned, Argon and the rogue were gone. They paced the streets nearby ready with a linen rag and stout rope to seize the boy. They met up with Argon, who stood in an alcove across the street from an astrologer's door. The building was two story, attached on each side to comparable structures. To the left was a fletcher's shop, obviously barely in business. On the right was a button maker.

"He went in there," said Argon.

Béjart entered the astrologer's room and, forgetting his objective, was captivated. Purple satin curtains trimmed with silver; carnation velvet carpet, flame, ginger, scarlet and green; white satin tent overhead. Silk scarves and pillows on the settee, which was upholstered in Holy Mary blue. And on a mantle, vials of irregular shape with smoke curling from the mouth. A dim light flickered from a candle. A scent could only be described as celestial oranges.

"You wish to see into your future?" the voice was neither male nor female. The astrologer's headscarf was wound in intricate convolutions with gold threads clearly visible.

"My dame, I am interested, but I have a worthless past. My future is no doubt likewise."

"Ah, I see in your eyes the burnish of extravagance."

"Alas! Worthless is perhaps too slight a word."

The astrologer cackled. "For a sou I will tell you if your future is worthless."

Béjart came to his senses and said, "For a sou, I will tell you if your future is worthless." He whistled. In came Argon and Samuel. They hesitated but when Béjart motioned them to the rear of the room they found the stairway to the upper level.

"Your boy stole a psaltery from me," said Béjart.

The astrologer sighed. "I have no boy. No psaltery."

Argon thundered back into the room. "The boy escaped out the window on to the roof. Should I find him?"

Béjart looked at the astrologer. "No boy, you say?"

The astrologer shrugged. "They sneak in here when I am asleep."

Béjart said to Argon, "Search for the psaltery upstairs. I'll search down here." He threw off the satin cloth covering the round table, but found only the astrologer's sandal-shod feet underneath. He opened trunks and gold laminated boxes. There were masks of the sort used in mimes. She—or he—was probably an unemployed actor.

The astrologer stood and said, "I will make us a cup of tea."

"You'll sit with your hands on the table, or you will lose a finger." Béjart pulled his knife.

Argon appeared with the psaltery, Samuel with an armload of things which he plopped on the table. Falconry gloves, periwig, two condoms of animal bladders, hair powder, knitted stockings, leather girdle, ankle boots. Argon disappeared and returned with scissors, table cloth, tennis balls, hide of a rabbit, a looking glass, a knife the size of a large needle.

"It is a gold mine up there," said Samuel.

Béjart picked up the wig, a modest one for casual wearing, hair tied in back with a ribbon. He turned it in his hand. The periwig he was wearing smelled of mice despite washings with vinegar and rosemary water.

"I'll take the boots," said Samuel.

"Nay. Take nothing that can be identified by an owner." Béjart put down the wig.

They left with not only the psaltery but as many treasures as they could hide in their cloaks.

For the remainder of their shows, the merchants proved to be well paying. The takings from their performances calmed complaints about the cold nights in the caravans.

✳

They awoke from a restless night of dreams of warmer beds. With the horses hitched to the caravans, they resumed the road to Chateau Durckheim. Béjart, who rode in advance, turned back to the wagon Argon was driving. "We should arrive at Lord Birague's chateau before nightfall," he said.

"What particulars are required to be admitted?" Argon was coming to realize that a stage appearance was only a small measure of what it took to produce entertainments, much less manage a troupe.

"I will enter the chateau first and settle with his lordship."

"We want rooms with feather beds and warm fires." Argon gave voice to a common dream.

Béjart glanced at Argon with mirthful eyes. "There are numerous houses on the grounds. One … or two of them … the Marquess will assign for our accommodations. Any bed is better than a canvas covered wagon. Be grateful for a roof."

"He may put us in a dungeon," said Argon.

Béjart laughed. "Or a garderobe."

"You will introduce me to the Marquess de Birague?"

Béjart gave him an amused glance. "Neither you nor I will introduce anybody to the Marquess. He makes acquaintances as he pleases."

"You have seen the chateau's Great Hall?" said Argon.

"It is magnificent. The ceiling is so high you will have to speak from your gut to be heard." Béjart had high expectations for *Mirabelle*'s performances, for a wealthy audience meant good prospects. "You will see. Lofty buildings on all sides of a quadrangle, some with spires. A fish pond in the middle."

"I wonder if the man knows how many rooms he owns."

"Be assured he does. They say he can tell you how many eggs his chickens lay on a given day."

In the caravan behind them, Isabelle sat on the bench beside Eugene, and though she had no quill in her hand, she was writing a letter in her head. *My Lord Dubois, Are you aware of a conspiracy to break your spirit?* Was this sufficiently dramatic? A sentence to make his hand flutter if not tremble? One to give him a taste of the discomposure he had caused her?

When the caravan was within a league of Chateau Durckheim they made camp for the night. The following morning, Béjart saddled a horse and made way for the chateau to arrange with the Marquess's steward for their arrival.

"Monsieur Béjart?" said the steward. "An instant." He closed the door but returned in a matter of minutes. "Hélas, his lordship has installed Le Petit Theatre for the winter term. They arrived not a week agone."

Béjart's disbelief turned to anger. "Look you here!" he snapped before catching himself. Despite experience to the contrary, he believed the nobility capable of greater integrity than the commoner. And despite years of their disdain, he expected fair treatment. "His lordship needs explain. He bound his word to the Augusto Troupe before ever Le Petit Theatre."

"Alas, the Marquess has no need of two acting troupes." The steward made no move to invite him inside.

"Does he make a liar of himself?"

The steward was closing the door. Béjart stuck his boot into the opening, holding up his palms in supplication. "Prithee, request for me an audience with Lady Birague."

"She has allowed no visitor for a fortnight." The steward loosened his hold on the iron latch while Béjart stood in the door frame.

"No ill fortune, I hope." Béjart removed a sou from his pouch and rubbed it between his fingers.

The steward eyed the coin. "Ah, good sir, ill fortune has followed her. Even her servants mislike to attend her apartment." His face winced from his narrow nose to his puckered lips.

"When I visited before, she was ill disposed..." He raised his nose, sniffed, and wrinkled it at the taint of a bad odor.

"Helas, 'tis true. Even the queen's perfume cannot disguise her difficulty." The steward looked at the floor, as he usually did to show shame for having so spoke.

"Hapless woman. Surely in need of a comedie to raise her spirits." Béjart was less than sympathetic despite his words, for he had been stung by the ill treatment.

"She does not leave her chamber. She must sit the stool." The steward was eying the coin Béjart played with his fingers. "She says the devil entered her womb with birthings and disabled her fundament." He shuffled, preparing to close the door.

Béjart held up the sou. "Perchance she will hark back to my visit and be reminded of her merriment. She may choose to abandon her solitude for me."

The steward glanced at the sou and said, "I will return with her answer." He prodded Béjart outside and closed the door.

As Béjart stood waiting, scattered snowflakes drifted from a leaden sky. In the alcove that led to the servant's entry, he paced and stamped his feet, going numb though clad in wool stockings and leather boots.

The steward returned with a stony and flat "no" from the Lady.

Putting aside his acid disappointment at having been mal-treated, Béjart consoled himself that he didn't have to endure the Lady's smell.

He sat his horse so angrily his periwig shifted over an ear. Rather than becoming hardened to the condescension of self-important men, Béjart had grown hostile. Only by drinking liberally from his horn mug did his chagrin recede as he followed the route back to the caravans.

On his return, he did not mention to the Troupe that he had been sent away like an unwanted thimblerigger. He explained the changed circumstances. Explained that he had had no success pleading their agreement with the Marquess nor with dislodging Le Petit Theatre. The actors sat around their open fire, and to ease their bone chilling indignation, they passed a flacon from hand to hand.

"The man's a worm," said one.

"A frog."

"A poltroon."

"A pox on his pillicock."

"May pigs set upon his children."

Louise, with Georgette's help, put oats, beans, and peas into the pot to cook for their supper. Argon watched Béjart, and at the opportune moment summoned him aside. "What will we do if we find no winter patron?"

"No need to reckon that. There are other chateaux. Other nobles squeezing for status, willing to risk poverty trying to prove their wealth."

"We have not had a winter in the caravans," Argon said, referring to the Augusto Troupe. However, prior to the Troupe, he could recall a wool stapler's cold loft and the smell of sheep. One winter spent in an upper closet of a tavern. Once he had slept on a pallet in a cruck hut.

"No. And we will find a place before snow sticks to the ground."

"I have heard of troupes forced to disband for the winter."

"A portion of them do. We have had good fortune."

"Samuel says he will go to Paris if we find no patron."

"Paris…" Béjart scoffed. "Samuel will beg employment and, if fortune smiles on him, he will survive as a curtain raiser."

"Better raising a curtain in Paris than sleeping in a caravan with ice in your nose and a frozen prick."

"When spring comes, what of his prospects? He will besiege traveling troupes until one gives him temporary quarters." Béjart clutched his son's shoulder. "I will go the morrow and I will find winter quarters."

Argon overcame uncertainty and said, "Prithee, allow me to go with you."

"You are needed here. To watch over Isabelle. To keep the Troupe together. Actors are fickle. Samuel is not the only chary one. Allow no foolish talk. Promise them anything you have to."

Argon made no reply. He was chary himself. He had no confidence in his ability to keep Samuel with the Troupe. Or Louise. Or Hubert.

"Keep the caravans moving unless you get permission to perform in a village. Do what you can to keep the actors performing — wayside taverns or hamlets. Anywhere. If I have not found you in a week, send an outrider to Troyes. I will meet him there at the tavern nearest the cathedral."

ා Scene 12 ൙
unmollified vexation

Argon hardly slept the night. Nor did Isabelle. To her, this turn of events had the rotting scent of nefarious manipulation. She suspected Lord Dubois. Thwarted lovers, in particular men of high position, did not forgive the unavailing temptations of a coquette.

In the early morning light, she spied on Béjart until an opportunity arose when she might occupy his sole attention. As he headed off to water the horses, she wrapped in a blanket and took a cup of tea from the pot sitting in the embers. At the nearby rivulet, she said, "How did Lord Birague explain his deceit to us?"

"I gained no audience to the Marquess." Béjart's breath blew clouds in the air.

"And the Marchioness, did she not remember you?" Isabelle gazed at him.

"She was indisposed. The poor woman flushes her bodily wastes like her monthly courses." He sipped from the steaming cup, aware of Isabelle's vexation.

Isabelle's distaste at *bodily wastes* was only a momentary distraction. "Then we are to have no explanation, just a freezing December in our wagons?" She clutched her blanket to dramatize their cold plight.

Béjart heard well her accusation. "I take leave today for Chateau de Bucey-en-Othe." Though the chateau was not one he had heard well of, a mirthful shoemaker who had repaired his boot declared it had drawn visitors from England. That it was located in the environs was its strongest recommendation.

"If I don't succeed with the baron at the chateau, I will go to Arcis. I know of a wealthy knight there who by reputation patronizes actors. He may steer me to prospects." A mist clouded the trill of water where the horses drank. Only Béjart knew the wealthy knight to be Leon's father, a discovery he had made in his travels. This information he kept to himself, for Leon rarely if ever spoke of his family.

Béjart's narrative neither verified nor negated Isabelle's worries about Lord Dubois. She said, "Lady Birague, poor soul. Her condition, by chance, made her deny a visit from a man such as yourself."

Béjart lifted his chin as he listened. He would not allow the failure of securing the winter appointment be made accountable to him. "Such as myself?"

Isabelle, aware of his vanity, said, "Being a woman, she may allow my presence. In particular, if I offer her a gift." From the Marchioness at Chateau Durckheim, Isabelle planned to discover whether or not Lord Dubois had been a visitor of late. Whether or not he induced Birague to rescind the Troupe's contract. Whether or not she might discover a contact to him.

Béjart handed her the cup, took the reins of the horses, and headed back toward the camp, his boots squeaking in the grass.

Isabelle hurried along with him. "I will beg an audience with her."

"What gift, pray tell? A cure for her disorder?" Despite the damage to his pride, he was a practical man when it came to the Troupe.

Isabelle made the answer that won him over. "My perfumed gloves, the ones made in Paris."

He knew how much they meant to her. "Take Argon with you."

Béjart departed for the Chateau de Bucey-en-Othe. The Augusto actors faced a bleak December. Most nobles had already engaged winter entertainments, except those chateaux spurned by acting troupes, such as Chateau Voisin, where actors were used as targets for archery practice. Or Chateau Evremonde, which treated actors as pimps and whores. Or Chateau Dreux where an actor was thrown into a well for failing to address a duchess as "Your Grace."

The prospect of disbanding grew as the temperature dropped.

Beyond the immediate prospect hovered a potential wound to Béjart's ambition to stage his play at the Palais Royal.

Though they had no side saddle, Isabelle insisted on riding a horse to Chateau Durckheim rather than taking one of the wagons. She borrowed Leon's steed. Argon took one of the draft horses. The two of them rode past fields peppered with stubble where crops had been harvested and where cows or pigs now roamed. The sun lightly stroked vineyards of pinched vines.

At the Chateau, the clop-clop of their horses' hoofs resounded from the stone covered yard to the massive stone structures. Opposing the entry gate stood the chapel, its door watched over by a metal cross two toises high.

Stretching the length of the courtyard was the chateau proper, crowned with three turrets, the center one soaring above those posted at each end.

Isabelle led the way toward the center turret which sheltered a citadel with a front door big enough for a catapult.

"Wait with the horses there until I return." Isabelle pointed to a walled alcove on the side.

As Argon entered the alcove, a peacock flapped briskly out, cawing shrilly. Could he get the peacock, a favorite Noël dish, into his saddle pack? He lunged for it. It screamed. The wing was in his grip.

A scullery maid opened the alcove door. He dropped the wing. The peacock leapt, hopped, and fluttered away.

Carrying a wood bucket, the maid eyed him suspiciously.

"Give you good day," he said, but she pinched her eyebrows and looked ahead as she walked into the courtyard. He led the horses into the alcove and sat on a stone bench carved to the appearance of a tree stump.

Isabelle waited at the door rehearsing what she would say. With no introduction and no entourage, the outcome turned on the name Dubois. The steward opened the wooden door, hung on iron pintels and not well fitting into the stonework. Isabelle said, "I am here at Lord Dubois's insistence. He is anxious to offer my service to amend Lady Birague."

The steward hesitated, appraising the cost of her shoes, which had fancy buckles. "One moment." He closed the door. Isabelle sipped from a flask she carried in her cloak. He returned, motioned her inside saying, "Madame, if you please, follow me."

He led her down a hallway and up a stone spiral staircase to the Marchioness's bed chamber. Isabelle bowed and extended greetings from Lord Dubois as if she were his envoy. "My Lady, I am a healer, much respected by Lord Dubois." She suppressed a gag at the strong and competing scents, at once sweet and sickening. "And I have come at his behest to offer my services."

The chambermaid, who sat by the fireplace embroidering the edge of a veil, gave her a condescending look.

The Marchioness was standing by a window with leaded glass. Wrapped in swaddling, she was able to move about the room, and her favorite place was at a window with a view of the dairy and beyond that, a field extending to a forest. "Madame, the brews of Aeschylus cannot restore to me what has been lost. You may serve your master, but your service to me will be unavailing."

Isabelle had a moment of envy for the grand bed, big as her caravan. Her fingers clenched the silk bag containing Maud Fras's elixir in her pocket. "I am here to make your forthcoming days charitable and happy."

"Alas! Even the Bishop cannot make me happy."

"Your Ladyship, if I fail to please you, Lord Dubois will curse me with God's nails," Isabelle said.

Lady Birague sighed. She could care less about curses on this woman, unashamed of her body and capable of controlling its functions.

Isabelle, who detected the Lady's disinterest, stepped closer and said, "Have you ever faced Lord Dubois's unmollified vexation?"

Lady Birague faced nothing but unmollified vexation. From her husband. From her father. From her servants. From God Himself!

"You know nothing of vexation." She hardened her heart against an onset of sniffles. By the saints in the Vatican, she would not whelp a wad of tears.

"Ah, your Ladyship. Rid yourself of vexation by casting it out."

Lady Birague turned and looked out the window. "You see my condition. I should cast myself out this window."

Isabelle was struck with dismay. She removed the red silk bag with the vial from her pocket and held it in her grip, wary of its strength and determined to use it. "Alas and alak, you cannot yet forego a taste of a nostrum powerful enough to give you flight without landing." She persuaded her Ladyship to call for wine for the two of them.

Lady Birague motioned to the chambermaid her intention to sit. The maid discretely removed undergarments and adjusted the overflowed skirts as the Marchioness straddled her stool.

Isabelle gazed out the window, hardly able to wait for the wine to arrive. "What Lord Dubois wishes me to convey to you is confidential." She looked from her Ladyship to the chambermaid.

Lady Birague, whose love of secrets was as keen as any, sent her attendant from the room as soon as the wine was served.

"This," Isabelle drew the vial containing the elixir from the shiny bag, "contains a rare potion known only to healers trained in sorcery. It has been passed down from Nostradamus." She opened the cork and tipped a drop into her glass of wine. "The ingredients were raveled in the Quatrains." Isabelle put a drop in Lady Birague's glass.

They sipped the sauced drink. A sensation of pleasure flushed their veins.

"Lord Dubois sends this?" Lady Birague held her glass for Isabelle to refill it.

They were giddy, lured to euphoria by the potion.

"Dare not whisper this to a soul, but ..." Isabelle paused suggestively. "Lord Dubois is smitten by a madame in a theatre troupe."

"Ah, his weakness is actors. And he is often smitten." Her

Ladyship's hand pressed on her midriff. The moment passed, projecting noxious gases.

Isabelle snickered and raised her wine glass. "A toast. To my Lady's disarming odor."

They laughed. Lady Birague said, "The sweet savor of the day is but a relief from the stink." They drank heartily.

"You, my Lady, have good humor as you sit at stool."

"Like spitting in a spittoon." She smiled broadly at her simile.

But it wasn't like spitting, but neither of them wished to change the mood.

Isabelle wished to comfort Lady Birague, but she didn't say *Why grieve about our flaws?* for she knew in her heart that the Lady had every right to grieve. Every right to cry out in anger to God. Every right to rid herself of a life too unwholesome to live.

They sat in comfortable silence.

"His attentions are intense, as if he may lose his mind if he lose the actor," said Isabelle, quoting from one of Lord Dubois's letters.

Lady Birague raised her plucked eyebrows. "The stage at the Salle des Machines in Paris employs strumpets he makes love to. They soon fall into disfavor, mayhap with the assistance of Lady Dubois." She summoned the chambermaid for another bottle of wine.

"Lady Dubois … poor petite. One needs be clever to beguile His Lordship." Isabelle restrained a giggle.

"She is his equal. Her renown for causing misfortune is well earned."

"As I live, am I treading upon thorns? Dare I worry that her foolish presumption will turn him against me, his hapless messenger?"

"Be wary. Lord Dubois only thinks of living joyously." Lady Birague looked at Isabelle and smiled. "Does his wife know of your service?"

The wine arrived and the servant poured with more attention to the two women than the drip of wine. She dallied serving the glasses. Upon her dismissal, she listened at the door to no avail, for the thick oak wood broke off sounds.

Isabelle sipped and said, "I have never attended the Lady, nor has his Lordship requested my service on her behalf."

Lady Birague tilted her head and said, "And have you rendered service to Lord Dubois?" Her look gave Isabelle to understand she did not mean a healing service.

Isabelle drank from her glass more liberally than she should have. "My Lady, I am a healer, not a harlot."

Despite Isabelle's acting ability, Lady Birague detected a ghostly disquiet. "If you think Lady Dubois does not know everything her husband does, you are mistaken." She said this with warmth, for she had enjoyed a time free of her burden. She had believed she would never laugh again, and she had.

Isabelle added a drop of elixir to each glass and in a rush of generosity, handed the vial to Lady Birague. "Take no more than a drop at a time. And take no more today."

"What a lovely bag." The Lady had noticed the shiny red silk.

"This bag once contained precious gems from an admirer. They are gone now, but in their stead I have a chateau unlike any other." Isabelle didn't dare mention that she lived in a caravan that Béjart bought from an Italian merchant who said it once belonged to a sultan. The claim was credible, for the interior gleamed in candlelight. The wall shelves, trimmed with carved wood and gilded with gold, were imbedded with pearls, crystals, and other stones. Paintings of satyrs and nymphs on the walls. There had been a glazed window, but after a thief broke in they sealed it.

It took Isabelle some time to figure out how to pose the question she had come to ask, but after more merriment and blathering and sideways maneuvers, she said, "How does Lady Dubois know all her husband does?"

Lady Birague tossed her head back and laughed. She had waited and chatted and wondered if this strange and beautiful woman was Lord Dubois's mistress. "Beware of his page. The boy is liege to Lady Dubois."

Lady Birague thanked Isabelle for the elixir. She had relented and allowed this one visitor and for that she was happy. Isabelle had brought her a present she sorely needed.

Outside, Argon paced around the alcove and stamped feeling into his numb feet. He had visited the fish pond and counted the fish, most of them as motionless as the water. Incidental servants appeared in the courtyard and scuttled from door to door.

He hummed, eventually it was a tune. The notes turned from back to front until he realized the song was one he had heard before. "Come all you jolly drinkers, come listen to my song." Into fragments he interwove his lyrics. "Of ale as dark as night and a shapely maid …" Before he knew it, he had a new song derived from an old one. "But I'll not be married and saddled with a wife …" With no quill, ink pot, or paper to write it down, he looked into Isabelle's saddle pouch on the unlikely chance she had them.

Her leather waterskin. He chewed on icy water from it and replaced it in her pouch. From deeper down he withdrew a collar of pearls and a bundle of curly hair, which smelled sweetly of citrus blossoms. When he sank his nose into it, Isabelle arose in the scent and filled his head with affection. He found a wrapped morsel of bread, which he ate.

He brought out a small box which contained the perfumed gloves. In a moment of incertitude, he started for the front door with it, assuming she had forgotten the gift she had come to deliver. However, much time had passed. He paused before the door. She would have realized her mistake by now and returned for the gift. He went back to the alcove and replaced the gloves.

As they were riding back to the Augusto Troupe's camp, Argon said, "Were your gloves well received?"

"The wine she offered had a savor of smoke and leather … extraordinary. Never have I tasted such." She giggled. "The effects are still upon me."

"Were you so overcome by wine you forgot to present the

gloves?" Argon looked for signs of surprise, or dismay, or some indication that she had forgotten them.

"A great liveliness corrupts my mind." Isabelle laughed and slipped to the side of her saddle and caught herself.

"In your liveliness, did you remember to query her about the Marquess's deception?" Argon said.

"Lady Birague is affected with black flux. Alas, her troubles are greater than ours."

"Will the Marquess allow us room and fare?" Having stood outside, hungry and cold, Argon dreamed of the warm fires and velvet-padded chairs inside the Chateau Durckheim.

"She did partake of my pleasure. As did I." Isabelle righted herself in the saddle and sat up as if she had won applause.

"What benefice did you gain? What advantage?" Argon added spitefully, "Other than 'extraordinary' wine for yourself?"

"Chateau Durckheim is cursed." Isabelle mumbled. "Poor femme. The rot she has to live with." She pulled tight the reins and stopped her horse, dismounted, and wobbled as she walked to the nearest evergreen and disappeared behind it. When she returned, she attended the horses while Argon peed.

Argon gave her a leg up as she lurched into her saddle. When the animals fell into a rhythmic gait, he said, "I stood in the cold till the sun shriveled and to what advantage? Did your skillful tongue win nothing more than a taste of wine?"

"I have requested another audience anon. She will not refuse me that." Isabelle said forcefully as if to bind the Marchioness to her will. She had confidence that the elixir had the power to win the Lady's approbation. "She will give me her favor in due time."

"In due time I will freeze my arse off." Argon kicked his horse angrily.

❧ Scene 13 ❧
a witch's venom

While Béjart departed to pursue winter accommodations the following day, the actors, traveling without a destination, trailed behind Hubert's wagon. They passed a field where stubs stood in shadowy stances along the line of the reaper's cut. Where the road split was a sign for the local lord's millhouse. Argon said, "Perchance we will find a chateau near the millhouse." Hubert agreed and they turned in that direction. Argon urged his horse ahead of the caravans to see the way beforehand.

He had gone barely a league when he drew on the reins and stopped at a wood sign with a drawing of a skull. The skull's cavernous sockets would have unnerved a person of less fortitude than Argon, but his hardiness began in the womb when he withstood abortifacients that Isabelle had taken.

Argon ventured ahead more slowly when he saw a frightful robed spectre the height and shape of a human. Protruding from its mask was a beak bigger than the horn of an ox. It wore a wide-brim, leather hat.

With a gloved hand, the Huguenot leader inside the costume raised his spear-like pole with a point of wings. "Do you not see the sign?" he said in a stifled voice, not that he was nervous but the mask obstructed his speaking.

Argon tightened the lines on his horse, which pranced backwards, and but for his tight control, would have galloped away. "Of what sign, my good man?"

"The warning." He gestured with his spear.

"What ill will brews in this hamlet?"

"The ill will of God himself," said the Huguenot aloud and in silent prayer begged forgiveness for ascribing to God the King's ill-will. For it was the King who had forced his people out of their homes and censured their trade and commerce.

"God be merciful to us poor sinners." Argon found such invocations promoted good will. He suspected from the costume that the man was an actor himself, but to what end he could not imagine.

"My good man, begone before God's breath brings on you a curse of boils and swellings." The Huguenot seldom had to encounter a traveler, for the plague warning usually frightened them away from their colony of worshippers.

In a sudden move, his horse wheeled in a circle, and Argon saw Hubert walking toward the two of them. He raised his arms and waved Argon nearer.

"God be with you," said Argon to the spectre as he turned back and met Hubert.

Hubert said, "It is a plague doctor. Let us begone … and with haste."

"The plague? 'Tis not now a danger. He wants us begone for some other reason."

"What would that be?" said Hubert with winded breath.

"Perchance he is an actor of another troupe, an outrider awaiting their arrival."

"And for what?" said Hubert.

At a distance, the plague doctor's metal-ringed eyes stared at them from behind glazed circles. He grasped his spear, turned, and glanced behind him. Out of view but hardly a furlong away was another Huguenot poised to rush back and assemble the villagers, dressed as plague victims, in places where strangers would see them.

Argon said, "Winter quarters, just as we are. The lord owning the mill will have a nearby chateau."

Hubert moved around so that Argon and his horse were between himself and the plague doctor. "There's the skull. Now this. Nay, 'tis the plague."

"By the rood, does this doctor heal using terror?"

"The beak mask is stuffed with herbs to keep him from breathing foul air. I'll not chance an encounter with the plague." Hubert headed back toward the wagons. "Pray that the plague is not rising again." The heaviness in his steps had origin in a memory. Picking mushrooms. A vile smell had warned him. He had thought it the remains of a goblin. Until he recognized her shoes. The breasts he had lusted after were drooling black effluvium. "Have you touched it?" His mother had squealed. She ran from him. Made him sleep in the stable.

Argon clucked his horse. "That be a doctor to frighten a sufferer into hell."

"No nostrum stops the plague. A doctor such as this only counts the dead."

At Hubert's insistence, they drove past sundown, putting distance between themselves and the mill hamlet. A buzzard flew over their wagons as twilight gave way to darkness. Georgette was reminded of buzzards that perched on her childhood home. So many, her father had fallen from the roof trying to get them off.

The moon's phosphorous glow crept through hazy clouds. As the horses plodded the road through wintry woods, cold shadows appeared and moved with the clouds.

The flicker of lamplight drew them to a peasant's lodging, which smelled of pigs. The house, made of planks covered with mud, had a thatched roof. Numerous heads poked into the doorway from the large room fronting the road. Inside, a fireplace served to warm the living quarter as well as a barn, attached to the rear of the house where the animals spent the night.

"Kind sir, I pray thee, a place to park our wagons for the night," said Hubert.

With the farmer's permission, they settled in the yard. In the darkness, the actors wrapped in sheepskins and huddled in their cots. Agnes could be heard worrying. "The skull has cursed us."

"Who will it be?" whispered Etienne.

"Be? Be what?"

"Who will get the plague?"

"Go to sleep and worry not yourself," said Argon.

"It means nothing," said Leon from his caravan.

"A skull means death," said Agnes.

"I have a lump on my neck," said Etienne.

"Holy Mother of God! Where is the tinder?" Georgette said.

"Wait till the morning," said Hubert.

"Nay. I must have a see." Georgette arose, fired a splinter at the tinder box, and lit a candle.

"Ow!" said Etienne.

"Quiet! I am only having a look. Be still."

"It is sore. Ow. Do not do that!"

"Quiet! You will wake the farmer," said Argon. "And that will surely bring us ill fortune."

"This is no bubo. 'Tis but a pimple. Go to sleep," said Georgette.

"We must go to the apothecary for the root of a mandrake to protect us," said Agnes.

"Your blather will sooner curse us than the skull," growled Leon.

"Speak no more of curses," said Hubert.

Agnes moaned. She would have said *God save us*, if she had been a good Catholic. The wagon boards creaked getting colder, sounding to her like the approach of cloven hoofs.

Etienne touched his inflamed pustule, the work of either God or a demon. Had his stomach not pinched with hunger, he would have fallen asleep before concerning himself.

Eugene, sleeping in the caravan with Argon, sensed a familiar aura that caused a sizzle in his nose. The twitching started. His tongue curled. He moaned.

"By the mass, 'tis cold," Argon said.

But Eugene's shaking was not from the cold. Upon realizing that, Argon climbed into his friend's cot and wrapped himself around Eugene until the quaking stopped. Argon had gradually come to understand that Eugene had a God-given malady.

Argon climbed back into his cot but didn't sleep. He wished to ignore Agnes, who had a way of provoking whatever she claimed to be avoiding. If Béjart were there, he would dispel fear and restore calm. But Argon could not reckon Béjart's whereabouts or circumstances; whether he had met with success or misfortune. There were times when Argon wished a curse on Agnes's tongue.

The actors awoke to an iron sky. In the night, water buckets had glazed with ice. With no destination, there was no need to hurry. Once on the road, they plodded along in a drizzle of water and sleet. Splashes washed up the horses' hocks. The wagon wheels squished in mud and reminded Agnes of her mother's gasping.

During the following days they traveled from village to village, and wherever possible, put on bawdy shows of trifling amusement — ballads, dancing, acrobatics. The locations varied — a tavern, guild hall, hamlet, or manor house.

They began to make their way to the point of rendezvous with Béjart. Audiences grew thin, the sou-cup sounded hollow. The actors hustled through their lines to warm their blood.

In the afternoon on the eve of Noël, they stopped and camped in a farmer's fallow field. "By cock, I'll go back to the tavern and get a proper bed," said Leon, who refused to remain in his caravan another cold night. He left for the Bon Vivant Inn, located at a crossroads they had passed earlier. Others would have done likewise, but the cloud over their future made them frugal.

While they sat about the open fire wrapped in blankets, Hubert remained in his caravan on his cot, sick with fever and fearful of his breath. As night approached, the young men opted for the Bon Vivant, where ale was plentiful and the fire warm.

"Bring half a score of dates from the inn, should they have it," said Georgette, taking over as cook from Louise, whose efforts had produced bland potage and brutalized meat.

At the tavern, Argon, Eugene, and Samuel met Leon, who sat at a table near the vibrant fire. "What provisions for Noël dinner?" said Leon, who had not decided whether he would take the meal at the tavern or join the Troupe.

"Georgette is making boiled capon with pippins," Argon said. He asked the tapster about dates but, being the eve of Noël, the man refused to bother the owner's wife.

As they sat at table and warmed to the brew and fire, the groom who managed the stables entered, stamping his feet and blowing his hands. After he quaffed of ale, he said, "The village bells tolled today."

"The Catholics tolling Noël," said Leon peevishly.

"Nay, 'tis no holy day this," said the groom.

"Who is the unlucky soul?" said the tapster, a burly man who spoke better Spanish than French. After a battle injury in the Fronde, he had been abandoned by the retreating Spanish forces.

"Lady Birague of the Chateau Durckheim, God bless her soul," said the groom.

"Perchance she will agree to associate with Jesus Christ," said the tapster. The Lady had earned a reputation for being haughty because she did not attend church and made no appearance outside the castle.

"There is a breath of odium withal," said the groom.

The room awaited an explanation while the groom stood at the fire and turned from back to front until his breeches steamed. "The lady's chambermaid was forced from the house. The Marquess has in his mind that his lady died most unnatural."

"And what is meant by unnatural?" said the tapster.

"The chambermaid said a witch visited ere the Lady died. And thereafter, the Lady laughed most unnatural. Was given to reverie. Like a person cast in a spell."

Though the other actors merely listened averagely, Argon realized Isabelle had been a visitor, perhaps the presumptive visitor. He took a draught of ale. Isabelle was of a hot-blooded temper. She, perhaps more than the others, abhorred the Marquess for the treatment they had received.

She had not given the gloves to the Marchioness. She had not admitted it. Argon tipped his tankard to drain bits of grain or a bug, which lingered in his gorge. Despite what appeared to be an unconcluded mission, Isabelle had considered it a success. He reckoned her innocence or guilt. As a given, innocent was not a word that attached itself to Isabelle. He ordered another ale. That she might have poisoned the Marchioness entered his head despite his avoiding the idea.

The actors walked in pitch dark back to the camp and ate heartily of what remained of the capon. Later, when only Agnes and Etienne were awake and sitting near the fire, Argon lit a candle from the coals and, with it to light the way, went to Isabelle's caravan where he knocked on the shutters of the door.

"Be gone. I am asleep," she mumbled from inside.

"It is Argon." He was unsteady from ale.

"Come back the morrow."

"No. Open the door."

A rustling of woolens sounded from inside, the latch clicked, and the door creaked. Argon ducked as he entered the low overhead, lower than other caravans with canvas covers. He put the candle in a holder and said, "Lady Birague is dead."

Isabelle's face, covered with pomatum containing fat, bees wax, and spermaceti, glowed like another candle. "God's wounds! She must have taken too much."

"Too much what?" As Argon sat on the empty cot, he was relieved to see her astonishment.

"How do you know she is dead?" Isabelle sat on the side of her cot.

"I heard it at the Bon Vivant. It is bruited about that she was poisoned."

"Poisoned? Who said?"

"The Marquess himself is dubious. He sent away the Lady's chambermaid. And the maid is telling of a witch who visited and cast a spell on the Marchioness."

"They will blame us."

"Should they blame us?"

"Argon, we have to move the caravan the morrow. We cannot stay here."

"What did you give Lady Birague instead of the gloves?" said Argon.

"How do you know I did not give the gloves?"

"It does not matter. What did you give her?"

"Have you been spying on me?" Isabelle put her hand to her chest.

"That is no answer."

"This is no small pain from a son I so love." Her voice choked.

Her words wounded him, but he suspected her of deliberately distracting him. "You visited her. She turned into a lunatic. And now she is dead," said Argon.

"Are you accusing me?" Isabelle's eyes glistened black from the white pomatum mask.

Argon loved her, but ordinary love did not get her attention. "What did you give Lady Birague?"

"Nothing of ill purpose." Isabelle was of many minds, but one certainty prevailed. Sorcery meant a bonfire with villagers gawking at a body going up in flames. And proof of sorcery required a mere accusation, she well knew. She had only to recall the Ursuline nun's few words that had sent a priest to the stake.

"Béjart will know how to get a straight answer from you." Argon picked up the candle.

"No!" She came to her feet beside him and, in the confined area, leaned backward to keep from bumping into Argon. "You must not tell Béjart." Isabelle's wide eyes blazed.

Argon brimmed at the terror in her voice. "Tell me."

She clasped his free hand. "I gave her a potion. To amend her stricken body."

"Potion? Or poison?" *Poison* emerged from his lips without intention. The word burned his gullet. He swallowed hard.

"By my troth, it was not poison!" Her theatrical voice, scornful and incredulous. "Surely you do not think that of me!"

"No." Argon put his arm around her shoulder. He wanted her arms to enclose him, but she braced herself and with a deep breath stiffened her back. He said, "The Marquess thinks it was poison."

"It was a potion to lessen pain. I have taken it myself," Isabelle's tone demanded that he listen.

"We have to tell Béjart."

She reared back. "If you say eversomuch as a word, I will quit the Troupe. I will never speak to you again." Isabelle's jaw hardened in taut lines. She heaved a breath. "I happened to visit her at a hapless time. But how was I to know she was going to die?"

"It is an unseemlie thing for us." He reached for the door.

"You will not talk to Béjart!" Isabelle watched him descend the ladder steps.

Argon left without pledging his silence, walked to his caravan, and climbed inside where Eugene snored in the cot atop a trunk. Argon lay on the cot athwart the small space and let the candle burn itself to a viscous puddle. He stared at the canvas cover and wondered about bad luck.

Isabelle lay in her cot but could not sleep. She had to take flight. And quickly. In a wagon. That she had never hitched one to a horse kept her awake. She needed a plan.

The following day the word *witch* spread among the actors, some of whom whispered that Isabelle had been to Chateau Durckheim. Agnes, whose jealousy exceeded her admiration for Isabelle, knocked at Isabelle's caravan door.

"Enter," said Isabelle, who was considering which outfits to take with her and which to leave behind.

Pleasantries aside, Agnes said, "It was sorcery, they say, about Lady Birague. But it was not a taste of mine." She often led people to false conclusions about herself in order to establish a confidentiality in the hope that confessions would flourish.

"And how does yours taste?" Isabelle held in her hand a taffeta doublet. She was choosing between it and a satin cloak. A caravan as a means of escape was too complicated and too noticeable. Her departure on a horse was possible. But she could only take what fit into panniers.

"Not so bitter as yours, if your reputation proves your character." Agnes made the remark expecting to be either slapped or ridiculed, which made no difference. She loved surprise.

Isabelle did neither. She continued to sort her costumes as if searching for something in particular. "So well do I appreciate how you inform me frankly of the truth." The mockery in her voice was near impossible to ignore, but Agnes did.

"No magician is ashamed to aright the devil's obstructions. 'Tis due time justice was meted out to the Marchioness." Agnes glanced at Isabelle for signs of her approval. "Little by little I have educated myself to herbals. I have much to learn, if you but teach me." Her single experience with potions had been to feed consecrated wafers to a frog which she burnt to a powder and surreptitiously added to her mother's vial of water.

"Mayhap." Isabelle turned her back to dismiss Agnes.

Agnes, to whom *mayhap* meant *certainly*, was uplifted as she left. Better than a life on the stage was that of an herbarian. As any but an actor knew, it was easier to learn the intricacies of medicinal herbs than lines in a play.

Before midday, Argon was confident Isabelle had no such malice as to poison Lady Birague. In the afternoon after a mug of wine filched from Hubert's supply, he became uncertain. Isabelle's passion ran deep. This made her a commanding actor. It also made her willful and protective of her reputation. That Lord Birague withdrew his invitation had jeopardized not just her reputation but the future of the Troupe. She was capable of exacting revenge, but would she do it?

The entire Troupe faced shrinking prospects. Having to huddle in a caravan in snow storms. Tasteless suppers of beet skins or cabbage cores or salted onions. Other actors had been forced to Paris and whatever fate they could find. Isabelle was not the only one who shriveled at the idea if it meant emptying privy buckets for other actors.

On the other hand, Argon held dear his dream of the Palais Royal, becoming a member of Molière's company, appearing before the King. He hesitated and took another draft of wine. The Marquess's betrayal had put their dreams in purgatory with no priest to pray them out. The sense of loss sloshed in his mug and he drained it.

All of them teetered on the brink of a winter more profound than the weather. Argon bit his lower lip. He came to the view that if Isabelle had poisoned the Marchioness, he was glad.

☙ Scene 14 ❧
hanging perilously at an angle

The tangle of oak and beech branches brought Béjart closer to his childhood, a time when he had traveled with his father and camped in the woods. Though most people heard only silence in forests, he knew the creak of cold limbs, the moan of the wind, the silvery pitch of dried leaves.

Near the Chateau de Bucey-en-Othe, he guided his horse from the packed dirt road. Behind a stand of holly bushes flush with evergreen leaves, he transformed himself from a mere paysan into a man of substance. Off with the wool tunic and on with his haute waistcoat and high heeled shoes.

Guided by the periwig's part, he adjusted it to his crown and tightened the ribbon knots. With his panniers repacked with his common clothes, he returned to the road, mounted his horse, and continued toward the Chateau. Restless clouds moved swiftly overhead, momentarily translucent in the sun's illumination.

The avenue approaching the castle gate welled with clumps of weedy roots. Stark briars grew on the barbican wall. Musty stones arched over the gate, coated with brown moss. Littered about the courtyard were oddments — an axle, broken stones, iron bars, barrel staves, wagon wheel spokes. As Béjart walked his horse to the well, the wind swept up sand and spewed it across the yard.

He looked into the well. Far below, the black shine of water rippled as if harboring a living force. Without a bucket or pulley, he had no way of getting a drink for either himself or his horse.

Vines climbed like chains up the wall of the chateau and grew into the storied windows. Sunlight streamed through rifts in the clouds and showed the patchwork tiles on the roof.

Béjart tied his horse to a tall larch tree in the courtyard and approached double doors of a size to allow a trebuchet passage. He turned away from the iron lock, big as a horse's hoof, and calling, "Ave, a-va," cautiously walked to the rear and gained entry to a labyrinth of passages which opened into a vacated room with a massive chest.

A purple curtain's loose threads waved in a breeze that came through the open window. From the cathedral ceiling echoed the scraping of his boots on the grainy floor. Of what good was a king and his regime when the poor farmer could hardly afford a roof over his head while such a chamber as this moldered?

He strolled into a room with scattered pieces of cloth and a long table with a broken leg. From the spiral stairway, hanging perilously at an angle, a bird as big as a falcon flew out the window. The fireplace, choked with ashes, needed but cleaning, kindling and wood. He could almost feel the blazing warmth. His Troupe might survive the winter in such a room.

Béjart wandered from room to vacant room, kicking aside leaves that had blown in through the windows. Tracks in the dirt banked against the floorboards betrayed habitation by animals. A restive air whistled in the shutters.

The stairs to the cellar were well worn. As he descended, no cobwebs netted him, evidence that footsteps had trod the passageway. Beyond the buttery and larder was a dark undercroft where light from a glazed window defined shadowy objects. Béjart stood still, anticipating movement. Only scurrying mice.

Disarrayed, open-lidded wood boxes of a man's size, some stacked on others. As he walked closer he realized they contained human remains. A woman's torso clung to a sideboard as if climbing out. Béjart stepped away, momentarily confused about whether she had moved. On a dust covered table beneath the window were skulls and other bones.

He cautiously moved from one coffin to another — emaciated faces, long hair, a fortune to a wigmaker. He had no heart to collect it from the skull despite its value.

A gray headed body's overlapping teeth disconcerted him. He saw his grandfather's smile and teeth, despite knowing those bones lay under a linen cloth just outside the hamlet of Champmol in an unconsecrated grave Béjart's father had dug. His grandfather had become no mummy, not like the ones in this cavern. He liked to think the rain had borne his remains into the soil that had trickled down to the stream where he had been fishing. Where he had caught a big one.

"Come here, help me get him out of the water," his father had said, tugging at the body.

Béjart had run away and crouched behind a tree.

"Come here!"

"No. No. No!"

Water splashed. His father had fallen into the stream trying to drag the body to the shallows.

"Papa..."

His father's wail had reached the tree tops. An eagle flapped its wings taking flight. Birds fluttered away. Distressed by his father's sobs, Béjart crept to the stream. The two of them trawled the body to the shallows. His father sat rocking himself, his hands on his head.

Béjart had sat on the soggy bank and stared at the body. A mess on the back of the head. The stream flowed peacefully about the arms and legs. A dragonfly landed on the tunic. A small fish nibbled at the bare skin above the sodden boot.

Béjart's father rubbed his face and cleared his throat. "Help me get him on the bank."

"No. I'll not touch him."

"Then what will you do? Leave him here for fish to nibble off his flesh?"

Béjart had cried.

"Here, boy. Papa is waiting for us to take care of him." His father turned the body over on to its back. The lips were parted. A salamander spilled from his mouth. His overlapping teeth glistened as if oiled by the sun.

They didn't talk about his grandfather's death. Despite the wound to the head, Béjart had assumed he had drowned. Years later he came to realize that when the crowd had shouted "Three Faces!" at his grandfather, it had been a death sentence, pronounced by rabblerousers and executed by the same.

✳

Béjart moved from one mummified body to another. One wore a periwig much like his. Suddenly a tongue appeared in the mouth, redder than burnt blood. Béjart shuffled backward and bumped into a coffin, which collided with another.

He stared in disbelief at the tongue, which crawled out of the mouth as a large, roach-like bug. It crept across the leathery chin, across the yellow neck, the sunken chest. The biggest bug he had ever seen. Its antennae twitched and pointed at the mummy's hands, which clasped a crude book.

Béjart took a deep breath. The bug was indeed the tongue of the mummy speaking to him. He reached into the coffin and as he took the book, the mummy's hands folded prayerfully. The bug scurried underneath pieces of the winding sheet and disappeared.

His horse neighed in the courtyard. Footsteps scrubbed the stones outside. He stuck the book into his waistcoat, hurried upstairs, and entered the great hall as the opposing door opened. In lurched a man with a scarred beard and oily hair last washed when it rained. Béjart stopped in mid-step and affected an air of nonchalance despite facing a powerfully built ruffian with the torso of a Tartar warrior.

"Look you here! Where go you?" The man's upper lip curled. His eyelids sloped.

Béjart leaned forward and touched the concealed hilt of the stiletto in the baldric under his waistcoat. "How now! Where is the baron?"

"I am the baron."

"And I am King Louie," said Béjart.

The ruffian guffawed, showing a broken front tooth. Béjart paced unobtrusively, putting distance between himself and the man. As a boy, he had seen the guts ripped from a man lulled by a congenial assailant.

"I have a message for the baron," said Béjart.

"Then you have a hapless task ... and will meet with much peril."

"Do you say the baron is a threat to such as a mere messenger?" said Béjart.

The ruffian paced in Béjart's footsteps. "Nay. But alas, the baron's wife is Dutch. They have returned to Amsterdam."

If that was the case, the owner was one of many merchants who, faced with the King's hostility toward the Dutch, had left France. "Ah, bien sûr. I hear that the King will send his men with shovels and pickaxes to throw Holland into the sea," said Béjart.

Curious about the ruffian's warrant to occupy the manor, Béjart said, "Are you the caretaker?" Minor chirrs and scrapes from other rooms, though only the wind, raised in him the thought of other possible occupants.

A casual grin twisted the man's lips. "The answer be well worth three sou."

Béjart smelled his sour breath and backed toward the door. "Yea, truly, that be an answer. The gentilhomme of this chateau would not hire a caretaker so cheap."

The man roared with laughter. "Look you here, it is well you're here. Take a cup of thankworthy wine with me."

Béjart's mouth was as dry as a catacomb but he needed no time to consider the invitation. "Gramercy. But I am on a mission." Without turning his back on the man, he talked continually, making his way to the back door. "My lord needs find other means of dealing with the master of Chateau de Bucey-en-Othe." Stepping outside, he said, "I wish a good day to you, sir."

He watched the door as he threw himself into his saddle. Watched his rear as he rode out of the courtyard. Moderated his vigilance when he was back on the high road.

Béjart took the road to Arcis, but sundown came betimes, and though he had slept on a sheepskin on the ground many a night, the cold of winter too easily got into his bones. He rode until distant torches informed the dark of a manor house. In the courtyard, alight with numerous torches, were several carriages hitched to horses dutifully awaiting their owners. From inside the manor came the strains of Noël music.

"Hoy! Who comes there?" said a groomsman strolling bow-legged from the stable.

"Hail, good man, I am a traveler too far from home and seeking cover for the night." Béjart rubbed a sou between his thumb and fingers.

"God's pity! 'Tis a curse to be dickering and doddering this night afore the onset of Noël." With fingers stained a hue of leather, the groomsman motioned Béjart down from his horse. "Follow me." He led Béjart and his horse to a stall in the stables. "There is hay for your horse. And straw for a mattress," he said with cheerful good will, pocketing the coin.

Béjart lay in the hay and took restful ease as bursts of laughter came from the manor house. The groomsman, preoccupied by ale and the scullery maid who brought it, disappeared. Soon enough the guests descended the manor and claimed their carriages.

Béjart, unable to sleep, overheard a lady taking to a carriage with her husband. "Heigh! How lavish the tongues tonight. Did you hear of the Marquess de Bouligneux's expected visit to the Chateau de Giffaumont?" She laughed merrily. "And Count de Gondrin was taking his winter in Paris..."

The man laughed. "Has the count returned to Giffaumont?"

"Certes, I would imagine so."

"He will revive the kitchen fires posthaste."

"And order wine."

The voices trailed away as did the clomping of hoofs heading out of the courtyard.

The following morning, Béjart paid the groomsman, watered his horse, and returned to the road to Arcis. Church bells gonged Noël from one hamlet to the next, which Béjart heard more as reproach than a celebration, for Augusto Troupe still had no winter quarters.

After passing through the gatehouse at Arcis, Béjart dismounted and awaited a procession led by two monks and the local priest. Musicians marched and played variously a recorder, shawm, and tabor. Villagers, wrapped in wools and furs, waved flags as they accompanied a rolling platform pulled by horses and bearing an effigy of the baby Jesus in a cradle. Holy Mary, standing on a platform, was carried by six men robed in purple satin. Children whirled scarves and danced. At the cathedral, the procession halted and the holy men mounted the steps. Clang, clang! The tower bells rang continuously.

The production of mystery plays had been undermined by the rise of Protestants, but they reappeared during the season of Noël. Whatever Béjart thought of the church, its mystery plays had paved the way for the theater, whether traveling companies or the Parisian stage.

Béjart threaded his way through the crowd and continued on the cobblestone street. Shops were closed. Tavern doors locked. The inn likewise closed, but his sou prevailed over custom, and he was given a bed. For an added coin, the innkeeper took care of his horse.

Though he had not observed Advent with fasting, his meals had been meager. His mouth watered at the aromas — roasted chines, mutton broth, pasty venison, pheasants. With the promise of deniers, the maid servant brought him a minced pie.

In mid-afternoon as he lay abed, the noise outside faded away only to be replaced by the creak of a coffin lid. The mummy climbed out. It hovered over Béjart, breathing on him. Hot breath. Soughing. He sat up directly, still under the spell of his dream.

Something important was unfinished. He drank wine from his pouch. The mummy's book was on the straw-strewn floor beside his bed. He picked it up.

The ink reeled across the page producing uncertain sentences. Reading the words was an exercise in interpretation. "Am held captive in a dungeon far from my rightful home." Or perhaps it was "Beheld captives domiciled far from righteous honor."

As Béjart accustomed himself to the writing style, he read with greater confidence. "My tongue molders but not my words. Heed me, I pray." A glacier crept into Béjart. A dread that the spirit of the book had the power of a curse. His eyes watered. The diary shifted in his hand. He put it down and wiped his slippery palm.

"What nonsense," he said to himself. He flipped pages quickly, catching glimpses of the content. Words came and went. The longer he flipped, a pattern of repeating words emerged: *herein, revealed, evil, herein, vice, revealed, herein evil, vice.* Though Béjart was no more superstitious than any other actor, an inspiration overcame him. He got it into his head that the spirit of the book was beseeching him to write its story.

A packet that had been sewn shut was wax-sealed to the back cover. He fingered the powdery contents and noticed its dainty inscription, "cross of François des Loges."

In the street, children shouted and chased about, and parents conversed at one another's door. Béjart went to the stable, watered his horse and gave it an apple he'd cadged from a yeoman. From the brief talk he had overheard about visitors to Chateau de Giffaumont, Béjart reckoned a possible opportunity and visited the apothecary. "Has the major domo for Lord Gondrin been in for theriac?"

"On what account?"

"Ah, it is whispered that he makes haste to Chateau de Giffaumont. Caught unawares by a marquess's visit."

The apothecary shrugged and had no report that was helpful.

Béjart wondered aloud to the blacksmith about a loose horse-shoe and mentioned the Count de Gondrin's return from Paris.

"Marry!" The blacksmith pointed at a carriage parked against a wall cluttered with hanging hooks, chains, buckles, barrel hoops, and such. "His marshal would have his carriage repaired afore the light of day. I rouse before the sun, work displeasant and forceful on his axle, and yet no one from the chateau claims it."

With that, Béjart's ears quickened. He called on the tallow chandler. After buying a half-score of candles, he said, "Do you know a cuisine in need of plentiful provisions? I raised an over-supply of hares for Noël."

The chandler tipped his chin up and bethought but said nothing.

"Does the Count entertain at the Chateau de Giffaumont this Noël?"

The chandler revived as if awaking. "Some celebration is afoot belike. But two days agone, the major domo ordered a hundred candles."

With confidence that the Count had returned from Paris and taken residence at his chateau, Béjart saddled his horse and presented himself at the gate house.

The steward allowed entry and guided him to the master's chamber and the Count. In a performance worthy of the Palais Royal, Béjart declared the entertainments his troupe provided. He acted a comedic servant worthy of Arlecchino; he sang "Ce Fut en Mai" as well as ever did Folquet de Marseille; he performed a Moorish dance. The Count, who did not admit to needing anybody or anything, leaned in his chair as if bored. He dismissed Béjart with, "Go to the kitchen. The cook will give you a hearty meal."

Béjart was not discouraged. He had met the likes of the Count before. Many a noble inflated their reputations by belittling the efforts of others.

After a meal of three collops of bacon in the servants' dining hall, he was escorted to the door and bade farewell by the steward who said, "My Lord will provide accommodation for your best diversions." Béjart hardly heard the enumeration of conditions the Count imposed upon the Troupe's behavior and performances. Lightheaded with success, he headed back to rendez-vous with the Troupe.

ꙮ Scene 15 ꙮ
Isabelle attends a funeral

In Troyes near Chateau Durckheim, Noël activities—processions, mystery plays, musicals—came to a halt on the fourth morning of Noël. A single church bell tolled a mournful cadence and continued unceasingly for hours. The cathedral door was draped in black. One of the monks arriving to assist with the funeral informed the priest that a rumor had spread about a witch having visited Lady Birague.

The priest had poorly handled a previous accusation, made by a peasant about his wife. There had been no evidence to the peasant's claim that she chewed on the bones of cadavers. The woman had no teeth. When the Church had investigated and found no evidence of sorcery, the husband had bruited it about the village that she had stolen the child that had come missing some months previously and carried it off to a cave beneath the earth.

This had set off an uprising of indignation and a demand that the Church hold another trial. The priest had suspected the peasant of making false claims to rid himself of a wife, but his call for reason had not been heard above the clamor of local yeomen. While he had been indecisive, villagers had dragged the woman out of her hut and hanged her at the town gates with cries of "Begone! Demon's shape!" "Devil take thee!" In the aftermath, many of his parishioners lost respect for the priest.

When he heard the monk's report of another witch, he went forthwith to the Marquess de Birague. "I know every family in this village and comté. There are no witches here."

The Marquess, despite his affection for his wife, was glad to be rid of the foul smell in his manor and feared his lack of mourning might show in his demeanor. "I do not say witch. I neither saw nor met the stranger. My steward warrants that a woman visited and thereafter my wife behaved as if under a spell."

"In his despair, the steward has in all likelihood exaggerated. It is an ignorant mind that deceiveth himself," said the Priest.

"That is possible, but she never sang to herself before. Nor called for a troubadour."

"Why did your steward not advise you of this before this dreadful moment?" The priest involuntarily shook his head.

The Marquess recognized that the priest offered an enlightened way to discredit his steward's report. Nonetheless, he said, "My steward is an honorable man, if somewhat timorous."

"God in His infinite mercy impaired Lady Birague. Wherefore could she go for companionship with other noble matrons? With good reason, she grew longsome and apt to display a changing spirit."

The Marquess knew this to be true. He pitied the life his wife had led, a hapless woman laden by a wretched disorder of the body. He was overcome with heartache, not for her death, but for her life. He had no voice to speak.

The priest measured his words. "Let us be prudent in our thoughts and words. Appearances are oft deceiving."

Lord Birague understood the priest's intimation. He knew of the woman hanged because her husband accused her of witchcraft. He also knew that the husband had remarried to the tavern keeper's daughter within the month.

The priest left Chateau Durckheim encouraged. He had not been forced to resort to threatening the Marquess with a mortal sin.

Morning light appeared but the sun did not. Under a shroud of clouds, Lady Birague's cortege left Chateau Durckheim and traveled to Troyes.

As they neared the village, thick clouds became mist and then a drizzle. A pack of children rushed to shelters at doorways where they crowded together. The overhang dripped on the toes of their ragged shoes. Dressed in black robes, the funeral party chanted with woebegone voices, "Take notice, such of you as are faithful, to pray for Lady Birague's soul." They were paid by Lord Birague, for the funeral reflected the family's status.

Isabelle stood nearby wrapped in a blanket and wearing a black oilcloth with hood. She had stayed with the Troupe. Her disappearance would have attracted attention and brought suspicion upon not just herself but the Augusto Troupe as well.

In any case, Isabelle had no safe place to go, save a nunnery, and her experience in one motivated her to come up with a plan, which led her to attend Lady Birague's funeral. It was her only chance to regain Lord Dubois's favor.

Yeomen, wearing oilcloth capes provided by the Marquess de Birague, crowded under whatever cover the frontage of the shops provided. A second bell joined the first, an indication that the funeral procession was entering the village.

Isabelle pushed her way through the crowd, glancing right and left for an urchin with a needy and bumptious look. A stabbing elbow or charging hip tried to block her way. She grabbed the coattails of a begrimed youngster kicking his way underfoot. Isabelle flashed a sou, more than he'd make picking pockets, and whispered in his ear, "A sou for you, if you stay near and do my bidding."

He gazed at the coin and nodded. The mist trickled grime down his cheek.

"Hold on to my cape," she said as she shoved denizens aside and nudged closer to the church steps. "Oh, la vache!" "Fie on you!" Curses didn't stop Isabelle.

Only the torches of mourners standing under the portico were burning. Isabelle hardly heard the doleful chanting of the hired villagers. Their prayers ebbed and flowed — "Mary, Matilda, Mark, martyrs, and all the saints…"

The priest and monks, wearing long black and wet robes, marched into the square and mounted the cathedral steps. The ostiary opened the heavy wood doors, and as they awaited the coffin, a chantry priest from a neighboring church raised his singular, high-pitched voice in a prayer for Lady Birague.

The hearse, bearing the coat of arms of the Birague family, approached drawn by decorated horses, ornate in black hoods and blankets. Several men removed the coffin and situated it on their shoulders while other mourners held the corners of the pall.

Isabelle edged past mourners who had been promised a sou for their services and stood near the barrier of soldiers. She cupped the boy's cheeks in her hands and looked into his eyes. "This letter is for only one person." Her fingers slipped on grime as she pinched his cheek. "Yes!" he groused. She said, "His wife must not see you. Nobody must see the letter."

She had spent hours deciding what and how to write. Without revealing her source, she explained to Lord Dubois that his wife read his letters, delivered to her by his page. Isabelle's note that this was "common knowledge" was a double-edged insult, but she optimistically expected Lord Dubois to see it as a naive lapse on her part.

The letter of my devotion to you is in Lady Dubois's possession belike. And the letter you received under my signature was written by your wife. Isabelle would have admired Lady Dubois's cunning had she not been the adversary.

Notwithstanding the dreary mist, the procession into the church moved slowly. Because of his social position, Lord Dubois was among the first mourners following Lord Birague.

Isabelle lifted the urchin above the backs of other mourners and whispered, "Him. The man wearing the black cavalier hat with black ribbon band." She hitched him onto her hip and pointed. "He is wearing a pearl earring. Push your way to his side before he enters the church and put the letter into his pocket."

The boy took the envelope and forced his way past mourners and to the rear of the hearse and horses.

Isabelle edged from side to side and watched his seedy woolen cap as he dodged capes and approached Lord Dubois, who had paused at the bottom of the church steps with the cortège. Dubois's cloak had no pocket as such. The urchin fumbled with the cloth.

Isabelle held her lips to keep from crying out. She was too close to let the moment slip away.

Lord Dubois looked down at the urchin. Isabelle's breath caught in her chest. The cortège began to inch up the steps. Lady Dubois, despite decorum, walked ahead of her husband. He paused and pushed the urchin.

Isabelle squeezed between a short, flabby woman and a dried-up peasant.

The urchin jammed the envelope at Lord Dubois, and Isabelle swallowed a prayer. Lord Dubois, his hawkish eyes dazed, took the envelope and stuffed it into his waistcoat.

Isabelle panted and stumbled back, turned, and wended her way out of the thicket of mourners. She paid the urchin and retrieved her horse from the stable at the inn. As she headed back to the caravans, her heart was light. Lord Dubois was not a man to ignore a letter surreptitiously placed in his hand. She recalled a moment when he had taken her ungloved hand in his and said, "You have the power to distill in me a wickedness." An intensity of longing so overtook her that she whipped her horse into a gallop.

A cold mist seeped into Isabelle as she rode back to the caravans. It was well past the hour to light candles. The darkness was so dense her horse realized they were upon the caravans before she did. She dismounted and, by listening to rustling and snorts, made her way to where the animals were tethered. She found her caravan, went inside, removed her damp clothes, and fell into her cot.

She wasn't asleep when Argon and Samuel returned from the Bon Vivant Inn, both of them tipsy and without a sou. She twisted and turned on her feather mattress and listened to their commotion. She heard Argon singing and playing the lute. The breathless croaks of his once masterly voice distressed her. What they had seen as a brilliant road for his future had run into a mire. She discerned the lyrics of a strange song she had not heard before.

> *Two doves sat a-shakin in every limb, on a dark and wintry morning. The first dove could not his ma find, not his ma find. The second ate the other, ate the other ... on a dark and wintry morning. Then it wasn't there at all, not there at a-a-tall. And that's all I know of the dove, I know of the dove ... on a dark and wintry morning.*

☙ Scene 16 ❧
Count de Gondrin's blazing fire

When Béjart returned with news that the Count de Gondrin had engaged them to present entertainments at Chateau de Giffaumont near Dijon for the winter season, the actors burst forth with hoorays. They hitched up the horses and took the southward road.

Stubble remained in grain fields. Except for oaks, the forests were webs of bare limbs. The clean smell of cold conifers quickened the air. Only the coo of the Gallic wind could be heard. From the ground a ghastly chill arose turning mud to ice.

Béjart had arranged for Argon to lead the convoy and for Samuel to drive Louise's caravan. He tied his horse to the rear of her caravan and pulled Louise from the driver's bench to the interior.

On her cot, the physicality of heated touches revived a feeling of unity and rebirth. Béjart's cold nights and lonely days of frustration dissipated in the fierce tenderness of her skin. The bugbear of failure had been dispelled. The sinews binding him with worry and disappointment unraveled and he felt wide spaces in his heart.

Tears came to Louise. The open spaces in herself swelled shut around him. Whether or not she loved him, she loved having a helpful man in her cot. She loved the Troupe. For the first time, she had a family. Her heart expanded, her arms tightened, and she received him gratefully.

✳

At Chateau de Giffaumont, instead of driving the train of caravans through the drawbridge, Béjart halted them in the meadow outside the curtain wall and rode his horse inside. A pack of hunting dogs bounded at him. His horse reared and turned. A shout came from the castle keep followed by a whistle, and the dogs retreated to the trainer standing in the portal.

From a corner tower strode the steward, dressed in livery, who greeted him and led him to the Great Hall where the Count de Gondrin sat at a blazing fire and drank from a chalice. A hairy dog, which had been lying at his feet, stood and barked. It was of a size and appearance to terrify a child. "Heigh! Sit!" the Count said, and the animal obeyed. Béjart warmed at the fire.

The Count sorely needed entertainment for his guests. In a fit of anger, he had booted out the small band of jugglers and dwarfs he had hired earlier. Even ample wine had not made their withering humor appealing to his guests on the Twelfth Night fete. The festivities had been saved from utter boredom when one of the dogs ripped the skirt off a lady. The party incited her with cheering and whooping until she disrobed completely. The Count's reputation as a man of culture and art had been upended.

"The Augusto Troupe will provide superlative and refined per-formances as I require," he said. "My guests are people of quality." He licked his thick lower lip. "Nobility. And I do not mean petty nobility." He sniffed, wiped drool from his mustache and smeared it on his chausses. With an intonation suggesting an important announcement, he added, "I have entertained Turenne and La Grande Mademoiselle." He paused for effect. "The Chevalier de Lorraine."

Béjart had been impressed until the Count threw in the Chevalier de Lorraine, a name many a noble used to elevate their social standing. Béjart considered his employer a pompous boor.

The confines of the inner court required that the caravans park outside the curtain wall. The horses were led to the stables, located inside the wall but outside the moat.

The farrier, drayman, and other servants hauled the trunks from the wagons up a cramped spiral stairway. The actors eagerly followed as they made way to their quarters, located in a building near the chapel in the rear courtyard. Grit scraped under their boots as they ascended the steep, cavern-like chemin de ronde. At the uppermost level, they passed through a tight opening to a narrow passageway with an arched stone ceiling of a height that the men kept to the center to avoid bumping their heads.

"Gramercy, it is as cold in here as in the caravan." Agnes pulled her wool cloak to her bosom.

"Here is a stove, in this chamber." Samuel had bounded ahead and looked into their quarters. Their space was little more than a gallery with open closets that formed the upper floor of the tower wall. To the left of the entry were two rooms with doors.

Stretching beyond the area allocated to them were other gallery rooms, some empty, some with military equipment—clubs, maces, halberds, helmets, bolt heads. One contained a small catapult, an outdated and useless weapon. Another room was devoted to a collection of flintlock muskets.

The actors went directly to the hot coals in an iron tub serving as a stove, shuffling together as near the heat as possible. Argon said, "This is my room!"

"Mine too," said everybody.

"There are three cots in here," said Béjart. "And one of them is mine."

"I need extra cots for my costumes," said Agnes.

"I need a stove and a door," said Isabelle, laying claim to one of the private rooms.

"Perchance you can coax Lord Gondrin to provide more stoves," said Béjart.

"Thankfully we are not at the mercy of the rain," said Georgette.

"In good earnest, I could not abide another night with frost in my nose," said Hubert, who had suffered fevers.

With three cots in each small room, most of the trunks were stacked in nearby empty spaces.

No sooner had they been installed than Lord Gondrin sent a servant to fetch Béjart to the Great Hall—a large rectangular building as high as the gatehouse and dominated by a fireplace the size of an oxcart. A large cavernous chamber of greater length than width, it adjoined the centrally located tower, creating a partition between the front courtyard and the rear one.

"Here now!" Which was how the Count launched into conversation, "Can you ask for a finer Great Hall!" His waistcoat, of such hardwearing leather as to be armor-like, fit tight over a paunch.

Béjart gazed up at ceiling beams so high bird nests perched in the joints. "This doth show you to be a man of superior taste." His tone had the ability to flatter without seeming to grovel.

The Count, who was accustomed to lickspittle, ignored the compliment. "The troupe that performed for Twelfth Night was much affected by the grandiosity of our Great Hall. The actor in chief," he paused to add an aside, "something of a mountebank I needs say," an insult actors often heard and which Béjart ignored, "was overawed. He bellowed like a goat, 'What stupendous entremets!'" The Count clapped his hands. "Their show was exceptional. My guests could hardly drink their wine for laughter."

Béjart's intuition recognized a false intonation often found in les grands, among whom arrogance was a virtue. At the same time, he understood the Count's expectation of adoration, which sank in like a pinch to his ears.

"Gold chandeliers." The Count looked up as they ambled about the room. Hanging from the ceiling were four gilded chandeliers, each with three-score candles, and placed equidistant from the corners of the room. An indoor venue lit by candles was unusual territory for the Augusto Troupe, a matter for consideration in staging their entertainments.

The long table of polished oak with chairs of carved wood and red upholstery suggested lavish suppers. There being no heat for the spacious rear of the room, Béjart requested an iron stove. He knew that a shivering actor was icily motivated. "Mayhap near that elegant tapestry."

On the distant wall athwart the fireplace was a wide doorway of over a toise in width and overspread with a heavy tapestry. Considering the Count to be a man requiring flattery, Béjart said, "Those brilliant threads of gold and blue carry on the splendor of the Grand Hall."

"Made in Brussels. There is no equal, not hereabouts. Mademoiselle de Scudéry wants to copy the colors for her salon. I have put her off." The Count sniffed as if the Mademoiselle's request was an offense.

"The Gondrin coat of arms?" Béjart said of the tapestry design — a gold crown with inset gems above a shield on which was pictured a cross encumbered by a dragon.

"The Gondrins have a history of bravery dating back to the Crusades." The Count pulled the tapestry aside to reveal a spacious alcove. "When an actor disappears behind this, he will know who pays to provision him."

The tapestry's thick threads grazed Béjart's cheek, a coarse stroke. He hated the glaring coat of arms that exaggerated the Count's claim to superiority. He hated that *Mirabelle*'s scenes must compete with this aristocratic claptrap.

To discover the routines and character of the chateau, Béjart called on servants such as the steward, water carrier, and carter. One after another gave him bits of information about the Count's habits. "He is the most martial of men," said the butler. The cook, with a tongue of imprudent wit, said, "He is one of good appetite but poor mettle."

With the Count's permission to use the Great Hall for rehearsals, Béjart went to the kitchen, located in the undercroft of the Great Hall, where the actors were eating. They chewed into sausages and dark bread as Béjart bellowed. "Rehearsal in the Great Hall as soon as you finish!"

With full bellies, they refined short burlesque acts. Agnes and Argon bantered bald jokes. Samuel practiced balancing a book on a pole. Leon, who was eager to introduce "flying blades" as a skit, threw his stiletto at a target, frightening the servant minding the fire.

Following mornings were spent the same way, in the Great Hall perfecting entertainments. After a few days, the chamberlain entered and relayed a message, calling Béjart to the mews where the Count was with Philippe, his huntsman, who had arranged the construction of several addtional cages specially made for the falcons.

The Count turned away from the falconer and the mews. "This forthcoming Saturday, I have arranged with a wealthy mercer for your troupe to provide jovialities at his chateau. He will entertain a trader with connections to the Fuggers. The mercer is a simple man of no cultured taste. If you throw somersaults he will laugh to the hilt. However, the Fuggers have generations of wealthy forebears and require exceptional diversions. More than mere tumblers and jugglers."

The Count rented out the Troupe to other affairs. One was a cathedral celebration of Candlemas. Béjart became more confident of Louise's ability as an actor after she played the Virgin Mary. He did not realize that his portrayal of Gabriel to her Virgin had inspired her with confidence and a belief in herself and him.

Béjart, required by the Count, entered the lord's chamber and stood as the Count, a silver mug in his hands, sat in a fauteuil with gold threaded upholstery. "I have guests coming for celebrations before Ash Wednesday. They will be of exceptional rank. Lord and Lady Bouligneux." He stood and puffed his chest out. "And the Duke de La Fare." He leaned forward and, putting the mug to his lips, sipped. "Nothing less than exceptional entertainment will suffice."

Béjart hardly flinched, but excitement brewed in the possibilities this presented. Never before had his troupe performed for a duke, a noble of heraldic authority and influence, not to mention wealth.

The Count's voice hardened into a command. "I will suffer no leaden tongues!" The words inflated his lips and cheeks. "There needs be laughter and merriment through and through."

That Béjart's troupe had not staged *Mirabelle* recently gripped his stomach no less than undigested sausage. He was confident of the actors' ability to perform short burlesques, music, and acrobatics. His priority became *Mirabelle*.

He retrieved the painted canvasses used as backdrops, which had been hastily rolled and stored, and cleared out shriveled worms, bugs, leaves, and a dead rat. There was no abiding the faded paints drawn to represent a chair and chest. The lines of a window were hardly visible, not to mention the view. After a trip to Dijon for paints, Béjart, along with the actors, refreshed colors, drew sharp lines, and painted detail.

Béjart realized he had to make changes to the script of *Mirabelle*. A frightfully ugly countess who mistakenly thought herself ravishing had brought rollicking laughter from yeomen. But such wit would fly like pudding into the face of a countess, especially an unattractive one.

He read a deceptive nobleman's lines, "All my happiness is in praise of truth," which were aimed at flattering the hideous Mirabelle. Béjart smiled to himself at the incongruity. However, nobles would not smile nor see the incongruity.

Little by little, he changed the script to mock wealthy merchants and farmers. Mirabelle became the widow of a rich chancellor. Her paramours, who courted and connived with her protégé, became affluent commoners with estates.

෨ Scene 17 ෧
Béjart says no

The actors hovered near the embers of the fire in the Great Hall. Béjart explained the revisions. "Isabelle, your role remains the same, only now you are a chancellor's widow rather than a countess. Leon, Agnes, all of you, you will address Mirabelle as *Madame* rather than *My lady*."

Isabelle took Béjart aside and argued for the role of the beautiful protégé, which either Agnes or Louise played. Isabelle's dissatisfaction with wearing a wax wattle and a nose mask big as a plague doctor's had increased along with her interest in Lord Dubois.

"I have played the hideous countess long enough!" Isabelle's voice rose above the mumbling of the other actors and descended from the ceiling beams like God's wrath.

"It is the leading role…" Béjart avoided vexing her. He was worried enough about the changes he had made and how they would be played. It was not just a matter of figuring out entertainment of excellent merit. It was a matter of pleasing the Count, and as far as he knew at the moment, those might be opposing aims.

"Give Mirabelle to Agnes." Isabelle knew Agnes, who sat at the wood table, would hear and take this as a compliment.

Béjart turned his back on the actors and said softly, "She does not have the force of voice, as you well know."

"Georgette can take the role."

"She is half the comedian you are. Why give up a role you play perfectly?" said Béjart.

The Troupe's noisy banter quieted as they realized a storm was brewing. Argon walked from the fire to where Béjart and Isabelle were talking. "Do I have time to curry the horses before we begin?"

"Nay, we will begin anon," said Béjart. "Have patience."

"Why not start now?" said Argon.

"Practice a ballad… Bedlam Boys… with Eugene," said Isabelle.

Argon slunk away like an unwanted hound at a hunt.

Béjart said, "Is this because you do not want to play an ugly female?"

Isabelle turned her face aside and considered her answer. "Why should Louise get the beautiful role?"

Béjart avoided going where Isabelle was leading. Though his affairs with women had brought on Isabelle's accusations before, he refused to recognize her enmity. "You know not your own mind. Mirabelle is the leading role of the play. The entire story revolves around her!"

"But she is ugly!"

"She is ugly, but she is the most important character in the play."

"I would rather be beautiful and unimportant."

Béjart could hardly contain his disdain. "There is nothing comedic about three courtiers courting a beautiful woman."

Argon returned. "How long do we wait while you two fight like horned goats?"

"Argon, leave us be," said Béjart.

"You deal with me as if I am a half-wit," said Argon.

"This is between Béjart and me," said Isabelle.

"Does it not concern the Augusto Troupe?" said Argon.

"Enow! We begin erelong," said Béjart.

Argon stepped back and turned aside but remained close by.

"Forsooth, would you have us rehearse well forward in the night while you learn another part?" said Béjart.

"I practically know the protégé's lines already."

Argon looked at Isabelle. "What? There is no comedie if you do not play Mirabelle," he said.

"You would have Georgette in the part? When will she learn the lines?" Béjart brushed his hand over his head. His hair, usually cut to a nap, irritated him, for it had grown long enough to curl. "Bumbling is not comical."

Argon leaned forward and said, "Georgette cannot play Mirabelle."

Isabelle's décolletage expanded as she swelled with breath. It had not bothered her to be the unattractive countess to an audience of rustics, but nobles of the realm were another matter altogether. Acting talent hardly drew a second look, but beauty did. "I will train Georgette to the role."

"You cannot train a horse to be a crow," said Argon.

"How should you know?" said Isabelle. "I have been a horse and a crow, and it is time I have a chance to be a peacock."

"Would you be a peacock at the moment when *Mirabelle* may be seen by confederates of such as Molière?" said Béjart.

Argon cleared his throat and cursed his oily voice. "Molière?"

"This may be my chance to get *Mirabelle* to Paris!" said Béjart.

Isabelle brightened at this news, which gave her even more desire for the role of the protégé. "What is the point of my going to Paris looking like an ugsome crone?"

"You put your vanity afore *Mirabelle*. Afore me! Afore our troupe!" Béjart paced to relieve his resentment, circling away from Isabelle, who dangled the future of the Augusto Troupe from her little finger, and with it, whatever hope he had for his play. "Georgette is not going to take the part," he said.

"Then *you* take the part!" Isabelle said to Béjart.

Argon scoffed. His mother was poisoning their comedie. "You have gone mad."

Béjart had reached a decision and was prepared for the consequences. His lips parted with easy assurance. "Either you will play Mirabelle or we will pack up the caravans and leave the morrow."

Isabelle gazed at him with glacial fury. She turned away and joined the other actors.

Béjart approached the actors. "Let us get started. Act One. On stage!"

Isabelle sashayed to the stage with her enormous nose upturned, setting the tone for her acting. Standing upright as if she had an iron backbone, she opened her mouth wide and read with piercing deliberation lines from what was presented as one of the courtier's letter, "My chere ami, I adore your great head. Your large cleft chin. Your rather flat lips."

Hoofs thundered on cobblestones as the Bouligneuxes arrived. Splendid horses dressed in gilded bronze harnesses pulled the carriage into the front courtyard. The Augusto musicians played lutes, tabors, and pipes as the visitors descended from their carriage. They played loudly to distract from the ill effects of fingers raw in a cold wind. All due respect was shown rather quickly as the grandees marched inside for the comfort of a warm fire.

Béjart expected every actor to show up at the Great Hall regardless of whether they had a part to play in a skit. On evenings when the Gondrins invited nearby peers or wealthy merchants for a social with the Bouligneuxes, the Augusto Troupe provided music and burlesque, acrobatics as well. It was on one such a night that Louise noticed Philippe paying undue attention to her. Before the entertainments ended, her eyes met his.

The Count's chamberlain delivered to Béjart the message that the much-anticipated Duke de La Fare was expected forthwith. The chamberlain gasped at the presumption of uttering the name of such a luminary. Recovering his voice, he commanded, "The Count expects two nights of trifles. On the third, a theatrical comedie worthy of the Palais Royal." His gaze was meant to give Béjart a sense of do-or-die.

The time was coming for the Augusto Troupe to present *Mirabelle.*

෧ Scene 18 ෴

missed cues and stumbling

Isabelle and the other women of the troupe gazed from a window of the keep in anticipation of the Duke's arrival. For some, it was their first encounter with glazed glass windows, which kept out the wind and birds. "Paris has no better lodging," said Georgette as she stroked the clear magic of the glass.

A sheep horn sounded from beyond the barbican. Argon, Samuel, and Etienne, wearing madcap costumes, stood inside the gatehouse with tabor, timbrel, and bells. Upon hearing the horn and thudding of hoofs, they savagely employed their instruments. The carriage roared through the gates.

Isabelle, Agnes, and Louise watched as the shiny black carriage with gold crown and gold wheels entered, drawn by velvet-trimmed stallions. It came to a halt in the front courtyard beside the master apartments. There stood Béjart and Eugene with lute, Georgette with psaltery, and Leon with pipe playing melodic strands, despite fingers tight with cold.

The Count stood formally dressed in a tabard and slops. The Countess stood beside him in a surcote with sleeves that dangled to the ground. She had taken all day to dress for the Duke. Her chambermaid, a niece of the Count's brother's wife, had made ready her toilet. She plucked the hairs of her underarms. Washed the skin with white wine, rosewater, and cassia ligna. Washed her mouth with watered vinegar and, to assure a sweet breath, rinsed with a concoction of aniseed and mint sodden in wine.

Vitriol oil exfoliated her face. Wash balls cleaned her skin. With the water dish removed, the chambermaid had presented a toner of bran and lemon juice. She rubbed white pigment into her cheeks while staring into the looking glass. She faced the Duke with con-fidence because her skin was as shiny as ivory. Her wig came from the king's wig maker, Georges Binet, and the gown from Madame de Montespan's dressmaker in Paris.

The Count bowed and Lady Gondrin kissed the cheeks of the arriving guests.

The Duke de La Fare and his wife wrapped their fur surcotes against the biting wind. Gold ribbons of the Lady's headgear glinted in the sun, creating something of a halo. The Duke's ordi-nary stature was elevated by high-heeled boots and a cavalier hat of beaver fur. As they entered the lord's chambers, the servants unloaded trunks and trucked them to the guest chambers.

Argon and the musicians shuffled out of the courtyard and

hurried to the warmth of a hot stove. With Louise as their emissary to the steward, they had managed to get additional stoves for their quarters.

For two days the lords went hunting for deer, ending at night in festivities at the Great Hall. The count's man, Philippe, organized the hunts. He and his servants, mostly garçons, withheld food from the hounds to intensify their search for prey. He assessed the grounds for quarry and by studying tracks, broken branches, and droppings, he discovered where to find the deer. His uncle, who had been the previous animal trainer, had taught him the craft. Upon his uncle's death, he had inherited the position. Philippe sought to make his situation secure. He did not want to end up in the Count's fields with his brothers.

Gondrin's party hunted not to kill the most game, but to enjoy the ritual. The sound of the horn, the stampede of horses, the barking of the hounds, the firing of crossbows. When an animal of ten tines was killed ballyhoos echoed in the trees.

In the evening while the huntsmen sat at the big table and gorged themselves on stuffed veal, boiled partridge, and jegote of mutton with anchovy sauces, the actors leapt from behind the tapestry and juggled flaming knives, sang love ballads, danced, and enacted farces.

The more the wine flowed, the more the room exceeded in merriment, so much so that the actors made bold and approached the grand table with their singing and dancing. Argon filched a bottle of wine, which the actors swilled behind the tapestry. Soon a second one appeared. Louise, while twirling about the diners, saw a guest whose modest habiliment distinguished him from other men. It was Philippe. He returned her smile.

As the candles burned down, the actors took as much warmth from their wine as they did from the small stove in the alcove. With the wind groaning in the eaves and the night spitting cold, the party of revelers finally retired to the guest chambers. The actors left by the door to the rear courtyard, except for Louise, who met Philippe in the forward courtyard and accompanied him to his chamber. His room, unlike that of other servants, was located in the wing with the guest chambers.

In the privacy of his chamber, they drank wine, ate cheese, and talked. He told of training a young falcon recently brought from Holland. And how he accustomed it to his commands, to perch on his hand, to hunt prey and then return. For the first time in her life, Louise initiated a kiss. She told of the Troupe, the actors, the acrobat, and how they regarded one another as family.

Louise told him that she liked the excitement of moving from village to village. "I have seen more of France than my mother or father." Not wanting to ruin her chances with him, she quickly followed with, "Though I do not want to be as old as Georgette and still acting."

"Mayhap you will find a village you like and stay there," he said, knowing the actors would leave when the weather improved.

Louise sneaked back into her cot, warmed with the hope that she might find a home even better than the Augusto Troupe.

At daybreak on the third morning, the actors laid the stage floor in the Great Hall in front of the Count's tapestry. They hammered pegs into hewn timbers. Raised frames for the backdrop. With help from Argon, Béjart attached the canvas to the frames. Every madcap, whether somersaults or satire, had entered the Great Hall from behind his lordship's coat of arms. There wasn't a guest that had not seen, if not appreciated, evidence of the Count's nobility and prominent rank.

Béjart's hope of staging his play in Paris soared when he heard during a trip to Dijon that the visiting Duke had relations with Charles Varlet, known as La Grange, the actor who spoke to audiences and introduced Molière's plays.

That afternoon, the cast gaped at Isabelle's costume. It was so elaborate Samuel performed a backward tumble. "Did you empty the coffers to pay for your paints?"

Her complexion, covered by tin glass, gave forth a metallic shine. A mixture of lead and vinegar whitened her neck and bosom.

Dragon's blood on her cheeks. Blackened eyebrows and eyelids. Jeweled décolletage, fingers, and shoes. Robe of red velvet trimmed in gold. Her appearance teetered between spectacular and ludicrous.

Leon said, "Have care of your wig, that it does not catch fire in a candelabra."

"Take care of your wit. It may earn you a chine bone from Lady Gondrin."

Isabelle had heightened her wig with sheep's wool and added ostrich feathers and ribbons. Her paints and brilliant garments were devised to shift the eye away from the false wattle and deformed nose.

Upon seeing her, Agnes hurried back to her trunk and lathered on more paints and replaced her green overskirt with a brilliant orange one. She retained her red bodice and returned looking as if her costume were going up in flames.

Louise, who was delayed by the attentions of the Count's animal trainer, arrived at the Great Hall merely minutes before the assigned time and was dismayed, for her maquillage paled in comparison. The perfection of her oval face and averting eyes, though admirable, were not stage-worthy.

Agnes secured a mouche on her cheek and passed the looking glass to Hubert, who pulled locks of his periwig to his forehead and passed it to Georgette. From hand to hand went the looking glass. Leon adjusted his powdered wig of twig-thin curls. He used a pasty scar and eye patch to disguise himself off the stage as well as on. Argon, mustachioed and in a lion-sized wig, wiped excess wax from the tufts covering his chin.

The Count strutted into the Great Hall early, took one look at the stage and canvas backdrop, and roared in a fit of rage. "By whose authority was this placed afore my coat of arms?"

Béjart took a breath. "My Lord, the canvas cannot approach the tapestry for beauty. But a comedie forgoes beauty for the ridiculous."

"Remove that wretched drapery of no import." The Count's face was red.

"Good Sire, would you have every ridiculous comedian enter and exit with notice of your coat of arms?"

"This comedie will not deny its debt to my heritage." The Count pointed his finger at Béjart.

"Truly, then, bear us no grudge if sod-witted, bate-breeding oaths are uttered well-nigh your coat of arms."

The Count waved forward Argon, who stood by the stage as if protecting it. "Garcon! Remove that brittle bush from afore the tapestry."

Argon looked at Béjart but did not move.

"Sire, reason. Mayhap it will serve us better to remove the stage with backdrop to yonder corner." Béjart indicated with a hand he hardly kept from trembling. Under his breath he cursed the Count.

"'Tis to your account to preserve the coat of arms in clear view. Do with the stage as you will, but I will not delay supper on your account." The Count turned and with each footstep drew a creak from the wood floor as he departed.

"Dunderhead!" Argon said so loudly the actors froze for fear the Count had heard.

He had heard but not perceived it, troubled as he was by the actors' impudence. "Such worthless paillards," he mumbled.

"The dunderhead is Béjart," said Isabelle. "The reason for the Count's entertainments is to flaunt his rank, not to mention his coat of arms."

"His rank will be much afflicted if *Mirabelle* fails to please his visitors." Béjart's sweat had made trails in his face paint, despite the crisp air in the Hall.

"Let us not worry over the curse of crows or rooks," said Georgette.

Béjart glanced at her with appreciation. "We will detach the backdrop and move the stage en bloc," he said.

Argon fetched their tools from the alcove and they set to work. As they detached the cumbersome backdrop, their headpieces slumped and toppled. It took the effort of the entire troupe, men and women, to surround the stage and shuffle it in the direction of the corner. Pantaloons snagged on splinters. Vermillion cheeks became vermillion ears. Bum rolls shifted. Bone stays stabbed midriffs. Velvet hems got caught under shoes. Leon took off his periwig. Georgette removed her shoes.

A servant entered and added wood logs to the fire. In a matter of moments, he returned with more logs. He sat at a table and warmed his back. The intrigue of the letter in his purse little interested him, but the sou that had been promised him did. As his eyes followed first one actor and then another, he listened for names, in particular the name *Isabelle*.

"Careful. Just a few more steps," said Béjart.

Agnes stumbled and let go her grip. But for Argon, that portion of the stage floor would have fallen away rather than dipped.

"Turn. No, the other way." Béjart's voice drew up nervously as they wobbled and seesawed to the corner. The stage floor timbers had shifted and some overlapped. They hastily leveled the floor and worked to reattach the backdrop.

Two more servants entered the Great Hall. They went from one candelabra to another with a torch and put light to the candles.

The servant at the fireplace stood and poked smoking wood and roused the fire. He noticed when Isabelle, along with the women, left the men and crossed the Hall toward the alcove. He quickly stepped toward her with the letter concealed in his coat and said, "Madame Isabelle?"

Isabelle, in bad humor, paused. "And what does the Count demand now?"

The servant looked about as he palmed the letter to her.

Isabelle overcame her surprise, secreted the letter in her sleeve, and laughed loud enough for Agnes and Louise to hear. "Of course not, you foolish garçon!" she said as if he had asked a favor.

In the privacy of the alcove, the actors made proper their costumes as best they could. Isabelle pulled the hair of her wig over exposed wool and, while Agnes and Louise primped, she secured the letter in her velvet chemise.

At the sound of boisterous voices in the courtyard the actors scampered from the Great Hall into the alcove as the Count and his guests entered.

Hardly had Hubert closed the tapestry behind him when he said, "By God's teeth! We need a drop of ale!" He wiped black paint off the white paint on his nose. The black had moved from the mustache he had drawn above his lip.

The Count sent the signal to begin. Argon swallowed an oily potion to prepare his throat for singing. He strolled into the Great Hall playing the lute loudly. In the alcove, Eugene slurred notes on his lute as Argon played broken chords and sang lyrics that arose with uncertainty. "Three ravens sat on a tree…" Eugene, from the alcove, brought forth what could be called a musical exclamation from the lute. Samuel danced out and turned somersaults around the tables. Argon's voice, though breathy, kept to the melody. "Down a down, hey down, hey down…" The harder he forced the lyrics the more a gall swelled in his throat until the song slipped into a raspy whisper. "They were as black as black might be."

The guests muttered. Whispers became laughter, to Béjart's chagrin. Dressed in character, with silk breeches, brocade waistcoat, and a daunting aristocratic wig, he stepped into the Great Hall and joined Argon in singing, "With a down … derry, derry, derry down …" He paced in Argon's footsteps and, in a lustful voice powerful enough to awake the passions of scullery maids in the kitchen, sang, "No other fowl dare him come nigh, with a down …"

Behind the tapestry, Leon arrived with two bottles of wine. Nobody asked where they came from. Though Isabelle had imbibed from a supply she kept in her purse, she took a share of the wine as well. The mystery of the letter in her waistcoat consumed her. Lord Dubois perhaps, but other quarry had entered the picture. Perhaps it was from the Duke or Lord Bouligneux. She dabbed a handkerchief on her chin. She was as unsettled as the other actors.

Because the stage was now removed from the tapestry and alcove, the actors were unable to share the task of prompter. Béjart assigned it to Samuel and stationed him behind the backdrop for the entire play. Samuel's parts in the play were taken by Etienne. Though Etienne could not yet read ably, he knew the lines well enough to play small parts with the prompter's help.

At Béjart's signal, Leon quit the alcove, marched to the stage, and banged the tabor. Béjart followed him. Leon twirled the drum sticks and beat the tabor until the guests quieted. In the momentary silence, Béjart announced, "Good gentlemen and ladies, the Augusto Troupe presents the acclaimed comedie *Les Propheties de Mirabelle*, a witty sport for your pastime."

From the behind the tapestry, the musicians struck up melodic mayhem. Isabelle strolled across the floor from the portal to the stage, took her position and, when the music stopped, declared her lines. When it was time for Louise to enter, she advanced from the alcove to the stage. As the play progressed, the distance from the alcove to the stage amounted to a protracted announcement of entering actors. Béjart spat on the coat of arms each time he passed it.

Georgette swaggered with unexpected enthusiasm and bumped into Hubert, causing him to forget his lines. He did not hear a prompt from Samuel behind the canvas and worried that his ears were not working. A dreadful silence ensued. The players obviously had lost their lines. The dinner guests coughed. Began to talk. Toasted one another.

Behind the canvas backdrop, Samuel, who had spilled his tankard of ale, was excitedly shuffling the wet script pages trying to find the place.

Hubert cupped his ear, leaned rearward, and said, "Ah, my lady! What sweet bitterness is the remembrance of music."

Argon, dispirited about his hoarse voice, searched for the wine bottle and did not hear the signal to dash onstage with music. With no immediate rescue, Hubert said, "Who calls me yonder?" and stepped off the stage, leaving Georgette, playing the mistress, alone to figure out what to do next.

Béjart pushed Argon out of the alcove but without his lute. He

turned back just as Leon leaped out playing the pipe. Béjart turned
Hubert back to the stage.

The musical interlude lasted until Hubert, with lines from
Samuel, roared, "The flirtations of courtiers do not make more
beautiful her face."

"By God's piss!" mumbled Béjart. The actors in the alcove gave
him wide berth as he stamped about, muttering, "Damnation.
We are but a rabble of blackguards posing as actors! Samuel is a
lethargic slug!" He kicked a wood box storing ropes.

When Louise stumbled over an uneven board on stage, Leon
caught her. A taste of salted fish rose in her gorge and she thought
of her mother who had eaten salted fish and got a bone caught in
her throat and her throat swelled shut. Now Louise could not speak
her lines.

Samuel, by now in control of the script, whispered, "You have
no right to be very familiar with me." But Louise did not pick up
the line.

In the ensuing pause Leon carefully brushed off her dress,
giving her time to recover, but she was thinking of her mother.

From behind the backdrop, Samuel voiced her line more loudly.

Leon grabbed Louise by the shoulders and said, "Mayhap you
think I have no right to be familiar with you, but I will die of
sorrow if you discourage my favor."

Louise rallied and the act continued.

From time to time, the Count and his guests chuckled and
murmured. There were no surges of laughter. Isabelle performed
with stately competence, but was preoccupied with the thought of
the letter. At the conclusion, the audience applauded with restraint.

ꙮ Scene 19 ꙮ
two-faced, weak, and illusory love

After the subdued conclusion of *Mirabelle*, the Count's party
resumed high spirits as maids came and went refilling glasses.
A servant lugged wood to the fire. The actors, rambling about the

alcove, complained of boredom, but Béjart fended off their requests to leave. As several guests suppressed yawns, the Count stumbled to his feet and roared. "Music! We will have music!"

Béjart strolled into the smoke-filled Hall playing the Drunken Maidens ballad. Argon and others followed. Their growly voices punched at the lyrics, their fingers flailed their instruments. Etienne and Agnes trailed them playing timbrel and bells.

> *Three drunken maidens*
> *Oh where are your mantles so rich and fine?*
> *They've all been swallowed up*
> *in tankards of good wine*

The Count wanted dancing, and the Augusto Troupe switched to an instrumental, "Tre Fontane." However befuddled by wine, the men were fastidiously aware of rank and chose suitable partners to form double lines. They dipped and swayed a personalized if unique version of the sarabande, for the revelers could hardly keep on their feet much less keep tempo. For the first dance, the Count chose as his partner the duchess after which he took turns with other wives. Bodies wove and swayed, lurched and stumbled.

The musicians strolled about the table, now strewn with wafers, tarts, fried oranges, and flagons filled with sweet red wine. They moved in and out, filching a sugared slice of bread or cream fritter.

The Duke pranced over and took Louise for his partner. The Count grabbed Isabelle's arm and pulled her into the line of dancers. The Countess and other wives retired to the table where they watched, bleary-eyed, and fanned smoke from their faces.

The Duke's dance steps were those of a gentleman, practiced since childhood. In the King's company, clumsy steps led to disfavor. To keep on good terms with the court, the Duke, like other nobles, was expected to perform with grace and style branles as well as pavanes.

The Duke paused, held Louise to himself, and said, "Your finely tuned voice has given me taste for more. Pray perform for me in my chamber." He put his hand under her chin and brought her face up, but she closed her eyes rather than look at him. He was not amused at her modesty. He twirled her with a spin that left Louise unbalanced. "My chamberlain," he indicated a man standing at the door, "will show you the way when the banquet is done."

"Prithee pardon me, but my contract with the Augusto Troupe forbids otherwise performances." Louise looked for Béjart, but he had partnered with one of the wives.

The Duke laughed. "Ma cherie, a troupe is nothing without a plinth from some grandee. In your case, Gondrin. And Gondrin squirms to get his foot under my table."

"My lord, I have a husband of fierce ire and a babe." Louise had not lied, at least not by her count. Béjart was as much as a husband and she had birthed a baby.

The Duke's complacent smile proclaimed that his desire was by far more important than a common peasant's complaint. "I will make you sing like never before." He pinched her cheek, bowed, and gave her a turn away from him and called to a servant, "Beg leave, a drink!"

A dance ended and the guests wobbled to seats near the fire for refreshed drinks while Béjart and Argon produced dulcet tones on their lutes. Others of the Augusto Troupe trailed behind the tapestry to the gallery and munched on the tasties they had stored in their pockets. Georgette, holding a grudge against Hubert for leaving her alone on stage, was not speaking to anybody.

As frost descended on the roof, the nobles and their retinue meandered out of the Great Hall following the linkman, whose torches enlivened the darkness as they crossed the foremost courtyard to the lord's chambers and guest rooms. The actors split into teams, one to distract the servants and the other to steal bottles with leftover wine. Isabelle left as soon as the Count and his party.

Louise was distracted and anxiously glanced at the door in expectation of the Duke's chamberlain. Uppermost in her mind was a need for a male defender who might support her wish to refuse the Duke's advances. Knowing of Béjart's jealousy, she eyed him with growing despair, for he was consumed by nervous excitement. Béjart had no authority with the Duke, but he was the only person who might approach the Count on her behalf.

The Troupe converged in the gallery with their loot. Béjart was stricken over their production and the reception of *Mirabelle.* "A pox upon Gondrin's coat of arms. May his urchins be barren." He threw his wig on the floor, kicked it, and denounced the actors as incurable amateurs. He said Agnes played her part no better than a milksop. And to Georgette, "What dumbfounded you?" And to Samuel, "Think you a statue?"

The embers in the stove, without refueling, sighed and went out.

"It is a game with the high-born. They show their social station by withholding approval," said Leon.

"Have you ever seen a nobleman display excitement in any measure? Except for the king, of course," said Hubert.

"Our hour of promise is over! My hopes have become fears!" Béjart marched back and forth. "We will be in blighted woods until spring comes." He kicked an empty wine bottle so hard it hit the stone wall and broke.

They finished off the wine and returned to the Great Hall for whatever warmth remained of the fire. Without more wood, dying coals bristled in the hearth. The actors stood close and absorbed radiated heat from the hot stones. All eyes gazed hypnotically at the embers, as cold air chilled their backside. Overhead, candles burned to stubs and began to flicker. Argon and Eugene sat on top of the grand table despite the authority of its ornately carved banding. "Do you think the Count will turn us out?" said Argon.

"He cannot hire other entertainment at this late date." Hubert stuck a boot close to the embers.

"He will return to Paris." Eugene yawned.

"Mayhap Louise or Agnes can show him favors to detain him here." Leon's glance lingered on that of Agnes. She turned aside in mock embarrassment and wondered if this was a signal that he was taking an interest in her. She hoped that she might one day be able to deny him her favors.

"He would not know an offer if it came on a silver platter," said Louise, in an effort to get Béjart to look at her.

"Nay. Every man knows an offer," said Hubert.

"Mayhap. But the Count is one with a cold bed," said Louise.

"How do you come to such wisdom?" said Argon.

"Hers is wisdom." Georgette spoke her first words since her last line in the play. "Some men are lovers of women. Some of piety. Some, prestige. Some of money."

"And the Count?" said Leon.

"Did he enter with his wife? Sit near her at the supper table?" said Louise.

Béjart wandered through smoke to the cold, dark stage and sat on the raised boards. Louise followed him.

"Did he jest with Lady Bouligneux or Lady Fare?" said Georgette.

The men were made aware of what the women already knew. The Count had surrounded himself with men throughout the supper and had required a female only when he danced.

The few candles still alight sputtered. The actors began to wander out the door leading to the rear courtyard. A torch appeared as the door to the front courtyard creaked open. In came the Duke's chamberlain.

"Béjart," said Louise, "Prithee intervene for my sake."

The chamberlain was crossing the room, his eyes on Louise.

"For the sake of Zeus! What for now?" Béjart stood on seeing the man's approach. Red threads circulated his eyes. His nubby hair showed filaments of gray.

"My lady," said the chamberlain as he bowed to Louise.

"If you please, take a mild respite while I bandy with Monsieur Béjart." Louise looked at Béjart without a glance at the chamberlain.

The chamberlain merely posted his legs and stood, waiting.

"Yonder. Rest yonder at the dressoir," said Béjart pointing to an ornate cabinet with shelves displaying silver drinking cups. As the chamberlain stomped and farted away, Béjart said, "What vice is this?"

"The Duke requires me to his chamber." She looked imploringly at Béjart.

"Faugh!" Béjart was annoyed but it came to him that this was not a bad development. "The Duke? Perfumed cox-comb!" He rubbed both thighs as he considered what words to best use.

His hesitancy distressed Louise. She said, "You must go to the Count. You must tell him that I am not a puteresse for the pleasure of some villainous duke."

"Nay, nay. Be not so hasty." Béjart stood, his eyes gleaming in the dim light as if he'd remembered something. "The Duke's attentions are noble. Just yester night he gazed at you and said, 'She is a goddess!'"

Louise stared at him.

Béjart grasped her shoulder. "This he said to me treblefold."

"Yes, no doubt. To make of me a yielding girdle!"

"The eye of a noble is nothing to scoff at," said Béjart, who would have himself gone to bed with the man to gain his advantage.

"He is a lecher and a scourge to womanhood!" Louise said, for she knew well that the outcome of a tryst was of infinitely greater risk to a woman than a man. Did Béjart not care about that? Was the Duke's good favor of greater importance than whatever happened to her? She turned from him and walked toward the rear door, now obscured in darkness. Her belly had borne that weight before. And she lived every day with the burden of what she had done. The cold air got into her eyes. Her feet were numb. The floor was distant but her feet found it.

Béjart caught up with her. In the darkness his voice came as a warm rush of breath on her face. "There is no choice here. Do you not see?"

"You abandon me. You choose the Duke's favor over me." Louise hardly knew herself as she forged ahead.

"What is a fuck to your future? The Duke will ruin you. Not just you but your family." Béjart did not know of Louise's mother, father, or relatives. He did not know that Louise would wish ill fortune on her father. Béjart had not inquired of her past and she had not said.

"My family is the Augusto Troupe. And it will have to survive without my swiving with a lecher." Louise stumbled and surprised herself by catching on the door. She found the latch. A gale of icy air rushed her face.

"We will be in the caravans with snow on the ground. It will be the end of the Augusto Theatre. We will freeze to death!" Béjart walked with her into the rear courtyard where there was cold light from the moon.

"I am not a doxie," said Louise.

"I will tell the Duke's chamberlain that you will come the morrow night. That you have scrofula. That if it please him, send dwale for your easement."

"I thought you cared about me," she said. Louise had thought Béjart loved her. But the lessons of her past had been forgotten. Love as she knew it was two-faced, weak, and illusory. She chastised herself for believing in him.

The actors returned to their chambers, and each took a hot stone from one of the stoves, wrapped it in a blanket and placed it in their cot. When Béjart came in, he took what comfort he could from Louise, albeit she only offered her rear. In the dark, he did not see her pale face and red nose.

The solace he found in that physical pleasure did little to relieve the misery of his situation. His diminished hope for his comedie *Mirabelle* was complicated by the threat of revenge by the Duke.

While the other actors fell into uneasy sleep, Isabelle's candle glowed well forward in the night. The letter was from Lord Dubois.

She put her nose to the delicate paper and the spicy fragrance aroused a passion for Lord Dubois. His words inspired her dreams of Paris. *My chere amie, let us forget evil spirits that have poisoned our intercourse in the past. I am in despair without you. I submit to my passion for you. Will you gratify my feelings and accept my advances?*

He had made arrangements to visit the Count de Gondrin during Mardi Gras for the purpose of taking her away to Paris. He implored her to leave the Augusto Troupe. *Your beauty will shine more brilliantly in the apartment I have prepared for you alone*, he wrote, though he did not mention that it had been the domicile of his previous lover whose illness made her unfit to remain his inamorata.

Lord Dubois preferred in his bed a woman who aroused his peers in Paris. He relished actors in intemperate attire. The more an audience adored his paramour, the more passionate their trysts following her performance. Other men were wealthier, other men exceeded him in influence and power. But his stable of courtesans exceeded theirs, and when he shared them, doors opened.

Isabelle was awake into the night after her warming stone went cold. She knew that if Béjart had a prospect of playing in Paris, he would leave her without regret.

℘ Scene 20 ℘

I will have her off

Béjart awoke and peeked from his blankets. Felt for Louise. He was alone in his cot and his toes were cold even though he was wearing wool socks. The servant had allowed the fire to go out in his stove. A breath of air chilled his lungs. And this, he reminded himself, was warmer than a caravan.

He wrapped in a blanket, lit a candle from Argon's stove, and stomped to the kitchen, wondering if cold ashes were Gondrin's way of booting them out. Nonetheless, he heatedly bellowed at the scullery maid sleeping by the overnight fire, "You worthless loiter-sack! Farting by your fire." When she tumbled to her feet, he said with mild bellowing, "While I fart and freeze my arse."

Back in his closet, he swathed himself in woolens and pulled from a coffer the papers containing what he had written of the mummy's script. The knight's voice had come to him in sleep, a title of his script—"King Claudius' Knight." Though Béjart knew not what the mummy had in store for his knight, he sensed the King's villainy. His head was full of conversation.

The servant delivered lively embers to his stove and added coal.

He dipped his quill in ink and wrote. Setting: tavern. Knight and eight soldiers. Knight collapses.

Knight (mumbling feverishly): "God be buggered." Groans.

Soldiers hear, withdraw, shocked.

Béjart impatiently wrote lines for the soldiers.

"What does he say?"

"'Tis heresy!"

"Our feet will burn."

"You won't have any feet. They will hack them off."

"No, first they cut out your tongue and cook it."

Louise crept past his doorway on her way to the cot where she often slept. Béjart put down his quill. The centuries-old passageway closed dark and cold stones about them.

"Where have you been?" he said without much hope that she had changed her mind and spent hours, or minutes as the case might be, with the Duke.

"It is none of your affair." She climbed into a cot and pulled a sheep skin up to her neck.

"My feet got cold without you." Béjart retained his claim on her irrespective of the Duke.

"I am tired of cold feet." She turned to face the wall. She did not mention that she had discovered that Philippe, the animal trainer, had warm feet. Or that his bed, curtained in green velvet, was even warmer.

Georgette, in the other cot, snored in snorts.

Béjart pushed Louise aside, sat on the cot, and whispered, "You are favored by the stars, my petite." He had come to realize Louise's rebellious streak raised the possibility of her abandoning the Troupe. Whatever the future, he was determined to keep the actors together, to keep Louise in place. She was needed in *Mirabelle* as the beautiful protégé.

In a moment of confusion, Louise wondered whether Béjart's "stars" referred to himself or the Duke. Since it was with Béjart's sanction that she was retained in the Troupe, she said, "And of all the stars, you are the most glorious."

He brushed hair from her face, bent over, and kissed her forehead. It remained to be seen whether the stars favored the Augusto Troupe, whether the Duke had countenanced her excuse.

A cheerful morning light came through the window, falling on the bleak stone floor. Béjart dressed and went to the Great Hall where he disassembled a panel of the backdrop. In the front courtyard, boots scrubbed against cobblestones. Clothing swished. Servants clamored. A coachman drove an empty carriage through the portcullis and parked near the guest rooms. The restive horses, groomed to a sheen, snorted. Geese sounded like flatulence. Another carriage arrived. A wagon.

Guests were leaving. One departure often led to another. Béjart paced to and from the window, taking a drink of sour wine with each glance into the courtyard. He watched for signs of the Count's carriage, a possible departure he was not willing to think about. The sun was mid-morn and still none of the actors appeared at the Great Hall to help dismantle the stage.

Servants hauled ornate wood trunks into the coaches. The horses were blowing white clouds of steam. From the kitchen came a shrill complaint and the clanging of pots. Dogs barked in the kennel. A servant drove a cart of cut wood to the kitchen door and toted an armload inside.

Béjart crossed the rear courtyard and climbed the cramped stairway to the actors' chambers. An icy serenity had settled into the stone walls. The only sound was a gasping snore from some congested nose.

He sat at his chair, opened the mummy's diary and read several pages. He put it down and took up his quill. As if he were still reading, words came into his head.

Soldier One to others: "It is not a question of whether *he* knows what he is saying. *They* know! *They* know that *we* know!"

Soldier: "We will be blamed."

Another Soldier: "Because we are his men."
Soldier: "His guilt will be ours."
Any soldier: "We will be tried and burned."
Any soldier: "Unless we stand against him."
"Unless we put him on trial."
"We must cut out his tongue."
"No we must execute him for heresy."
"Execute! We are not judges!"
Béjart scribbled excitedly.

Leon stuck his head in the open doorway. "What is the order of the day?"

Béjart put away his quill and papers. "Help me dismantle the stage timbers and haul them to the back gallery." Angling for a clue as to where Louise had been overnight, he said, "Mayhap your nighttime wandering is leading the innocent astray."

"There is an innocent among us?" said Leon.

Béjart ignored the sarcasm. "We cannot afford to lose Louise."

"Ah, has the maiden drifted?"

"Did you see her about the rooms this night?"

"Perchance she found the Count's cold bed not so cold."

"She has not the trickery to gain his bed."

"Or she changed her mind about the Duke's behest."

"Nay. We await the Duke's displeasure."

"Women are born with the eyes of an angel and the heart of a serpent." Leon assumed every man of reasonable intelligence knew this.

Béjart gazed past him as Hubert entered, one eye swollen. Béjart said, "What befalls your eye?"

"Georgette had a bad dream," said Hubert.

"Her dream gave you a black eye?" said Leon.

"Her elbow. She said it was a bad dream." Hubert sorely needed a cup of hot chocolate.

They went to the kitchen, which was a flurry of activity, and poured their own tea. Scullery maids drove them from a table where they were packing cold meats, sausages, bread, and bottles of wine into baskets for the departing travelers. The cook's hip shoved first one actor, then another; her elbow gouged Hubert's ear.

The actors left. On the way to the Great Hall, Béjart encountered the potboy carrying two chamber pots which, judging by the smell, were fully charged. "What causes the excitement?"

"The Marquess de Bouligneux and his party are leaving today."

"And the Duke de La Fare?" Béjart walked beside the servant who neither slowed nor stopped on his way to the privy by the moat. "Is he leaving?" If the answer was "yes" the actors should steal as many blankets as they could.

"For aught I know he's snoring in his bed of feathers," he mumbled. He only knew what he had overheard from the maids. More immediately, the chamber pots were heavy, had to be emptied, and the quicker he did it the less he hated it.

As Béjart and the actors stored the final planks of the stage floor in the gallery, coachmen rowled the horses. "Geeyup!" the Marquess de Bouligneux's loaded carriages rattled on the courtyard stones, followed by empty silence.

That night, the Troupe performed skits, songs, and tumbling acts for the Count, the Duke de La Fare, their wives and newly invited guests, a mercantile agent and his paramour. However, without the Marquess's party, the revelry lurched from boisterous to subdued. Because Leon had found a buttry maid with a weakness for his charms, the actors were well oiled with wine by the time the performances began. Despite their uproarious nonsense, the spectators snuffled more than laughed and chewed seriously on venison and duck. Béjart was aware that the Troupe had not yet repaired its reputation.

At the end of the night, Gondrin swaggered over to Béjart. "It is well and good to have secret liberality of ladies, but there is no favor found in ill purpose," he said brusquely for he had no sympathy for an arrogant moll who would deny a noble his will. "One of your doxies is most offensive to the Duke." He looked for but didn't discover her among the actors preparing to leave the

Great Hall. He would see her face when he said, "Explain yourself! Are you a scornful hufty tufty?" And when she cried, he would say, "You are banished from here for now and forever." He was confident this would prompt pleas for forgiveness. She would agree to accommodate the Duke. He sent a servant to rustle out bodies in the gallery.

To her good fortune, Louise had sneaked out of the Great Hall during the final entertainments before the guests departed. The actors remaining in the Great Hall dallied in order to eavesdrop on the conversation but as the fire waned to embers they gradually took leave.

Béjart's heavy eyebrows stretched and drew together. Though he wanted to save Louise, he was no better than a vagabond in this dispute. "Fie! Nary a person has ever before found fault with her." He guarded his words, for his wig was taller than the Count's, a risk in itself.

The Count growled at the servant leaning on the long handle of a candle snuffer. "You, knave! Find the coquette!"

The Duke's displeasure weighed heavily on the Count, who said, "Mayhap she is swiving with some garçon as we speak." He was in a quandary about how to appease the Duke and turn his visit into a success. The Count repeated what the Duke had claimed. "It is winded about that she besets herself on the dull-witted as well as the high-born."

Obviously a false accusation, but Béjart dared not suggest the liar was the Duke. "Sire, we serve at your pleasure. I am the master of actors, but only for our divertissements."

The servants returned without Louise.

"Where is she?" The Count sputtered. His wine sotted breath met Béjart's. "This is the way I am repaid for my generosity. Sweet blessed Virgin! She is not to have chamber nor rations from my chattels." This was not going the way he had expected.

Béjart noted the exaggerated use of the word *chamber* for the communal closets they slept in. "As you wish."

"I will have her off. My steward will see her out the portcullis the morrow." The Count had convinced the Duke that it was too severe to put her out in the cold night. In any case, he was not going to search every corner of the chateau for her at that hour.

Béjart attended in suspense. When the Count turned on his heel, he relaxed. Gondrin did not deny quarters to the Augusto Troupe. As the heavy wood door slammed shut behind the Count, the servant put out one candle, then another. The cavernous room lost its high rafters and its spacious walls as darkness closed in around the dying embers in the fireplace.

Béjart walked through the rear courtyard and returned to where the actors hovered near a stove drinking from a wine bottle.

"What did the Count say about Louise?" said Leon, who had stayed longest in the Great Hall.

"Where is she?" said Béjart.

Georgette took a swig and handed the bottle to Argon. She had no obligation to tell Béjart that his paramour's nighttime absences were likely because of a young swain.

"Maybe she changed her mind about the Duke, the way he ogles her," said Samuel, who was standing on his hands.

"The Duke was looking at Isabelle," said Hubert, who knew how much Isabelle needed to hear this.

Isabelle smiled as she stood and said, "I bid you good night." With the expectation of the arrival of Lord Dubois, she was more conscious than usual about her appearance. She could not afford red eyes from lack of sleep.

"The Count has demanded that Louise leave," said Béjart.

Every one of them had suffered the eccentricities of the nobility at one time or another. Isabelle stopped in her tracks. Samuel eased into a backward flip, turned, and stood. Leon caught the handle of the knife he had tossed. Argon gulped the last of the wine. Eugene took the bottle and sucked on the lip. Each one felt a chill and leaned toward the warm coals.

"What about us?" said Agnes.

"Just Louise?" said Hubert.

"Just Louise." Béjart saw in their faces both relief and sympathy.

Agnes struggled to put on a sorrowful face, but a surreptitious grin conquered her lips when she thought of this development. Without Louise, the role of the beautiful protégé was hers alone.

"Just Louise?" said Samuel.

"Aye," said Béjart.

"Because of the Duke?" said Hubert.

"Offense to the Duke," said Béjart.

"Gallous buffoon," said Argon.

"Worthless blackguard," said Eugene.

"Lecherous knave," said Georgette.

"The steward comes for her the morrow," said Béjart.

"And take her where?" said Eugene.

The candle was sputtering into a puddle of wax. Georgette went out and returned with another one.

"Outside the chateau wall," said Béjart.

"And where is she to go then?" said Georgette.

"The Count said she might walk to a farmer's house, two leagues distant," said Béjart.

"And where to then?" said Argon.

"We have to give her a horse," said Isabelle.

"She will freeze to death," said Béjart.

"Give her a wagon," said Hubert.

Several smirks. "She will freeze slower," said Leon.

The hot coals hissed and popped an ember on the stone floor. Béjart crushed it with his boot. "We are not going to sit idly while the Count dispatches Louise." Having said this, he realized that if the Augusto Troupe departed with Louise the weather would force them to disband.

"What did she do?" said Agnes.

Béjart gave her a brutish look with his dark eyes, but she did not falter. She said, "What? The rest of us need to avoid it."

"You do not have to worry about it," said Leon. The men snickered, Argon among them, for the Duke's advances had been whispered one to another.

"Either we leave with her or we get her back inside," said Béjart.

"I am not leaving," said Agnes.

"Louise brought this on herself," said Leon.

"Better one freeze to death than the entire Troupe," said Samuel.

"Easy for you to say when it is not you," said Argon.

Isabelle said nothing. As soon as Lord Dubois arrived, she expected to run away to Paris.

"What do you mean by getting her back inside?" said Hubert.

He did not know what he meant until he said, "When Louise leaves with the steward, she will walk to the copse of linden trees and wait there until dark." Béjart concocted a plan and revealed it as he spoke.

Agnes said it was too risky. Eugene thought Louise was too frail. Argon wanted to go with her. Samuel said she would drown in the moat. Georgette agreed if Béjart promised to take care of her and Etienne if the plot failed and the Troupe was thrown out of the chateau.

Hubert said to Georgette, "What about me? You negotiate for your safety without me?"

Hubert and Georgette clashed, accusing each other of selfishness and spite.

"The Count is not so stupid he will not figure out Louise is back inside the chateau," said Leon.

"Are we not masters of disguise?" said Béjart.

It was well forward in the night when Béjart heard Louise sneak into Georgette's room and rustle into the cot. He arose and went to her. Without a word, he mounted her and spent himself until he was weary. He nodded off. After a time, he awoke and said, "Come to my cot." The dim light of a candle reflected in the doorway.

"I am too tired," she mumbled.

He stood. "Come..." He pulled her arm but she resisted.

"We are done, do you not know?" she said.

He picked her up in his arms and carried her to his room where a servant was shuffling fresh embers from a bucket into the stove. He deposited her under blankets and slipped in beside her.

When the servant took the light and left, Béjart said, "The Count has banned you from the chateau." He explained that the steward was to escort her through the drawbridge that very day.

This development threatened an end to her hope for a future with Philippe, who served at the Count's pleasure. "I needs gather my things." Louise tried to push him off, but he used his weight to keep her in place. "Prithee! Your force is offensive." She was desperate to get to Philippe's chamber, to appeal to him to rescue her. Her arms flew wildly into Béjart's face.

He grabbed her hands and felt the tears that dampened her temples. In the darkness, he was so close his breath blew into her face as he said, "Hark to me now! We will take care of you. We are going to get you back into the chateau."

She stopped fighting and started crying. When the sobs were spent, she listened as he explained the plan.

୬ Scene 21 ୧
Isabelle's letter

The following morning Béjart was unusually solemn when the actors asked if they were to perform that night. "No. The Count has made no order for entertainment."

"He'll find other entertainment," said Hubert.

"We might as well pack our trunks," said Samuel.

"It's Louise's fault," said Agnes, who by this time had heard of the Duke's rebuffed advances.

Isabelle did not dare relieve their anxiety about the Count's intentions, though she knew he had need of entertainments. He had invited another guest, Lord Dubois, who was expected to arrive for Mardi Gras. She kept his letter hidden in her bodice and the information it contained under her tongue.

A rash had developed on her complexion, and she employed the excuse that her pot of pomatum was empty to borrow a wagon for a trip to the apothecary. For at the village tavern, Lord Dubois's servant, a replacement for his treacherous page, awaited her letter of reply.

With Eugene to accompany her, they took the rock-riddled road to a hamlet near the Abbey of Saint-Seine. Such a figure as Isabelle was a rare sight in the environs. She was better than hand-bills at advertising the Troupe. Her momentous wig, iridescent skin, and sparkly costume inspired either awe or suspicion. Many a person held their wallet closer to the breast. Some avoided stepping in her footsteps. But every yeoman and livery maid stared.

After a moment's confusion, the apothecary loosened his tongue to offer his advice for whatever ailed her. She described the cream she required. He puckered his nose, nodded his head, and recognized the ingredients as those of a white paste he sold (at an exorbitant and unwarranted price) to the local baroness and the printer's wife. "Madame, only the best pomade for you. Which, I must profess, is incomplete without the white excellence of mercury."

Isabelle already had an ointment of mercury. "You are well spoken and solicitous to a fault, but prithee, no mercury." She used the power of her smile to persuade him to set aside his professional pride long enough to agree to omit it. With ostentatious precision he stirred together fat, bees wax, and spermaceti.

With her pomade in her bag, Isabelle walked to the tavern where Eugene sat with a tankard in the company of the one-legged beggar who had been sprawled at the entry of the public stable. The beggar, a former soldier, was telling of the siege of Maastricht. "Calvinists be our ruination. It's the gospel, so says good King Louis," His clothes clung in wrinkles melded with dried mud.

"Have you the sou to favor a drunkard by his cup?" Isabelle knew of Eugene's tenderness for beggars.

The beggar stiffened his back. "Upon my salvation, what benefit me to fight for good king Louis? Months in a trench! A mortar from the Royal Artillery! The bastards bombed the fourth-parallels!" He had already told this story, not just to Eugene, but to anybody and everybody and himself if there was nobody. He arose in his seat, leaned for his crutch, and wobbled it at Isabelle.

Isabelle drew back and looked at Eugene. "Perchance you could devise a ballad and make known the fair cavalier's story."

"The king's appetite for war is our ruination," said the beggar.

Eugene looked about the room, as did Isabelle, to ascertain if this man's words had been heard, but no head had turned. No eyes inspected them. The charge of sedition was of such consequence that Eugene said, "My good man, do not increase your injury by bitter charges against the King."

Isabelle turned to Eugene. "Prithee, fetch my gloves from the wagon." She deliberately left them in order to send him away while she inquired about Lord Dubois's servant, whose only choice of lodging was a rented bed in this solitary tavern.

The alewife said, "How should I know where he is? I am not his keeper!" She had a ruddy face and cheeks like curds of cheese.

At the stable Isabelle approached a young boy filing the hoof of a Percheron draft horse.

"Sir, I cry your mercy. Have you seen a traveler, a stranger to this locality, a garçon of your age?"

The stable hand, who was of an age to ride but not old enough to grow a beard, mumbled something incomprehensible. Isabelle sniffed and cleared her throat of the manure smell. She placed her foot in straw that looked the least primed and moved closer to hear him repeat, "What causeth me to remember?"

She dug into her reticule and produced a sou. In spite of the choking smell, she chanced to open her mouth and say, "A show of more than hope."

The boy pocketed the coin. "Mayhap at the skinner. He has gone there before." He nodded his head toward the corner, which Isabelle took to mean she should go in that direction.

On the walls of the skinner's shop were hanging squirrel, fox, and badger furs and cow hides. Stretched across the wall behind the counter was a bear skin, one big enough to subdue freezing nights.

Isabelle would have coveted the bear skin had it not been for Lord Dubois's letter. He offered her the possibility of ermine blankets.

The skinner's prominent eyes fixed on Isabelle as she asked about the Dubois servant, who, as it turned out, was entertaining his daughter in the loft. The skinner turned and disappeared behind a horsehair drapery and could be heard, "Alain, down to the nethermost!"

A boy new to Isabelle, name of Alain, entered the room. She led him to the street, for she durst not hand over the letter in the presence of the skinner or any other person. Every word she had chosen had been weighed and appraised. *I thought I would die of sorrow*, she had written. *But my joy is returned with your billet-doux.* She had enclosed a perfumed handkerchief.

Alain followed her to the street, pulling his tricorn hat over hair that thrust from his ears like tusks of a wild boar. "My lady." He bowed. Though his thin nose and narrow face gave an appearance of a shyster, Isabelle had no choice but to trust him with her letter.

She pulled the envelope from her cloak sleeve. "For his lordship and no other." The boy reached for it. She held on to the letter until he looked at her and nodded. His protruding teeth, had they been straight, would not have bothered her. "Go directly to Paris and place it in his hand posthaste." She held on to the letter.

"Paris? Wherefore Paris?" The boy was confused. He was a scullion at a chateau in the region of Burgundy and had been hired by a guest to fetch the letter. The boy's home, the chateau where Lord Dubois was visiting, was but a score of miles distant.

"Is Lord Dubois not at his Paris abode?" Isabelle had to wonder if he was a messenger of Lady Dubois. She refused to be foiled a second time. She jerked the letter from his hand.

The garçon, afraid he had let slip a secret, whined. "My lady, bear patience!" Without the letter, he forfeited the promised gratuity. He cocked his head to the side. "The nobleman will have your letter from my very hand, or my tongue be cursed with boils."

"Did the nobleman wear a wig? Color of..." Isabelle searched her mind for something as dull in color. "...a carp?"

The boy nodded.

"Curls on the crown and all the way down?" She motioned below her ears.

He licked his lips. "Yes. His eyeballs bulge like a toad," he said, inspired to salvage the exorbitant fee he had been promised. "A winged mustache. Short pointed beard. And a mole on his cheek." He pointed below the corner of his left eye.

She was satisfied and handed him the letter. He bowed again and with awkward steps headed toward the public stables.

Isabelle's future, like the billows of a blacksmith, was expansive at one moment and crushed in another. Her letter disappeared in the possession of a person with little to recommend him. Her heart faltered. It was her fate to exercise little jurisdiction over her own welfare.

☙ Scene 22 ❧
the shadowy figure of the towering keep

Before morning light Louise slipped away in search of Philippe. He had raised her hopes, despite her knowing that men played at love with less jeopardy than women. She hurried to his chamber to tell him her fate, for he of all persons had reason to support her refusal to bed with the Duke de La Fare. Little did she realize that Philippe would in no way endanger his position as the Count's animal trainer. Upon entering his chamber and seeing his four-poster bed empty, she had no choice but to return to the actors' quarters.

Early in the morning, Philippe heard of Louise's banishment from the kitchen maids as he took bread and hot tea. His throat narrowed and he felt a sorrowful weight press on his eyes and nose. The fresh excitement of her beauty brought him joy. He had doubts about whether Louise was the quality maiden to choose for a wife, but he had been dazed when she returned his admiration, and when he overheard the Count speak of the Augusto Troupe as quality entertainment, surpassed only by the Hôtel de Bourgogne, he became even more enamored of her. He had declared his love for her. He drank tea. He gulped. He swallowed a future he dared not pursue.

At the falcon tower, he let no disappointment interfere as he prepared for the Count's hunt. He warranted the jesses and hoods for the birds and leather gloves for the hunters.

After an early breakfast with his guests, the Count arrived and the two of them decided which birds to fly at the hares. The party of hunters mounted their horses and loped off, surrounded by yapping dogs. At the moment when other servants were witnessing the expulsion of Louise from the chateau, he sat his horse in the Count's forest and watched a hawk circling hundreds of feet in the air as it waited for the dogs to flush out a hare.

His thoughts were not on the hawk nor the hare. He pictured Louise walking from the courtyard out the gatehouse and was overcome with a sense of loss. Had things been different, she could have been the joy of his future. But he need not think on that. Without his position at Chateau de Giffaumont he had no future. The falcon plunged from its height. Death came to the hare at the speed of lightning.

The steward marched Louise from the back court through the Great Hall and front court, out the gates, and over the drawbridge. Without so much as a "fare thee well," he returned through the gates. Actors, in his view, were lechers and parasites. With the discharge of one of them, the chateau improved in morals and security.

Doors of the heavy wood gate creaked and grated shut. Louise stood on the drawbridge. She put down her basket of goods and pulled close her woolens, fur-lined cape, and bed coat. She looked back fretfully, for she had been unable to notify Philippe of her situation.

Facing her was a barren field where nubbins of wheat stalks stood in hoary silence. Her woolen stockings and thick underskirts held off the frozen whiskers of the ground as she made her way to the forest.

Jots of powdered snow clung to knobby roots and sunken holes. She wrapped the cape around her midriff and sat in the sun on a fallen beech tree. A shy wind passing through the branches ennobled a chilly loneliness. Louise ate bread and sausage that Georgette had filched from the kitchen. She leaned over and took a nap.

Upon waking she arose and stomped feeling back into her legs and feet. To restore blood to her body, she trod about the naked trees, staying within sight of the chateau. Memories of warm coals bristling in a stove made her light-headed.

She supposed Philippe had not heard about her. She supposed he would learn that she had been forced out in the cold. She supposed he would be alarmed. He would be angry. He would look for her. He would find her. He would wrap his arms around her. "You are safe with me, my darling," he would say.

She wandered about the beeches. Rime ice created brilliant blurry lights in the trees. "You are safe with me," she murmured to the icy leaves autumn had forced to the ground. The sun crept farther and farther away. Twilight creaked into the limbs. Louise grew uneasy. She paced and stomped and gazed into the gloaming. Her eyes burned. Alone as dark descended, she pretended to be unafraid, to ignore legends of the dark. Well she remembered the priest's incantation at the end of day for protection from diabolical forces that emerged in the absence of light. Demons disguised as animals.

Dogs barked, alarming Louise. She crept within view of the field. Hunting dogs were traversing the field toward the forest, in her direction. From the party of hunters on horseback came a shout, "Heigh! Here!" It was Philippe's voice. Except for the lead dog, they turned back. "Beau! Here!" Philippe kicked his horse to a canter and chased the dog back into the roadway. They disappeared in the chateau gate.

Louise saw Philippe turn away. She felt her fate was to die alone here in the woods despite Béjart's plan. Did she not deserve it? The prayer she mumbled stung her stiff lips. "Forgive me, little one." She asked for forgiveness, not from a God she did not trust, but from the baby she had left on the cathedral steps. For him there had been no justice, nor love, nor comfort. "It is right that I should know how you felt, lying in a basket alone on cold stone steps." She turned her ankle on a snow-covered stone. "But it wasn't all my fault." Her eyes took on a glazed look.

"It was not my fault," she said to the ashen trees.

They answered her "Whoose then?"

"It was Thomas. It was his fault. He seduced me." The wind turned frozen briars into needles that pricked holes in her stockings.

The trees whispered, "Nooooo. It was youuu."

She fell to her knees crying. "Yes, it was me. I wanted his love."

"Louise!" Argon's voice wafted through the silvery trunks. Upon seeing her on her knees, he said, "Surely you did not lose hope of my coming." He helped her up and would have enclosed her into his arms but for Béjart's shadow. He wiped her moist cheek with longing fingers. To avoid perilous implications, he smiled and gave her a handkerchief. "Verily, God does not hear your prayer unless you forswear being an actor."

She blew her nose. "Do you believe that?" She drank heartily from the bottle of wine he brought.

Argon broke loaf bread in half and gave the larger piece to her. "Béjart says the Church has God in a prison. And if you want to know God, you have to go to prison."

The moon gave light enough for them to see ghostly outlines. They wended their way toward the shadowy figure of the towering keep. From the field, the exterior curtain wall presented a towering barrier of rough stones. However, inside, stables adjoined the wall at a certain point. They walked along the exterior searching for that point, but every section of wall seemed identical to the next.

"Look for a rope," said Argon. The wall cast a shadow in the moonlight. They ranged their hands along the rough stones, feeling for the rope Béjart had secured to a roof strut and dangled over the side.

"Here!" Argon grabbed the knotted rope. He looked up the wall and said, "Béjart!" his thick voice whispery.

At the top of the wall, darkness took form. Béjart appeared.

"The knots are for grip," said Béjart.

Argon squatted to the ground and said to Louise, "Get on my shoulders." He picked her up. "Try to hold your feet to the wall. It will keep you from dangling. And pull yourself up. Béjart and Eugene will draw on the rope from the top."

Louise stood and balanced on his shoulders. Gripping the rope, she lifted her feet to the wall, and with her back to the ground, started her trek up the wall. Béjart and Eugene pulled faster than her fists advanced up the rope. At mid-way and thereafter, she dangled. Her palms burned. Her arms trembled. Béjart and Eugene groaned and tugged. When she was within reach, Eugene clutched her hand. Béjart hauled her over the top. They dropped the rope back to the ground.

Argon climbed while the three at the top heaved on the rope. Once he was on the stable roof, they scrambled over the eave and in through a window. Eugene returned the rope to a coffer containing horse equipment.

In the actors' chambers, Louise stood at a stove and revived herself in its flow of warmth. Once warm, she lay in her cot and fell asleep. In the morning before daybreak, Béjart woke her. "Go to the chapel. The mass is over, and the servants have left." He turned to Etienne, who held a torch. "If the priest is about, wait with Louise in the corner tower until he leaves."

The two of them left for the chapel and, finding it vacant, went inside. Etienne departed with the torch. Louise inhaled cold moments of stony darkness. Windows vaguely appeared. She tried the locked doors behind the altar. Saints gazed down at her from the walls. She tried to pray, but Jesus, painted like a skinned animal, was dying on a large gold-rimmed cross behind the altar. It gleamed with accusations. She had prayed for help, but Jesus had never been with child without benefit of a bed to sleep on.

The priest had said her sins were twofold, cudgeling wantonly and enticing a young boy into wrong-doing. Yes, Thomas was younger than her. He was of a respectable family and he had treated her kindly. She thought he would rescue her from her father's pandering. The priest had warned her that to say the name of her baby's father was a sin against God.

The penance for absolution had been to attend mass every day until the baby was born. She had not done that. The priest had made arrangements for her to enter a convent. And she had not done that. Her soul was damned. Eternal fires. Hell. She sighed. Had she been a horse, she would not be condemned for her baby. Or if she had been a dog. Or a cat. Or a chicken or goose. Their gods did not make sacrifices of women.

The poor state of her soul passed from her mind with the thought of Philippe. She sat on a kneeling bench and considered how to get a message to him. Despite the Count's ire, she believed, or hoped, he would marry her. She dared dream that with his support she might prevail upon the Count to forgive her. After all, Philippe was valued as an animal trainer and had some sway with the Count.

She curled into a corner, drew her fur-lined coat about her, and fell asleep. She was awakened by the scruff of footsteps on the stone steps. Without a sound, she slid through the linen cloths covering the altar and hid underneath.

In trudged the friar who had stayed at Chateau de Giffaumont weeks longer than he had intended. Now the weather aggravated his cough and his leather boots were thin. A boy servant accompanied him and placed candleholders, chalice, cruets, and paten on the altar. With the candles lit, the priest began in a nasal twang, *"In nomine Patris et Filii et Spiritus Sancti, amen."* The hint of a scent he didn't recognize confused him.

He sang, "Glória in excélsis Deo." A wisp of sound leaked into his piety and he stopped suddenly. A shy silence. Noticing the altar boy wipe his rheumy nose, the friar accounted him the transgressor. However, he was bothered about something and forgot to kiss the Bible. Only after the altar boy began *"Credo in unum Deum"* did he chant the profession of faith.

Louise remained tense and quiet, but the sound of the friar's chants brought to mind her lost soul and the eternity of hell. The sniffle she smothered had caused her nose to bleed.

As the friar broke the bread, he had a strong sense of another presence. Thinking it was a benediction, he blessed and broke bread several times. He refilled the chalice and drank the sour wine. To the altar boy's astonishment the friar sent for more wine.

After mass, the altar boy returned to the kitchen and warmed at a fire. "Strange, Father drank the chalice dry and asked for more. Kissed the altar as if it was Jesus' feet."

☙ Scene 23 ❧
the dog's chair

Following two days of inactivity, Béjart received a messenger while he was currying his horse. Hay stalks and spikes poked through cracks between the loft boards. Chips of tree bark overlay the floor. A satisfying grain scent surrounded him.

"My lord wishes to see you in the Great Hall," said the chamberlain.

Béjart threw the currying brush into one of the wood compartments built into the wall and led his horse back to a stall. The return to routine that followed after Louise came back into the chateau gave him confidence that the problem was satisfactorily under control. She spent her nights in a warm cot in the actors' rooms. As soon as morning mass concluded, she took a blanket and went to the chapel, where she remained during daylight hours.

On the day Louise was banished, Béjart and the actors arranged to perform their entertainments without her. Between Agnes and Etienne, who wore a wig and mounds of makeup, the shows continued without disruption.

Béjart reckoned that the Count's summons meant that either he was returning to Paris or he was requiring a night of divertissements. Should it be about Paris, Béjart braced himself for the ice-sealed axles of the caravans.

Aside from the Louise dilemma, Béjart had been ambivalent about whether the Count would continue to employ the Troupe following the misadventures of their performance of *Mirabelle*. With so many distractions, he had little time and less inclination to continue the story of "King Claudius' Knight."

He had read and reread portions of the mummy's diary only to sense the depths of the grave and the desperation of unfinished work. Words escaped into hollow caverns. He had neither sharpened a quill nor refilled his ink pot. Moreover, he reasoned with himself that it was all for the best. The plot of the play was not just problematic but perilous. He had been driven to write of a knight sent by his king to capture a convict who was morally superior to the king—a plot to enrage King Louis.

The Count, attended by a nearby servant, sat in an upholstered chair drinking ale as he leaned toward the fire. A dog with eyes hardly visible beneath its inordinate fur lay on the seat of the armchair. It stood up and uttered a desultory bark.

"Calme-toi, petit monsieur!" said Gondrin. The dog looked at its master and curled back into the seat. Béjart stood awaiting removal of the dog, but the Count launched into praise for a comedie he had seen at the chateau of an associate. "A gentilhomme of brilliant taste."

Béjart realized he was expected to stand while the dog took the seat. This was too much for his pride. He clutched the back of the chair and tipped it forward, dislodging the dog, which thumped on the wood planks of the floor. It ambled over to the Count, who rubbed it behind the ears. "Poor Fabby. No chair for you."

Béjart bit his tongue. Poor Fabby was fat and lazy and obviously didn't hunt. What it deserved, Béjart thought, was a kick in the ass.

A blazing ember spit from the fire and landed in the dog's fur, which smoked up. It yelped and ran, causing the smoke to blaze and dispensing an execrable smell. The servant chased the dog, which by this time was flaming around the Great Hall.

"For God's sake, catch him!" Gondrin stood up and shouted to his servant, who was trying to do just that. Another servant opened the door, his arms laden with cut limbs for the fire. The flaming, howling dog bolted out the door, followed by the servant. The entering servant screamed, dropped the wood he was carrying, and fell backward onto the stone step.

The Count hastened to the door, stepped outside, and stood watching until the animal ran into the keep and out of sight. The howling was replaced by silence. In a matter of moments a stir of voices arose about the inner courtyard. Servants went to the keep. Somebody cried out amid high pitched voices. The Count marched outside, leaving Béjart standing and warming his backside to the fire. In the Great Hall, a cloud of foul smoke obscured the ceiling timbers.

The Count returned. Slammed the door. "Shit!" He sat and stared at the fire without another word. The dog's death was tantamount to losing a signet ring. He had impressed many a guest with a casual anecdote of how Marc-Rene had gifted him with such a shoddy animal. *Gifted* was an exaggeration the Count no longer discerned. In reality, he had happened upon the street when Marc-Rene demanded that somebody remove the puppy from his path. The Count admired the puppy that had obstructed the nobleman's way. He took it home and grew fond of the dog's slavish devotion.

"Lackaday, my lord." Béjart said nothing more. To sympathize about a dog was below his dignity. It was no secret that the Count held the dog in greater esteem than most people, including the actors.

The Count sighed. "By God, I swear, such a cherished dog never smelled so putrid." The dog had made up for poor hunting skills by lying at the Count's feet on cold nights and keeping them warm.

A servant, with tentative footsteps, entered and took his position in the corner behind the Count. Without turning to the servant, the Count said bitterly, as if he had suffered an injustice, "Here, you hedge-born scut, have they put Fabby in the stable?"

"Yes, sire." The servant's voice adequately conveyed a sense of mourning.

Béjart swallowed air that gave him a nauseous taste. A log

sizzled as it ebbed and fell through crumbling cinders. He sorely needed a noggin of wine.

"By cock! This had to happen now." The Count looked at his fingers. "My Fabby. Gone." He glanced at Béjart with resentment. The dog would still be alive if it had remained in the chair, a consideration that had not escaped the Count's notice. He looked at the actor with grim disdain, as if Béjart was guilty of a preventable tragedy, guilty of Fabby's murder.

The revolting scent of burning flesh drifted from corner to corner. There was no escaping the Count's insinuation. Béjart was deciding whether to choke his pride, offer an apology for taking the dog's seat, or otherwise attempt to appease the Count. After all, the Troupe depended on him and he needed Gondrin's favor. On the other hand, let this coxcomb kiss his own ass.

The Count turned to the servant. "God's teeth! Bring more ale!" He tipped his nose up and sniffed the air as if Béjart was the source of the smell. Tragedies came and went in his life. He couldn't mull over every one of them.

The servant shuffled on quiet feet to refill his goblet. Béjart swallowed his spit.

"That *Mirabelle* comedie. Three days should be adequate time to turn your piece of trumpery into a comedie worthy of an audience. Excellence this time around or your reputation is not worth a cock's crow."

Béjart's concern for his own reputation left little room to think about the Count's, which was languishing despite his efforts to impress the Duke.

Gondrin's thick lower lip sheened with the moisture of ale. "More guests will be arriving. Get your actors in top form. No more of this muddling around and calling it amusements."

Béjart ignored "muddling" and heard what he wanted to hear. The arrival of more guests. More shows! Shelter from the elements. Despite the Count's deprecating tone, Béjart left in a cloud of enthusiasm.

The Troupe gathered in the Great Hall for rehearsal.

ා Scene 24 ൙
voice of vapor

Into the inner courtyard clattered a carriage, the wood about the crown and door elaborately carved with fleur-de-lis. Chickens and ducks scurried from the hoofs of four groomed horses prancing in synchronous high steps. Dogs in the far kennel rioted. The driver's gold-trimmed livery was no less impressive than the carriage's velvet curtains and upholstered seats.

Inside sat Lord Dubois, without the company of Lady Dubois. When she had inquired about accompanying him, he had constrained her with a reminder of the Count's hounds. Lady Dubois, who treasured her lapdog, loathed hunting hounds. Her dog had fits, set off by, among other things, the barking of dogs.

When the carriage came to a stop a servant opened the door. Lord Dubois emerged, his high heels landing on the proffered footstool. He breathed deeply.

"Sir Thomas, it is my pleasure to welcome you to Chateau de Giffaumont," the Count addressed Lord Dubois. They bowed to each other.

"It is my good fortune to be in the environs." Lord Dubois swept off his plumed hat and with a gliding motion bowed and kissed the hand of the Countess, who stood nearby with an unflagging smile.

"Indeed. We exceed in good fortune, for the Duke and Duchess de La Fare are here for the nonce." Gondrin rocked on his heels in naming such prestigious guests. He gloated on seeing Lord Dubois's surprise. "Chambers have been made ready for you with every comfort you might require. Dispose yourself at your ease."

Dubois had not expected to encounter the Duke de La Fare at Chateau de Giffaumont. It had been dinned about that La Fare had traveled to the baths of Plombières with Duke de La Rochefoucauld, though how this affected La Fare's noble standing varied according to perspective and whether one forgave La Rochefoucauld's being a frondeur during the rebellions preceding Louis XIV's reign.

Nonetheless, La Fare had assumed the rarefied air of les grands. Dubois forgot about Isabelle and turned to thoughts of how he might impress the Duke and put himself to advantage.

Inside the Great Hall, Béjart, with the actors present and advising him, revised *Mirabelle* in light of the previous performance, taking out some lines and adding others. "Louise will return and play the part of the protégé," said Béjart.

Agnes, who expected to be the lovely protégé, was bewildered. "The Duke will recognize her. He will know we tricked him by bringing her back."

"You will play the opening scene. Louise will come in as the protégé in the second scene." Béjart gave her a peremptory look.

"If we are found out, we will be banished," said Samuel.

"She will put the rest of the Troupe at risk," said Agnes.

"Somebody in the audience is bound to know it is her," said Leon.

"You have not seen the costume Hubert is making for Louise," said Béjart.

"Humph! The Count is not blinded by a costume, I trow!" said Agnes. What she intended for a gracious smile was more of a smirk. In watching Isabelle, she had come to realize that anybody might become an adored actor with the proper paints and wigs.

"The parts are decided," said Béjart.

"It was not proper to take the role from me in the first place. I played it better than your strumpet," said Agnes. At a time when she needed better parts, Béjart favored Louise, who knew more about Béjart's cock than she did about acting. A nauseous wave passed as Agnes thought of Béjart's groping hands under blankets.

"Fie on you! Be glad you have any role at all." Béjart saw in her eyes the hooded gaze of resentment.

Isabelle brightened from head to toe at the rumble of a coach on the cobblestones outside the Great Hall, surely the arrival she eagerly awaited. "Phew! The fire fills the room with smoke," she said, giving her a reason to go to the door where she could see outside. "It is giving me a chin cough." She shoved the heavy wood door slightly open. When she spied the dapper figure of Lord Dubois, she heaved a sigh of euphoria. Her fervor for his attention was rekindled, as was her impatience.

Louise entered the Great Hall followed by Hubert. She stood a handspan taller and sauntered by necessity, for her feet were not accustomed to elevated shoes.

Leon said, "By my trowth, our beautiful protégé has lard-bloated bosoms."

"A bonny maiden too taken by the supper table," said Samuel.

Hubert had padded one of Georgette's costumes and enlarged Louise's bosoms with inflated pig bladders. She wore a red wig that Georgette had dyed and fashioned. Wisps of red hair spiraled onto Louise's forehead and temples. Thick twirls swept to her neck and shoulders. Her cheek bones, given an overlay of wax, took on a chiseled look.

"This is the beautiful protégé men fight over?" cried Agnes. "She will be laughed at, yes! Pilloried!"

"Even with her costume, Louise does not have lips like a mouse," said Argon.

"Or eyebrows like an owl," said Samuel.

"Enow! We begin. On stage!" said Béjart.

As the rehearsal progressed, the actors strutted across the platform, raising a murmur under their feet. From one jest to another, the characters of *Mirabelle* met folly with sarcasm and mockery.

Argon was downcast. His role as a manservant had been reduced to hardly more than a walk-on because of his thready voice. Gone was his best scene, one with a beautiful maid played by Agnes. It had been an excellent stage moment, involving trickery and a fur-lined shawl. He could not help but remember that the hoarseness had turned worse after the incident of Isabelle's potion and Lady Birague.

Despite what other owners of the Troupe might wish, Béjart

reserved to himself decisions about the fate of lines and scenes. Many a dispute had arisen while traveling in the provinces about who or what instance had caused rotted foodstuffs to fly at the stage. Only a good reception by the audience preserved any single actor's right to the stage.

This rehearsal took on more importance than any other. He shouted "Foul pig!" or "Ha! Indeed!" depending on the actor's delivery. They arranged Louise's scenes in such a way to display her profile, the better to reduce the risk of her being discovered.

Despite Argon's effort, his voice vaporized like steam from a pot. Béjart would have no more. To keep his son on stage despite his impaired voice diminished him in the eyes of the other actors. "Au diable! What happened to your speech!"

"It is worse in sound than I have ever been," Argon said.

"Mayhap you take a different dodge. Mime or acrobatics." Béjart expected his son to accept his suggestion.

But it embarrassed and angered Argon. "It is a curse belike. And I will be at the bottom of it." The words sputtered out.

"Did you not say so days already gone?"

Argon could hardly come up with a reply. "I will have my voice!"

"And how? With concoction from an enchanter? Or at a house of whores?" Béjart's habit of belittling dissenters was more effective on peasants than his actors.

"Nenni! That is your domain." Though Argon intended this as an insult. Béjart, if anything, took covert pride in his reputation for virility when it came to women.

"When you have the voice, you will be back on the stage." Béjart realized this meant Argon would join Eugene as a backstage member. The size of their Troupe could little afford two such members. Eugene, whose talent with the lute entertained them both on and off the stage, had made a place for himself in the group. But Argon was another matter. Béjart thought quickly. "I know a jongleur with a pair of monkeys. I will buy one. You will have time to train it to do tricks, mayhap before the spring comes."

Argon's anger was upended by dismay. Because his early success on the stage had been met by boisterous hoots and shouts of approval, everybody assumed he was fated for an extraordinary future. He had hopes of playing at the Palais Royal in Paris. Béjart's suggestion of a monkey turned him to stone.

Béjart took his son's silence as acceptance and was satisfied with his suggestion.

When it was time for the manservant to appear, Argon, brimming with anger and resentment, stood aside and watched Samuel deliver the lines in his place.

Eugene quietly plucked notes on his lute and said, "Argon, can you play a violin?"

"Who gives a fig?" mumbled Argon, listening to lines Samuel spoke loudly but with little talent.

"I saw one in a Troyes shop." Eugene tested a gut string for pitch. "I'm thinking of buying it." He figured that if he learned the violin it would make Argon's lute more necessary. At the moment, it seemed that Argon needed to be needed.

"I'm going to train a monkey," Argon said bitterly.

Though there was no audience in the Great Hall, Isabelle, as the chancellor's widow Mirabelle, delivered with mockery the words of a love letter she assumed was for herself though it had been written to her protégé. It was so perfectly nuanced Béjart guffawed. The rehearsal ended and he was in good spirits. With two more days to practice, he felt confident.

The Troupe, excepting Louise, clamored to the kitchen for their meal. Chairs scraped loudly against stone as the actors sat at stark wood tables. The Augusto Troupe, since arriving at Chateau de Giffaumont, had benefitted from meals with meat, often brought in from Gondrin's social hunts. Etienne had lost his gaunt look. Hubert had grown stronger and Georgette fatter.

That evening the Troupe put forth bawdy skits and musical interludes. As wine fuddled the heads of the Count and his guests, the more lewd the comedy, the louder the laughter. While Isabelle and Leon acted out a fabliau, Béjart chanted rhythmically. In Eugene's hands, the lute made innocent or eager or erotic music. Thus a lusty young blacksmith's story was told.

> *… to him a buxom young damsel came smiling*
> *and asked if to work at her forge he would go.*

Leon pounded on a table with a hammer. Enter Isabelle dressed as a peasant,

> *They stripped to go to it, 'twas hot work and hot weather.*

Isabelle removed her blouse showing her tightly-strapped bodice and a wanton décolleté. Leon wiped his sweaty brow.

> *She kindled a fire and she soon made him blow.*
> *Red hot grew his iron, as both did desire,*

Leon slipped a huge sausage from his side to his crotch. Isabelle ended the ditty with:

> *What I get, I get out of fire,*
> *Then prithee, strike hard and redouble the blow.*

As Isabelle swayed and bumped Leon's groin, she caught the eye of Lord Dubois. "Lo! Yes!" ascended into the nether regions of the smoke-shrouded ceiling. Her cleavage swelled and in a frolicking twirl her nipple peeked out to bursts of nickering appreciation.

That Isabelle had the eyes of every man in the room excited Lord Dubois, who gave a self-satisfied chuckle. The evening was going well. The wine suited his taste, not that it was superior, but because he could congratulate himself on serving better quality at his chateau.

Outside snow began to fall, but in the Great Hall the fire roared. Samuel performed a tumbling extravaganza around the grand table. The actors joined in an ensemble Arabian dance. The Count stumbled to his feet and gave a toast to his guests as if he hadn't already toasted several times. As he began an ale-soused speech, the actors gathered at the tapestry and quieted. Eugene quietly plucked the lute.

The guests variously nodded and slumped in their chairs to the sound of the Count's droning. He wobbled forward and fell onto the table. Servants helped him up. They loaded him on a chaise a porteurs and carried him to his chamber, returning for others doing their utmost to avoid falling on the floor. As the last of the guests exited on chaises, the maid servants picked up knives from under the table, retrieved bits of goose or marrow bones or capon pies that had dropped out of fingers. They wiped up puddles of wine and piss from the wet floor. Carried goblets and plates to the kitchen. Removed the sauced tablecloths. Hurried to discharge their duty before the fire went out.

The following morning the Count and his guests were off for a day of hunting. He had ordered another evening of musical interludes to accompany their supper. "Prepare your spectacular comedie for the morrow," he said in expectation of a triumphant meal of wild game.

Béjart roused the actors, eager for another rehearsal of *Mirabelle*. Time was short to assure that Louise accustomed herself to her costume and avoided standing full front to the audience. Béjart had made a decision about Argon and waylaid him in the rear courtyard. Argon, coincidentally, was looking for his father.

Argon believed his performance, even taking into account his voice, was superior to that of Samuel, whose physical talent as a tumbler was superior to his acting. "Samuel's shrill-gorged lines are no better than my efforts," Argon said. He controlled his temper enough to refuse the words, "By cock!"

"He has twice the breath for voice." Béjart boomed as if to illustrate what an actor should sound like. "The problem with Samuel is that he does not look the part. Give him the costume you wore, the scarlet cape with satin laces." He motioned laces with his hands.

"His weedy body will appear ever the more insufficient in my costume."

"Hubert performs miracles with his sewing needle. Or if need be, a buckle or laces," said Béjart.

"My costume belongs to me, not the Augusto Troupe!"

"Alak! And whose sou paid the mercer for your cape?"

Argon, being a minor in the company, had yet to pay for his costume, but he had filched costumes and props that others in the company used. "Did I not add to our coffers? I have claim to Leon's snake-toed shoes and Etienne's silk tunic with brocaded flowers."

"Give Samuel your periwig, too. You can have it back when your voice is of substance."

Worse than the humiliation at having to give up his costume was the threat to Argon's confidence that he might never recover his voice. "I'll have no monkey!" He turned away before his father could see the fury in his eyes, swearing to himself, "A pox unto thee."

Leaving his father's troupe had never entered his mind, but Argon refused to prance about with an acrobatic monkey. Better to work the audience selling flags or magic beryl stones, or carved roots like the boy Etienne. With some despair, he realized he had no token and nothing of value to vend. It occurred to him to steal money from Béjart. At least enough to get him to Paris.

The actors lumbered into the Great Hall. Rehearsal began without Argon. Béjart hurried them through *Mirabelle* in order to make changes to that evening's entertainments.

When the audience did not vary from one performance to another, it was necessary to vary the amusements or risk boring the onlookers, in particular the Count. Béjart changed the ensemble dance into a mock ballet performed while Georgette sang a ballad about cock fighting.

Leon suggested that he perform the stabbing and recovery trick, since he had a sheep's bladder.

"What stabbing?" said Etienne, who was keen to hear of a stabbing.

"I'll fill the bladder with vermillion water and bind it to a wood plate and fasten both to my midriff." Leon took his knife from his boot and pointed it to his torso. "The knife goes into the bladder." He touched his knife to his doublet. "I bleed like a pig and howl like a werewolf." He groaned. "But the plate protects me. I get over the groan, belch out loud, give the crowd a triumphant look, and dance out of sight."

"Washing that doublet will cost you more derniers," said Georgette, who knew that red color was hard to remove.

"Argon and I have rehearsed a mime. We could performed it," said Louise.

"No. We take no more chances with you being on stage," said Béjart.

That night the actors sang lustily even if the ballad happened to be the wrong one. The mock ballet was more of a tumble-about on toes. Agnes stole a jellied eel from the table and choked trying to eat it and dance. Leon accidentally cut his girdle. But it was no matter. The Count and his guests, exhausted from the day's hunt, were hardly awake.

◎ Scene 25 ◎
Argon's twitch of the fever

The following day when the actors gathered in the Great Hall to rehearse *Mirabelle* for the final time before their performance, Argon had little to do. Feeling useless, he took Béjart's horse Borgia without permission and rode to the nearby hamlet. No person was about the road, in the main because snow crusted the ruts and obscured the rows where barley once grew.

The tavern, however, was alit with burning logs and lively paysans. Argon resented the wrongness of life more acutely as he sat and drank ale, in particular the injustice of his flawed voice, for he was blameless. It was the doings of the God of the voice. Next to him a callow goatherd, with a voice to make goats follow and men listen, rambled about a woman made bald when she washed her hair with a potion her husband gave her. That the goatherd should have the voice Argon needed proved God's recklessness. Would Jesus be the God of the Church if he had lost his voice?

He could afford to play card games with laymen, for the stakes were in sou rather than écus. At that, he won enough to keep his ale cup filled.

As Argon waited at the bar for another mug of ale, his gaze fell upon the maidens. He was angry at God and needy in the crotch. A drink of ale coated his bitterness and blended well with his thoughts, which returned to the females of seductive lips and witless talk. Of those with lips he could possibly put to his, he noticed one who had all her teeth, such as they were. She withdrew from a roaring boy with bristles for a chin and headed for the door. Argon intercepted her.

"Stay a while. I will order another ale."

She smiled at him. "Flat cakes too?"

Argon nodded her toward his table just as a lout was stealing into his seat. He rushed ahead and tumbled the lout on the floor.

"Whey face!" The lout jumped up shoving his shoulder into Argon.

The muscles in Argon's arms brimmed. "This be my table, you worthless palliard!" From his belly to his throat, his blood scorched his veins.

The lout stumbled away, mumbling, "Pigeon-livered loon."

The maiden sat and drank his ale while he fetched flat cakes and more ale. He returned and quaffed his ale more quickly than he intended. After she ate the flat cakes, Argon said, "Your fair comeliness captures many a suitor, I dare say."

Her eyes sparked with excitement. "Are you wooing me?"

"I cannot resist your captivating…" He was looking at her bountiful cleavage.

She leaned forward, exposing more of her assets, and kissed his nose. He took her hand and caressed it, gradually becoming forceful.

She laughed. "You make the stars shake."

"Aye. My horn is made of thunder." Argon took words from a ballad he often sang. It well described his need of the moment. "Thunder I stole out of heaven."

"And so you crave a tempest?"

"Come. Let us find a corner where thunder meets lightening." Argon hardly noticed as a couple of brawlers entered the room and demanded beakers of beer.

"Did you bring silver?" she said.

He nodded.

"Let me see," she said.

Argon hesitated, reluctant to expose sou. One of the brawlers, a man noticeable for scars in his beard and boulders for shoulders, pushed through chairs and approached their table. "Ah, my fair wench!"

"Fie and aroint with thee! I never again will drink with you!" said the maiden.

The brawler bellowed, "And you drink with this dunderhead?" He shoved Argon and his chair, which fell backward and knocked into a customer sitting at a nearby table, knocking over his mug. Argon and the customer stumbled to their feet.

The customer said, "Alak! Jolt-head! You spilled my ale." He let loose a fist aimed at Argon, who ducked, and the blow landed on the brawler.

The brawler jockeyed his fists toward both of them. Argon reeled behind the customer, now fuming at the mouth. The jostled customer tussled with the brawler and the maiden climbed out a window followed by Argon, who lost her in the gloom.

Argon fetched Borgia from the stablehand and rode the lonely wagon road back to Chateau de Giffaumont. The moon rose in the sky. He wondered why his journey as a human increased in disappointments. What had happened to the time when there were daily chances for triumphs? A cold breeze obstructed his thinking. Frozen pebbles crunched under Borgia's hoofs. Nothing moved except himself and his horse. The woods and meadows offered only forlorn variations.

They passed from ghastly forests into the open range of a snow-covered field. A menacing darkness was relieved by moonlight that layered the ground with ghostly silence. He had dallied longer than he intended at the tavern.

A snap of a twig echoed as if a highwayman stalked them. He looked fore and aft and saw only shadows. He kicked Borgia to a canter. "Let us ride at a rattling pace," he said. Upon hearing his own hoarse voice, he repeated as loudly as he could, "At a rattling pace." He was not too ale-wrecked to realize it was foolish to travel alone, especially at night. He was paying for his folly with moments of terror.

Borgia stumbled in a trench. Argon slipped from the saddle as the horse went down on his side. "God rot it!" Borgia righted himself on all four legs. Argon stroked the blameworthy leg good and gentle, lifted the foot and lightly rubbed from foreleg to hoof. With the horse at his side, he hand-walked him a distance on the road and soft talked. "Without you, my good and faithful Borgia, my arse will freeze along with the grasses and stones."

When Borgia put his head down and exhaled sharply through his nostrils, Argon took a deep breath and climbed back into the saddle whispering, "God save me from freezing."

The horse regained confidence before Argon did. He ignored a dull click behind him, crouched in the saddle, and looked ahead, his eyes nipped by the air. Shadows whispered. The road itself swelled and squirmed like a snake slithering. A pale light prowled from one bush to another. The reins cut welts in his glove.

He patted Borgia's neck and felt the warm muscles. He trotted as if parading in sunshine with nothing but flies to fear. The horse's assurance calmed Argon. "Shadowy woods. No more than childhood fears."

What he might rightfully worry about was his voice. He had, from one time to another, used elixirs, but with mixed outcomes.

There had been only momentary restoratives. What he needed was an enduring cure.

Isabelle came to mind. In particular, her elixir. Or elixirs, for she was rumored to have a casket of them. Should he ask her about an elixir? Agnes had said, "Be careful of Isabelle. She is jealous of your talent. Remember what happened to Remy when he stole her applause." Agnes hadn't needed to say the singer and his remarkable voice had met an early death at the bottom of a well. Despite what Agnes said, Argon did not believe Isabelle had put a lizard under Remy's cot.

He heard a noise and pulled Borgia to a halt. Without the clop of hoofs or the squawk of leather or the shiver of metal reins, the world was utterly silent. A breath cut a cold trail into his chest. A chill mounted to his brain and flushed his cerebral apartments. He decided to petition Isabelle for a curative potion.

Argon thundered on the chateau gate until the gatekeeper unlocked the door. He gave Argon an impatient look and said, "Fusty want-wit! Have you no fear of falling from a horse?"

Argon stabled Borgia and went upstairs to the actors' quarters. He stumbled through a dark room before coming into candlelight where Georgette, sitting on a cot, squinted into a mirror and plucked hairs from her forehead. Her brass tweezers had belonged to her mother, who had also extended her forehead despite the Church's warning that it was a mortal sin.

Louise, who often shared Béjart's chamber, lay in the other cot. From a room further down the passageway came loud snoring.

Georgette, admired for her ample physique, was well known for bedlore. Though Hubert was her husband and helpmeet he could only trot out his post for a twitch. As long as she respected his flagging pillicock, he did not deny her the commerce she craved from other men.

Argon sat on the cot and nuzzled her ear. "Do you think I could be man enough for you?"

She turned and gave him a kiss that trailed from his lips to his ear. "No." She turned back to her looking glass.

"I will please you, whatever your bidding."

"Desire comes not with bidding. It catches you unaware."

"I have desire enough for both of us." The virility of his libertine muscle knew no restraint.

She looked at him in the looking glass. "I will not go to the expense of dubious advances."

"By Saint George, you have it in your power to make certain our advances."

"Helas, nay. I will draw breath of easement this night."

"Your ease is a baleful night for me." Instead of leaving, Argon crept near Louise's cot. "Louise?" he whispered.

She appeared to be asleep.

He whispered in her neck, "If you could but love me." He longed to climb under her sheepskin and press himself to her.

She roused and turned her back to him. He stroked her hair.

"Go to bed before you get yourself into more trouble than you can get out of." Georgette sighed, blew out the candle, and climbed into her cot.

In the darkness, Argon put his arm over Louise and lowered his head on to her shoulder.

"Go you hence. Louise has troubles enough," said Georgette in a thick voice. Argon took to his own cot.

Louise lay quietly but she was by no means peaceful. Argon's love would be but another curse. Love was an empty cup you filled with disappointment. Her letter to Philippe had gone up in flames, cast into the fire by her own hand. Not only had Leon refused to deliver it, but he had explained, with all due severity, her mistake. Philippe would not stand by her as long as she was undesirable to the Count. Did she not realize that one's security was more important than love? That love, if anything, was temporary and, like an earthen ridge, susceptible to crumbling under weight? Leon merely pointed out that Philippe was like every other man, not the magician she had imagined.

☙ Scene 26 ❧
oysters and roast boar

Devil's hand!" said the Count. Following a late noonday meal, a card game in the solare proclaimed the good and bad luck of the Count and his guests. "Left-handed luck!" Because nobody dared win more hands of brelan than the Duke, they roared with dissatisfaction at their bad luck. "Another round!"

In the Great Hall, a butler, shined and polished in blue velvet, entered and arranged bottles in the wine casket. Servants hauling baskets of herbs scattered lavender and thyme across the floor. Dapper maids in embroidered aprons unfurled scarlet tablecloths. Others brought in silver plates and Venetian wine glasses. The linkman placed on the tables candelabras, each with a dozen candle cups or more. A porter brought in firewood and added it to what was already an inferno. He remained in the shadows of the fireplace, continuously adding wood.

The actors returned to the Great Hall dressed in their costumes. They stood near the fire's feverish vitality and basked in the heat. When the tower bell sounded the evening hour, the servants hurriedly finished pampering the table and exited. The actors retreated to the gallery behind the tapestry.

The Count swaggered in the door with a confidence that his hall's lavish accouterments, though not of royal measure, adequately insinuated wealth and prestige. To erase any doubt of his status, he wore a gold-threaded waistcoat and doublet laced with jewels. Had he the power of a wizard, he would magically fetch from his Paris manor the bust of himself. The Duke would be forced to admire his superior discernment. As he flicked his head, the jeweled ribbon binding the strands of his wig glinted in the candlelight.

His wife glided forward as if on winged shoes, her red velvet overskirt billowing open to reveal a black satin forepart edged in pearls. The Countess de Gondrin awaited an opportunity to explain her gown, for she had it copied from a portrait of the Countess de Soissons. Two large emeralds shone in her ears.

Lord Dubois, aspiring to prestige, arrived in a quilted and embroidered doublet, which tapered at the waist and flared at the hips. The skirt provided no coverage and, in such weather, one wore hose that were held up by straps. He wore long, pointy-toed shoes of a style called poulaine, which was meant to suggest the size of the wearer's penis. The longer the point, the more virile the man. His moustache, with the aid of gum, stretched out in stiff flourishes.

The Duke and Duchess appeared in jeweled needlework, gold buttons, and silver ribbons. Her long cashmere shawl dragged the floor collecting herbs into its folds. Each arm was encircled by a gold filigree bracelet set with opals.

Servants stood in attendance at every corner of the room. The actors gathered around the stove in the back gallery, except for Béjart, who waited at the tapestry with his eyes on the Count. When the Count nodded, Béjart and several musicians strolled into a corner of the room and quietly plucked and strummed Italian love songs.

The Count and the Duke praised the comely costumes of each other's wife while the women distinguished themselves at the fireside and drank wine. A carriage arrived in the courtyard followed by another. Outside, hearty greetings could be heard as visitors were met by the marshal and numerous servants. Guests entered to the outside rumbling of their vacated carriages departing for the curtain wall where they would be guarded by the Count's footmen.

Visiting drivers returned quietly to the inner courtyard and went to the kitchen where they crowded at the table and warmed at the cook fire.

Inside the Great Hall, polite greetings and deferential bows to the Duke and Duchess turned to cagey chatter and cheery smugness as guests milled in the warmth of the wood fire. As the wine flowed, guffaws and laughter arose.

Below in the kitchen, cooks, maids, butlers, carvers, and spit boys scrambled about the work tables, whispering orders and complaints. Fat dripping into hot embers billowed the scent of seared porcine skin. A saucier spooned a garlic and lemon sauce on oysters arranged on silver platters. A servant peeked in the door, giving the signal to a second contingent of Béjart's musicians, who were awaiting the conveyance of food to the Great Hall.

The actors struck up a tune and led the porters upstairs, trailing citrus and garlic aromas. With tabor and pipe, they dramatically introduced the oysters. Argon's lute mellowed the music as guests tried to outdo one another in delicacy while slurping oysters. A visiting lady attempted to pierce them with a knife, but more slid off than reached her lips, and more often than not landed on the floor.

A merchant's wife whispered to a table servant that the Duke, managing slippery oysters with his fingers, lacked a fork or knife. With a puzzled look, the servant trotted off to the dressoir, returned, and offered the implements to the Duke whose face turned sour. "I require no fork or knife!"

The lady said, "Your grace, the garçon's concern is to keep your elegant fingers unsoiled."

"My lady, my fingers are not nearly so elegant as those of the King, who eats with his."

He exchanged a glance of smug superiority with his wife. The woman had obviously never been in the presence of the King.

For a second course, the musicians heralded tureens of stewed broth of mutton marrow bones. There followed a parade of courses: capon larded with lemons; pigeons with gooseberries; veal in sharpe broth; sheep's tongues with herbs, vinegar, and butter. After soiled plates were removed and replaced by clean silver ones, the Count nodded his approval for the grand course.

Playing exuberant music, the actors entered ahead of two porters carrying a platter too heavy for one. The music swelled portentously as the porters hefted a roasted boar with an orange in its mouth on to the table before the Duke.

Despite the Count's effort to remain nonchalant, his eyebrows twitched at the bronze seared skin and magnificently displayed animal. He cleared his throat and stood. "Good sires and madames, a drink to the health of his Lordship, by whose hand we have this boar for victuals this good evening."

The company stood and raised their glasses. "To your Lordship, The Duke de La Fare!"

The Duke nodded his approval to the great satisfaction of the Count, whose glass was empty again, and in such a short time he wondered how it had happened.

"Prithee, recount the hunt and your pursuit of this savage animal," said Lord Dubois, maneuvering to ingratiate himself to the Duke. His elementary knowledge of firearms had put him at a disadvantage in conversations with the Duke, who talked of little other than a new styled breech-loading flintlock.

Lord Dubois's unrestrained enthusiasm was a tone the Duke took as warranted adoration, which he often encountered. Of the numerous listeners, only the actors heard it as lickspittle.

That Lord Dubois had seized attention for himself annoyed the Count, who had expected to lavish praise on the Duke for his hunting mastery. A moment on center stage was the least he expected after his huntsman had all but delivered the boar to the muzzle of the Duke's musket. A servant quietly refilled the Count's glass.

The Duke casually leaned back in his chair, only willing to speak when given ample adulation and rapt attention.

"Never saw so large an animal in these forests," said one guest.

"It takes a shrewd hunter to bag a wily boar," said another.

"Please, your Lordship, do not keep us in abeyance," said another.

He licked his fingers and gave his backbone a stretch. "We were in Bosquet Forest. It was late of the day." He turned from side to side so that all might hear. "The hounds were tired. I had already brought down a two-point buck with my musket…" During the Duke's prolonged description of his unrivaled mastery of the hunt, the Count drank three more glasses of wine. The boar's meat was growing cold, but he dared not interrupt the Duke.

At a point when the Duke paused to drink, the Count seized the opportunity and said, "Garcon! More wine for His Lordship!" He stood up. "For your pleasure, my Lord, you shall be first to savor the quarry." He nodded to his carver who slashed a slice from the roast's shoulder and, with flourishes, placed it before the Duke.

The slashing continued as meat disappeared from the wild boar's bones. First one and then another guest stood and raised their glass with a salute to somebody's health. When the skeletal boar was borne from the dining hall, in came jellies and dishes of chestnut pudding and macaroons.

"Most especially to my Lord and Lady de la Fare." The Count stiffly tipped his glass, spilling a jot. "Fare-thee-well on your travels the morrow. Pray, grace us with your presence anon." Applause down the table. He motioned to Béjart to begin entertainments.

Béjart turned to his players and whispered. "Now stands the hour. Good sirs and madames, make waste sobriety!" He pranced on stage and announced the opening scene of *Les Propheties de Mirabelle.*

Argon, Leon, and Georgette gamboled to their music to open the show, quickly on and off the stage. The courtiers, played by Béjart, Leon, and Hubert, each in turn pursued the vain widow's wealth. Béjart had expanded his role to the point that his man-servant, played by Etienne, had hardly a complete sentence to say.

"You are a nymph, white as alabaster, and with an … unsurpassed … nose," said Leon as he dodged Isabelle's fake nose to bow to her. Murmurs and chuckles from the table.

One after another, the courtiers fell in love with the lovely protégé Louise, who pitched her voice high to avoid sounding like herself.

As the widow, Isabelle twisted, dipped, bent and bobbed to get around her enormous nose, which was liberally complimented. She looked at herself in a mirror. She puckered her lips as if to kiss her image. A ripple of amusement from the audience. "My modesty is my great weakness," she piped as her gaze ranged into the Great Hall in search of Lord Dubois.

He had sent her no communication. His chamberlain was nowhere to be seen. Her tension had turned to nervous speculation. She wondered if his renewed wooing was a ruse or some sordid vengeance. The worry that he might have come with the intent to disappoint her was relieved with a potion of dwale she had sipped with wine.

At the interlude, Béjart and Leon strolled on stage playing their instruments and singing. Hubert and Georgette added harmonies as well as rhythm with tabor and bones. The Count and his guests stood and warmed at the fire. The elevated pitch of conversations bespoke a good reception for the *Mirabelle*.

Isabelle was beside herself. From her pocket she removed the letter she had written earlier in the day. *My lord, you have made all the advances in our affair. It is unmanly to play with love.* Her hand trembled. Her head was spinning. Should she have the letter delivered to him? Should she ignore his affront as if it were nothing?

One after another the bottles of wine Béjart had procured were opened and shared. Isabelle drank more than her share. Once drunk with wrath, she became drunk by her cup. Given wine's wisdom, she realized that accusing a lover of wrongdoing was a route to humiliation. If a paramour was inattentive, a woman of substance found one who was. Any clever woman would not be hurt by a lover's wayward behavior. She would be disgusted. Whatever Lord Dubois's ploy, Isabelle dared only a mute response.

Before she returned to the stage, Argon adjusted her fake nose, made of chewed paper that had been molded into shape and lacquered. "You are entrapped by much wine. Will you know your rhyme and meter?"

"My ducky, I will play my part."

"Is that what you do? Is that all that you do?" Argon took the bottle of wine that she was about to finish off.

"What else is there to do?"

"How can I know you if you only speak lines that fit a part?"

"You speak as if there is more to know."

"Can you be nothing but an actor? Is a cook nothing but a cook? A peddler nothing but a peddler?"

She looked at him with amusement. "You are an actor whether you are on stage or buying cheese from a cheesemonger."

She returned to the stage on cue and did not falter even when she bungled her lines. Agnes, playing her servant, was forced into a moment of dumbstruck silence as Isabelle went off-script to say, "Thy ass savors of rosemary and mint." A rumble of laughter.

Agnes smoldered at Isabelle's flamboyant insult, albeit couched in a scene on stage. As the play progressed, she could hardly follow the accustomed script for thinking of ways to repay Isabelle.

In a scene with Leon, Isabelle added, "'Tis a vice you commit entering a house of ill fame." To which Leon responded, "The vice lies not in going in but in not coming out."

Despite the jovial response of the audience, Béjart kicked the wall of the gallery as if it were Isabelle. He gripped a bottle and swilled wine.

In the end, the boisterous patrons frolicked on stage with the players. Argon started up a dancing tune on his lute and was joined by Leon with the pipe. Eugene played the shawm in the shadows. The Great Hall turned into a festival, much to the satisfaction of the Count. Those guests, nobles, and hosts who did not dance, drank and engaged in breathtakingly trivial conversations.

Those actors not providing music returned to the gallery behind the tapestry. Béjart jerked Isabelle aside, dislocating her fake nose. He said, "Damnation, you bring my play to heel! You doom me to a cursed life!"

"It was the wine. I overdrank to calm myself." Isabelle removed her fake nose. With a calmness that belied her spirit, she placed it in the casket containing her necessaries.

Despite her seemingly penitent manner Béjart said, "Are we to be content because your demons sacrifice the work we have labored over for weeks? months?" He clinched his fist as if to punch Isabelle's now naked nose.

"I have served you and the Augusto Troupe with my heart and soul," said Isabelle.

"We will be better served if you abide by the script. Your variants are maddening to the actors." He paced about her. "Not to mention the agony they bring to me!"

Argon pulled aside the tapestry and said, "The Count's chamberlain is here for you." Béjart jerked away the tapestry and entered the Great Hall.

"The Count is weary of such lively tunes. He requires melodic music," said the servant.

Béjart joined the musicians in the Great Hall and led them in dulcet songs, with more from the psaltery and lute. Eventually boisterous conversations softened to whispers, and the nobles swayed precariously in their chairs.

The actors made their way to their quarters. Louise had performed beyond their expectations, as if she were a person they did not know. Isabelle drank herself to sleep. As Argon lay in his cot, the face of one of the visiting nobles stirred a memory. He had seen the mustache before. On the face of a peasant attending one of their shows. Was it in Bourges? Auxerre?

❧ Scene 27 ❧
Eugene at risk

The following morning the sun shone with no promise of warmth. In the inner courtyard, the Duke and Duchess made farewell speeches as their coach and six awaited. The Count, his wife, and numerous servants clamorously bid them fare-thee-well and lord-keep-thee.

Agnes wandered among the grandees and servants mixing in the courtyard. Upon spying the well-fed boy known to be the Count's messenger, she said, "Sirrah, prithee, may I buy your favor to deliver a letter to your master?" She held a sou in her open palm.

Without a glance at her, he pocketed the sou and took the letter.

The horses whinnied. As the carriage containing the Duke rumbled out of the courtyard, the Augusto Troupe struck up a rousing strain, testing the range of their bells and cymbals. Dogs barked. Air so cold it gripped noses and squeezed throats contributed to loud and dramatic disharmony. Chickens clucked. Sheep huddled against their lot fence and bleated.

The following day, the Count avoided the inevitable letdown of the Duke's departure by traveling with Lord Dubois to visit a wealthy mercer who owned a nearby chateau. Beforehand, he warned Lord Dubois that the mercer's inflated politesse inevitably turned into sniveling flattery. "It will be your magnificent cloak, or elegant doublet. He has gone so far as to opinionate on my breeches. It is his backhanded strategy to peddle his goods. Even before you quaff a dram of wine, he will say, 'Prithee, let me offer you a view of the spectacular goods I have just procured,' and off you will trot to see his velvets and silks, with him declaiming, 'Have you ever seen such resplendent color? Made by weavers of Milan' … or Florence or whatever loom is the latest to serve the King."

The Count's carriage was brought around, and the two men settled comfortably into fine velvet seats fitted with cashmere quilts and foot warmers. "Geeyup!" cried the coachman. His silver-handled whip spun an elegant halo over the horses and away they headed for the gate at full tilt.

The actors took advantage of the absence of the Count, sleeping in until noon, except for Louise who arose earlier and hurried to her hideaway in the chapel. After devouring coarse bread lathered with hog's grease, the actors went to the Great Hall and dismantled the stage and stored it in the gallery. They practiced ballads, poetry, and acrobatics. Hubert stitched up a rip in the crotch of Samuel's costume, the first of several sewing projects. Leon rode to the hamlet and sold wood carvings of crosses and penises. Samuel accompanied him and hawked old coins, magic moon stones, and Georgette's ointment for hiccups.

Béjart bartered a carriage lantern he had found in the stables for paper and ink. He grumbled to himself about his need for more paper. He was no Shakespeare who, so people said, never crossed out a word once he scripted it. In a fit of anger he had ripped to shreds three entire pages — pages in which a whore of Babylon crept into the lines without his permission. In the alehouse he consoled himself with ale and a wench with exotic eyebrows.

Isabelle lay on her cot in her room. Tied under her chin was a cloth containing a maceration of cowslips. She had noticed that her chin's hint of a dimple had a hint of a wrinkle. Her fingers prodded stones in a jeweled coronet, a gift from a former admirer. She wondered about the value of the stones.

Argon knocked on the door. She didn't answer. He entered anyway, pushed aside the wig she had worn the previous night, and sat on the opposing cot. "*Mirabelle* has turned you into an idler?"

Her look gave him reason to get to the point.

He sat forward with one hand clasping the other. He twisted them together, thinking of a way to begin. "Béjart would make me a monkey trainer."

Isabelle sat and leaned against the wall. She would have covered her head to get away from everything, even Argon.

"It is because of my voice," he said.

Isabelle tossed the coronet and it skidded across the floor. "Well-away, we all have moments of disappointment." She considered his problem momentary while hers was for the rest of her life.

"You have potions … elixirs. Mayhap one for my improvement." He watched her face for he knew not what.

"'Tis but a passing thing." She sighed.

"If it pass more slowly, I will be your age before I return to the stage."

"My age … marry! Age is a hideous disease to women and a feather bed to men."

"Your casket is filled with potions and pomades. Is there not one for remedy?"

"I am in need of remedy. If I had an elixir I should take it myself." Her sculptured eyebrows knit together.

"The crone who made the elixir you gave to Lady Birague, surely she can cure me."

At the mention of Lady Birague, Isabelle's countenance darkened. "I was a fool to give her all of it."

"It was a powerful elixir?"

"That it was."

"It is what I need."

"She is a day's journey." Isabelle had no intention of going anywhere as long as Lord Dubois was near.

"Béjart and the troupe will entertain without us." Argon was well prepared for a day's journey.

Isabelle's possessions were packed into two trunks, awaiting word from Lord Dubois about where and how they were to depart together. "Mayhap he could do without one of us, but not both of us."

"We will not be missed." Argon could not decipher her peculiar gaze, but he wondered if sorcery engaged her spirit.

A loud thump interrupted Argon's thought. Boots shuffled on the gritty floor outside. "Do you hear that?" Argon arose, looked out the door and left. A waxwing had swooped in an open window and was beating its wings against the stone ceiling of the passageway.

Isabelle shut her door behind Argon. Whatever the commotion, her skin treatment was more important.

Argon followed Samuel hurrying into Eugene's room. The stove had overturned and Eugene lay on the stone floor, his arms and legs locked and quivering.

"Hey?" Samuel, coins from sales he'd made in the hamlet still in his leather bag, stopped and stared.

"What goes there?" Hubert entered followed by others.

Hot coals bristled on the stone floor. The spectacle of Eugene's spasms bewitched them. Hubert kicked the glowing chunks together in the middle of the room.

"God's pity!" said Samuel.

"Get halberds from the guardroom! Make haste lest the fire spread!" said Hubert.

Eugene's condition raised fears. Bizarre behavior was the devil's work. Even ignorant yeomen knew of the book *Malleus Maleficarum* and its stories of demonic possession. Under evil spells, a person might thrust out their tongue, spit excrement, or more to the point, shake and tremble.

Samuel rushed in with two halberds. He and Hubert forced the hot stove upright. With the blades, they gathered embers and dumped them back inside. Others stomped out random sparks on the pavers.

Goat-like noises gurgled from Eugene. His teeth grated. His eyes rolled.

Whatever the actors believed about devils, not one in the room would place a wager against their existence. Hubert had traveled with his grandfather to Loudun and witnessed witches wallowing ecstatically in uncontrollable frenzies. Most of the actors had heard of the Loudun nuns, taken to churches where they spoke strange languages, screamed blasphemies, and levitated. Spectators had flocked to see their obscenities and animality.

Georgette shoved past them to enter the room. "Begad! Argon and Samuel, pick him up and put him on the cot."

Argon had not seen Eugene have a seizure so severe. He overcame his fear and grabbed Eugene under the arms.

"Some mischance will befall us!" said Samuel.

Georgette hit him on the head with one of the halberds. "Aroint thee!" She chased him out of the room. "Hubert, pick up his feet!"

Etienne cried, "Help him. Somebody help him or he will die."

In the passageway, the bird thumped from wall to ceiling, unable to find its way out the window.

"Quiet!" said Hubert. "The servants will hear."

"Die? He is possessed of demons!" Agnes clamped her lips shut to keep evil spirits from getting into her mouth.

"By the Mass, keep your tongue!" said Argon.

"For God's sake, calm yourself," said Hubert.

"It is said he has falling sickness," said Georgette, who had heard this rumor but had never seen Eugene incapacitated.

"If a servant finds out, the whole of the village will come for him," said Argon.

Agnes clutched her stomach, her vitals bewitched. "We must fetch a priest!" She shoved into Leon, who had entered the quarters. He obstructed her way as she tried to make for the door. "What hot bile moves thee?" he said.

Georgette said to Agnes, "Forsooth! A priest will torture him in the name of God."

Agnes jerked away and stumbled into the passageway, terrified of being near Eugene and whatever possessed him. The waxwing gyrated wildly about the ceiling and swooped into her coif. She frantically slapped her crown with her hands. The bird fell to the floor.

Its small beak opened and closed. Agnes thought of her mother lying on a mattress of hay, her mouth working open and shut with the effort to speak. Tears rolled down Agnes's cheek and fell on the immobile bird. She touched the tawny feathers. Overcome with a sadness she could not explain, Agnes picked up the bird and put it into her pocket.

"He will over it forthwith," said Georgette. "Leave him quiet." She ushered the actors out of the closet. Whatever the illness, her ministrations began with a warm wet cloth applied to the affliction.

"I will stay with him," said Argon. It was with difficulty that he watched tremors stun Eugene's body. In his heart, he knew Eugene to be helpful and compassionate, but this, this was otherworldly. "Eugene…" Argon approached. "Eugene…Answer me."

Eugene's eyes rolled demonically.

"What is this that possesses you?" Argon's breath stifled his words, hardly loud enough he could hear himself.

In came Georgette with a pail of warm water. With the refreshed cloth she wiped his face, ears, neck. "Isabelle has henbane oil. Get some from her."

To Argon's surprise, Isabelle's door was fixed shut. He banged on it. "Isabelle, wherefore this barred door?"

Hubert came near. "What is this?"

"Her door is shut."

"Shut? Does she think she is a précieuse?" Hubert shook the door until the iron hinges rattled. "Open the door!"

"Aroint thee!" Isabelle said from her cot.

"We need henbane oil for Eugene. He is gravely stricken," said Argon.

"I am gravely stricken. I needs guard myself from being overwrought."

Georgette came to the passageway. "Gramercy, Eugene has calmed."

Eugene lay still on the cot, pale and listless, but sensible and focused. Georgette gave him wine from a cup.

"Ave, good friend. It is well you are back," said Hubert.

"You frightened us by falling away," said Argon.

"Helas, my malady." Eugene raised his head from the cot and looked into their faces for signs of fear … fear of himself. "Was I a spectacle?"

"Not to worry," said Georgette.

"Your condition was seen by the others," said Hubert.

Eugene closed his eyes and laid his head back. He swallowed painfully, for his tongue was cut and bruised. It was dangerous for him to remain in the Augusto Troupe. Returning to the nomadic life of a lone troubadour was a miserable thought.

❧ Scene 28 ❧
a falling star

On his return from the hamlet, Béjart sequestered his leafs of paper in a casket under his cot. As the actors headed for the kitchen for supper, he was detained by Argon, who greeted him with tidings of Eugene's malady.

From around his neck, Béjart shucked over his head a small bag that he wore as an amulet. "If it happens again when I am not here, make a fresh cut in this root." He handed the valerian root to Argon. "Put it to his nose. The smell helps."

"I have never seen him so transfixed," said Argon. "There are those in the Troupe afraid his affliction is the work of demons."

"Demons sooner inhabit one of them than Eugene." Béjart made light of the actors' fear for his son's benefit. He had not forgotten a scene he witnessed as a youngster. A crowd had quickly turned into a riot when an old woman had been accused of witchcraft because her red eye gazed toward her nose. She had been dragged into the village square and hanged. "People destroy what they cannot understand," Béjart's father had said.

"He was much afflicted," said Argon.

"In the main, Eugene feels it coming on and gets away from people."

"The reason his caravan gate has a latch?"

Béjart's glance said *yes.* He went into the room where Eugene rested on a cot. "Wellaway, Argon says you were overruled by the falling sickness."

"Aye, and taken as by demons. So reckon the others." Eugene was wan and listless.

"Actors themselves are suspected of baleful spirits. Rest your mind, for we will not desert you."

Eugene trusted Béjart to be as good as his word, but Béjart was not the worry. Actors were a superstitious group. Rather than face them in the kitchen for supper, he rested on the cot.

✳

Another day passed without a message from the Count. Béjart sought out the steward and said, "Will Lord Gondrin require amusements this evenfall?"

"Nay, he has not yet returned from his travel." The steward continued crossing the yard toward the bath house where a large tub of warm water awaited him. Seasoned with herbs, St. John's wort, and mallow. He was given priority, the first to take a bath. Further, his preference decided the order for those servants who took baths. And for those who didn't, he had the authority to require one, should a bodily stink become offensive. This was a privilege he guarded like a treasure.

"When do you expect his return?" Béjart walked beside him.

"When his wine cup is dry and the jests dwindle to naught." He strode ahead, proud of his clever repartee.

"Might the actors be allowed in the bath before the servants?" said Béjart. Previously the bath water had been grimy by the time they had a turn.

"Nay. 'Tis more seemly to clean the sweaty armpits of toiling servants before lazy actors."

In the kitchen, a scullion maid plonked a bowl of chewet of stockefish on each end of the table where the actors sat. In turn, they scooped portions into their bowls and began to eat. Béjart reported that no entertainments were required that night and secondly that the bath water would be cold. He waited for them to eat before pronouncing tidings the village troubador had made known.

Isabelle resented having to eat from a wood bowl. More than that, she begrudged Lord Dubois's indifference. While others supped on chunks of fish, she said to the scullion, "This malodorous hogwash is too displeasant!"

The servant took away her bowl of chewet, added wine and salt, and returned it to Isabelle.

Béjart cleared his throat. "I have grave tidings from a troubadour in the village." He gulped ale. "The actor Molière is mort."

Argon spat a fish bone on the floor and said, "Wherefore?"

"Horrible!" said Hubert.

"Mayhap the Marquess de Montespan revenged himself on Molière for ridiculing him," said Leon, the Troupe's sporadic source of information about the Court.

"Montespan? Who is that?" said Samuel.

"Montespan's wife was taken from him to be the King's courtesan," said Leon.

"Apparently it was not a violent death," said Béjart. "Moreover, Montespan is in the Bastille."

"Molière was not an old man," said Georgette, who suffered age and sought to mitigate it. As long as she wasn't as old as the dying, she saw fewer wrinkles in her face.

"Fifty-one years old," said Béjart.

"Only fifty-one," said Hubert, whose shoulders felt the burden of having lived longer than Molière ever would.

"He barely got off stage at Palais Royal. Was taken to his home. Coughed himself to death." Béjart did not mention the reported convulsion because of Eugene. "He was playing the part of an invalid in one of his plays."

Isabelle was crestfallen. The Paris she had hoped to gain had lost its most brilliant star. The Palais Royal without Molière was like Fontainebleau without the King. In a stroke, her dream had dulled.

A pall overcame the table. They exchanged murmurs.

"I wish I could have seen him act in one of his plays," said Georgette.

"They say his acting wasn't elegant," said Hubert.

"Not classical." said Leon.

"What does that mean?" said Argon.

"He did not thunder and spout," said Leon.

"How do you know?" said Samuel.

"I saw him play the part of Sganarelle in *Don Juan*," said Leon, whose own adventures were not far removed from those of Don Juan. Many eyes turned to him in disbelief.

"Without 'thunder and spout'?" said Isabelle.

"High-flown, yes. Bombastic, nay."

When called upon for particulars, Leon said, "He was of good height and manner. Had thick eyebrows. He used them to advantage in ways few actors can."

Béjart said, "One of the actors said he looked ill before the performance."

"God rest his soul." Georgette wiped her nose on her sleeve. "Would that the Pope should usher his soul into heaven."

"Blackguards wearing robes..." Béjart mumbled.

Samuel slurped from the edge of his bowl. "Wherefore blackguards?"

"No last rites is what the minstrel said." As Béjart chewed fish a bone lodged in his mouth. By the time he coaxed it out, the bone had dragged a sore in his cheek.

The actors listened for Béjart to explain. "The Church refused a Christian burial until the King spoke up for the family. Even then, only a burial at night at Saint Joseph's church with no mourners. A grave in the pauper's cemetery."

"Does that mean he is damned?" said Etienne.

"The cassocks be damned," said Leon.

"God have mercy on his soul," said Hubert, picking his teeth with a fine bone.

"The bishop treated him like a common palliard. But it is Moliéré who makes Saint Joseph's Churchyard holy," said Béjart.

"If the great Molière's soul goes to purgatory, what hope is there for us actors?" said Agnes.

"Your soul is hopeless, even if you get last rites," said Leon.

She gave him a poison-arrow look. "You are inflated with ignorant opinions."

"Is there one here who is not daft when it comes to God and death and the hereafter?" said Argon.

"The Church as much as we," said Isabelle.

"A priest once saved my life when nobody cared whether I lived or died," said Eugene.

At this they mumbled sourly.

"If the Church be godly, it will excommunicate the priest who refused last rites to Molière. And if God be godly, that same priest will go to purgatory," said Béjart.

With no amusements required, Argon and Eugene groomed and fed the horses. In the rear courtyard Samuel tossed two flaming swords, added another one, dropped it. Started again. Georgette took bread and cheese she had filched from the kitchen to Louise in the chapel. Leon saddled his horse and left for a merchant's manor house and a game of brelan. As Béjart crossed the back courtyard, Etienne approached and handed him a paper. "Prithee, read to me the writing hereon."

Béjart took a look at the paper. He so pursed his lips that his thin mustache advanced to his nose. "Where did you get this?"

"It was lying under the kitchen table."

"It is but a list of things, strainer, tongs, skimming spoon, cheese grater. Mayhap the cook's order for utensils." Béjart folded the note and placed it in his hat.

Etienne's interest escalated upon seeing it secluded into the hat. "It is my paper!" He read well enough to know Béjart had not rendered correctly the words.

"I will keep it safe for you." Béjart had every reason to retain the message he had not read to Etienne.

"Nay! I will have it back. I found it!" Etienne reckoned it was valuable, if for nothing more than as a leaf of paper.

"And what will you do with a note you cannot read?" said Béjart.

"It is not writ on the verso. Louise will buy it."

Why Louise would need paper was a question Béjart ignored. "What is it worth?"

Etienne knew not, but his eyes illuminated with prospects. "You shall have it good and cheap."

"I shall pay a dernier — more than it is worth."

"Dernier? A sou, if it please you." Little did Etienne realize that Béjart would have paid twice that.

"For so much I might have a score of papers." Béjart slapped a sou into Etienne's open palm.

Béjart went directly to Agnes. She sat at a table making her toilette, for she expected to be summoned by the Count, whose return to the chateau was expected anon. She had painstakingly combed her wig into furrows which she sprinkled with a scented powder made of clove, nutmeg, watercress, and galangal.

"What is the meaning of this?" Béjart shook the paper in her face.

Agnes stood, read the first lines, and with a shock of recognition suppressed a cry by swallowing powerfully. Her plan to earn his Lordship's favor was exposed in the writing. With all the control she could muster, she took a careful breath and brushed away his hand holding the paper. "What has this to do with me?" She sat at her glass and tied a garter around the coif covering her sprigs of hair.

"Is that not your name? Agnes?" Béjart pointed to the signature.

"You have been led amiss. I know nothing of this." She placed her wig over the coif and adjusted it.

"Then who signed your name?"

"I cannot say what I do not know."

"And what does this signify?" Béjart read the note aloud.

> *My Lord Gondrin, You are a man of great virtue and it grieves me that there are those of the Augusto Troupe capable of doing you an injustice. With your vow that my name remain secret, I will explain at your behest. Your humble and admiring servant, Agnes.*

If the look in his eyes had materialized, it would have hit her like an iron mace. "What treachery are you plotting?" His voice boomed so loudly servants in the rear courtyard paused their devoirs. Isabelle, in a nearby room nursing a headache, took notice as well.

"Where did you get this?" said Agnes. In a moment of inspiration, she added, "Do you think Lord Gondrin is so clumsy as to let fall into your hands such a notice?"

"Can you deny that this be intended for his eyes?"

Under his glowering gaze, Agnes said, "Why would I dispatch a note to him when he is not here? Your presumption is an injustice to me and a pain to my heart."

"I will show this to every actor. We will discover your intrigue."

Agnes, seeing this as the servant's betrayal, cursed him under her breath and said, "That is likely planted in your hands by Lord Gondrin's chamberlain. He has plagued me with his lovemaking. He warned me that his passion will not be denied."

Béjart, who little noticed romantic alliances of his actors, paused. That he had not noticed the servant pursuing Agnes did not mean it hadn't happened. However, other actors would have noticed. "We shall separate trickery from truth," Béjart said and left the room.

Agnes chewed her lip, sniffed, and paced. Her brain worked feverishly. Black smoke engulfed her and unless she could control the drift, it would consume her. She might deny the missive, insist on its being forged, and attempt to stay with the Augusto Troupe. Or she might go straightaway to the Countess, tell her that the Troupe was hiding Louise, and ask for protection. In the end, she reckoned she had no choice.

Béjart stopped at Isabelle's room and knocked on the door. Upon seeing the note, Isabelle wondered if Dubois had exposed to Agnes their plan to decamp to Paris. She said, "Mayhap Lord Dubois has inspired her with some intrigue." Or had Agnes otherwise discovered their secret? Her knees were faltering and she sat as naturally as possible on the cot, barely able to maintain her composure.

What Isabelle said struck Béjart as irregular. Why did she think Agnes had Dubois's confidence? This flew against what he knew of

Agnes. Isabelle's white cheeks darkened his mood, for there were secrets afloat that he did not know.

☙ Scene 29 ❧
Agnes knocks at the countess's door

How did Béjart get his hands on my message?" Agnes muttered to herself as she hastened across the rear courtyard, for she had no time to wait for the Count to return. "That logger-headed messenger!" Her breath quickened as she clambered through the keep. "He must have given it to Béjart instead of the Count." Agnes's head was spinning. She made a fist as if squeezing the poison from a toad. She crossed the inner court to the Lord's chamber and banged on the heavy door. She would have to apply to the Countess.

The steward stuck his head out, trailing a savory smell.

"Prithee, I must see the Countess. Her livelihood is in danger." Agnes did not have to act to appear anxious.

"Who are you?" In the gloom of sundown, he gazed at her with weak eyes.

"Lord Gondrin's favored actor, of the Augusto Troupe."

"What is the meaning of this?" He waxed lofty as if he himself were of noble blood.

"My good sir, it is of a delicate nature." Agnes put her handkerchief to her nose and glanced down in a pose of embarrassment.

"Go away and come back the morrow." He stepped back to close the door.

"It will be too late!" Agnes rushed forward, her voice trembling. "I will not have her blood on my conscience!"

The word *blood* gave the steward pause. "Bide here an instant." He slammed the door.

"Prithee! Make haste!" Agnes called into the crease where the door met the facing. She blew on her bare fingers, stamped her feet, and looked about the wintry courtyard where snow banked in the corners.

The door opened and the steward escorted Agnes through a sitting room so red and gold she temporarily lost her senses. She breathed in mesmerizing wisps of citrus and cloves. Light beamed from the chandelier and reflected off shiny surfaces of the marqueterie. She stumbled on the leg of a chair cushioned in gold-threaded velvet. The chimney piece, carved with acorns and ivy spiraling from a crown, impressed her with the Count's noble heritage. Being in such a room gave her a sense of spiritual elevation. If only God had given her a life such as this. She walked slowly and glanced about but did not see an item small enough to tuck into her pocket as a reminder of this moment.

The lady's chamber was no less luxurious. The Countess sat up in a bed big enough to accommodate three fidgety actors. "What do you know of danger to me?"

The tone of her voice brought Agnes to her senses. A chambermaid with the rosy cheeks of a favored child stood in attendance on the far side of the bed.

Agnes had practiced an emphatic opening, but the chambermaid distracted her. She took a chance and said, "My Lady, ave and good health. But for my welfare and yours, prithee dismiss your servant." She refused to look at the chambermaid, whose malice showed in her eyes.

The Countess turned her ear as if she had trouble hearing the request. Her hesitation was followed by a wave of the hand. The chambermaid, as envious as a dog, nodded at Agnes with obvious ill will and left the room.

"I have stumbled upon the knowledge of a witch at Chateau de Giffaumont." Agnes had come to the view that Louise actually was a witch, for that accorded with the gravity of Agnes's situation.

"Witch? How do I know you are not a witch?" Lady Gondrin pointed a careless finger and stared.

"Truly, I make no lies to myself! She is the wench my Lord banished from Chateau de Giffaumont."

The countess did not believe this outsider, but it came as a surprise that her husband had discharged a woman from the chateau. The mischief of that claim prompted her to listen further.

"Go you to the chapel posthaste. The witch is there for the nonce. Under the altar." Agnes paused to see how her ladyship was responding.

"And how did you discover her?"

"I was praying to Saint Cecilia on the chapel steps." Agnes was careful to say she had not entered the chapel, which was forbidden to the actors. "When of a sudden there came a disturbance in the air. A whirlwind blew open the door, and I was compelled inside — forgive my impudence, my Lady. The altar cloth billowed out and … I saw a figure … crouched under the altar!" She stuttered. Her eyes, glazed with fear, opened wide as goblets.

"What sort of figure?"

"By my troth, it was the witch. The woman the Count banished. By her sorcery she has returned."

Whether or not there was a witch, the Countess came to believe Agnes was afraid, which indeed she was, though not of a witch. Such visceral terror could not be ignored.

"You will accompany me to the chapel," said the Countess, miffed at having to leave her cup of warm chocolate.

Agnes fell to her knees and held her hands to her head. "No! Prithee! Have mercy! The witch will know it is I who divulged her hiding place!"

Agnes's performance dissuaded the Countess, now concerned about the situation. "Alors, go to the kitchen. I will attend to the affair and will send for you." As Agnes wiggled to her feet and backed out of the room, the Countess attired herself in a fur robe and sent for Chaplain Chastellain. The messenger returned without the chaplain, who begged leave to remain in his chamber on account of roaring bowels. The Countess sent for the steward. Twilight brought a blindness across the castle's keep and towers. The steward held a torch as she followed him through the court-yards to the chapel.

※

As soon as he left Agnes, Béjart motioned to the actors dallying in the rear courtyard to follow him into the arched doorway of the Great Hall. He withdrew the note from his pocket and read it aloud.

"Where did you get it?" said Eugene.

"I found it!" piped Etienne, taking credit. "It was on the kitchen floor!" His voice pitched to a level of excitement.

"What does it mean—injustice?" said Argon.

They looked at one another with questioning eyes. Perhaps it was the wine they stole, the cakes. Spitting on the tapestry? A violated servant? Missing jewelry? A complaint from a peddler? Eventually their reasonings led to Louise and the chapel.

Béjart expressed what they were coming to realize. "Agnes is going to tell the Count about Louise."

"We will be back in the caravans," said Samuel.

"Has the Count seen the letter?" said Georgette.

"He has not been here for two days," said Béjart.

"And if he were here, would he find a note in the kitchen?" said Argon.

"Why was it in the kitchen?" said Leon.

"That's not important. Agnes is going to betray us," said Béjart.

"Agnes is a bitch, but Louise caused this," said Samuel.

"Alak! You would have Louise swiving with a lecher?" said Georgette.

"The Duke was a mere stallion requiring entertainment," said Samuel, which Georgette denounced angrily, joined by Eugene.

"Damnation! Stop the harebrained arguments. We needs find Agnes!" said Béjart.

"Before the Count returns," said Argon.

"Before she can tell anybody about Louise," said Hubert.

"We have to lock her into a room and keep her there," said Béjart.

ᔐ Scene 30 ᔑ

is she dead?

Hubert, standing on the covered battlement, spotted the Countess with the steward in tow crossing the rear courtyard. He hurried to Béjart. "The Countess goes to the chapel!"

Béjart said, "We must warn Louise to get out."

They hustled the long gallery toward the chapel only to realize the Countess and the steward had already entered. Béjart hurried down the winding stairs.

Inside the chapel, the Countess said to the steward, "Kick the cloth."

The steward flinched. The cloth was embroidered with a sacred heart and draped the floor with crosses. Was it not a sin to kick it? "My Lady, is it not sacrilege to kick the altar cloth?"

"Kick the cloth. Or I will summon the marshal."

The steward, accustomed to absurd commands, kicked the cloth.

"Do you feel a spirit?" said the Countess.

He wondered if his mistress had undergone a religious experience, in which case she expected something other than *no*. "My lady, my boot does sense a warmth there under."

"Remove your boot and kick again. Indeed, kick two more times."

He was loth to take off his boot, for the stones had known weeks of freezing weather.

Béjart hastened across the courtyard, skipped up the chapel steps, and cracked open the door. "My Lady! Prithee! Our boy Etienne has fallen into the well! Make haste!"

The actors watched from a window in the covered battlement. Etienne said, "What ho! I am not in the well!"

"Shhh! Not so loud. Use your noggin! Béjart is trying to get the Countess out of the chapel," said Eugene.

The Countess turned to him and said. "Then remove him! And be quick about it!" She was mildly curious as to why the boy made no crying.

"Alas and alak, but how shall I remove him?" called Béjart.

"Get thee to the stable for a rope and bother me no more!" The Countess turned back to the steward. "And shut the door!"

Béjart had no choice. He closed the chapel door.

At the altar, the steward had hesitated on the chance that the Countess might forget about a bootless kick.

"Sirrah, off with your boot. Let us settle this mystery," she said to the steward, withering in the icy light of the torch.

He loosened the laces and removed his boot. His woolen sock drew a frigid wave from the stones into his soles. With a kick, his foot encountered a decidedly warm presence. He backed away from the altar, his eyes wide. Something was sequestered under the cloth. He could only think of escaping. His tongue gave vent to a pretense. "My lady, do you not hear horses approaching in the courtyard? Mayhap his lordship returns." He grabbed his boot and hopped toward the door, preferring the Countess's wrath to whatever his foot had encountered.

"What? I hear nothing. Here now!" she called as he disappeared out the door and into the courtyard.

The steward's foot nigh froze on the stones as he ran across the outer courtyard, unseen by Béjart, who was collecting pebbles near the gatehouse.

Inside the chapel, the Countess stood like a statue. The torch, secured in a wall sconce, cast curdling shadows. Her intuition sparked with warnings. The altar cloth swished on the stones. The smell of smoke charged the air. Her robe brushed the floor as she stepped back-and-to and paused and listened. Breathing, barely discernable, no more than that of a mouse.

A sudden clack sounded above her and echoed in the rafters. Another clack, as Béjart threw pebbles on the roof.

The stones crackled on the tiles as if cloven feet trod there. The Countess's tongue grew numb and expanded in her mouth.

She couldn't move even after she realized her breath was a flurry of noise.

Louise, crouching under the altar, lifted her face from her knees. The whisper of the Countess's robe on the stones unnerved her. A corner of the cloth twitched as if a hand might pull it up. She took a deep breath. With a fury, she grabbed the altar cloth and wrenched it from the table as she leapt from underneath, pulling the cloth over her head. "White-livered, dog-hearted, canker blossom!" She choked out the words as she jumped the steps descending from the sanctuary and ran down the aisle. "I will not give you my blood!" Once at the door she dropped the altar cloth, swallowed hard, and plunged down the front steps.

Béjart grabbed her arm and they ran to the actors' quarters.

The Countess lurched backward in utter terror, fell down the sanctuary steps, hit her head on the stone floor, and heard nothing at all.

In the kitchen, the scullery maids washed dishes and shuffled embers of the fire. A doe-eyed servant entered carrying a cage with pigeons. The cook begrudgingly warmed chocolate for the actor who, favored by Lady Gondrin, sat at one of the tables. She sloshed the mug in front of Agnes.

"And I will have bread as well," said Agnes, who expected the Countess to discover Louise's hiding place at any moment. "You will owe me respect when my Lady comes hither," she said, presuming the Countess's gratitude.

Agnes sipped chocolate, mindful of outside noises in case Louise screamed or cried out as she was dragged from the chapel. At every sound she turned to the door expecting the Countess's chambermaid to enter and request her presence. More sweet than the chocolate was the expectation of being in the lavish bedchamber, the Countess awarding her with compliments.

Agnes anticipated becoming a servant at Chateau de Giffaumont, perhaps a napier or an attendant to the table. But not in the kitchen. A smell of blood tainted the air as scullery maids chopped off the heads of the pigeons one by one. Agnes had had her fill of gouging out entrails and plucking feathers. The smell of blood made her gag.

A commotion arose outside in the inner courtyard.

"Now what is that noise?" said a scullery.

"Mayhap it be my lord returning," said another.

"Nay. The sound is someone in quiet shoes," said another.

Several of them went to the door and peered through the darkness to the fluttering light of a torch. "Some malt-worms barely afoot from too much ale," said one as they dispersed to their tasks.

Agnes stood and brushed crumbs to the floor. She assumed that Louise had been exposed by this time. Where was the Countess's chambermaid? What was taking so long?

The steward returned to the chapel with the marshal and Philippe, the gamekeeper. Upon seeing the altar cloth strewn on the steps, his fears increased. He picked it up and looked at the two men. "What does it mean?" He stalled and entered the chapel behind the others.

The light of their torches illuminated the shadowy vestry with lectern and stalls. Near the altar lay the Countess on the floor. "By the Rood, what has happened to her ladyship?" said Philippe.

"God's death! What?" The steward gasped at the apparent misfortune that had occurred in the short time he had been gone. He squinted to see the bare altar table, no visible fiend underneath. "It is the work of demons," he said, believing his foot had encountered one.

He sent the marshal to fetch salt of hartshorn and brandy from Lady Gondrin's chambermaid. As the man left, the closing of the chapel door echoed like the clacking of a prison cell. The light from the torch whipped against the stone walls. The steward's eyes rounded in their sockets at the sight of lively shadows playing against the murky gray walls.

They bent to the Countess reverently, Philippe leading the way. Blood trickled from her nose. Her eye wells were dark and fleshy.

Kneeling beside her, Philippe wiped her forehead with the fur of his glove to no effect. The steward drew near Philippe as much for protection as to attend to her ladyship. He knelt and called with increasing intensity, "My lady... my Lady! My..."

Philippe blew his breath on her eyelashes. The steward did likewise, but she did not feel their breath, nor their touch, nor did she hear their voices.

"This is as deep a swoon as ever I saw," said Philippe.

"They say God be near those in swoons," said the steward, aware of a spirituality in the room and afraid it was a mouthless hairy creature. He tried to pray but he couldn't think, couldn't remember the words, *Miserere mei, Deus.*

"Why did you leave my lady alone in here?" said Philippe.

An unknown darkness closed in behind the steward. Philippe's voice brought him back to the problem of the Countess. He was not nearly as distressed with Philippe's question as he was with the knowledge of facing that same question from the Count. "She ordered me to fetch help. I insisted that she accompany me, but she sent me away forthwith. What could I do?" He kept his eyes on the creeping dark of the chapel corners.

"Why did she send you for help?" said Philippe.

"I know not her intention." The steward, who grew increasingly anxious, said, "Would you dare question her?" More than his position was at stake should it become known that he had left without her permission.

The door creaked open. Footsteps echoed into the room as the marshal entered with smelling salts and brandy. He was followed by the chambermaid.

"Mon Dieu! What befalls my lady?" She took tentative steps near the motionless figure but kept her distance, ever cautious of fever and the plague.

The steward's hand trembled as he extended salts to Lady Gondrin's nose. "My Lady! For the love of God, awake!" His voice strained, his brow creased with tension. He attempted to administer brandy but spilled it.

"She isn't dead, is she?" said the chambermaid, suddenly uncertain of her future, for her position depended on the favor of the woman lying on the floor.

Philippe took over and poured brandy in her lips but it ran down her cheek. "'Tis of no use," he said.

The steward, whose concern verged on derangement, paced and shook his head. "God defend us! Not a word of this to any other person!" he piped to the chambermaid.

For a moment Philippe suspected the steward and the Countess of cudgeling, but that idea was too curious to entertain. He said, "That goes for the rest of us. The Count must decide who to tell and when. If this is dinned about, we face being flogged, hanged, or banished. Or all three."

"We must take her to her chamber," said the marshal.

"Clean the blood from the floor," the steward said to the chambermaid.

The three men picked her up and carried her to the door. "Outen the light," said the steward. "We carry her in the dark."

"I will fall down the steps," said the marshal.

"Better you fall down the steps than that we be seen carrying my lady to her chamber," said the steward.

In the kitchen, Agnes, with growing disquiet, watched the scullery maids. One took a bucket of offal to the dogs; another poured suet into a bronze pot; another sharpened knives; one removed the cleaned pigeon carcasses to the cold storage room. The cook prepared leavened dough and set it aside to rest for the night. They shuffled among themselves, chattering. Agnes sat before the fire and waited.

ꙮ Scene 31 ꙮ
something amiss at the altar

At the merchant's manor some fifteen leagues distant from Chateau de Giffaumont, the Count and Lord Dubois took spiced wine and dipping toast with the merchant while their trunks were being packed. The merchant regaled them with tales of shipping silk from Florence, silk that excelled that from Holland. A knock at the door and the steward stepped inside.

"Master, one of Lord Gondrin's horses has turned up with the colic."

The Count went to the stables and found his horse rolling and groaning. He might try to make it back to his chateau with three horses, but that could wreak havoc on the driver. Or he might rent a horse from the village ostler. Or he might borrow a horse from the merchant, which, if experience proved the case, would expect the horse to have improved on return. In the end, he bought one from his host.

The two men sat in the carriage's velvet-lined seats while their chamberlains climbed into the open-air bench at the rear. Once on the road, the carriage wheels squeaked on the icy ruts. The driver shouted, "Geeyup!" more than once at the errant new horse. "Worthless arse! Back in line!"

As they bumped along, the Count called to mind a visiting nobleman's son who had been robbed and left to freeze to death on the very road they traveled. They brought out a flagon of wine and drank to the son's bad luck.

The luxury of upholstered seats and leather interior did not soften the jolts as they rode a rough road. The Count and Lord Dubois sat under blankets and talked, each more effusive than the other in praising the hospitality of the wealthy mercer. After a time, the cab settled into silent pauses and comfortable yawns. Dark descended. The driver lit the carriage lanterns from the tinderbox.

Lord Dubois stuck his hands into the pouch of the muff he wore around his neck. He had bought from the mercer pieces of fine fabric — velvet, tulle, and moiré. And an especially elegant seawater green satin for Isabelle, since he had given the pearls to the Duchess de La Fare. His investment in green satin was meant to endow Isabelle with such splendor as to dazzle the haut monde at the Hôtel de Bourgogne.

Lately, he had grown tired of even his most accomplished coquettes. Isabelle brought forth the possibility of a delicious game. Her command of the Troupe's amateurish stage was overtop. As much as he enjoyed her saucy ripostes, he liked even better her conquest of her audience. She was the temptress to awaken the desires of his youth. The jezebel to ignite the fervor that once brought him pleasure. Little did he notice that the pursuit of other courtesans had begun with similar expectations.

Since the Duke had departed Chateau de Giffaumont, there was no reason for Lord Dubois to delay his absconding with Isabelle. With his boots comfortably resting on the foot-warmer, he said, "I cannot conceal my desire to remain longer at Chateau de Giffaumont, but affairs in Paris draw me yonder."

The Count was not surprised at Dubois's announcement. In absence of the Duke's eminence, there was less purpose for lavish dress, conversation, and jests. He himself was thinking of returning to his manor house in Paris.

The horses drew the carriage at a faster pace as they approached the Chateau. Upon entering the gate, lights glared from flambeaus of the inner courtyard. "Ho! Ho! Arretez!" called the driver as they came to a halt. He breathed into his gloves, which eased the cold sting upon his nose. The passengers disembarked to a warm welcome by the servants, who had been nodding in the kitchen.

Installed in the master's apartment, the Count and Lord Dubois warmed at a roaring fire and drank to each other's good fortune while their chamberlains withdrew to the kitchen where they prepared warm water scented with rose petals and fetched white linens.

The two chamberlains commiserated, juggling bits of information, testing each other. Each compared the nature of his servitude to that of the other. Lord Dubois's chamberlain had to tolerate insults regardless of how carefully he undressed his befuddled master, often much flown with wine. The previous chamberlain had been dismissed for accidentally pulling off Dubois's ring when drying his hands.

The Count's chamberlain had avoided being dismissed but barely when he spilled snuff on his lord's fur cloak. He had accustomed himself to onslaughts of "idiot!" or "luggerwort" or "stampcrab," especially if warm water splashed as he poured it over the master's hands.

In his apartment, the Count sat back in his chair, warm wine in his silver cup, and said to the servant, "Here, boy, bring cheese and bread. And send for a musician."

The Count's steward paced about the outer chamber, indisposed and worried about how his master was going to react once he discovered Lady Gondrin's condition. He dared not deliver such news in Lord Dubois's presence. A servant arrived with a message. When the steward saw it was for Lord Dubois, he nodded to allow a knock at the master's door.

The letter, written in haste by Lord Dubois's steward, informed him of a gathering of dissatisfied farmers who worked the lands he owned near Limoges. A ringleader was urging them to slaughter their oxen for food. Heavy taxes had taken their toll on the harvest and some families faced starvation.

Lord Dubois folded the paper into his pocket. His dissatisfaction came to rest on his steward, whose missive implied the farmers were Dubois's problem. The problem, however, was the steward's, who was neglecting his duty to properly supervise the farmers. Lord Dubois twisted the tip of his mustache, much vexed that the messenger had come at such an hour. He sipped wine, emptied his cup, and rolled it in his hand.

Gondrin sent his servant for another bottle. Lord Dubois hardly noticed his host's muddled conversation, carrying on about his dog Fabby, smoke, something about a wretched smell. Dubois was considering whether to travel with his doxy back to Paris or leave her and go to his fiefdom and set his steward aright.

In the antechamber, the Count's steward approached the servant who exited the master's chamber. They walked to the undercroft, the servant after more wine. "How much longer?" said the steward.

"Draw a steady breath."

"But we needs send for a doctor posthaste."

"Should I tell his Lordship?" said the servant.

"Nay. That is my task." The steward guarded to himself communicating vital information to their master. The guest complicated things. The longer Lady Gondrin lay abed without sensibility the greater the risk of discredit to the steward.

When the Count and his guest warmed to a sleepy comfort, they retired for the night, Lord Dubois to his guest chamber. As the servant exited with a bottle of unfinished wine, the steward grabbed it from the tray and gulped it down.

He knocked on the Count's door, made a servile salutation, and said, "My lord, Lady Gondrin is stricken with we know not what."

The Count, upon seeing his wife, sent for a doctor. Outside her chamber door, he inquired of the steward and the chambermaid, "What was she doing in the chapel?" He swayed. Leaned on the stone wall and anchored himself.

The steward, his breath expelling steam into the candlelight, said, "She said she would settle this twaddle once and for all."

"What twaddle?" His perpetually stern gaze had a decidedly bloodshot aspect.

"I know not what she meant," said the steward. He had to work to come up with words. "For some reason she troubled herself about the chapel and required that I accompany her there."

"What was so bothersome that it did not await morning light?" His twisted lips gave life to a dull mustache.

The steward swallowed dry. "I did not ask, my Lord. I obeyed her instructions."

The chambermaid, seizing the opportunity to put herself to advantage, spoke up. "Just at nightfall an actor in some alarm was allowed into my Lady's chamber."

The Count turned his cold eyes on the steward. The candle atop the torchière gleamed fitfully like icicles aglow.

The chambermaid suppressed a triumphant smirk at exposing the steward's mistake of allowing a commoner to enter the Countess's chamber.

The steward inhaled and said, "The actor said it was a matter of grave danger to my lady, which I repeated to Lady Gondrin. And she required that I usher in the actor."

The chambermaid said with no little annoyance, "So fraught was the actor that she refused to speak until my lady sent me away." She pulled her wool shawl close to her chest.

"Who is this actor and what was the purpose of her visit?" The Count stared at the steward.

"She gave her name as Agnes. My lord … on private matters, my Lady confers not with me but with her chambermaid." He nodded toward the chambermaid, hopeful of getting the Count's dour gaze off himself. Wintry weather, instilled in the stone walls, pervaded the antechamber, but the steward's face glistened with sweat.

When Lord Gondrin pursed his lips and turned to her, the chambermaid said, "My lady uttered no word about a concern. After the actor left, I fetched her robe and she left with the steward."

The Count turned back to the steward.

"I carried the torch. She was out of countenance, but for what reason I could not tell." He wiped his watery eyes with a cold glove. "I lit the sconce inside the chapel and she walked ahead to the altar." With some effort, he glanced into the intense eyes of his master. "Of a sudden, she reared aback, but I could see nothing out of the ordinary." He cleared his throat. "She said something was amiss and sent me for help."

"Something was amiss?" The Count, warmed by the wine he had drunk, didn't notice the steward and chambermaid shivering.

"Something about the altar. She told me to get the marshal posthaste." He had devised his story with care for fear he would be accused of failing in his duty. "When I returned with Philippe and the marshal, she lay on the tiles."

"She was alone?"

"Yes, my Lord."

"And you saw no one?"

"No, my Lord."

"No sound? No footsteps? A door closing?"

"There was nothing."

"Do you ..." he looked from the steward to the chambermaid. "Either of you ... have an explanation for the condition of your mistress?"

Shaking from cold and fear, the chambermaid said, "My Lord, Mistress Gondrin's welfare means more to me than life itself, but I will not disobey her. When she told me to remain in her chamber, I did not go to the chapel." Tears rolled down her cheeks. "Please forgive me for obeying her."

"God rot it! Do not speak of yourself in a superior manner." Lord Gondrin's spittle landed on her robe.

"My lord I am not the one who left her alone in the chapel!" She covered her mouth and awaited a blow.

The steward, taken aback by the chambermaid's bold accusation, said, "My Lord, I too obey her ladyship without question. How can I do otherwise?" He shriveled, awaiting Gondrin's temper.

"Where was this actor while you were neglecting your duty to your mistress?" said the Count.

"My lady sent her to the kitchen. The actor requested that she not be sent to the actor's quarters," said the steward.

"You will both go to the chapel and spend the night there. You may leave when you discover what drew the Countess there."

The chambermaid shrieked and began to cry. The steward's gorge rose and he hurried to find a chamber pot.

Lord Gondrin called his chamberlain. "Make certain that the flambeaux at the gate is burning. The doctor will be arriving."

☙ Scene 32 ❧
I am sent for Agnes

Lord Dubois lay in his four-poster bed with the velvet curtains drawn. The window glass was plowed with trails of ice. Sleep escaped him, but not because of the cold. His chamberlain kept the fire. The wine warmed him and made his sleepy. But the thought of what to do the following morning concerned him. The distance to his fiefdom in Limoges was twice as far as Paris. And there was no way of knowing the weather in Limoges, whether there was more or less snow, whether or not the roads were passable. If he traveled to Limoges instead of Paris, he needed to call his chamberlain and halt the plan to stow away Isabelle.

At Lord Gondrin's return the servants in the kitchen had darted into the inner courtyard with torches and chants of "Welcome home." It was late but their work wasn't done. Agnes sat in the midst of the hustle and bustle, watching quietly and wondering what had become of Lady Gondrin. The cook prepared a tray for the master and his guest using butter and aged cheeses from the larder. Bread warmed in the oven. Several scullions, claiming exhaustion after refilling the hogshead with water from the well, were allowed to go to their quarters for the night.

The firewood carrier brought in faggots and while mending the fire said, "Lady Gondrin is indisposed."

This gave Agnes confusion. "Wherefore?"

He glanced at her without answering.

A scullion said, "How do you know?"

"I was not allowed to tend her fire. Had to give firewood to Brother Chastellain." He added logs to the kitchen fire.

"Lo! Brother Chastellain?" said a servant.

"Doth she need a sacrament?" said another.

"I asked Brother Chastellain, but he only said, 'I give you good-night and Our Lady's blessings.'"

The cook paused, a roll of raw dough under her hands. "The steward will know."

"I could not find him."

Agnes, alarmed by the talk, lit a torch and made her way up the stairs and outside to the inner courtyard. She stuck her hand in her pocket and felt the waxwing. Though the bird had been dead for hours, its body was not cold. Having lost the strength of thought, Agnes was ill with dire premonitions. She worried that she was the victim of black sorcery. She breathed shallow, afraid a foul spirit surrounded her. In the dark courtyard, shadowy creatures appeared as if drawn from the cobblestones. They played lutes, juggled swords, danced around a fire. In their midst a flame whispered and consumed a blur in chains.

She was terrified. Did she dare attempt an audience with the Countess? Too much dark power blinded her, drained her of her senses. Despite the deepening of night she did not return to the warm kitchen. It was unsafe. But where to go?

She slipped along the inner curtain wall and climbed the steep steps to the bell tower where she crouched in one of the stonework corners. She surmised that Lady Gondrin had been so distressed upon discovering Louise she had taken to her chamber. Or perhaps she had taken Louise to her chamber for interrogation.

Agnes kept alive the torch, which offered poor warmth but at the risk of exposing her hiding place. When she peeked over the stone panel and saw the marshal march across the courtyard with his torch, she snuffed her light in the sand of the corner.

✳

Despite the late hour, the marshal was ordered by the Count to fetch Agnes. He went first to the actors' quarters. Hubert was abed, suffering from catarrh. Isabelle had secluded herself in her room. Others, including Louise, had crowded into the two rooms with stoves and were drinking wine and having salted fish and loaf bread, which Etienne had filched from the kitchen.

Argon was the first to notice the approaching light of the marshal's torch. He stumbled into the marshal before he could enter the gallery. The two of them fell backward down several steps of stairs, gaining time for Louise to sneak away and the others to hide the food.

The group made merry in the gallery like a noisy herd, creating a screen as Louise ran toward the garderobe in the outer wall.

They helped the marshal to his feet, and the actors cursed Argon, "Malt worm!" "Lick wimble!" "Rummy!" as if he were drunk.

The marshal proclaimed, "I am sent for Agnes."

The actors looked at one another. "Have not seen her," chorused several.

"Wherefore do you require Agnes?" said Béjart.

"Lady Gondrin is most anxious for a private visit with her." The marshal, who expected every actor to be two-faced, said, "My lady cannot yet sleep this night. And entreats Agnes to recite poetry."

"If you please, I will recite for her," said Georgette.

The marshal cleared his throat. "She particularized Agnes." Disturbed embers crackled and spat from the stove.

"Then you needs search elsewhere," said Béjart.

"I must be satisfied she is not here." He trekked from one small chamber to the next. Isabelle's door was closed fast. "Open the door in the name of Lord Gondrin!" His fists thumped the wood plank.

The door swung open and Isabelle stood, dressed in a satin over-skirt with puffed sleeves. "Make your search," she said and stepped back from the door as he marched in. "Mayhap something is hidden in my underdrawers." She unlaced her bodice, dropped her costume on the floor, and stood stark naked, her nipples pointy and shining.

Breathing puffs of fog into the night air, the marshal spat at her.

"Brassy bore. A pox upon thee!" He searched under her cot and slammed the door going out.

His search complete, he reported to the Count. "She was in the kitchen earlier, but the cook and scullery maids have not seen her since."

"Did you look in the Great Hall?"

"Yes my Lord."

"The actors' quarters?"

"The servants' quarters?"

"The storage rooms?"

"Did you look in the chapel?" said Lord Gondrin.

"Yes, my Lord. She is not there."

The Count stared at the marshal.

"She was not there," the marshal repeated.

Lord Gondrin gazed with a look sufficient to rowel horses.

"Is my Lord displeased?" said the marshal.

"There was no one in the chapel?"

The marshal breathed easier. "Yes, my Lord. The steward and my lady's chambermaid.

✳

Agnes trembled uncontrollably. She blinked her eyes. Deep night had set in. A winter silence had befallen the courtyards. She sat and waited, unable to think or make a decision. Neighing horses aroused her from a stupor.

"Open the gate!" rang out. Carriage wheels clacked on stone.

Her hips ached. She arose clumsily on benumbed legs and felt her way down the stone stairs, barely able to balance her feet on the narrow steps.

A carriage brought lantern lights into the inner courtyard and came to a stop. It was met by a servant and linkman. Agnes hovered at the keep's archway and gazed across the yard. She was unable to see the far side of the carriage where a doctor descended with his bag. Afraid of freezing to death, she trod into the yard, waving her arms.

"Ho! Who goes there?" called the coachman, a sensible man, but one who believed in spirits and had communicated with his dead wife. "The curse of a coward on my head! A shade from another world!"

With one arm raised, she hailed the men. "Prithee, good sirs, I have a message for the Count."

"By cock, woman! What are you doing out here at this hour?" said the doctor.

The servant, who recognized Agnes, swallowed a bolt of excitement. "My good woman! Lord Gondrin awaits you." He rushed to her and helped her inside behind the doctor. She sat and warmed at bristling embers in the Gondrin apartment.

In Lady Gondrin's chamber, the doctor greeted the Count and gazed upon Lady Gondrin. Her eye sockets were swollen and black, signs of blood at her nares. When he perceived no swellings in her armpits nor rashes about her arms or legs, he approached closer and opened the lid of her eye, looked into her ears and throat, and put his ear to her chest.

He asked the circumstances of Lady Gondrin's falling ill. Lord Gondrin recounted what he had been told. From all appearances, the malady was not plague, typhoid, leprosy, venereal disease, dysentery, or a stone. As so often happened, the doctor arrived at a diagnosis by a process of elimination. "The immediate infirmity is a head injury, perhaps brought on by a faint, or some other malady which caused her to collapse." He recommended bleeding. Upon the Count's approval, he removed a lancet and prepared to breathe a vein.

❧ Scene 33 ❧
dead bird

After the marshal left without Agnes, Isabelle withdrew to her closet and read the letter Lord Dubois had sent by messenger earlier. He endeared her as *ma petite minette*. "I have been governed by caution in contacting you." More importantly, the missive said:

> *I can no longer abide our separation, even at the risk of insult to the Count. Your sublime performances have excited my desire. I must have you to myself.*

On a separate leaf of paper that had arrived hours earlier, he instructed her to pack a trunk and await his chamberlain, who would meet her at the lower gallery of the actors' quarters that night.

Isabelle looked at the two trunks containing her basic necessaries. No woman of any repute maintained herself on what she could put into one trunk. However, she expected that Lord Dubois would supply whatever she needed — farthingales of silk, jeweled garments, satin cloaks in purple or scarlet with gold laces and buttons, cashmere scarves. How paltry her costumes compared to the ones she would soon own. She could leave this trunk behind.

However, she could not part with her chalk powder, cork plumpers, dried roses, oil of vitriol, borax, and mercury, which went into a separate trunk. Her pomatums contained spices and oils she had acquired from hags and sorcerers. On top of these vials she packed her favorite undergarments. Without these, she couldn't imagine facing Paris's social life.

The trunk, packed tight as pigeon feathers, wouldn't close. She removed a corset and stomacher. Removed a farthingale and bum roll and squeezed the top down, sat on it and forced the latch. That Agnes would likely get the wig, silks, and satins she left behind gave Isabelle a moment of dismay. On consideration, it might well be Louise. She felt a moment of pity for Louise, for her expectations of love from Béjart. Perhaps she would never discover that Béjart was incapable of loving another person more than himself.

After the actors went to bed, Isabelle waited at the window in her room in the dark and watched shadows disturb the courtyard. A snore came from Béjart's closet. She sneaked near and warmed by his stove. He slept fitfully, mumbling what sounded like her name. As she stared at him sleeping, a flicker of the love she had had for him brought tears to her eyes. He had loved her as best he could.

✳

When the Count entered his apartment, Agnes stood up. Following him was the steward, recalled from the chapel. Agnes recoiled, not only at the steward's presence but at his appearance, one eye a squint away from shut. He walked as if impaired in the knees. Without a peruke, his head shrank, his hair, what there was of it, was frazzled. Lady Gondrin was nowhere to be seen.

Instead of speaking to Agnes, the Count turned to the steward. "Is this the actor?"

"Yes, my Lord."

Agnes backed away, holding her hand on the waxwing in her pocket. "Where is Lady Gondrin?"

"What were you doing in the chapel?" The Count leaned back and stroked the fur of his robe.

"Chapel? Me? Louise was in the chapel."

"Is your name Louise?" The Count hardly knew one name from another, in part because their craftiness was aided by masks and maquillage.

The steward skirted behind the Count, for he had inklings that this actor's magic allowed her to become dual personages.

"Nay. You yourself banished Louise from the chateau. But she did not leave. Ask Lady Gondrin. She knows the whereabouts of Louise." Agnes looked from the Count to the steward.

"Did you persuade Lady Gondrin to go to the chapel this evening?"

Agnes realized she didn't know what was going on. "I risked the

Augusto Troupe's vengeance and went to Lady Gondrin in good faith to oblige you. Does she say I persuaded her to the chapel?"

"Do you pretend you know nothing of Lady Gondrin's condition?"

Agnes gasped. "Let me speak with her. She will set you aright."

"You spoke with her already." The steward, eager to diminish his own culpability, spoke in his most accusative voice.

"What did you tell her?" said the Count.

Agnes's fingers felt her life blood slipping away. Rather than looking at a reward, she faced something gigantic, inscrutable, and threatening. She bit her trembling lip. Fear created a maelstrom of incoherent words. The waxwing in her pocket moved. It pecked her hand. She choked a cry.

"Bring forward whatever is there!" The Count pointed to her pocket.

Agnes didn't move. The Count held out his hand and waited. Agnes stared.

The steward gasped. "She has a mandrake!" He would have bolted from the chamber had he not heard the Count's angry command. "Take whatever she has in her pocket."

The steward crossed himself and, despite his panic, approached Agnes.

"I thought it was dead." She removed the waxwing and placed it into the steward's cupped palm.

He jerked his hand back and yelped. The dead bird fell to the floor.

✳

A glimmer across the courtyard set Isabelle's heart to pounding. Lord Dubois's chamberlain crossed the open yard and placed his torch in a tall, narrow urn at the bottom step and mounted the darker and darker stairs.

Awaiting him at the top was Isabelle. Together they carried her trunk down the steps. From there, Isabelle held the torch while the chamberlain hauled the trunks to the carriage, parked in the inner courtyard. He returned to the stairway for her pannier and a leather bag containing more belongings.

With the trunk stored in the driver's stall, the chamberlain climbed into the passenger compartment and raised the cushioned seat to reveal an empty chamber underneath. In it was a bear skin. As Isabelle climbed inside the chamber, she felt the warmth of a foot warmer on the floor. Her wig veered to the side. She gathered and tucked layers of her overdress and surcoat inside. The chamberlain lowered the lid. She curled into the small space, feeling more like a prisoner than a runaway.

So solid was the darkness, her excitement turned to unease. In moments when she felt the enclosure crushing her, she breathed with difficulty. Her elbows scrubbed the walls as she withdrew a vial of wine from her purse. She drank it down to the last drop and rested her head on her arm.

Despite being constricted and cold, she fell asleep. In a dream, silence took form and stretched across a desert-like plane. It changed its shape to a lonely but lovely song. It became more distinct as her body slipped away from her. What remained was the song, which had more beauty than ever her body or soul.

The ostler shouted, "Come! Come!" Horses neighed. He hitched first one horse and then the others to the carriage. Porters transferred Lord Dubois's trunks and panniers from the guest apartment to the headboard of the carriage. Isabelle awoke with a sore neck and aching legs, but the discomforts were of no consequence, for she was at last on her way to Paris.

In the master apartment the Count and Lord Dubois sat at a table in the warmth of a fire and took ale and buttered pancakes.

"Lady Gondrin sends her apologies. She's feeling poorly this morning." The Count would have described her as feeling "poorly" however dire her condition. Though she had opened her eyes, she had showed no signs of recognizing him. Her gaze was fixed on the distance. Her few sounds were incomprehensible.

"Prithee, convey to her my wishes for good health." Lord Dubois, oblivious to what had befallen the Countess, drank heartily, amused with the secret of abducting his paramour. "When you return to Paris, you must see my latest discovery. She is an actor par excellence. Has that spark of fire that puts fever in the loins." In fact, his loins at that moment felt a rush of heat.

"A shadow falls on the theater without Molière's amusing nonsense. Such a loss…" The Count had proved his cultural sensibilities by attending comedies at the Palais Royal.

"Yes, we will have to settle for Racine's glorified lines."

"Lately he did *Britannicus,* but I care not for his turn to Roman history. He needs write of French royals." The Count took smug satisfaction in being au courant about the theater.

"Pray we do not have nobles such as Nero and Agrippina." When Dubois heard the play was about a possessive mother and an assassination plot, he had chosen to not see it.

When they finished their ale, Lord Dubois, done up in fur from head to foot, walked with his host to the courtyard and the carriage where the driver awaited, reins in hand. The Count motioned forward several kitchen maids with baskets containing stuffed veal, boiled partridge, quince pie, breads, cheeses, and other foods, as well as bottles of wine. The servants curtsied and gave the baskets to the chamberlain, who, after installing them inside the carriage, hoisted himself to the seat situated at the rear of the cab.

The Count made his farewell saying, "My dear wife insists that Lady Dubois accompany you on your next visit to our modest domicile."

As the carriage clamored across the cobblestones, Argon, Eugene, and Georgette played a lively tune. Inside the secret confine, Isabelle heard the music, which brought tears to her eyes. Her heart raced with thoughts of Argon, playing the lute without knowing it was their goodbye.

✳

The carriage bounced on the stone-paved road. Lord Dubois took pleasure in sitting atop Isabelle, knowing of her discomfort as they lunged back and forth. He coached his concubines to be submissive to himself, but imperious and coy to others. It was a matter of pride that les grands were envious of his paramours.

Isabelle grew more impatient the longer she thumped against the sides of the wood case. Sufficient time had passed that they were well away from the chateau and among rustics, should they meet passersby. With every minute, her resentment grew. The carriage bumped into a crater. She pounded on the lid and shouted, "Gramercy! Halt this instant!"

Lord Dubois thumped once on the underside of the driver's seat. The stallions slowed their pace, but the bumps continued.

"Prithee! Stop and rescue me!" Isabelle called from the casket under the seat.

Lord Dubois chuckled. He thumped thrice.

The driver called, "Yo! Sonipes! Ho!" and engaged the brakes. The carriage rolled to a stop.

Lord Dubois stepped outside into a winter field where peaks of black soil rose above melted snow. The chamberlain lifted the lid of the seat.

Isabelle was breathless with anger and humiliation but she swallowed her spit and smiled. "My Lord, I am wounded by my eagerness to see you. Prithee, pardon my discomposure." Her wig was askew, her rouge smeared, her white paint smudged, and the black around her eyes had drifted.

"Ma petite minette, you grow even more lovely." The ridicule in Lord Dubois's smile cut Isabelle to the core. "My pardons. We passed a troop of the king's soldiers." He reached over and tweaked her chin. "Am I too cautious? I will not chance your safety." His genial manner was like salt in a wound.

Isabelle grew more furious, but she endured his lies calmly. She reached into the carriage for her pannier of maquillage, but Lord

Dubois put his hand on hers. "Let us be on our way." He motioned her into the passenger compartment.

"Prithee, ere we resume, I die of shame until I repair my appearance." Isabelle firmly took the pannier handle into her hands.

"We've no time for vanity. We depart posthaste." He shoved her aside and climbed into his seat.

Isabelle stood outside trembling with fury. "I'll not be taken for a bedraggled termagant!"

Lord Dubois sighed. "Ma petite minette, as long as you're with me, no one will dare think you a termagant." He motioned her to the inside seat.

"My Lord, I'll not abide insulting you with my disagreeable appearance."

Lord Dubois reached for the carriage door. "Then must I abide the loneliness of continuing without you?"

Isabelle saw her predicament. She climbed into the carriage. Lord Dubois thumped the underside of the driver's seat and they were off.

❧ Scene 34 ❧
a sour apple's worth

In the morning light of a sunny day, gossip passed from the master's apartment to servants in the kitchen, in the stables, the mews, the laundry: Lady Gondrin had been lured to the chapel and stricken down by an actor; an actor who carried in her pocket a dead bird.

The laundress said the dead bird was a sign of sorcery. Some thought it was a curse. Some feared a witch. Or conjuration. The butler fell ill with shooting pains in his hip. The scullery maid refused to take food to Agnes, who had been sent to the guard room. The porter took no charcoal embers to her stove.

The Count retained the doctor at his wife's bedside by promising a sizeable gratuity. It was to Gondrin's advantage to keep the doctor out of sight and away from the villagers. Despite his efforts, the rumor of a witch traveled past the chateau walls with a servant who fetched herbals from the apothecary.

The Count called his chaplain from Lady Gondrin's apartment and conferred with him. Chaplain Chastellain saw in the situation an opportunity to call upon Father Rozmital, a priest he knew and admired, not least because he had exorcised demons from the soul of a peasant's wife. The wife had attacked the kindly father with spit, snot, and feces. Despite this, Father Rozmital had chanted the *Vade retro satana* for hours until her frenzies disappeared.

"I pray the actor is not possessed," said Chaplain Chastellain, "but in my judgment, you would be well advised to act as though she were…if for no other reason than to calm your household." He bowed ever so slightly, believing only a Bishop merited a full bow. With each mass he prayed for the Count's continued benevolence, by which he meant but did not admit, the abundance of the feast table.

The Count was reluctant to take the Chaplain's advice, which he saw as an admission that the girl was a witch. However, when several drunken villeins pounded at the gate shouting, "By God's wounds, send out the witch!" he dispatched a messenger to fetch Father Rozmital.

By noon, servants had taken notice that the doctor and chaplain remained in the Countess's chamber. Because they were aware that Lady Gondrin was indisposed, but uninformed of its nature, rumors spread that she had grown feathers; that she voided excrement through her mouth; that she violently thrust out her tongue.

The Count left his wife's bedside and gave Béjart an unenthusiastic order for entertainments at the supper meal.

Etienne rushed across the courtyard and up the winding stairway. He stopped in the corridor to catch his breath. "Agnes is locked up." The actors were sitting on the floor around the stove.

"Wherefore?" said Georgette, who didn't believe him. Neither did Hubert. Nor Argon.

"She is in the guard room. I heard her crying," said Etienne.

"Let her cry. She deserves it," said Samuel.

"I thought the Count would have set up a search for Louise," said Argon.

"Louise is hiding in the garderobe," said Georgette.

"Ha! So that is the cause of the stink that clings to her." Leon had been wearing a mask since he returned from a day's absence.

"If Agnes exposed Louise…" Eugene stammered, unable to complete his thought.

"The Count would be looking for Louise," said Georgette.

"Something is amiss. Agnes betrays Louise but Agnes is the one locked up," said Leon.

"But did she betray Louise?" said Georgette.

"We all saw the note she wrote to the Count," said Béjart.

"But we saw it before he had a chance to," said Eugene.

"Mayhap the letter was a trick, written by somebody else," said Georgette. "Like Agnes said."

"It is dinned about that Agnes is a witch," said Etienne.

"Wherefore is she called a witch?" said Argon.

The actors looked at Etienne. He mumbled, "One of the scullery maids said she cast a spell on Lady Gondrin."

"We needs find out the charge against Agnes," said Béjart.

"And where is Isabelle?" Georgette looked at Béjart.

Béjart wondered the same. He had not yet admitted to himself that one of her trunks was missing.

✳

After a fitful sleep, Agnes awoke to the smell of wet hay and the moldy walls of the guard house. She wondered how she had ended up in such a place. The damp air clung to her. It got inside her nose, inside her throat and chest. A pan of hot coals rested at the foot of the board planks that served as a cot.

The voices outside the room came and went with the changing of the guard. Agnes grew hungrier by the hours.

Georgette arrived at the guard house and spoke to the servant guarding the door. "I wish a good eve to you, sir, from her who sends greeting to you," Georgette handed him a note.

"'Tis a sour apple's worth you bring." He glanced at the note.

"Nay. An admirer seeks your favor to visit," said Georgette.

The guard hurled the note back. "I want no admirer nor note."

Of course he couldn't read. Georgette said, "Come with me into the light. I will read it." She strolled past the stairway to a window cove, looking back at the guard with a captivating smile.

He stared at her.

She tilted her head to say, "come hither."

He stared at her.

She turned toward the window and read, "Forgive my forwardness, but I can no longer hide my desire for you." Georgette paused and gazed back at the guard. The guard swallowed and looked at the floor. Georgette read, "Prithee do not laugh at my confession. I beg you to read me with good humor." She looked at the guard, who had relaxed his hold on his flintlock. He left his post and stood behind her as she read, "I have admired you from a distance but cannot contain my desire to see you. I love you infinitely and I will be inconsolable if you deny me the pleasure of a visit. Please consent and send me a letter."

While the guard was dictating a letter as Georgette wrote, Eugene sneaked into the guard room with bread and water and a lump of cheese for Agnes.

In the still of night, Agnes heard sounds as if a cat were speaking through a crack in the door. With her ear to the rough hewn wood she heard but didn't understand what was being said. She put her lips to the crack. "What has happened to the Countess?" The utterance turned to a snarl and stopped. "Come back, prithee …"

The silence was steeped with spirits generating blasts of cold breath. When Eugene next sneaked into her room she said, "Bring my wool-stuffed quilt."

She only kept it for a night until the guard took it and said, "Lo! this will sprighten the eyes of my doxy."

Agnes found three feathers in her pocket. They smelled of carrion. She had felt an evil presence from the moment the bird had flown into her coif. It was a familiar, sent to curse her. But who sent it? Who was the sorcerer?

She asked herself how Louise remained free while she was imprisoned. The light from the one high window cast shadowy messages on the wall. Her throat was dry. She was hungry. The shadowy messages got into Agnes's eyes and made them quiver. The messages snickered. They said that Louise was favored. That Louise had cast a spell on Lady Gondrin. That Louise had known of her plan.

Agnes sat on her cot, hunched over, her arms wrapped around her knees. She rocked herself, becoming ever more alone and nervous, loathing Louise all the more.

The guard opened the door and dropped a morsel of bread in the fetid rushes on the floor. She pleaded for an audience with the Count. He looked with one eye and said, "How be it a sorcerer cannot deliver herself?" The afternoon guard said, "Make a familiar of a rat and send the message yourself." The evening one said, "Forswear your magic, disrobe, and I will give you audience." He grinned, aging yellow skin on his teeth.

☙ Scene 35 ℮

Father Rozmital

The longer Lady Gondrin remained sequestered in her chamber, the more fraught the gossip despite the Count's efforts to contain it. He sent the chambermaid to a nunnery near Paris with the explanation that she was of unsound mind and affected by wild excitement. The new chambermaid, a maiden with a superior upper lip she cultivated for effect, whispered to the sewer that a black vapour arose in the air above the Countess. To the cook that Lady Gondrin had been cast into a deep sleep by a spell.

Too late the Count realized that Father Rozmital's passage through the hamlet vitalized gossip about a Giffaumont witch.

In the kitchen, when the actors gathered for their meals, the cook noticed the absence of the actor she enjoyed watching, the woman who gave as good as she got from the men and had the wit to insult without injury. Knowing her place, the cook refrained from questioning members of the Troupe. Instead she placed an extra bowl at meals until one of the actors said, "Wherefore this empty bowl?"

"For the lady with the big bosom." The cook looked about the faces for a sign, some hint as to what had happened to her. To her disappointment every one gazed into their bowl as if they hadn't heard.

"She is visiting her sister in Amiens," Béjart said in the hope that she had gone there, for she had spoken of a sister in Amiens.

The actors, who bent over their potage of peas and slurped loudly, knew not whether Béjart was telling a fabrication or an explanation. Argon, preoccupied with his spoon, turned a glance of disbelief on Béjart.

After the meal, Argon rushed to catch up with Béjart. "You have tidings of Isabelle and have not told me?"

"Nay." Béjart's footsteps pounded the stoneyard as if they might loosen the grip that disquiet had on his vitals. "There is nothing."

Argon needed to hear more. "Where is she?"

"She is with her trunk and I know not where." The words marched out with precision.

"Her trunks are in her chamber," said Argon.

"Not all of them."

Argon rubbed the scant whiskers he expected to become a mustache. "I have searched everywhere for her, the stairs, the closets."

"Yes, I know," said Béjart.

"Mayhap she walked out of the chateau, fell, had an accident."

"Mayhap, but I doubt it. She cannot walk far carrying her trunks."

"You have good reason. She might have been stolen away. A highwayman. Another acting company."

"Stolen? Not likely. After all, she packed her trunks."

Neither of them had the heart to suggest that Isabelle had elected to leave them. Argon squeezed his eyes against the prickles gathering there and sucked up his breath. His footsteps came to a halt as Béjart continued to the stables where he found a way to avoid thinking by currying the horses.

Argon paced out of the chateau and to the woods and the place he had rescued Louise. He sat on the trunk of the fallen tree where she had prayed. If Isabelle had but left him a letter, a note, something to keep away the fear that she had met with violence or trickery. As it was, there was only conjecture. A big void. Nothing. Just what was left of her belongings, as if she had been a phantom all along.

A coach rumbled into the inner courtyard, its doors painted with a brilliant coat of arms featuring a cross. Father Rozmital, a man of arrogant carriage, descended from the coach. Lord Gondrin bowed stiffly and kissed his ring. In the kitchen and about the servants' quarters, the priest's arrival confirmed their suspicions of sorcery.

Chaplain Chastellain welcomed Father Rozmital hesitantly. He overcame the impulse to embrace his friend and instead offered a greeting padded with religious conviction and gratitude. Whatever the problem in their chateau, God's messenger had arrived and the solution was at hand.

The chaplain's effusive praise of the priest's miraculous deeds only increased the Count's doubts. He was not certain he wanted a remedy from a man well versed in the *Malleus Maleficarum*, a book that had sent many a witch to the fire. He tugged at his mustache and sighed. At the moment, there was nothing for him to do but welcome the priest into the chateau.

The chaplain attended Father Rozmital to a guest apartment

as servants hauled in his trunks. Eager to resume their friendship, Chastellain praised the Father and brought to mind their previous endeavor. "The gentilhomme yet remembers with gratitude that you delivered his wife of the demon Asmodeus." The chaplain's heart quickened at the memory of the woman's obscenities, porcine grunts, and grinding teeth.

The priest detached the clasp at his neck that held his cloak together and placed it on the table where the sparkle of its diamonds gave spirit to the polished veneer.

"Poor man, Monsieur Beloquin," said Chaplain Chastellain. "The indecencies he endured before you performed the exorcism."

"Ah, the wife. Receptacle of sinful vigor. In the end, her vigor turned to vinegar," Father Rozmital said as if the woman had become a shrew, and as if a shrew found little favor with God, as if he thought his work had hardly been worth the effort.

The mystery of the insinuation escaped the chaplain. "Praise God, you are able to undo the work of the devil."

Father Rozmital removed a large ring with a precious stone. He held his hands over a bowl as a servant poured warm water, still steaming from the kitchen, over them. The water that fell into the empty bowl turned grimy with dust. "We are artisans for the gain of the Church. I take no credit."

"Yes. I regret that my sins are great. But alas, no one understands this heart." The chaplain pounded his chest. He wanted to confess that his passionate love of the priest had had moments of physical longing, but Father Rozmital murmured, "We all pay the debt of nature." Still wearing his velvet tunic with silk lining, he lay on the four poster bed and fell into a deep sleep.

Leon and Samuel were at the village tavern playing brelan. Leon's mask was gone. The skin of his face, coated with pomatum, showed little sign of healing scratches. A less than willing trollop had had fingernails like cat claws. Leon had need for women but no love.

The treachery of his brother's wife, a woman he had thought he loved, wounded him in a way that would not heal.

The two actors exchanged secret signals, finagling for three of a kind, as they sat at a table with a carter and a hay merchant. Into the room came the miller, carrying a sack of flour. He crossed to the kitchen and returned without the sack.

The tapster said to the miller, "'Tis bruited about that witchcraft lamed your horse."

"Came lame, I swear, after standing in Chateau de Giffaumont's courtyard."

Another customer leaned closer and listened.

The miller looked about and said, "I took flour to Lord Gondrin's kitchen, came out, and behold, my horse, fine enough for the Lord's stable, could bear no weight on his front leg."

Another listener joined them and said, "I seen a bird drop from the sky. Right there at the chateau. The cook said it fell on the witch's quarter."

"My wife says Lady Gondrin needs a magical healer to lift a spell."

"There's an actor at the chateau with an evil eye," said another.

"The magistrate says one of the actors is a demon."

Leon looked at Samuel. Samuel looked at Leon. They finished the game and headed back to the chateau.

✳

"They will hang her," Leon said to Béjart.

"If not one of us," said Samuel.

"By my cup, let them hang her." Béjart, sustained by a steady flow of wine, didn't care. He could no longer avoid the fact that Isabelle was gone. He drained his mug, the third since his meal. It had become known to the other actors that Isabelle had departed. Whispers came and went: Béjart had driven Isabelle away, she had been lured to another acting company; she decamped with a lover; she sought an abortifacient; she had the pox.

The name "Isabelle" struck Béjart deaf and mute. In the presence of others, he neither heard nor said her name. He demanded solitude and muddled over "King Claudius' Knight."

"You can't pretend she never existed!" Argon had said.

"Mayhap you can't." said Béjart.

"Then I would not exist. Is that what you want? You want me to go away?"

"You are man enough to do what you want." Béjart had enough troubles without his son's problems.

"What I want is to act with the Troupe like any other member."

"Do not chivvy that. It is settled."

"If not acting, then what trade am I to work at?" In his worst moments, Argon had figured he might get a position with a printer as a compositer. He had seen how they picked up, arranged, and distributed letters. However, there was no person to recommend him to a printer.

Béjart said nothing.

"I will not train a monkey." Argon thought of a bear. Perhaps he would train a bear. "At least you still have Louise." If Argon had Louise, he would not be so bereft.

"Yes. That you know and must remember." In the past, if Béjart suspected another player of flirting with his paramour, that actor's role dwindled regardless of talent, and if his suspicions endured beyond his infatuation, the rival's roles disappeared altogether. "But Louise is no Isabelle and never will be."

Argon did not say, "You do not value Louise as you should." He walked away, jealous of Béjart and angry that his father had a strong voice. Angry that he had Louise, the finest female the Troupe had employed. And what did Argon have?

"We have to get Agnes out of the guard room," said Eugene.

"Wherefore? She betrayed us," said Hubert.

"If that be so, the Count would have rewarded her," said Georgette.

"The Count didn't see the note belike. He was away when Etienne found it," said Argon.

"What was the 'injustice' she was going to reveal?" said Leon.

"Our hiding Louise, by all odds," said Béjart.

"And the Countess went to the chapel. Wherefore? Did not Agnes tell her of Louise?" said Hubert.

"Agnes was not with her," said Béjart "Only the steward."

"Louise, was Agnes in the chapel?" said Leon.

"I did not see anyone. I heard two persons talking." Louise, in her state of hiding and running, had had no occasion to look on any person.

"Did you hear Agnes's voice?" said Argon.

"Nay," said Louise. "But the Countess thought somebody was under the altar."

"She thought it was you?" said Eugene.

"She did not say my name," said Louise.

"Do we dare beseech an audience with the Count?" said Eugene.

"To what end? To ask him if Agnes has confessed that we have sheltered Louise against his command?" said Leon.

"We dare not question the Count. There is much disorder in his house," said Béjart.

"The dairymaid says the Countess has lost use of her limbs," said Etienne.

"The water carrier says her fingernails grow like claws." said Samuel.

"Has the water carrier or the dairymaid seen the Countess?" said Leon. He spat as if the gossip gave him a bad taste.

"Idle talk," said Béjart, but he listened with interest.

When the actors got wind of whisperings about the doctor's arrival, they came to the conclusion that some mishap had befallen the Countess. The secrecy surrounding her chamber led Hubert to say, "The plague?"

The actors looked at one another. Béjart said, "The most likely explanation is that she has been so frightened by Louise as to take ill."

But why had Agnes been accused of being a witch?

None of the members of the Troupe would have been surprised if Agnes had betrayed them to curry favor with the Count. However, an actor accused of witchcraft cast a shadow over everybody in the Troupe.

Samuel said, "If we rescue Agnes and hide her, they'll hang all of us."

"Indeed," said Hubert.

Georgette nodded. "This is not Paris. We do not have the King's favor."

"Nor a nobleman to protect us," said Hubert.

"Chaplain Chastellain will not defend the Augusto Troupe," said Leon.

"We can appeal to the Count. He has enjoyed our entertainments," Eugene said.

"But if his wife suffers fearfully of a witch…" said Samuel.

"You are a fool if you think he will concern himself with actors." Béjart sank on the nearby cot.

"And if the villagers storm the chateau?" said Leon.

"Let them storm it. I hope they break through the gate house and burn down the place." Béjart said.

"Before they do that, the Count will give up Agnes and throw us in for good measure," said Leon.

Agnes was an actor, and a group loyalty prevailed. Béjart, who came to his senses, said, "Whatever predicament she has got herself into, we have to get her out of it."

ꙩ Scene 36 ꙩ
Agnes's soul

When escorted to Lady Gondrin's bed chamber, Father Rozmital, who was not a bishop because of a powerful duke's machinations, bowed to the Count with the chagrin he held for all lords and peers who, by virtue of their wealth, assigned ignorant nobles as bishops of the Church.

The Chaplain had prepared the requested materials. Father Rozmital took from embers of the fire an iron ladle containing molten lead and held it over Lady Gondrin's head for the length of three breaths. He poured the lead into a bowl of water at the bedside.

"Mmmm." Watery figures appeared as shapes such as spikes and hairs. "I see by the signs that this malady is not natural." He blew waves on the water. "It is suspect."

Upon seeing what the priest interpreted as signs, the Count turned and paced to the fireside, staring at the meager flames. He had no more confidence in the priest than in witchcraft, but the opinion of the villagers and his servants weighed heavily on the situation. Since they submitted to the will of the Church without question, the Count had no advantage in raising doubts.

Father Rozmital rubbed his thumb over the pectoral cross containing the relic he had traveled to Sebourg to get — threads from Saint Drogo's robe. Like Saint Drogo, Father Rozmital's mother had died birthing him, but unlike the Saint, Father Rozmital did not blame himself, nor did he concern himself about guilt. He had been told by his father that his mother's foul smell had ruined his business. It had driven travelers away from their inn. His father had been relieved that she had died.

Saint Drogo appeared to Father Rozmital in dreams — as a shepherd shrouded in mists. Each visit brought the Saint closer but the closer he came, the thicker the mists, which concealed his deformed face. Father Rozmital lived in perpetual doubt about whether he was being shielded from the saint's smile or scowl. He told himself at morning prayers that the Saint's presence was a sign of approval, that it protected him from demoniacs.

✳

The Chaplain remained outside Agnes's door as Father Rozmital entered the closet and placed a chalice of water on the floor by the door.

Agnes sat up on the cot when she heard voices. They belonged to neither the guards nor Eugene. Distant and recurring shouts of "Au diable! Evil one!" had unnerved her. She half expected to be dragged outside and put to a fire or hanged.

The priest remained near the door with his staff in hand and gazed at the grimy creature with burning eyes. He fingered the cross about his neck and approached. "Have no fear. I come as legate of the Count to see to your welfare."

Had Agnes not been lonely for human companionship and needful of help she would have said, *Go away!* Instead, she said, "Where is the Count? I have information. He will reward me when he hears what I have to say."

"Whatever you tell me will be whispered forthwith into the Count's ear."

"I am but a feeble maiden, more feeble now that I share morsels of bread with rats and vermin. Is the Count so fearful of such as I that he refuses to see me?"

"By what right does a commoner such as yourself expect an audience with the Count?" His clean shaved face was a conscious effort to impart a nonjudgmental temper, but Agnes was repulsed by his thin woebegone lips.

"I wish to serve him. He is sorely used by those he has trusted. I only wish to discharge my duty as a loyal servant." She glanced at his pupils, which took black to a depth she had never seen before. She forced a coquettish smile to her narrow lips.

The priest sighed. "There are many who wish to serve him. He chooses."

"Then I wish to know why he keeps me imprisoned." Agnes choked on anger but outed the words.

"Will you take holy water?" Father Rozmital motioned to the chalice he had placed on the floor. A smile wrinkled into his flat cheeks.

Agnes had had nothing to drink for hours. When she reached for the chalice, Father Rozmital intervened, picked it up, and sprinkled water on her forehead. "In the name of the Father, Son, and Holy Ghost."

"By the teeth of God!" She fell backward in utter surprise.

"*Vade retro satana…*" He stepped forward shaking more Holy water.

"Prithee, Begone!" Agnes wiggled backwards, screeching.

The priest interpreted this as her escape from the Church's blessing, behavior consistent with a demoniac. He called to the Chaplain to unlock the door. "See that the woman has a noggin of water," he said and descended the narrow stone stairway.

In the afternoon, after a servant placed a chair in Agnes's room, the priest entered with a mug of ale and a chunk of bread and sat. In stubborn denial to his status, she did not rise from the cot.

She looked askance at him, vaguely aware that if she were pummeled by bits of bread she might catch some in her mouth. Her feverish eyes burned holes in her head. She considered over-throwing his chair and grabbing the bread.

"Your thoughts are evil-boden," he said as if he had intercepted her musing.

She blinked. "I am but a poor sufferer." She stared at him.

His dreadfully sad eyes fixed on her. He was displeased that she gazed at him as if he were the cause of her suffering. "There was a promise that you made." He broke off bread, put it on his tongue, chewed it.

Her mouth filled with saliva. She swallowed futilely. His hollow eyes splintered her ability to think. Without a robe, he might have been taken for an imbecile. "This is the message from the Count?"

She leaned back on the cot, wondering for the first time if Louise had actually been in the chapel. Wondering what artifice was at work. The countess's chambermaid came to mind.

Father Rozmital tucked in his slight chin. "Your eyes betray the torture of the nights. You are ill-treated by your dreams?"

"If it were only dreams …" Agnes reached out her palm for a bit of bread.

The priest gave her what would fit into a bird's beak.

"My message to the Countess was true. I broke no promise." She swallowed dry and gazed longingly at the mug.

When the priest sipped at the mug, ale trickled from the corner of his mouth. He was disappointed that her behavior had so far given limited evidence that she was a witch.

"Prithee, a drink." Agnes brushed hay from her hair, grown long enough to curl.

"This ale will be a blessing for you once you have confessed your sins."

Agnes, who did not dare admit her mother had been a Huguenot, made a clumsy sign of the cross and mumbled incoherently with sounds similar to "sorry, sin, forgive."

Father Rozmital understood hardly a word. "My child, have you no regret for having struck down Lady Gondrin?"

Struck down? What was this? The priest accused her of harm to Lady Gondrin? Or was the priest sent to deceive her? Agnes, who had committed harm, to her mother in particular, saw no advantage in admitting it. She scratched her scalp. Her fingernails snagged a mite. "Has Lady Gondrin accused me?"

"There is no person without sin. Yours is all the greater for your weakness. Weakness is used by the devil. The first step to ridding yourself of a demon is to confess and ask God's mercy."

Father Rozmital persisted with questions. Hunger and thirst impeded Agnes's thought. She confessed that for want of food, her stomach was possessed of a demon growl. Her throat was parched by a scratchy demon. She shivered with a bone-chilling demon because some jaded fop in the chateau refused her a sheepskin.

"Look elsewhere for a demon. Look to Louise! She has cursed me. She goes freely while I suffer this filthy cell crawling with cockroaches. Yes! She is the demon!" She lunged at the priest, screaming.

Father Rozmital held out his pectoral cross which cracked into Agnes's forehead. She whirled backwards. The priest said, "I will return. Think on the evil you have done."

When the priest didn't come, Agnes had only the rats to talk to. A small one hardly escaped her grasp and darted into the wall. "Come, come," she talked to it at the crack in the stones. "There are no wounds in my words, not for you." She wiped her nose on her sleeve. "The devils are outside. Listen." From a distance came shouts, "Rope, short drop, no grave." She had not a friend in the world. Even the rat avoided her. Her soul was old and wrinkled.

Grainy footsteps sounded outside the door. The latch clicked, and in came Father Rozmital. His scarlet cape of velvet made her so angry her head felt nauseated.

He sat on the chair he brought and began to pray. Had Agnes known Latin, she would have cursed him. However his soft and sweet way of speaking blessed her ears. His voice swelled and dropped with lofty and magnificent words.

He droned downward to a whisper. "*Sicut erat in principio, et nunc, et semper, et in saecula saeculorum.*"

Agnes couldn't make spit. Could hardly breathe.

The priest had not expected her calmness.

"Did the Countess find the witch in the chapel?" Agnes said.

"You know the answer to that question."

"Yes, yes." Agnes agreed. It had been Louise. "The witch cursed me."

"Confession will subdue the devil's will," he said. "The devil is present even when we sleep."

Agnes supposed he knew of her terrifying dreams. That he was showing her the way to rid herself of them. "I have peccant humors. Comes from my mother. It wasn't my fault." Grief swelled like a tumor in her chest.

"To receive God's mercy, we must admit our faults."

"But it wasn't my fault." Agnes gulped. "I didn't do anything." Louder came her breath. "She shouldn't have been so close to the fire … it wasn't my fault." She choked out the words. Her mother's flaming dress had disappeared from her memory. But now the flames came back and consumed her. She remembered her mother's screams, her flailing arms, the smell of burning flesh, the horrifying moans, the horrifying silence. Agnes was shaking uncontrollably.

The priest broke off bread and offered it to her, but she fell to the floor in a swoon. Her eyes rolled.

The priest stood over her chanting, "*Vade retro Satana! Nunquam suade mihi vana! Sunt mala quae libas. Ipse venena bibas.*" He waited and she twitched. With a sigh he paced to the door, picked up and ate bits of bread, drank the water. He turned the handle on the door.

"The girl's appearance goes beyond light suspicion, but without a more definite finding, I cannot declare it a vehement or strong suspicion. An inquiry is necessary." Father Rozmital sat at the table with the Count in the privacy of the master apartment and minced a portion of loin of veal. His delicacy with a knife testified to an instinctive fear of anything sharp or pointed.

The Count, who disliked indecisive conclusions more than adverse ones, picked up a plover quarter and chewed off a chunk of meat. "There will be no inquiry at Chateau de Giffaumont. I'll not have village brawlers pounding at the portcullis. And my wife will not be subjected to that." The prospect of such an upheaval to his own tranquility intensified his pronouncement.

With that, Father Rozmital's anticipation of a public performance at the chateau faded, but he said, "Of course not. The Bishop will require an inquisitorial tribunal." His nose wrinkled despite his attempt to show favor to the Count. "It usually falls to one such as myself to manage that affair."

The public agitation over Agnes promised to make this an occasion for the Church to promote its authority. To bring about justice. To restore calm. As if thinking aloud, he said, "The tribunal might be held in the village. Is there a town hall?"

"In good earnest!" The Count pounded the butt of his knife on the table. "Take the girl elsewhere." He leaned toward the priest. "For the sake of my family and the girl. Take her to the bishop's chateau." The Bishop's Chateau de Brandon was one of the finest in the provinces.

Father Rozmital, who had no wish to surrender the proceedings to the bishop's oversight, said, "The bishop commonly defers to me in such matters."

"Whether the bishop defers is not my concern."

"I will pray for guidance in this matter. It is best to keep word of witchcraft from parishioners. It causes fear and turmoil."

"Such as we have here," said the Count. "All the more reason to remove the proceedings."

This didn't sit well with Father Rozmital. He twisted his glass and gazed at it, appearing to be in a pensive mood. "Whether the girl has entered into a pact with the devil will ultimately be decided by the Chambre ardente."

☙ Scene 37 ❧

Argon's nose was bleeding

Béjart looked out the window, thinking about the coming spring season and a possible itinerary for the Troupe. He and Argon had come to realize that Lord Dubois's appearance at the Chateau de Giffaumont had not been coincidental, and given what had transpired, his purpose had been Isabelle. Béjart's rage at her having abandoned them had turned to concern about the Troupe's performances without her. And without Agnes.

The stone floors were gradually thawing, and the Count's servants plied less charcoal to the fires until they replenished only the one in Béjart's room. He listened as one and another actor came into the room to warm at the embers.

"The Count does not want a horde of scoundrels pounding

on the gate demanding Agnes. He will listen to reason." Eugene looked from one face to the other.

"What reason?" said Hubert, pinching snuff from his box.

"If Agnes is not here, the problem will go away." Argon had to repeat himself to be heard.

"We must get the Count to grant her safe passage from here," said Eugene.

"And before more brawlers arrive," said Georgette.

"Will he not suspect that we are confederates to her deeds?" said Samuel. "Whatever she has done."

"He will not risk more accusations." Béjart took Hubert's snuff box and helped himself to a snort.

As Béjart walked into the inner courtyard, a stone fell from the sky and landed but three rods from his boot. "Foist the witch on a cross!" A shout from outside the curtain wall. "Get thee gone, gramarye!'" Another stone swooped over and bounced on the cobblestones.

Béjart pounded on the door of the master apartment. The steward opened it and took a dignified stand, his nose sniffing the upper strata. Béjart said, "Pray, forewarn the Count. There is a servant at Chateau de Giffaumont who conspires with the villagers and foments the hunt for a witch. This servant will unlock the gate and allow the brawlers to come inside." It was a ruse, but who could say there was no such a servant?

"How do you know this?" The steward glanced at the gatehouse. The gate was shut.

"Drinkers tipple freely at the tavern and secrets come to light."

The steward, who had no intention of delivering such a message to the Count himself, invited Béjart inside to make the announcement.

The Count listened, and though Béjart did not name the deceitful servant, the Count dared not dismiss the message. On returning from a hunt the previous afternoon, he had passed paysans skulking outside the gate house. He did not require verification nor proof that danger was imminent.

Having gained the Count's confidence, such as it was, Béjart followed his plan. "Prithee, we of the Troupe will convey her to a nunnery of your choice."

"I will see that she is sent to a safe retreat this very night," said the Count.

"Gramercy. It would gratify me to accompany her."

"Father Rozmital will safeguard her."

"The mask of night conceals many a brigand. A priest is poor protection against a hapless ambush."

"My coachman is no small man. And he employs well his sword." The Count grew weary of Béjart's persistence. "I am beholden to you for this intelligence." He walked, leading Béjart to the door.

"Pray, where will Agnes be taken?"

"Verily, I give you my word, she will be safe." The Count opened the door.

Béjart ignored the Count's intractable tone. "But where will her sister visit her?" he said as if Agnes had a sister.

"My steward will see you to the door." The Count nodded to the steward who tugged Béjart's shoulder urging him out. The door closed.

The steward escorted Béjart through the gallery and outside.

"I am not Jesus Christ!" said Béjart to the Troupe, though he considered himself the savior of this ragtag group of actors. "I cannot give orders to the Count!" He told of his attempt to insinuate himself into Agnes's removal. "The Count will not say where she is to be taken."

"The Count is a smooth-tongue poltroon. He will have her drowned in the Suzon River," said Georgette.

"I will follow Agnes and the priest … find out where they take her." Argon's voice had not improved, though the whiskers above his lip had turned into a perceivable mustache.

Everybody looked at Béjart, who shrugged. "And then what?" he said.

"Steal her away," said Eugene.

Béjart considered this an unlikely plan, but he had no better one. "In that case, I will follow them rather than Argon. I will find her whereabouts."

"You cannot leave us here. It has been a fortnight since we performed, and the Count may well require us to leave anon," said Hubert.

"Lent stretches before us. He is not likely to keep us for a Holy Week play," said Leon.

"There is risk in being off," said Louise, giving Béjart a curious look.

These things Béjart already knew, but he said, "Argon is too young and inexperienced."

Argon's back stiffened. His lackluster performance on stage had caused him to question his rightful place in the Troupe. This was an opportunity to make himself worthy of them. "What experience is required to follow a carriage? A goat can do as much."

"A goat is not likely to be set upon by highwaymen," said Béjart.

"Nor accosted by wandering soldiers," said Georgette.

"Only a half-wit will attack a carriage marked with a church's coat of arms," Argon said.

Against his better judgment, Béjart was talked into allowing Argon to follow Agnes.

That very night well after dark, a carriage with horses and a driver rolled into the inner courtyard and waited. Agnes, smelling of hay and excrement, wobbled down the many narrow steps and into the courtyard for the first time in days. She knew not where she was going. So debilitated from hunger and thirst, she cared not.

Father Rozmital's unrelenting instruction had opened her eyes to her own wickedness. He had explained her terrible dreams. She believed him when he said, "The devil sought you in your dreams." His sour breath had gusted into her face, penetrating her body with the need to confess her sins. That he had known about her hardened breasts before touching her was a sign of his holiness. He had known that her monthly flux no longer flowed. She believed his promise to rid her of the demon that consumed her blood and wracked her body.

Before she stepped into the cab, her hands were tied and a sack placed over her head. The steward threw a wool blanket into the seat beside her.

Father Rozmital entered the carriage after her and slammed the door shut. They rode for hours, stopping only to relieve themselves in the light of a looming moon. Father Rozmital sat with his face to the window. Shadows escaped into the dark woods. A wandering light blinked through a dismembered tree. The smell of horse dung assaulted his nose.

"Are you afraid of me?" Agnes said.

Father Rozmital said, "No." He feared no evil, confident that as he defended God, God protected him.

"Then why have you covered my face in a sack?"

"For your own protection. The paysans are afraid of you."

"But it is dark and they cannot see me."

"You can see in the dark, can you not?" Father Rozmital, confident a demon gained power in darkness, dared not allow liberties that might enhance Agnes's strength.

"If the villagers are afraid of me, they will avoid me."

"Oh no, my child. People kill what they are afraid of."

Neither the priest nor the groomsman noticed the dark figure following in the glimmer of an old moon.

※

Argon was able to keep focused on a road pocked with uneven stones by watching the light of the carriage lantern. More than once, he appreciated the new saddle. He was amazed that Béjart would forego use of it until he returned.

An eagle owl's whoop echoed in the stark trees. Argon whispered a senseless ditty to himself.

> *Carve your name on a moss covered stone*
> *On a moss covered stone*
> *A moss covered stone.*
> *Ding ding ding dong*

A wind, chilled and woodsy, rushed his face and ruffled his long hair. As they emerged from a canopy of trees into a spacious field, Argon saw more clearly and allowed greater distance from the carriage, worried that he and his horse might be seen. He smelled a pig farm before he saw gradations of darkness in the distant sky where smoke emerged from a chimney.

The road eventually wound into another forest. Argon let his mind wander. The horse stumbled in a crater. A roar grated from its throat. Argon was unprepared for the jolt and bolted upright. "Hoa, calm yourself," he said, pulling on the reins, though his palfrey had already halted. He dismounted, rubbed the horse's muzzle and offered it a turnip, but the horse was not comforted. "Steady … steady."

The coachman heard the horse and, assuming highwaymen pursued them, lashed the team into a gallop. The carriage bumped forward, thrusting Agnes into the priest. Through the cloth she felt his hot breath. His moan caught in her throat. The hood allowed her to escape her own identity. Without a prescribed visage, she was anybody, nobody, a mystery even to herself. A desire to be touched, handled, and caressed overwhelmed her. Her fingers fumbled into Father Rozmital. She blindly searched for his arms that they might embrace her.

He clasped her fettered hands and pulled them to his aching prick. He thrust open his cassock and rammed her hands on the source of his sore longing. Agnes's tears wet the cloth sack as she relieved him. She never wanted the sack removed from her face.

The carriage arrived as the sun rose above the tree tops at the convent where the Count's sister lived. Agnes, disheveled in spirit and appearance, was assigned to a small room with a cot and a chair. Her door was locked. Only Father Rozmital had the key.

Argon coaxed his lame horse, hardly able to touch its injured hoof to the ground, into the woods and tethered it to a tree. Taking his waterskin, he set off on foot, now far behind the carriage. Shadows clicked. He kept to the rut. The sniggers and grunts of wild boars, deer, and bears as well, the dislocated souls of dead persons echoed in the trees. Argon hummed the ditty, "Carve your name on a moss covered stone." Dawn inconspicuously crept out of the darkness.

A brick wall adjoined the road, high enough to keep out knaves and long enough to proclaim a nobleman's wealth. It protected vineyards Argon could see growing on the distant undulating hill. Installed on one of the elevated slopes was a chateau with a down-grade prospect of vineyards and, at its rear, a view uphill to fields back-ended by forests that grew on the gentle ridges. Argon walked until he found the gate in the wall and the rut road that led to the chateau.

The steward allowed him to refill his waterskin at the well. When Argon said, "Good sir, my horse drew up lame, and I find myself with no means of conveyance back to my home," the steward sent him to the groom.

Though the groom was not nimble in his physique, he had a well-filled head. "Young master, before nightfall a fueller will pass on the road to Vougeot. Do not mind his black'd beard or hairy ears. He is a good man. His cart has place enough for more than charcoal and wood."

Argon returned to the road and walked until he heard the scrub of hoofs approach behind him. "Hoy! Good morrow!" he said as he stepped out of the rut, and the cart drew up beside him. The fueller's unruly eyebrows were as dusted with grime and soot as his shocks of gray hair. Argon, after hours of walking, gratefully sat in the back of the cart.

In the village of Vougeot he searched out the owner of the public stables, who agreed to barter a donkey in exchange for Argon's lame horse—provided the butcher agreed to buy the lame horse and pay him. With such an agreement, Argon, along with a party including the butcher, his son, and the stableman, returned to his horse. Argon sat in the flat bed of the butcher's wagon, which was tainted with blood and smelled of moldering flesh. Beside him was the butcher's pikestaff, as long as a long sword. The stableman rode the donkey Argon had bartered for.

With professional alacrity, the butcher and his son removed one side board from the wagon as well as two wheels, allowing one half of the wagon to drop to the ground.

At the tree where the horse was tethered, the butcher said, "Ah, a fine saddle for my wife." He unbuckled the belly strap.

"Yours is the horse, not the saddle," said Argon, pushing the butcher aside.

The butcher pushed back. "Nay! The horse comes with the saddle."

"It by rights belongs to me," said the stableman.

The men spewed forth claims for the saddle. Argon prevailed in removing the saddle.

"Let us decide the saddle after we relieve this poor animal of its misery," said the butcher with a sly look at the stableman.

The horse, tugged and tempted with an apple, hobbled to the road where the men positioned it alongside the lowered side of the wagon.

So swift did the butcher's dagger cut the horse's throat that Argon was surprised when blood gushed and it swayed. They shoved the collapsing animal onto the lowered side of the wagon.

"Hoy, push all together. Push …" said the butcher, jockeying to get the horse as far onto the wagon as possible.

They men grabbed the lowered side of the wagon. "Hoist the wagon. Up … up … more," said the butcher. When it was of a height, the son positioned the pikestaff underneath the wagon and propped up the wheelless side. Thus, they replaced the wheels.

Argon grabbed the saddle and dragged it toward the donkey.

"That be the property of myself and the stableman," said the butcher, who had, in the meantime, covertly struck a deal with the stableman.

"Nay, the word 'saddle' was never spoke when we made the deal," said Argon, fending off the butcher's son.

"We would be fools to take the horse without saddle." The butcher grabbed hold and with his son's help wrenched it from Argon and threw it into the wagon.

Argon grabbed after it but met the son's fist and landed butt-first on the ground.

"Do not be a dunderhead." The stableman kicked Argon once and again.

The butcher climbed on the seat of the wagon. "Come on!" he said, spiriting the horses from their idleness. The wagon wheels grated. The stableman and son jumped on the wagon and moved the horse's carcass enough to make space for themselves at the back gate.

Argon's nose was bleeding. His head thundered. He pulled himself up and chased after the wagon. The son's boot smashed into Argon's face. Blood ran into his eyes. The stableman poked him with the pikestaff. He lost his breath and fell.

"Luggerwort!" shouted the son. The wagon gained distance.

"Pigeon livered arse!" Argon gasped.

"Worthless palliard!" said the son.

"Louse ridden knave!" Argon's front tooth was loose. Stink-fart!" He could not breathe through his nose. He sat on the ground. The wagon lumber away.

His donkey brayed long and loud. He recovered his waterskin

and gulped water, which cleared his head enough to consider whether to continue in pursuit of Agnes or turn back. He wiped his painful nose, bringing away a bloody sleeve.

✳

Agnes and Father Rozmital, by now past the town of Vougeot and rumbling at a fast trot on their way to the convent, were well beyond Argon's reach. Even had Argon been able to solicit information of the priest's carriage from the villagers, an unlikely event given his appearance, he had only a mule.

The loss of the saddle made returning to Augusto Troupe all the more difficult. As tempting as it was to strike out on his own, his hope of making a minstrel depended on a singing voice, which he no longer had. And his lute was at Chateau de Giffaumont.

He shook the coins in his leather sack, which depressed him further. Of what good was taking leave of the Troupe if he had little money and no means for making more? He refused a future of cutting grapes in a vineyard or plowing a barley field.

He balanced himself on the mule and turned back toward the chateau. Like a dog with its tail between its legs. Like a stammering village idiot. And his failure to find Agnes's whereabouts ached more than his head.

ꙮ Scene 38 ꙮ
caravans lurched and bumped

By the time Argon returned to Chateau de Giffaumont, he had removed his surcoat in the midday sun. He rode the donkey to the stables before crossing the moat and gate. Because there was no respectable way to explain his exploits, he moped as he rambled down a passageway and into the Great Hall. He encountered Leon and Eugene hefting a trunk containing stage props. "Move aside!" said Leon.

"Argon, you have returned!" said Eugene, who smiled broadly with the expectation of a cheerful greeting.

"Aye." Argon kept his head down and continued through the Hall.

As they exited the door, Eugene gave Leon a doubtful look.

"Some wench, mayhap," said Leon, who had experienced the damage one could do to the face.

Argon came upon Hubert, sorting theater equipment and packing boxes. "Where is Béjart?" He winced at the pain in his swollen lip.

"Off to Paris." Hubert continued his folding without looking up.

"Paris? Wherefore?" Paris, of all places. Argon flushed at a memory, or perhaps it was a dream, of the city. Because Béjart had left while he was away, Argon suspected it was a deliberate stratagem to exclude him.

"He will be back the morrow." Hubert did not mention that Béjart had taken Agnes's costumes and accouterments to sell, as well as a few of Isabelle's items.

"Mayhap he will perform a miracle and we will act *Mirabelle* at Palais Royal."

Hubert looked up and, despite his astonishment at Argon's black eyes and swollen nose, said, "Did you discover Agnes's whereabouts?"

Argon shook his head. He did not explain despite Hubert's quizzical look. "Alak, her fate is out of our hands." The furrow in his forehead meant an end to the conversation. Though he was tired and aching, Argon began to gather props and place them into trunks.

"Get thee to bed and rest," said Hubert.

Argon needed no more encouragement. In the quarters, the actors bundled hats, sashes, cuffs, jewelry, and such. They gasped at Argon's appearance. "What befell?" "Is this Argon?" "Begad! Bad luck?" "Who cuffed thy face?"

He ignored them and went to his closet. A numb peace

overcame him and he fell asleep to the sound of feet scuffing the floor, the clang of clasps, the swish of fabrics.

Eventually the entire Troupe knew of Argon's misadventures. Because the actors lived a life of comings and goings, they took the news about having lost Agnes with greater equanimity than Argon. Louise said she was a wicked woman. Leon said, "So are all women."

Etienne said she was indeed a witch.

Eugene said, "There are no witches."

"How do you know this?" said Etienne.

"From a man with a mind of much courage," said Eugene, who withdrew a small book from his cloak, flipped through well-worn pages, and read aloud. "People spend more time finding reasons for witches than finding out whether they are true."

"Who wrote that?" said Etienne.

"Montaigne."

"Who is he?" said Louise.

"You would prefer this scribbler to the Pope?" said Hubert.

Eugene had read passages of the book many times and with each time he had been puzzled about why Brother Vallans, a man of the Church, would give him such a book.

Béjart returned the following afternoon with proceeds from selling costumes, enough money to sustain them through the lean weeks of Lent. By promising to add religious instruction, he had been able to contract for performances at a chateau near Auvillars-sur-Saone on March 19. The Church paid little attention to Saint Joseph's Feast. Bishops feared a celebration might rouse heretics who questioned the parentage of Jesus. However, parishioners, who had a taste for greater stimulants than Holy wine, eagerly commemorated the day.

Béjart breathed a sigh of relief upon seeing Argon. He had regretted agreeing to Argon's travel without a companion. "Ave!

Odysseus has returned!" Upon seeing Argon's face he added, "Are these wounds by right or by wrong?" He clasped Argon's shoulders.

That Béjart had glimpsed Isabelle while in Paris was information he did not share with Argon. His self-respect had not yet recovered from the insult of her taking to another man, albeit a nobleman whose doublet of glittering threads humbled any costume in Béjart's trunk. He comforted himself that Dubois's gold attire did little to improve his unseemly visage. Upon seeing Isabelle dressed in elegant raiment, he was confident she had been won over by his wealth and position. Béjart hardly blamed her for it.

"My faults are coupled with no virtues," said Argon. He explained his lame horse, the fight over the saddle, his return with the mule. "When last I saw Agnes's carriage, we were on the Auxonne road somewhere near the village of Tavaux. They could have taken her to any of the villages thereabout."

"Have no regret. You chose well to return."

Argon was gratified to hear this. "Will the Count honor his word and keep her safe?"

"Agnes will take care of herself." Béjart said. He avoided speaking his mind, for he knew a nobleman's word was no more honorable than an ass's bray.

The actors loaded their trunks, backdrops, and riggings into the wagons. The following morning the sun vanished behind a heavy mist so dense Béjart could hardly see the horses hitched to the wagons. He waited until the fog cleared to knock at the Count's apartment for a farewell. The Count walked into the courtyard as if his boots hurt.

After an oration of gratitude, Béjart said, "Agnes is much on our mind."

The Count's page arrived and handed him a note, which he read, hardly hearing Béjart say, "We wish to visit her before taking leave of the hamlet. Prithee, where is she installed?"

Gondrin smacked his lips as he surveyed the notice his chaplain had written for him, an offer of a reward for the return of a recently purchased falcon that had flown the mews. "Post it in the village," he said to the messenger. "And pay the town crier for five proclamations."

"Where will we find Agnes?" Béjart kept his voice even.

The Count had more important concerns — packing their belongings, servicing and repairing the wagons. Getting a litter with feather-filled blankets and mattresses for the Countess, who remained much afflicted. The upholder he had hired to make cushions had not arrived as expected. That very morning he had sent a messenger to the butler at his Paris manor to make ready for their return. "That is no longer my affair!" He stalked toward the mews, seething over the loss of his falcon. A hunting party at the Duke's lodge loomed on the horizon, and he suspected sabotage by a competitor.

Béjart waited until the Count was at a safe distance and mumbled, "Foul reeking lout."

A nearby servant turned away and pretended he hadn't heard.

They set out for Auvillars-sur-Saône in the afternoon. The wagons jolted over cobblestones that speckled the dirt ruts. During long lapses with little conversation, the occasional horse snorted, iron hinges squeaked, reins jangled, the drivers nodded off.

Argon was not a person to think of the past, but a longing for Isabelle pulled him like a tether. Whatever he knew of home was embodied in her and Béjart. But he was losing her. He no longer smelled her scent. He found comfort in recalling her strut and plume as the vain countess of *Mirabelle*. But the sound of her voice grew distant. Despite their life of transient places and actors, it had not occurred to him that she might be transient. He had heard the gossip about Isabelle taking a lover. Nonetheless he held hope that she would return.

As the caravans lurched and bumped along the road, his mood varied with the scenery. A bird's song raised his spirits. The beauty of nubs of new leaves strengthened his belief in rebirth. The farmer steering a plow, the ox lumbering ahead, oppressed him. Clouds helped him overcome dismay about the incomprehensible expanses beyond the sky.

They passed plowed fields, reviving forests, pastures and rivers, and he came to appreciate the singularity of every tree. Every shrub. Every stone or hillock. Or cloud. The sky displayed differently from one moment to the next. Every barn was solitary. Every dwelling uncommon. Every village peculiar. No two cathedrals were alike.

The absence of Isabelle stretched the capabilities of the Troupe. In particular, it remained to be seen if they could stage *Mirabelle* without her. Louise, who now shared Béjart's caravan and feather mattress, was cherished for her pleasurable body and affectionate manner. However, what he required in bed was not what he needed in the role of Mirabelle.

Georgette had to play the part. She resisted, saying she could not learn that many lines, but finally gave in to Béjart's insistence.

Béjart made changes to the script. Despite his resentment, he scratched through words to shorten Mirabelle's part. As each word disappeared under black lines, he heard Isabelle cursing him with it.

Whenever possible, he removed the protégé from scenes, so that Louise could take over parts that Agnes had played. Little did they know that Agnes now played the part of a depraved priest's harlot, locked in a bare room at a convent. So changed had she become that she was hardly able to endure the hours until her next confession to Father Rozmital.

As they traveled from Dijon to Auvillars-sur-Saône, Georgette studied lines, recited them with Hubert, and forgot lines. Eugene coached her when Hubert was tired. He inked in clues beside difficult lines. She said the clues instead of the lines. The script was punctuated by her sighs.

Béjart brooded about the changes to the play, about whether

anything of substance remained. Could Louise play Mirabelle? And if that weren't question enough, could Georgette, whose figure gave little credence to youth, play the protégé? In desperation, he began to consider Leon for Mirabelle.

Georgette developed hiccups. She wandered the camp at night mumbling. Hubert went to Béjart's caravan. "Georgette can't play Mirabelle. She is not made for that sort of role."

Béjart listened to what he already knew. "Then she will play the protégé. That part doesn't have as many lines and there is respite between her scenes."

Louise believed herself to be the better choice for Mirabelle, but it still came as a surprise when Béjart came to her and said, "Here's the script for Mirabelle's lines. You can play the part better than Georgette."

In the evenings they sat under the stars and rehearsed Mirabelle around the fire as they ate roasted rabbit or barley porridge or frumenty, or whatever pot-pourri they could get their hands on.

⏴ Scene 39 ⏵

the gold mask

Upon arriving at the remote castle near Auvillars-sur-Saône, the Troupe drove through the gate and parked the wagons near the curtain wall. They rehearsed in the Great Hall that evening. Béjart, now dubious about performing *Mirabelle,* reminded himself that this altered version was temporary. It was only a matter of time until they added an actor capable of replacing Isabelle.

The following morning, visitors arrived in gold-trimmed carriages, ladies with lofty platform shoes, stiff and tight bodices, and uplifted décolletages. Servants unloaded trunks imbedded with jewels that proclaimed the owners to be grandees.

After several days passed with dinner performances of diversions such as acrobatics, dancing, music, and mimicry, the Troupe prepared to perform *Mirabelle.* Throughout the day, the kitchen scented the courtyard with singed meats and fresh oranges. Servants scurried to and from the Great Hall with buckets of soapy water and sweet rushes.

Béjart finished a third tankard of ale, opened a bottle of wine, and took a swig, which moderated the taste of theriac syrup. Louise's décolletage was no rival to that of Isabelle, who knew how to put her breasts to licentious exposure. It remained to be seen whether Louise, who had become adept at condescension and cunning, could excel in irreverent farce.

At dusk glamorous couples swayed across the shadowy court-yard and into the Great Hall, their laughter designed to be crafty. Under the flickering candles, *Mirabelle* began with Etienne playing Agnes's role of the countess's protégé. He wore Isabelle's wig, his lips blazing with vermillion paint, his eyebrows plucked and sculptured, his eyelids blue, his neck bejeweled, his body plumped with sheep's wool. In a soprano range, he said, "A footman is here and asks if you are at home, and says his master is coming to see you."

The sly humour of Louise's portrayal of Mirabelle escaped into ceiling timbers. The guests, besotted with the new sparkling wine called champagne, had too little sobriety to discern subtleties. Babbling and snickers arose from the table. Into the second act, a coxcomb approached the stage, grabbed Louise by the waist, and went at her like a rutting animal.

Béjart came between them. "My lord!" He would have cut the man's throat had he not been before an audience. He ushered Louise back, paced downstage, and orated his lines, "My lady, you have as lively towardness as a man could wish," The grandee stumbled off stage to coarse laughter. Béjart boomed his lines to Louise. "I am not master of the feelings of my heart."

Louise recovered, but the guests continued to laugh at one another's jests.

In the following scene, Hubert, playing a wealthy merchant, recited, "God has never bestowed such a great ring on a bishop," and stopped before finishing.

Leon waited for *as He has on me*. Leon paced. Stared at Hubert. Mouthed the words. Hubert stared back. The prompter, Samuel, didn't notice the missing words. Leon said, "A greater ring than on thy finger?"

In the third act, Etienne's long gown caught on the corner of the stage and ripped off exposing his lack of an under-skirt. By this time Béjart had guzzled the last of his several bottles of wine.

The play ended while the rowdy audience was goading one of the ladies to suckle a drunken guest. Béjart rallied his actors who provided their own applause. As they took bows to one other, they roared, "Yes! All hail! Hoy! Yo! Ho! Hey! Yah!"

In the light of morning, there were headaches to go around. Wigs resisted their places. The trunk lids closed crooked. A dead bat turned up in Samuel's closet. Hubert spilled coffee on Eugene's book.

In preparation for leaving, the men hitched the horses to the caravans. As Argon harnessed a draught horse, one of the traces broke. "Cursed hemp cord." He knotted the ends together. "What's to do without leather lines?" He mumbled to himself.

Leon heard him. "Hitching lines be damned. What's Augusto Troupe to do?"

They drove the caravans into the courtyard and parked near the postern they used. A horse stepped in a water bucket. Another on a hunting dog, which howled loud enough to wake the prophet Abraham.

Louise had not slept. The debacle of the previous night's *Mirabelle* had landed on her shoulders. Béjart had not come to her cot. She intercepted him at the well in the courtyard as he was drawing water.

Her thoughts had been driven out of control by fear at the prospect of being thrown out of the Augusto Troupe. However, she had learned that to show distress by word or deed heaped recrimination on a woman. Before she opened her mouth, she took breath. "Prithee, will Argon drive my wagon this morning?"

"Bien sur." He glanced at her with angry eyes. He preferred that she not be there. His attempt to turn her into the insolent, ribald Mirabelle had come to no good end. If he thought he had a chance of getting Isabelle back, he would go to Paris.

"If you drive my wagon, I can consult with you. About how to change my performance." She dared not risk rancor by saying *Mirabelle*.

"Argon will drive you." He poured water to the top of a firkin and secured the lid.

"I was afraid to give the character too much vigor. I will speak loud and lusty. I am unseasoned in the role. I will improve with time. I will grind and cudgel and swell the veins of pillicocks!"

He heaved the firkin on his shoulder and turned away from the well.

She walked with him toward the caravans. "Last night the audience was too pickled in liquor to follow the plot."

At the wagon, he loaded the firkin and took an empty one.

Louise said, "All is not lost because of one performance. Your comedie is a masterpiece."

He said, "Is your trunk ready to load?" He headed back to the well with the empty firkin.

Béjart tightened the saddle's belly belt on his horse. He led the caravans out the gate and toward the village of Brancion, which had agreed to amusements for the Feast of the Annunciation on March 25.

They passed fields of modest proportion that arched up rolling hills to the tree line. Those not planted as vineyards were undergoing the ox and plow. The fine sunshine did little to calm Béjart's disappointment. His morning meal of wine-soaked bread had been followed by wine. A waterskin filled with wine and tied to his saddle waggled with the horse's gait. He hadn't hated Isabelle for leaving until now.

Nearing the Saône River valley, stone-paved roads built by the Romans followed surveyed courses which went over hills and crossed rivers and ravines. Dry roads with drainage ditches.

Béjart halted the Troupe at the small village of Chalon Sur Saône on the chance of picking up a show. He convinced the priest of Cathedral Saint-Vincent that his amusements edified audiences with Catholic principles. "My musicians play like angels." He kept his breath a distance from the priest, for the wine that eased his anger had a burdensome scent. "Our spectacle glorifies the visit of the Archangel Gabriel to the Virgin Mary." He made a sign of the cross.

Upon winning the priest's approval, he hustled back to the caravans and hastily turned a farce about a constipated girl into one about the gravid Mary. The actors practiced their scenes into the night.

Louise played well the role of Mary. Béjart took the role of the Archangel Gabriel and wore wings Hubert fashioned from dried vines and silk gauze. Following the performance, the priest paid but a portion of what he had agreed to.

"Wherefore? The villagers favored us with ovations," said Béjart.

"Yea, doubtless because they recognized the tune of 'The Three Drunken Maidens.' It is blasphemy to put such a tune on the lips of Mary."

"The lyrics were from Church prayers," said Béjart.

"Even more your error. To cojoin holy words with an ale house chanson. And what of the Archangel's message, delivered to the tune of 'Itches In Me Britches?' Your troupe need not apply here for privileges. We will not be disgraced again."

The Augusto Troupe returned to the road, their wagon wheels grating against the stones. They stopped for the night where a farmer allowed them to park and partake of water from his well. They bought oats and hay for the horses. With the sunrise Samuel and Eugene hitched the horses to the wagons, and they followed a route through the undulating vine-clad slopes of the Mâconnais.

Entry into the village of Brancion was by a stone gateway built into fortifications secured into a hill, the wall high enough to withstand attack from a trebuchet. "It little and little distills into your mind fear," said Georgette, who walked afar from the road to avoid the dripping putrefaction of a dangling corpse.

The horses strained to pull the wagons up the steep road. Drivers stood down on the ground and urged them with "Gee up!" Along the route, villagers gazed at them from stoops. Children jumped to the beat of Etienne's tabor and chased about the steep road in a chaotic parade. "Gleeman! Gleeman!" they screamed. The wagons wound uphill past the Market Hall, an open air building which covered a furlong square and had low walls on all sides. Its deeply sloping roof dominated the center of the village.

The castle came into view, a stone monolith built into the top of the hill and separated from the village by woolly trees. By the time they reached the center and L'Église de Saint-Pierre, the horses panted. People surged about them, dancing and shouting along with the rowdy sound of their tabor and recorder. Brancion's consuls allowed the Troupe to park their wagons in the central courtyard.

The following day, the actors performed farces, ballads, and comicalities in the courtyard for a raucous crowd, some of them valets in the nobleman's household. Those in long gowns with high collars and beaver-fur hats were wealthy merchants. At supper in the village tavern, Eugene, rarely a person of enthusiasm, said to Béjart, "It is a mime unlike any other! The masks will astonish the audience."

Béjart tipped his bowl to his lips and sucked out what remained of leek pottage. He liked *astonish*. "We will give it a try."

The actors knew well of Eugene's work on a mime, even better the masks he had fabricated.

Though Argon and Louise had wearied of practicing the mime, Eugene claimed they needed one more rehearsal to manage the inevitable awkwardness of the masks. Argon said, "God's teeth! We're not playing the Palais Royal!"

Villagers gathered in the courtyard, attracted to the music as Béjart and Argon played the lute, Georgette the psaltery, and from behind sheepskins, Eugene the shawm. Before the mime, Samuel somersaulted on the makeshift stage and ate fire. He exited doing cartwheels.

Louise, wearing a loathsome mask with tangled eyebrows and red pustules, stepped on stage with Argon, who swished his velvet cape as became a swain. Louise was dressed in a robe with lavish folds where she could hide her mask. Loud lilting music accompanied them.

A second grotesque mask with a prominent crooked nose lay conspicuously on a table. Argon whimsically put it on and as he did so, Louise surreptitiously removed her repulsive mask to show her face. They danced, he with the grotesque mask and she as his beautiful partner. They turned and frolicked to the music in ways that enabled them to remove or add a mask.

Argon removed the big nose mask, and as he did so, Louise replaced her hideous mask. Whispers of disbelief arose from the onlookers. She danced ever slower, the musicians played slower, and using her arms and hands, she beseeched Argon to put the repulsive mask back on. Her motions were accompanied by a supplicating song played by Eugene on his shawm.

When Argon did as she requested, she removed her grotesque mask to reveal her beautiful face. The villagers gasped.

They danced, Argon wearing the big nose mask and Louise without a mask.

The music grew more lighthearted. Argon removed his mask and placed it on the table and as he did so, Louise surreptitiously put on the pustules. The musicians played a mournful song.

Louise proffered the big nose mask to him and with gestures, pleaded with him to wear it and return her beauty. After fits and starts, Argon agreed to wear the hideous mask if she married him. As he reluctantly put it on, Louise became beautiful when she removed the pustules mask.

From the sidelines, Eugene and Béjart played a wedding tune.

The couple danced, Argon hideous in the mask and Louise a natural beauty. When she spurned Argon and danced with Leon, who appeared on stage, Argon feigned removing the mask. She returned to his arms and they danced off the stage. The villagers cheered.

After the performance as the Troupe ate servings of pot-pourri at a tavern, paysans approached Argon and Louise and looked on them with wonder. "Begad! How now did your face change?"

There was no opportunity for the Augusto Troupe to get permission to perform at the Castle of Brancion, for the Maréchal de Montrevel was in the Low Countries fighting the Dutch with the king's army. However, the village courtyard was a seemly locale for a performance.

The success of the mime encouraged Béjart to reconsider staging *Mirabelle*. It had been overtaxed by ill circumstance, script changes, actors taking different roles. The problem was one of implementation. More rehearsals were required. Louise was proving herself more capable of ribald comedy. The actors grumbled but prepared for another *Mirabelle*.

During the performance, Louise delivered her lines with saucy disrespect, but when a rotted cabbage flew on stage she stammered. She stepped away from the audience. A soggy turnip smashed into Leon's velvet joupon. Béjart intercepted him before he stalked off the stage and pressed him into joining in a rousing ballad about a mourner who swived a priest at a grave site.

Béjart halted their performance of *Mirabelle* and they staged a profane skit Béjart had learned from his father, "The Crooked-Nosed Knave." Though the villagers cavorted to the music, the actors were eager to get off stage.

✳

Leon had no way of knowing it was a good time to take off when he had arranged to meet his brother at a hostel in the hamlet of

Chapaize. After greeting Pierre in a small room with six tables, he hailed the kitchen servant. The food of the night was spitted pigeon, which the two of them requested, along with brown bread and radishes.

After finding out his father had returned to Chateau Gaillard, Leon said, "Would it be seemly that I petition Father to meet with me?"

His question was with them every time they met. Pierre knew how much his brother wanted an affirmative answer. But changes that were occurring in the family were not to Leon's advantage. "To contact him is to risk a duel with Geoffroy."

"Will Geoffroy never forgive me?" Leon said, "Though it is his wife who needs forgiveness more than I do."

Pierre tore off a pigeon leg and bit into the chewy meat. "Father depends more and more on Geoffroy to manage the estates."

"Father must see that I can only return if he presses Geoffroy to accept my apology."

"Tamora will not abide it. And Father knows this."

At the mention of Geoffroy's wife's name, Leon spit a bone on the floor. "Has she enticed Father to her will?"

"I have in my pocket evidence that he has not forsaken you."

Before parting, Pierre gave Leon money from their father. Leon was coming to realize his time away from Chateau Gaillard was an irredeemable loss. And the longer he stayed away, the less retrievable became his home.

☙ Scene 40 ❧

diable driven away in smoke

In conversation at the Peauterpotte tavern, Eugene overheard a peasant speak of a man named Vallans. He gulped ale and asked the peasant for particulars.

"Nay, he was no man of the cloth," said the peasant.

Brother Vallan's absence, rather like a curse, had tugged at Eugene ever since he disappeared. When Eugene had been a child, the friar, a mendicant and a wanderer, had visited him regularly until one spring he didn't come. And just like that, Eugene lost the guardian who had safeguarded him as a child. If there was a chance, however remote, to see Brother Vallans, Eugene had to pursue it.

He visited the confectioner, soap boiler, poulterer, and other tradesmen with the same story. "I am come a great distance to find Brother Vallans. By chance did he come this way?" Finally, with information he gleaned from a midwife, that a friar said to be Brother Vallans lived some four leagues distant, Eugene arranged to borrow Béjart's horse the following morning.

"Come with me," he said to Argon.

Argon's money bag was virtually empty. The henbane concoction for his voice had cost what livres he had managed to save. "I can no more buy a meal than a periwig."

"I will provision you. If you can talk Leon off his horse."

Eugene, with Argon on Leon's horse, followed the midwife's directions to a hovel where he faced a stranger he had never seen before. A man he could hardly understand because overlapping teeth affected his speech.

Eugene remembered the glint in the midwife's eyes. Perhaps his credulity had been her amusement. Brother Vallans, the man who had found a home for him as he grew from an urchin to a stripling, was lost anew.

Eugene hesitated outside the doorway as the seer sputtered something about a burning wick for a heart. From inside came the bleat of sheep. "What is pressing on your mind?" said the seer.

Eugene looked at Argon who looked back. Argon cleared his throat.

"My towardness may relieve your disquiet." The seer mumbled something to himself and spat orange spit. "I am well willing to utter my mind. But if it is for sin, I will be of no help."

Eugene apprehended the seer's beneficent offer. "Will you tell us if our troupe of players will find royal patronage?"

The seer licked the unruly hairs of his mustache, which seemed to grow out of his nose. Instead of answering, he looked at Argon. "Me think this is the troubled soul."

Argon hacked and said, "I have no coins to pay you, good sir."

The seer shrugged one shoulder as if in disappointment. A sheep scampered from behind him and ran through his legs into the yard.

"I will reward you for your service," said Eugene.

The seer motioned for Eugene and Argon to come inside. They sat at stools surrounding a scarred table. The seer placed an adder stone the size of a pipkin on the table.

"Mayhap you have water to quench our thirst?" Argon's words came out as if birdlime coated his throat.

The seer raised the lid of a casket-like chest against the wall opposite the fireplace and removed an ewer. He carefully poured a small measure into a mug and handed it to Argon, who quaffed it in one go.

"You also?" the seer said to Eugene.

Eugene was no less thirsty. The seer turned up the ewer and emptied the remaining water into the mug, which he handed to Eugene.

The seer sat and blew his damp breath on the adder stone's glistening hollow. Where moisture beaded he rubbed his thumb. Lights sparked and crosshatched. He hoisted the stone to his one good eye and looked into the hole. With gnarled hands, he turned the stone in circular motion. "There will be a remedy."

"Argon will regain his voice?" said Eugene.

The seer studied something inside the stone. "The light dims. But the light is there." He gingerly placed the stone on the table and wiped mucus from his bad eye with his sleeve.

"How long will it be?" said Argon.

"I can only see the outcome." The seer picked up a straw from the floor and pulled it between his lips.

"Is there a way to hasten the outcome?" Argon said, despite his paltry money bag.

"Madame Helene is a wise woman. She has cures." The seer shook a few drops of water from the ewer into his mouth, wiped moisture from its rim with his finger, and put it to his lip.

"Prithee, where is she to be found?" said Argon, laying plans to borrow money from Eugene as he had done on other occasions.

The seer gave them directions to Madame Helene's place, some five leagues distant. "And good sirs, I am, wellaway, out of water."

"Where is your well?" said Argon, willing to fetch some.

"Alak! I have none. The woodward who lives next on this road has one. I can walk there and back in a morning, but with a horse it will take less time."

They strapped two firkins on Argon's horse, and he rode with Eugene to the neighboring well for water. The woodward, responsible for the noble's forest, was well installed in a domicile. Before returning with water for the seer, Eugene and Argon entreated bread, wine, and cheese from the good man, who charged them only a few sou.

"Gramercy!" said the seer upon helping to unload the casks. "Mayhap this will last until another rainfall." He counted the deed as recompense for his service and bade the two men farewell.

Eugene and Argon rode at a gallop, for the sun was well past its height. Madame Helene lived in a cottage with thatched roof. The straw-strewn floor retained such a scent of lavender and thyme that Eugene's head tingled, an unwholesome portent. He backed out of the room and gasped fresh air until the stir in his head and eyes calmed. He lay on the grass while the horses chomped nearby.

Argon sat in a rush-bottomed chair at a three-legged table across from Madame Helene. One of the walls in the room was painted with drawings of plants and creatures of mixed human and animal parts.

She studied a candle's flame and said that Argon was the victim of a curse. From skeins hanging from numerous knobs on a wall, she took a powder and dusted it into the candle's light, filling the hut with a virulent scent. Argon swooned and tumbled onto the floor. As the candle's light blinked to darkness, he worried too late about witches that were known to collect male organs.

Swells of unpleasant breath coaxed him awake. The wise woman's shriveled lips smiled in his face. "Prithee wait while I fetch a tankard of worthy tonic."

He felt into his breechcloth and was relieved to find his manhood undisturbed. She handed him what appeared to be a cup of bloody milk. As he took to his unsteady feet, a vague squeal came from the corner, followed by scurrying. As it darted away, a stream of light followed the rat's trail and faded to smoke. The tonic puddled in his throat. He swallowed with difficulty.

He took from his pocket a sash Isabelle had given him and held it for Madame Helene to see. "Be the devil in this sash?"

Her wandering eye turned from the wall in his direction. "Nenni! There is no diable here. Diable driven away in the smoke," she said, though murky air still whirled about them.

"This will return your voice to its proper place." She put around his neck a leather string with a lead circlet. On it was engraved the lettering of a language Argon had not seen before. A carved face with snakes curling like hair stared at him from the reverse. It rested on his gorge.

As he and Eugene started back to the encampment, he discovered his poor money pouch, which he'd hidden in his hat, was missing. He did not turn back or accost Madame Helene. The eerie swoon from her potion still affected him and he would not risk more magic.

After a period of going at a fast pace, they slowed the horses to a trot. The sun dissolved beyond the western trees. Argon's voice regained strength, and he tested it singing. "The gypsy rover came over the hill; Down through the valley so shady …"

A groan emerged from Eugene, who said, "For Christian pity! Quiet."

"He whistled and he sang till the greenwoods rang; And he won the heart of a lady." The song allayed the stillness surrounding them.

Eugene said, "You'll waken the dead!"

"A ley lu a ley lu a ley, a ley lu a lee ley ee."

An owl wailed. Like a baby's cry.

Argon stopped singing and they rode in silence. Clippety-clop. They listened. Saddle leather chafed. Night bugs thrummed. A breeze hissed. Finding his voice stronger, Argon could not resist hearing it. "I wonder where Isabelle is tonight. It is said that she joined the Troupe de Chatouilleurs." The moon cast shadows.

Eugene did not mention the rumor that Isabelle was in Paris. "Chatouilleurs is well admired in Orleans. And it is nearer Paris."

Argon said, "I can hardly blame her if she gets to play to bigger audiences."

"In truth, she excited any show." Eugene sighed and filled his lungs with cool sweet air.

"It is Béjart's fault." Argon's voice commanded the words.

"Wherefore say this?"

"He took the applause as praise for himself, even when Isabelle had the favor of the audience. He did not credit her." Argon was pleased that his words spoke out clear, like a man's.

"It was said by Leon that her magic bewitched men. Gave her power over them." Eugene's face glowed in the moonlight.

"Doubtless Leon knows about women. It is a surprise that he credits any woman with power over men," said Argon.

"Her magic once called down a curse on Béjart … after one of their disputes." Eugene had come to this understanding with help from Agnes.

"She cursed him with every argument."

"Nay. I mean she used sorcery."

"Wherefore? She is no sorcerer." Argon said this with greater assurance than he felt.

"She said to Béjart, 'A pox upon you and your script finger!' In a trice, his finger swelled so stiff he was unable to trim a quill."

Argon uttered a laugh. His throat gave it robust volume. "That was when Suzanne joined the troupe." What he did not say was that Suzanne, who preceded Louise, had become a memory. And was that to be Louise's fate?

"And Isabelle was skilled in reading palms." Eugene had learned from her. A break in a particular crease meant, "Your path will meet an obstacle." Or deep furrows, "Be on the watch for a faithless friend." A line separated into two, "You will face a difficult decision." Eugene was capable of interpreting palms in like fashion, but he had not the boldness to present himself in this regard.

"When she read my palm, she said I have interruptions in my life-line," Argon said.

"Interruptions? What does that mean?"

"She said I would have heartache," Argon said.

"Ho!" Argon drew rein the instant he glimpsed a crater in the moonlight. His horse whirled in a circle. He rubbed its shoulder. "Calm-toi! Calm-toi." It stopped reeling and they returned to the rut.

"Wherefore heartache, did she say?" said Eugene.

"Nay, but the line is not broken. Means I will over it."

๑ Scene 41 ๏
Madame Thibaut

By the time the players prepared to leave Brancion, their pouches of cash were lighter and that of the alehouse owner's the heavier. They packed up their property and turned their train of caravans southward.

The second day, dust, uneven paver stones, and a delay while awaiting the removal of a broken wagon, along with its spilled hay, from the road drained many a spirit. Béjart sent Argon and Eugene ahead in search of a farm where they might have water and rest and possibly quarter for the night. The two actors found a farmer who allowed them to overnight within his gates in exchange for ballads for the peasants.

The Augusto Troupe stole carrots, milk, and two chickens before resuming the road the following day. By afternoon, the two towers of Cathedral Saint-Vincent de Mâcon came into view. The aged village wall, oppressed by weather and wars, was cracked and crumbling. The wagons rumbled through the gate where years before soldiers had stood guard. On this day it was guarded by a wood cross, which leaned precariously to one side. Nearby, two human heads impaled on spikes attested to the law's presence, if not justice.

The actors took care not to sink into the ditch of ordure that streamed down the middle of the street. They attracted a pack of dusty urchins, dogs, pigs, and chickens as they made their way past alehouses to an innkeeper and a bath house, which enlivened the players with an expectation of a bath.

The spires of the cathedral towered over other buildings. People said the spirit of Queen Jeanne III of Navarre had haunted the nave since her visit in 1564. It so inspired the Huguenots they praised her as Queen of the Protestants. Eugene took off his hat at the cathedral, for of all the actors, he was the most attracted to the Church. When the bells began to toll the hour, the horses startled and darted aside, stepping high, frightening dogs, ducks, and children.

They settled for the evening with a writ allowing permission for them to perform on a tennis court propitiously located within sight of the cathedral towers. The following day they set up their stage.

Strolling about the shops, Argon handed out playbills and Etienne hawked hand flags. With growing bewilderment, Argon realized the effect of Madame Helene's potion and amulet had lessened. Did this mean he had to settle for a monk's voice? He took the shrill squeaks of the bats that whooshed from the cathedral belfry as evidence of a spiritual deficiency. As Etienne headed back to the wagons, Argon said, "I will be back anon."

"What's to do?"

Noisy bats flapped overhead and bobbed in and out of the

belfry. "I am going to look inside that door." Argon pointed at the rugged cathedral door.

"Nay! Béjart will strangle you!"

"If those bats can enter, why not me?"

"Better bats than actors."

"Do not betray me to Béjart!" Argon called as Etienne chased away.

Argon dragged the heavy door by its iron handle, opening it enough that he saw what might have been the habitat of a wealthy sorcerer. Shadowy, statuesque creatures lined the walls. Echoes lingered like a sinister wind. The holiness of the place chilled the air. He was awed by the space above him, where ceiling timbers claimed the authority of the sky. Arranged on either side of the aisle were rows of empty chairs leading up to an altar, where two old women in scarves knelt like wraiths.

A person clothed in a hooded black cape, sat near the back. Argon removed his floppy hat, crept to a seat behind her, and thought for a while. He had no idea how to pray, but he was willing to try anything to repair his voice. "God in heaven, or in this church, or wherever you are, tell me where to find a cure for this cursed voice. There must be a cure, but where? Where?"

A whispery breathing of "Ave Maria, gratia plena ..." echoed from the chair in front of him. The hood turned aside and a quiet voice with neither male nor female tones emerged from the hood. "Curses and cures are not of this world. Seek and you will find what you need."

The presence gave forth a smell of rabbit's fur. Argon slapped at a spider crawling on his neck. It tumbled into his lap. He took this to be a spirit warning him of danger. His chair scraped the stone tiles as he stood.

In a whisper, the voice said, "A spirit will cure your curse."

Argon sat down and leaned forward to the source of the voice.

A face, more womanly than manly, appeared from the cavernous hood, her skin so white it verily suffered even a winter sun. Wisps of white hair fringed her face. When she spoke, her thin lips stretched in a cheerless smile. He gazed at her purple eyes.

"'Tis no good, fair lad." She looked at the amulet about his neck.

He stared. "What do you know of a curse?"

She leaned closer to him. "You can claim the voice of a dead soul. Possess an amulet from its bones. The bone of a finger will suffice. Wear it close to your voice."

The woman pulled the hood down. She rustled from the seat and swished down the aisle toward the door.

In his confusion, Argon mumbled, "God of all saints, spare me from ignorance and folly." His head cleared. He told himself it was but an old meddlesome woman. However, she knew about curses. He stood to the rasping of the chair on the flooring. Going out, his boots crunched grains of sand into the hard stones.

He squinted at the bright outside light and surveyed the court-yard until he glimpsed the black hooded cape turn into a narrow cobblestone street. He followed her to a thick door like many another in a narrow row of attached houses.

He knocked and was admitted to her apartment, a room cramped with crucibles, basins of dried petals, hanging ceramic urns, herb sprigs, and animal pelts. On a wall was a painting of the pig-faced woman, known in the provinces as a wealthy damsel with a normal body who had been bewitched with a porcine face.

"Yes, you are a victim of sorcery." Madame Thibaut, for that was her name, draped her cloak over the table, covering powders, herbs, small stones, and several teeth.

"Wherefore? I have no enemy." Argon backed up to a wall after seeing a shadow disappear at the window.

"I heard the voice you once had. Its magic threatened those of lesser merit."

"How do you know the voice I had?" Argon overcame his trepidation and looked into her eyes.

"Your Troupe. It has played many villages."

"I have never seen you before." Argon was certain he would have remembered this white face, white hair, purple eyes.

"Nor have you seen the evil that cursed you."

"And you know this evil?"

Her laugh was mild and musical. She dipped her fingers into a pipkin and withdrew them, glistening with an infusion. She motioned Argon closer and lightly touched her fingers to his throat. He head went light from an overpowering burnt scent. A warmth spread from his neck to his belly. So stimulating was the sensation he had to resist taking her into his arms.

"The herbs will delay further damage." She licked her fingers.

"I will regain my power to speak?" Argon would have licked her fingers as well had he not recovered his senses.

"The obstruction is a curse merely swayed by potions. Forceful curative magic is needful. That will come with the help of Poquelin. Something of his — a bone, hair, a tooth. Take that and wear it at your neck. His spirit will draw nigh and your voice will recover."

As he walked back to the Troupe, he wrestled with notions. A cure that depended on securing a relic from the grave of Poquelin, know to all of France as Molière, necessitated a trip to Paris where the great actor was buried.

He felt confident his throat had improved and yelled "Hoy!" at a woman with a churn paddle chasing after an urchin. So commanding was his voice she stopped.

☙ Scene 42 ❧
an owl gagging on fetid air

The following morning Argon woke up and spoke, "I wish a good day to you, sir." The sound went from husky to breathy. He cleared his throat. "You do but small credit to your fame." Now it was whispery. "A pox unto those words! Will my voice ever be more than a plague sore?" He was shouting bitterly though feebly.

With no speaking role, his appearance or absence at the rehearsals was of less importance. He wandered around Brancion, mumbling with discontent.

At a tavern, he downed tankards of ale thinking of ways to get to Paris and Molière's grave. Through the door, he watched the Market Hall across the square where wagons came and went with an influx and outflow of casks of wine, and he had an idea. Paris had an insatiable need for wine. Because King Louis increasingly required nobles at his side, high-ranking peers in the provinces bought manor houses in Paris.

Argon approached a drayman loading wine into a wagon. "Good sir, have you need of a wagoner to deliver your wine?"

"Go-along, lout! I have no need of you."

After several days of drinking ale and offering his services to one or another merchant, Argon met a dealer willing to hire him. For seven sou, Argon delivered a dozen firkin to a chateau some five leagues distant.

When he failed to show up for an afternoon performance by the Augusto Troupe, Béjart said, "Hoy! Where were you?" He missed a second time and Béjart said, "Are you so certain of your comforts that you let slip your duty?"

Making wine deliveries and keeping in good faith with the Troupe became complicated. Argon explained his dilemma to Eugene, who had on occasion taken excursions away from the Troupe in his constant search for Brother Nicolas Vallans.

Eugene said, "Leon, were he not an actor, might well be a magician. His head is a map if you need directions. And he sees round every corner; can borrow anything from a needle to a tennis ball."

Argon cared not whether it was by cunning or chicanery that Leon convinced a local merchant to hire him to deliver wine to a cathedral in Paris. It was the opportunity he had hoped for, even dreamed of. The delivery made possible a trip to Saint Joseph's cemetery and Molière's grave. He broached the delivery mission to Béjart.

"Nay! Augusto Troupe needs you," said Béjart, who knew Isabelle was in Paris.

"What? To hawk phallic gourds? Portraits of dickheads?"

"By cock! Take a tack from Leon. More tokens mean more sou and a better supper."

"Sou! The merchant says the cathedral will pay me two livres to deliver the wine," said Argon.

"And abandon the Augusto Troupe? There is work for you here, to make our diversions work."

"Think on this. I will see troubadours and players as I travel. I will return with new plots and poems."

This idea appealed to Béjart. "Find somebody older to travel with you."

Eugene sat on a wagon gate reading Nostradamus's *The Prophecies*, which he had to return to the printer the following day.

Argon said, "I am going to deliver wine to Paris. Come with me."

Eugene held up the book and laughed. "Give an ear to this. 'A young child will be born of poor people. He who by his tongue will seduce a great troop.' Nostradamus here makes a prediction befitting you. You will have a great voice."

For Eugene, the prospect of travel was exciting as it meant the possibility of finding Brother Vallans, or at least news of him. He had come to realize the debt he owed the friar, a debt that weighed more heavily on him as time passed. He might well be dead but for the friar, who had taken him from his mother's graveside and secured him as a servant on a nobleman's estate. This good fortune had led to another, a fellow servant who played the lute. A chaplain who taught him to read.

In preparation for the Paris trip, Argon and Eugene removed a cot from the caravan they shared to make room for the casks.

"Your caravan is not well suited to haul wine," said Béjart. "In fact, it is only suited for traveling actors. Those gold and blue colors will attract the attention of thieves and whores. Children and dogs will follow you in the streets. If you're reported to the Church, you risk an inqusition."

"What do you propose?" said Argon.

"Take the wagon. There will be less displacement." The wagon had no cover and was used to pack their belongings such as pots, dishes, stools, and stage props.

"The wagon is wobbly. I would not wager a sou on its making the trip." Argon had no wish to sleep under it for a week.

"You underestimate it. It will serve you well."

"It will wear our asses to nubbins. And churn the wine to froth."

"Then take Samuel's caravan. You and your wine will sit in better comfort," said Béjart. The caravan Samuel slept in was essentially a wagon with a canvas top. It looked no different from that of a woodcutter or ragpicker. Because it was colorless he usually rode at the rear as they entered villages.

"Samuel's caravan is the smallest," said Argon.

"It is easier to steer in the streets of Paris."

"Truly, but we travel the streets one day and Roman roads for five," said Argon.

In the end, Argon and Eugene drove to the wine merchant's stall in the caravan used by Samuel, who was happy to exchange his for theirs, even if Argon had crowded into it the cots, baskets, and chests they removed from his caravan.

✳

Argon and Eugene loaded up barrels of wine and headed north toward Paris, some 300 leagues distant and about a week of travel. Too excited to be afraid of highwaymen, swindlers, or rogues, Argon pulled the reins this way and that. Fleury, a filly Béjart had won in a game of reversis, became agitated at Argon's hasty, sometimes conflicting, signals. He was apt to say "Alak!" at the animal's slight misstep. Followed by, "Hey! Gar! Get on with thee."

"Prithee, relax your bowels." Eugene volunteered to take the lines, but Argon held on to them.

As long as they had light, they stopped only to rest and water the horse. Come night, they parked the caravan on the edge of a vineyard behind a wine press and ate a mouthful from the bread they had brought. With hardly room under the caravan seat, Argon curled up for the night while Eugene slept underneath on the ground. From moment to moment Argon was startled and his imagination conjured up highwaymen or spirits, but he said, "It's only the wind," or an owl, or a fox to calm himself.

In the middle of the night a jingle of metal rings woke both of them. Horsemen on the road. Eugene hustled up and gently caressed Fleury's nose and ears, whispered to her, blew into her face if she moved unexpectedly, anything to avoid a snort that might bring on an assault. The jingle drifted past them. "Good girl, Fleury." Eugene walked around and around the wine press to relieve his tension.

In the morning he took a turn driving, and Argon settled down to the squeaking of the wheels. At a farmer's hayrick they found provender for Fleury. Wisps of clean air assailed them from vineyards where grape vines had begun to clutch wood stakes.

Only when the horse farted did Argon rouse from a dream in which his mother took off her wig to reveal a bald head that glowed unnaturally. After that, the two men took turns driving. As they trundled through small villages along the route, Eugene asked strangers for word about the friar he had known.

A prolonged silence stretched over leagues of pitted ruts and a sloping landscape of vineyards while the sun toiled in the sky. "I was but a forsaken urchin when Brother Vallans rescued me. Bound for a life of thievery." Eugene, with little encouragement, would have gladly volunteered his memory of the cold day when he dug his bare toes into a pile of dirt shoveled from a hole in the ground where his mother's body lay. A priest had stood beside him and told him to throw dirt onto her covering cloth. But he had been unable to move. The priest threw the dirt.

He tried to keep his mother in memory. Not the sick mother, but the one who sold eggs in the village until wolves ate their chickens. If a wind rustled her skirt, she wrapped a scarf around her face. "You shouldn't breathe the wind. It carries the wasted breath of everybody. Even animals. Even breath from years ago. From people who are dead. You don't want dead breath in your body."

Argon wasn't paying attention. Saint Joseph's, he understood, was where Molière had been buried. However, Paris had many churches, and Saint Joseph was a common moniker. Their time in the city was limited and he had much to do.

After a week of lumbering over stone roads built by ancient Romans and nights of taking turns sleeping under the wagon, they encountered increased traffic—road carts, carriages, and coaches.

Eugene arose as morning light approached the horizon beyond a paddock where they had slept the night. He shook Argon awake. They fed Fleury and hitched up the caravan. The vista of fields and forests narrowed. Distant manor houses turned into farmhouses which turned into cottages and as they drew nearer Paris, shacks along the road. After they stopped at the gate and paid the toll, barking dogs and rowdy children chased alongside them and made the horse skittish. They passed roadside stalls and a tavern. Peddlers wandered into their path—hawkers with baskets, apple-sellers, hucksters of relics and winged phalluses.

"Ail ... Ail!" trilled a tall vendor in a tricorn hat as he strolled among ragged children, hungry dogs, and garrulous men, his garlic ropes swinging from the staff on his shoulder. "Les liévres! Les liévres!" shouted another peddler whose hair bristled as if it was last washed by the rain. He carried a sturdy pole laced with rabbit carcasses.

Argon and Eugene felt the pinch of hunger, but they did not chance stopping at an auberge or alehouse, for thieves were as numerous as vendors. A vanilla scent wafted into Argon's aquiline nose. "Mmm. That recalls thumb-buttercakes at Fontainebleau's winter faire."

"I am hungry," Eugene took out a knuckle of bread which they shared.

An urchin carrying a large apple dashed in front of them. Argon had carelessly allowed the lines to fall loose. Fleury shied and clumped into the sewer ditch. In went a wagon wheel. Argon pulled up awkwardly and rasped, "Hoy!"

"A pox upon you, you witless grub!" Eugene called after the boy.

Fleury stamped in the drain. Argon gasped, "Hoy! Fleury! Attention!" The caravan tipped and swayed. The wine barrels rammed the rail and a froth seeped from a lid. Eugene jumped down, grabbed the bridle, and tugged the horse back into the roadway. He climbed in back and belayed the barrels.

At a tree-lined square, they circulated with carriages and wagons. In the midst of the square a minstrel juggled balls and sang of an arrogant noblewoman who charmed her lord with a willow twig. Argon guided Fleury out of the traffic and into a street stall where they parked and listened.

Argon handed the lines to Eugene and jumped down with their flacon. "I will get ale. And directions to Saint Joseph's."

"Saint Joseph's? We are bound to deliver the wine to L'Église Saint-Eustache," said Eugene.

"Yes, but first we must find Saint Joseph's and Molière's grave."

"Nay, beforehand to L'Église Saint-Eustache," said Eugene.

"Safeguard our wine. I will be but a moment." Argon turned and crossed the street, dodging carriages, horseback riders, townsmen, beggars, and brawling dogs.

A boy dressed as a jester handed Argon a playbill. In the crowded tavern, a crier was reading in a thunderous voice from a notice: "Arrival of beaver furs from New France at haberdasher. Beaver hats. Beaver oil for your hair now at Farfannchy apothecary. Oil excellent for memory. Improves hearing."

While the alewife filled his flacon, Argon said, "Good mistress, prithee, where can I find Saint Joseph's Cemetery?"

"By God, I swear, I never been there." She withheld the ale until Argon placed coins in her palm.

Argon drank from the flacon and, after looking about the room, approached a clean-shaven but scarred man and repeated the question. From a nearby table, a man whose nose jutted from a bristly mustache and beard, said, "Near the Palais du Luxembourg."

Because of the man's three pilgrim badges Argon judged him to be fairly honest. He gave directions by way of Boulevard d'Enfer which required several turns.

At the caravan, Eugene, who learned music without trying, repeated from memory the melody of a song a nearby minstrel had been singing. Had he brought his lute, he could have accompanied the minstrel.

Eugene slapped the lines on Fleury's hind and the caravan rolled out of the stall and merged behind a cabriolet into a line of moving conveyances. He hummed the melody and sang occasional words of the song until Argon caught on and hummed along. The two of them kept at it until they could remember the song. Eugene picked up the flagon, shook it, and said, "Lo! You drank the ale."

"Not all of it," Argon said. "Take a look at this." He held out the playbill.

As Eugene read, his face brightened. "Molière's *Misanthrope*. At the Palais Royal Theatre. If we could but see it!" He had never imagined himself so near such genius and beauty.

"We have to go," Argon said. He took the lines from Eugene and flapped the leather straps on Fleury's croup.

"When?" said Eugene with some incredulity. "And how are we to get in the door with hardly a sou in our pocket?"

"Tomorrow."

"And without so much as a cravat?"

"Not to worry, my goodman," said Argon.

"No wig?"

Argon didn't say that he had pilfered Béjart's locked chest and taken a gold medallion in anticipation of the unforeseen.

Fleury settled into the lively stir of moving vehicles. As occasion presented itself, they asked of strangers the whereabouts of Palais Royal Theatre. Upon seeing a handbill with a map posted at a chandler's shop, they ripped it off the wall and tucked it into the wagon.

Fleury's hoofs rose and fell. A church bell gonged in the distance. "We are near the relic that Madame Thibaut prescribed.

I can feel it," said Argon. He didn't say the word *Molière*, for fear the sound might attract adverse spirits.

He belched loudly, leaned forward, and pointed when he saw the Lamont Butcherie, the landmark he had been told to look for. "The butcherie. This is where we turn."

Fleury snorted and pranced and as soon as they were on another street, the bell tower appeared in dark relief in the sky. Argon gasped with elation. Never had he been so pleased to see a cathedral spire. The grind of carriage wheels and the rapid clop-clop of horses replaced hawkers and hucksters. Cobblestones settled into their beds, free of stagnant ditches and clotted vegetables. The massive stone buildings of engravers, goldsmiths, and avocats cast shadows over the muggish roadway.

"We are in the land of lords and ladies," said Argon, entranced by bronze statues, marble tiling, and gold leaf gates. When the caravan scrubbed against a carriage, Eugene took the reins.

Eugene slowed as they approached the cathedral. "Hoy, Fleury!" They came to a stop at iron gates. On either side was a rushlight held in a wall bracket, one of which was ignited. At the other, a bewigged sexton stood on an inside platform lighting tallow-dipped strands.

"Good e'en!" Argon called with all the force he could give his voice. "I have wine for the bishop, may his holiness ever exceed in glory." He motioned toward the barrels in the back.

Eugene whispered, "What are you doing? We can't leave the wine here!"

"What do you say?" The sexton held up a torch.

Argon turned to Eugene. "Don't worry. Tell him what I said. Speak up." His eyes pleaded with Eugene.

Eugene called to the sexton, "Wine for your holiness."

"And what are you called?" The sexton narrowed his eyes.

"I am the Lord's servant, Argon." Argon's gravelly voice waned as if taken by the wind.

"What say you?" The sexton leaned his ear forward.

The sexton's squinty-eyed caution was taken to account by

the two young men trying to look like wine sellers rather than minstrels. "Argon, kind Master." Argon whispered forcefully.

Eugene took a deep breath and called with more confidence than he felt, "Argon, kind Master. And Eugene. With the wine."

"Ah, bon! An instant." The sexton disappeared behind finials. In a matter of moments, the portal slowly opened inward. As soon as the horse and caravan pulled inside, the sexton closed and latched the gates. "I'll lead you to the cuisine." He walked ahead, motioning them to follow. Fleury was slow to start, tired from pulling the weight. They inched into the shadow of the cathedral steeple, and somberness descended like the presence of universal darkness. Argon shivered.

"What are we to say to the sexton at L'Église Saint-Eustache when we arrive with no wine?" whispered Eugene.

"We will leave but one barrel here. Saint-Eustache will not notice one missing barrel."

As they made their way around the cathedral, they continued past a clean stone roadway that veered right toward the steps. Eugene allowed Fleury's footsteps to dawdle in passing, the better to see the cathedral's heavy wood doors carved with jovial but savage creatures. A round stained window glared above the portico, whose columns brought to mind bared teeth. Spiraling from the tower into the clouds like a finger pointed to heaven was a cross.

The sexton motioned them to proceed across the ward to the manse. Eugene swallowed. "Onward, Fleury!" A stagnant scent troubled the air. A biting chill touched their faces, so spiritual was the place. The wood wheels creaked and groaned in a speech goblins might understand.

"Hark, an unfavorable wind behaves badly." Eugene rubbed his nose.

"The legacy buried in yonder graveyard will protect us," said Argon.

The sexton turned back to the caravan. "Be quick! Allons-y!" He motioned them forward though Fleury kept to a lumbering pace and snorted. At a stark chestnut tree, one of two that grew near the manse, they halted. A cloud of smoke arose from the chimney of the stone building of modest dimensions.

The sexton pulled open the door and eagerly ordered a man-servant to prop it open while he scuttled inside. Out came a man servant big enough to carry the barrel of wine on his shoulder.

Eugene and Argon followed the wine to the kitchen but the sexton was nowhere about. The cavernous room was alight with candles and bustled with scullery maids and cooks. The servant threw down the barrel into a trough near the water urn.

Embedded in the center of one wall was a wide, shallow fire-place with a hood that vented smoke from bristling embers. Neither Argon nor Eugene had ever seen so many wall shelves so over-burdened with food stuffs — ewers of vinegar, bags of grain, baskets of root vegetables, crates of nuts, boxes of dried beans, chests of spices, metal tubs of grease. Instead of the common trodden-earth floor was an amazing foundation of paved tiles.

A manservant hammered the plug of the barrel loose, and ex-tracted it. As he watched, Argon said, "By my tun, it is a luckless day! Our wagon wheel wobbles like a drunken duck. It is about to fall off."

The manservant inserted a hollow reed into the plug hole. "Aye, aye! And I have an ugsome master!" he said returning the complaint.

The baker tended a pudding, a maid strained milk, butchers decapitated plucked geese. A commotion arose at the wide open hearth where a servant stirred a smoking pot that smelled of charred flour. The cook slammed his knife on the table and said, "Hellbound dolt!" He threw the roux out the door.

A door on the wall opposite the caravan opened suddenly and the sexton rushed in. From behind him came pleasant musical tones. Holding a flacon to the reed, the sexton tipped the barrel until wine flowed into it. As he smelled and tasted it, his wig shifted on his dome. "The seigneur expects quality superior to this." He smacked his lips sourly. "The reckoning will come to less."

Eugene gulped at an approaching dilemma. "We will not leave without the reckoning our employer requires us to deliver him."

Argon's cheeks flamed. The trouble was that the church had not ordered wine, at least not from the merchant owning the barrels they were delivering. And they only knew what they were supposed to get, not what the church usually paid for wine. Wine was not the matter. They were there to get the relic from Molière's grave. "Good sir, pay us a fair amount. If our master disagrees, the adjustment will be made to your reputation."

The sexton took out his money sack and placed a coin in Argon's hand, a paltry amount. Eugene gave Argon a wary look.

Sweat beaded Argon's forehead. "Prithee, allow us to remain long enough to repair the wheel of our wagon."

"Whatever is wrong with your wagon?"

In rushed a servant boy, raising a cloud of flour from the floor. "Monsieur! Fie upon me, but the new boy dropped the salt-cellars in the cistern."

The sexton's heavily lidded eyes gazed down his nose at the boy. To Argon he said, "Very well. Be gone ere the bishop arrives."

"Gramercy. I will work in the graveyard where only the dead be disquieted," said Argon to the sexton's flapping backside as he pushed the boy toward the door.

Argon filched a flickering taper from a table and left unnoticed, along with Eugene. With the caravan's torch lit, Eugene sat while Argon grabbed hold of Fleury's bridle and led them to the dark side of the church grounds where gravestones cast no shadows. They made their way through a mossy aisle inhabited by vapors and hemmed in by cedars and gravestones. It was narrow and the wheels scraped the back of a gravestone.

Eugene gazed into the darkness with wide eyes.

Argon felt souls under his boots and heard sniveling. Fleury resisted his tug on the reins, stamped and halted. He whispered to the horse, "Passerby, give at least a sigh or two for this enlightened spirit." Fleury took hesitant steps forward. Argon murmured, "And say, approaching his grave, Farewell laughter."

"Are those Béjart's words?" Eugene said.

"They are his, but he is not the first to say them." There was so much pilfering of plays from one troupe to another hardly a versifier in all of France could safeguard his work.

"Alas! I have stepped on a grave." Argon stopped. He picked up his foot as if he'd landed in pig dung. To offset ill fortune, he released Fleury and walked backward in his footprints until Eugene said, "How far is far enough to rid your foot of a vengeful spirit?"

Knowing Molière's burial had not been sanctioned by the church, they trudged to the unconsecrated sector of suicides, unknown babies, and the unbaptized.

Argon shone his light on the occasional wood marker with a name carved into it. At the inscription "J. B. P." he took inspiration into his lungs. "This is it," he whispered to Eugene.

"What is this J. B. P. ?" said Eugene.

"Jean Baptiste Poquelin. That was his name."

"Why did he not use his name?"

"Ah, it is said his father was a person of high quality, not one to want an actor in the family."

They dragged their shovels from under sackcloth and dug by torch light. "Did you hear that?" Eugene paused, shovel in hand. Laughter came from different directions, as if a horde of spectral jesters shuffled through the cedars.

"It is the bishop's banquet … echoing in the trees." Argon's hands trembled under the weight of the mools. His brow burned with sweat. He wet his finger with spit and put it behind his ear to protect against sorcery. Their shovels gouged and chunked. And clunked into something. The earth underfoot creaked. "Out! Belay! Before it breaks in," said Eugene as he climbed out of the hole.

Fleury stamped and pulled at the reins tied to a cedar tree. "Steady, Fleury." Eugene caressed the horse's nose and ears. He broke a twig from a cedar and brushed the scent about the horse's neck and mane. "This grim shadow will pass," he whispered in her nervous ear.

Argon, who had also climbed out, turned back into the hole, cautiously placing his feet in two corners. He crouched down and dug with his fingers. The wind delivered an awful racket. They paused to listen. "Cats," said Eugene. Argon scraped dirt from a wood board. A crack groaned under his foot. Before he could jump out, the ground collapsed and his boot caved into a hollow. "By God's piss!" He hauled himself out of the grave.

"Merde!" said Eugene on seeing Argon's glistening boot. "What a stink!"

At first, even with torch light, they could not discern what they saw. Dirt. Splinters. They wedged a shovel under a board and pulled it up. Hair stuck to the bottom side. A ringlet. Several long black curls. The hair pulled free of the board and fell back into the coffin. Argon pulled up another board. Another. Putrid and noxious shocks of air blew into their faces. The two of them fell away and gasped for air. Eugene hurried to the far side of the caravan. When Fleury's high-pitched neighing threatened to expose them, he whispered, "Easy, Fleury. Aye. Calm-toi." He guided the horse and caravan down the tow path several rods distant from the grave. And there he lay on the ground.

"Tant pis! This is what has become of the greatest actor of our age." Argon hacked up spit until his throat was dry. Blew his nose on leaves. Wiped his face with his sleeve. Sat and stared at the open grave.

"I cannot go there," said Eugene from the dark.

Argon thought the same. But he must have the finger bone for his voice. He crawled to the edge of the grave. With his fingertips, he pulled a ringlet of hair and the entire mound moved. "Alak! It is beset by the devil!" He flung it back. "Damnation! It is a wig."

Though Eugene lay with his eyes shut, he could see the body in the coffin, the wig with a profusion of black curls. "Without a proper funeral but with a proper wig." He whistled through his teeth.

With the wig out of place, maggots gave motion to muck in the skull's pockets.

"'Tis a miserable lot, this dishonorable grave for one blessed by God with eloquence and talent." Eugene stared at the moon and held his sleeve across his nose.

"'Tis miserable the dishonor God has done to bring a body to this." Argon recalled the likeness he had seen of Molière on a frontispiece Béjart kept in his chest. "From this wretched mess, nobody would know of his proud visage." He rolled over to the edge of the grave, reached down, and touched the slick covering of a cheek bone. He withdrew his finger and rubbed it in the ground until dry. "Béjart said his nose was thick, his lips too."

An ungodly cry came from a towering tree. "An owl," said Eugene, "gagging on fetid air." A cloud's shadow glided through the moonlight. Fleury chomped and stamped. In a soft and reassuring voice Eugene said, "Not to worry, Fleury. The stink will not harm you. Nor the Gods of the dead. Keep your feet still, little one."

"They called him a foolish scribbler," said Argon.

"Damnation, let us be done with this." Eugene returned to the grave.

Argon tugged on the corpse's foremost finger bone on the right hand, but it was rigid. He tried the little finger bone, which fell away. So moist was the bone he dipped it in the freshly dug dirt, rubbed it with dirt, and put it into his pocket.

The corpse's lace collar of red silk appeared hardly spoiled, irresistible to Argon as more bounty. He tugged at it only to have the skull fall away, dribbling a wormy trail. The skull's flight was virtually into his hand. He took this as a mystical signal and reached down with both hands to remove it. "The skull will be the most powerful of any relic."

Its condition necessitated a quick and thorough cleansing in dirt. Argon stuffed dirt inside and scrubbed everywhere with a grainy wash until the skull's white bone shone in the moonlight.

Eugene had backed into the dark.

"Put this in the wagon," he put it forward to Eugene.

"Fie on you! I will not lay hand on it."

As Argon got up and tucked it into the compartment under

the driver's bench, a large toad hopped into and out of the torch light. He gasped at what appeared to be the Devil's mark on its back and scrambled clumsily after it. "God's Fury! This graveyard is polluted!" He stomped wildly but the toad disappeared, as if swallowed by the ground.

Argon took a breath, picked up his shovel, and flung dirt back into the grave. Eugene found his shovel. The noise of the bishop's party had died down. A breeze sloshed in the trees. The moon raised images in the grass.

The scrub and whiff of their shovels stopped at a sudden cry and loud rush. A nighthawk's wings flapped so near Argon's head he lost his balance and stumbled against the J. B. P. wood marker. It toppled into the open pit. "Arrrgh!" Argon barely saved himself from falling into the grave on top of it. "God's wounds!"

The J. B. P. wood lay wedged in the dirt above Molière's rib bones. Argon poked his shovel at it and tried to retrieve it.

"Do not trouble yourself with the marker." Eugene looked at the eastern sky. "We needs be at the gate before first light."

They shoveled more dirt on the broken coffin and marker. Argon said, "We will come back and put up a marker."

When the grave had been refilled, they spread mulch and leaves over the new-turned dirt. Argon climbed into the back of the caravan while Eugene walked them back through the headstones. Once past the graves, they set forth. "Ho, Fleury. Hie hoof!"

At the gate the sexton, his eyes red and veined, merely waved them through behind a sedan cab departing at the same time.

The light of their torch reflected off houses with dark windows that lined the quiet street. Chancing upon a park with an oil street lamp, Eugene pulled Fleury aside, tied the lines to a hitching post, squeezed in back with Argon, and fell asleep.

☙ Scene 43 ❧
stage of unsurpassed grandeur

Fleury's snorts woke Argon. He roused and saw two villains attempting to unhitch their horse. He yelled, "Fie and aroint with thee!" and chased them away.

The morning was well spent delivering the barrels of wine to L'Église Saint-Eustache. "Sirrah, there are but four casks of wine," said the cleric overseeing the wine cellar at the priests' manor house.

"Good sir, if you please, we were set-upon by brigands. We galloped to get away and one cask broke the back gate and fell out," said Argon. "Prithee, we were able to escape by grace of a company of dragoons, which frightened them away."

Eugene nodded his head, as if to swear the truth to Argon's fable. The cleric made no protestations, but deducted for the cask that had not been delivered.

With an empty caravan, they bumped more easily along the streets of Paris.

In readying to attend the play at the Palais Royal, Argon and Eugene resorted to thievery to improve their habiliment. For a sou, they hired young rapscallions to snatch two wigs from chance gentlemen on the street. They spent from their wine receipts to pay for a fish dinner in a fine auberge where they stealthily exchanged their cloaks for more fashionable doublets.

Afterwards they parked the caravan in a stall and dressed themselves. The two wigs, though obviously impressive, had to be cleaned of twigs and leaves. Without skullcaps, they applied hog's fat around their hairline. Eugene set on his head the massive wig with an over-abundance of black curls that covered his back and shoulders.

"I'll look better in that wig." Argon was trying on a full bottom curly wig but one not so high.

"Yes, you will." Eugene gratefully handed over his heavy wig, for he was getting a headache from just moments in its employ.

"In troth! My neck needs be iron to keep my head up." Argon tied the ribbons to secure the wig.

They examined the doublets, one of brocade and one of velvet, one large and one ordinary. Since the previous summer, Argon had grown to approximate Eugene in size. "Which one of us will look less ludicrous in a doublet too large?" said Argon.

"I will follow you this night. I will wear the big one," said Eugene.

They climbed out the door and woke up Fleury and traveled to a public stable near the theater where they left the caravan and horse in the care of an ostler. With tickets they bought at the door, they wandered among the early arrivals to the parterre, their appearance of a quality to raise no eyebrows as long as no gaze fell lower than the tail of their doublets.

Where they stood became more crowded as the hour neared for the opening scene of *The Misanthrope*. The more people, the more shoving closer to the stage. The heavier the air with flowery perfume. It was impossible to avoid being jostled. "There's many a pickpocket about the theater," whispered Eugene, knowing full well that Argon might be one.

"To filch our francs, one will fondle my breechcloth." Argon hitched up his male parts.

Candelabras with as many as fifty branches were lowered by pulleys from the ceiling. Pushing through the melee were two officials, one with a tinderbox and one with a taper. When a candelabra reached a reachable height, they lit the candles after which the candelabra was hoisted back up to a good distance above the hats and wigs.

The auditorium was of a height that three tiers of galleries shot upward on either side. "Have you ever seen a chamber so big?" said Argon. Nymphs, angels, and musical instruments in shades of gold and blue glowed in bas-relief on the balcony rows.

"My eyes are blinded by the gold." Despite poor eyesight, Eugene could see the gilded scrollwork framing the galleries.

"And the ceiling!"

Eugene tipped his chin up. "How did artists get up that high to paint those pictures?"

Argon's gazes took in galleries divided into loges teeming with padded women dressed in princess coats and long cashmere shawls. Never had he seen so many festooned women.

Even short men were tall with wigs and high heels, much in the King's fashion. Bejeweled jerkins. Flourishes met with bows. Elegant laughter was delivered with luster and brilliance.

Argon's wandering eyes halted at a gallery section near the stage, second tier. He gasped. Isabelle was entering ahead of the man he recognized. Argon swallowed to ease a numbing pain in his chest.

Eugene caught sight of Isabelle too. Her costume excelled in stiffened satin and padded sleeves. Her carriage hinted of triumph. The flamboyant waft of her feathered fan took attention from other patrons.

"It is he, Lord Dubois." Eugene nodded toward the bewigged man accompanying her.

"The gallery is full of lords. How do you know Dubois from another?"

"Do you not remember him from Count Gondrin's festivities?" Eugene mumbled.

"Oui, it is him. A dull witted buffoon." Argon had come to realize Dubois was the stranger who had pursued the Troupe well before Chateau de Giffaumont. "He wooed Isabelle even as she warmed Béjart's bed." Argon's blood rose in his veins for the insult to Béjart.

"He is not so dull witted. He charmed Isabelle into leaving with him," said Eugene.

"How can you be sure?" Argon's naiveté was his way of ignoring what he didn't want to believe, that Isabelle had chosen to abandon him and his father.

"She disappeared the same time that he took leave of Chateau de Giffaumont," said Eugene.

Argon looked at his grubby boots. At least Isabelle had won first class shoes for herself. "He is but Isabelle's chance to play a part such as Célimène in a room such as this … with gallery seats." Argon made no effort to strengthen his voice. "And on a stage of unsurpassed grandeur. Forsooth, a painted backdrop." His arm motioned toward the stage, accidentally brushing a man's wig.

The man turned. His blackened eyebrows twisted toward his eyes. His thick rouged lips spat out, "Shackles and the prison-house shall punish the next offence of this kind."

"God save me, monsieur, for in truth your injury is my grief." Argon shuffled to distance himself, taking care to remain in sight of Isabelle, who had taken a seat in a gilded loge.

From the moment the actor playing Alceste took the stage, Argon watched enthralled, overpowered by the excellence of the actors, the costumes, and the scenery. That the Augusto Troupe was no match for this level of entertainment came as a melancholy realization.

After overcoming the shock of seeing Isabelle, he understood her desire to be in Paris, in the company of celebrated actors. He shared her ambition to win the approval, if not adulation, of a grand audience.

Despite a flawless performance, he knew Isabelle could have played Célimène better. His throat ached as he thought of her watching the play, her heart beating with disenchantment as she watched an actor of talent inferior to hers play the part of Célimène.

The final scene was rewarded with gleeful applause. Flowers glided to the stage and landed at the feet of the actors. As they headed out, Argon said, "I have to find her."

"Wherefore? Even if she agrees to return to Augusto, Béjart will not take her back."

"I have to see her."

"For what? She has forsaken you." Eugene scurried to keep up as Argon, holding on to his wig, slipped through the throng of painted ladies and gallant gentlemen.

"You misjudge her. She did not forsake me," said Argon. The precious parties of gilded people gave way to him as if he were a crawling insect.

"Mayhap you think eternal thoughts like your horse." Eugene trailed behind him.

"Isabelle!" Argon called when her wig came into view. He hardly noticed the encumbrance of scarlet cloaks, gold embroidery, silk slippers, floppy hats, and turbans.

She turned toward him, and when her eyes lit on Argon she paused as Lord Dubois strode ahead. A puzzled expression came to her face. Argon waved, nodded to her, and smiled recklessly. Forgotten was his resentment. Forgotten was his loneliness for her.

"Argon! Ave! It is truly you," she said.

He approached and kissed her cheeks. The sheen of expensive pearl powder did not conceal the mark of time on her face. Nor did vermillion paint. Thus enameled, she gazed with eyes that had lost the gleam of mischief.

Argon wiped his nose on his hand, so strong was her perfume. "Will you come with me?" He blurted out without forethought. He urged her out of the grinding stream of people exiting the doorway.

"Is Béjart with you?" Isabelle's hand trembled as she fanned her face.

"No." Argon fought tears. Too many black patches were on her face, no mere beauty marks. Thick paste filled her cheeks. The powdered skin of her neck lacked firmness.

Eugene, who had pushed his way through the crowd, stopped beside them. "Isabelle." He nodded in greeting.

"We will be trampled. Let us go outside." Isabelle led the way.

The heavy scent of perfume dispersed. A carriage halted some three paces distant. Lord Dubois stuck his head out the window. "Are you coming with me?"

Isabelle waved to him and said to Argon. "Come to my

apartment tonight. Knock at the door: tap-tap-tap, tap." She whispered her address.

Argon and Eugene retrieved their horse and caravan from the stable and paid the ostler with wine money.

✳

At Isabelle's apartment, located above a printer's shop, Eugene waited on the street with the horse and caravan while Argon climbed the stairs.

"She made no answer," Argon said when he returned.

"Let us set off for Brancion," Eugene said, knowing in his heart that Argon was courting disappointment.

"We will wait." Argon sat on the caravan seat. Eugene crawled into the back and lay down and was soon asleep.

The moon came up so bright it cast shadows. Two workers left the printer's shop and joined stragglers on their way to their homes. The printer closed his shutters and locked his door. Fleury slept. Eugene snored. A man emerged from Isabelle's apartment door. It was not Lord Dubois.

"Eugene!" Argon shook his shoulder. "Be watchful while I am gone." Eugene climbed from the back and slumped in the seat as Argon crossed the street.

Isabelle stared at Argon. Argon swallowed thick and took her hand. She pulled his face to her cheek. "Do you hate me?"

Argon's feet caught in her ample robe of dense silk brocaded with gold leaves and red violets. "Do you love that fop?"

She stroked Argon's short hair. Leon had cut it short, for now he considered himself mature enough to wear a wig more commonly. "No. But he knows Claude Deschamps. He has promised that I will perform at the Palais Royal." Her buoyancy rang hollow.

Argon detected a note of despair. "You have yet to act in a play?"

"He says it takes time to arrange it."

Argon said, "Months, Isabelle?"

She was swaying. She sat on a velvet chair bordered with gold stitches. She swallowed as if to raise the energy to set straight her backbone.

"Come back to the Augusto Troupe." Argon did not sit in the lounge chair. Its red sheen was blighted by what could have been scum left by men.

"He will give me the chance I've waited a lifetime for. I cannot leave now."

"Do you not see? He is not an honorable man."

"Argon, you judge him harshly. When you are back at the Troupe, tell them I played the part of Célimène in *The Misanthrope* at the Palais Royale."

"Wherefore? It will only cause pain for Béjart."

"He deserves pain." She coughed as if a frog croaked in her chest.

"You judge him harshly. He loves you."

"He has too much love for himself to care for any other person."

"He is a better man by far than your royal asshole."

"At least I am not sleeping in a crate and rattling over the provinces. At least I have a feather bed!" She arose unsteadily, poured herself a beaker of wine, and drank.

"Will you come back for my sake?" Argon did not say he loved her, that he missed her, that he was afraid for her future. "We have a wagon. We can take from here belongings to make your caravan even more comfortable."

She gave him a wan smile. "I am sorry about leaving you." She looked away from him. She poured more wine. Drank more.

Argon's face turned pink. He rubbed his nose and stroked his whiskers. "Will you come with me?"

"The Palais Royale is planning to start rehearsals for *Le Cid*. Lord Dubois has promised that I will be given a role. Some day you will tell people that you are the son of the Grand Dame Isabelle. Who knows, I may play Célimène for the king."

As Argon wrapped his arms around her to say farewell, he felt a tremor in her heartbeat.

He returned to the caravan crestfallen and climbed on the seat beside Eugene. They drove the quiet street.

☙ Scene 44 ❧
bad meat

Argon and Eugene parked behind a public bath house and slept for the night. The following morning they got directions to the roadway that took them from the city. Vendors milling along the streets slowed their passage. The smells of smoke, horse dung, old sweat, and musty walls filled the air. An old woman, her head and shoulders wrapped in a woolen scarf, sat beside the road at a barrel of cabbages and shouted, "Aroint thee!" at a worrisome urchin while another stole a cabbage.

"Verily, *The Misanthrope* will abide in my dreams," said Eugene.

"Never will Béjart believe Isabelle is in Paris." Argon flushed with the excitement of horses, carriages, and shouting vendors surrounding them.

"Will you tell him?" said Eugene. Fleury snorted at a passing horse pulling a cart.

Argon stared ahead. "Mayhap Béjart can get her to return to the Troupe." He resisted the temptation to jump off the caravan and stay in Paris forever.

"You will tell him of going to the theater?"

"A whisper to Georgette and the entire Troupe will know. Béjart has ears." The sizzle of a pig roasting in a galley floated a mouth-watering scent. "Isabelle knew what she was doing," he said.

"Nobody mistook Isabelle for a doxy."

"Except me."

"What ho?" said Eugene.

"I thought she tormented Béjart about other women. But she wanted better lines, better comedy, better costumes."

They passed an open window where an entire cow, roasting

over an open pit, spit fat into a fire that sparked and hissed. Several customers lingered alongside the street slorping morsels of a hindquarter.

"Pull Fleury aside," said Argon. "I'll get a bit of meat." He bounced to the road and said to a broad-shouldered cook with massive arms, "Good sir, a portion of meat!" Argon leaned over a young boy wiping up drizzle from the ground with his fingers and sucking them.

With a cleaver the man carved off meat which he lapped on a trencher of bread. Argon offered several derniers.

"Don't insult me with derniers! A sou!" the cook shouted, withdrawing the meat in his leathery hand, glistening with grease, his fingernails horned with grime. "A sou! For the finest cut and my mother's bread!"

Argon's black, strongly marked eyebrows rose in disgust. Even he knew the price was exorbitant, but the smell of the charred meat cast a spell.

From the roadway came a shout of "Out of the way! Get along with you!" A driver in passing the caravan clumsily veered into a woodmonger's stack of faggots, knocking them into the street. The woodmonger shook his fist and shouted, "Accursed clout!"

Fleury reared. Eugene clenched his fists on the reins. "Ho, Fleury!"

Argon dug into the leather pouch hanging around his neck, paid the sou, and hurried back to the caravan, which had advanced perhaps a furlong down the street. The hot bread warmed his fingers. Before they reached the corner, he had gulped down several bites before offering it to Eugene.

Eugene was put off by the pungent taste. "What say? A strange flavor. Mayhap Spanish spices?"

"Verily, you have been gnawing hog jowls in the shires too long." Argon paused after a bite to inspect the appearance of the meat. He glanced at Eugene and, in spite of uncertainty said, "Ne'er so fine a fare as this in the provinces."

"If this be meat to fetch a sou, then turn my tongue to pigeon liver." Eugene spat out a mouthful that landed on the pavement where cats licked at it.

"Don't throw it away. I will eat it." Argon grabbed what remained.

Auberges and taverns gave way to cottages and farmhouses. "Hoy, Fleury! Prithee, more drama in thy hoof!" said Eugene. He slapped the lines and the horse picked up the pace. The road wound through open fields and thick woods. Argon finished what turned out to be a squishy blob of fat that oozed between his fingers. It slippered into his mouth as if such fare might calm the discontent roaring inside him. Leaving Paris distanced the dream of a lifetime. Losing Isabelle was no easier the second time.

"You fault Isabelle for leaving Augusto Troupe?" said Eugene.

"Béjart himself would abandon us if he had a chance to appear at the Palais Royal," said Argon.

The sun stretched the heavens. Flies curried Fleury's hair. The riggings grated. Argon's farts outsmelled Fleury's. Flocks of birds fed in the wheat fields. The day was growing long. Argon braced his hand on the rough wood of the seat and steadied himself. They needed rest to revive their weary bones.

Argon groaned and held his midriff.

"What befalls?" Eugene said.

"My belly goes to rot."

"Drink water." Eugene reached behind the seat for the jug.

"This rickety road bestirrs my stomach." Argon drank and spat water.

Sunset gave forth such reds and oranges to raise restless spirits. They passed a thicket of beeches and came upon a newly plowed field.

Argon doubled over, holding his stomach. "Begad! My belly's split with a spontoon."

"We will stop in a trice. Rest calm."

A commotion shocked the quiet field. The horse took to a gallop. "Steady … steady." Eugene clutched the reins. A covey of black birds flew over them, brought to light in the gloaming.

"Eaassy, eaassy." And Fleury settled into a trot. "Black birds ..." Eugene didn't like the looks of them.

Argon's bowels roared gaseous into his clothes and his belly churned. His fevered sight perceived ghastly formations on the horizon. He belched up a mouthful and spat on the ground.

"Mayhap this skull is enchanted with evil," said Eugene.

"Nay. It will bring us good fortune."

A looming object took shape, and as they advanced, a farmhouse stood silhouetted in the dark. They approached with the hope of finding safe quarter. Eugene knocked on the door. Argon, leaning on the wall, knocked louder. A sound of movement inside. A dim glow in a window. "Hélas, Goodman, excuse the hour and have pity on poor travelers," Eugene said.

The door cracked open. A candle appeared and bleary eyes stared at them from a face over flushed with cutaneous eruptions.

"Prithee, kindly allow us to sleep in your stable." Eugene spoke up, for Argon began to tremble. Fleury snorted and shimmied in the moonlit yard.

"By faith, garçon. You look like a specter in this light." The farmer held his candle up to Eugene's prominent nose. "But hear now, I am a man of charity, but I am no fool and this is not a monastery. By God's mercy, I have a stable, built with these hands." He displayed his knobby, scarred fingers. "And built a shelter for my livestock." The stubble on his chin moved with his lips, which barely covered his dark teeth. "And being of goodwill, I will allow you respite this night if you but show goodwill on the morrow."

"Aye. We will return your hospitality to great benefit," said Eugene, putting his arm around Argon, who was swaying.

"By the cock's crow, bring firewood from the shed to the trestle at the kitchen door. And be so good as to milk the cow and bring the pail to the back door."

"Gramercy, good sir," said both Argon and Eugene.

"There is water in the trough by the wellspring, good and free." The farmer pointed his chubby finger. "Hay for your horse, you shall pay a denier." He held out his palm. Whisperings echoed from inside. Eugene paid the farmer who closed the door.

As they led Fleury to the trough for water, Argon hied out of sight behind the barn. Moments later on returning, he spit several times and wiped his mouth. He leaned on the sideboard. "You will unhitch Fleury?" Argon said, obviously unable to do so himself.

"Aye. Give you good night."

While Argon went into the barn, Eugene parked the caravan on the far side of a dilapidated outbuilding near an oak surrounded by unused farm equipment—iron wheel rims, an axle, a plow stock. He unhitched Fleury, left the wagon, and walked the horse to the barn where he put it in one of the empty stalls facing a central aisle. From other stalls came the rustle and whinnies of the farmer's horses.

Argon lay in a stall with loose hay that was spotted with dried mud and other droppings. He belched loudly.

Eugene filled his flacon with water from the wellspring. "Here, drink this to your fill," he said to Argon. "Your belly be more swollen than the purse of a moneylender." After Argon took water, Eugene cratered thatch and sat on it near his friend. His head rested against the partition wall, his breathing went slow and deep. He closed his eyes.

Argon's hasty flight into the dark farmyard roused Eugene from a chase he was losing to an executioner. He roused from the nightmare at the sound of Argon's retching. In a matter of moments, Argon returned to the stall and collapsed on the hay. Eugene wiped his friend's mouth and chin with his shirt and gave him more water. During the night, Argon made more flights to the perimeter.

Like an orchestra tuning to begin, light played on the horizon. Several cocks crowed. Inside the farmhouse, the farmer ate a trench of bread with belly meat and drank warmed wine.

"You cannot leave me here alone with those men," said his wife, who had no courage for life since losing their one infant.

"What do you say? Who will take shovels to the vineyard and get the tillers at their task?" He sipped the sweetened wine.

"I will go with you."

"And leave the house to two strangers?"

Her lips quivered on her cup of warmed milk sweetened with honey. "Why do we not have a doorman? Your parsimony will be the death of me."

He stood and grabbed his hat. "Don't go so straight faced, my pet. I will return forthwith. Should the strangers fail in their tasks, do not attempt to put them aright. Have a care for your humours and do not invite too much choler with worry."

He slammed the solid door as he left and went to the barn for a horse. In the shadowy light of early morning he peeked into the stall and saw the travelers sleeping on the hay. A smell of vomit curled his nose hairs. With an expression as sour as the smell, he hitched his horse to his wagon, loaded shovels, and headed to the vineyard, some dozen furlongs distant.

Argon awoke, staggered up and slumped on the stall. Eugene grabbed around his waist. "Get me away," Argon moaned. He heaved mucus and dropped back down on the hay.

"Hoy, Argon, we needs find a doctor," said Eugene. "As soon as I do the farmer's chores."

With a sense of impending urgency, he hitched Fleury to the caravan parked near the oak. In the unused farm equipage, he spied a discarded ax with a cracked handle, which he put into the caravan. At the wood shed, he carelessly and hurriedly loaded split logs into the back of the caravan and carted them to the trestle at the backdoor. By stacking them unevenly, there appeared to be more than there was. All the while the cow mooed plaintively, but nature urged him to sit at stool, so he hid behind the barn.

On returning to the barn he encountered the wife with an empty milk bucket in hand. She had lifted the caravan seat, which was the lid of the trunk.

Eugene said, "Good mistress! 'tis unseemly to plunder what is not yours." He slammed down the lid, barely missing her fingers. Inside was the skull, put there in a blanket.

She shrank back. "What is this?" She pointed to the trunk.

Eugene said, "Medicinal potions, good wife. We have been on a quest to find a cure for my friend's bedeviled throat."

After a look at Argon, who was curled up and rasping through his nose, she backed away from them. "There betides more than an ill throat."

Eugene said, "He ate bad meat in Paris."

She shoved the bucket at him. "Lo! 'Tis behind time to milk the cow." She put the bucket on the ground. "Knock at the back door when you have the bucket full."

Eugene picked up the bucket and headed toward the cow barn which was beside a decrepit building with loose stones and a collapsing roof. The door, though hanging from its hinges, was nonetheless locked. A smell, perhaps wet feathers, made his nose tingle and he quickly turned away.

The miserable cow's swollen teats did not fill the bucket. He squeezed, pulled, tugged, and squashed the teats while avoiding her nervous hoofing maneuvers. After getting as much as he could, he filled his flacon with milk for Argon and knocked at the door with a bucket well nigh full after he had topped it off with water. The wife stuck her head out. "Leave the bucket on the stoop," she said, a kerchief to her nose and her eyes closed.

"Goodwife, have you a morsel of food you might share with us?" said Eugene, for they had nothing to eat.

"I will leave bread on the step." She blinked. It was common knowledge that underworld creatures charmed victims with their eyes and made people into slaves of darkness.

Eugene waited on the steps until she said, "Come back in a spell. I have to feed the cats."

With dogs and cats about the place, Eugene had sense enough to keep an eye on the steps for the bread. In the meantime curiosity got the best of him, and he returned to the decrepit building with loose stones and a caving roof and peeked through cracks in the door until the smell once again sent a tingle into his face. Rumors of wolves in the provinces came to mind.

The farmer, annoyed that the cart of manure he had ordered from the village ostler had not arrived, drove his wagon into the courtyard. His breathless wife met him and whispered urgently, "Forsooth, they have a skull. They are minions of sorcery."

He smelled the wine on her and said, "Ducky, you are more than half drunk."

"By my trowth, I saw it with my own eyes. You must get the priest," she said.

Eugene saw the farmer return and depart without so much as a word to either of them. His intuition was telling him to leave while hungry rather than wait for food, but he circled the yard, hopeful for a crumb from the kitchen. Just as he decided to get Argon into the caravan and leave, the wife opened the back door. "Here is bread for you and your friend."

She took care that her fingers did not touch his hands as she delivered a hard crust, no more bread than she fed the cats. "Come back, I have potage." Her upper lip twitched disagreeably.

Eugene tore off a bite as he left the door, his tongue gloried in the taste. Argon took a crumb, most of which either stuck to his lip or fell onto his shirt. He chewed so long he fell into a stupor. Eugene woke him with a nudge. "Swallow your bread!"

Eugene touched Argon's forehead but no demon of hell burned his hand. He knew his friend did not have plague, for he was acquainted with the telltale signs from Brother Vallans, who had attended sick beds. However, the finger of death was pointing at Argon. "God, the Father in heaven, have mercy on us," mumbled Eugene.

He awaited the wife's potage, for Argon needed nourishment. Eugene lay on the hay, for the odor of dried grain had turned into a smell of burnt wood, a smell he associated with moments he most feared. His arms twitched, his fingers tingled, his body, as rigid

as armor, thumped the floor. He heard Argon's groan as a clap of
thunder.

The farmer's wife reappeared with a bowl of thin broth.
"Garcon! Here is potage..." She looked wide-eyed at Eugene,
stifled a scream and dropped the bowl. The wood door of the
farmhouse slammed shut loud as thunder. Clink went the lock.

Eugene recovered his senses. Despite his weakened state, he felt
a premonition of danger.

Inside the house, the wife locked the door and pushed a table
against it. Clutching the rosary, she prayed with desperation, not
knowing whether the demon would want her for food or sex.

She peeked from the cuisine window. A person of raw nerves,
she dreaded people she didn't know. Though every door of the
house was a bastion of wood and iron, she went about to see that
the bolts rested in their retainers. She cursed her husband, notwithstanding that he was doing her bidding by fetching a priest.

Eugene brought the caravan near Argon and tethered Fleury to a
barn post. "We must be gone." He heaved him into the back and
closed the gate. By the time Eugene noticed the noise of a horse
behind him, he was knocked down by a blow in the back.

"Get up!" The farmer stood with two other men. One, whose
build and demeanor had a likeness to the farmer, said, "Grave
robber!"

"What are you doing with a human skull?" said the farmer.

Eugene swallowed a lump of fear and said, "It is the skull of
my father. I am taking it for a proper burial in our family tomb."
Argon, who hardly moved in the wagon, wheezed.

A carriage rolled into the yard with two more men, shortly at
the barn, one of them wearing the tunic of a priest.

"Where is Father Unity?" said the farmer.

"He is on a pilgrimage to Santiago de Compostela," said the
man in a tunic.

"Father Bastide is the vicar serving in his stead," said the driver.

"Father, may God protect us, this man possesses a human skull." The farmer opened the trunk of the caravan for the cleric.

"A grave robber, he is," said another.

Upon seeing the skull, the priest reared back and held up his pectoral cross. Others shuffled behind him.

"Nay! He misspeaks," said Eugene. "'Tis the skull of my father. With a seer's help I found it. It belongs in the grave our family made for him."

"May Saint Peter protect us," mumbled one of the men.

"This man is possessed of demons. My wife saw it with her own eyes." The farmer pointed at Eugene.

"Pagans!" one said and held up his wood cross.

"It is my mother's wish that my father's skull return to its grave!" said Eugene.

"He trembled and spat and rolled his eyes. He is possessed by the devil!" whined the farmer's wife.

"'Tis God's curse!" said one of the men, retreating near the portal. The others gave Eugene ample sphere.

"God's wrath." The men crossed themselves.

Argon, in a muddled state, groaned and farted a stink so disgusting it escaped from the caravan into the barn.

The farmer opened the caravan's gate. Argon lay on the floor.

"The plague!"

"Verily, he ate bad meat," Eugene said.

"They're demons!"

"Evil-boden."

"May God protect my home from the devil's minions." The wife crossed herself and kissed her rosary.

Father Bastide, holding up the cross, said, "Goodman, do you have a document of permission from your priest to disturb a grave?"

Eugene stepped forward as the men inched back. "Father, my priest gave his word."

"Wherefore is your parish?" said Father Bastide.

Eugene chose to avoid Brancion and said, "Paris."

"Paris is of numerous parishes, my goodman."

"Yes, it is Saint Joseph's."

"Who is your priest?" said Father Bastide.

Eugene provided the only name he knew. "Father Vallans."

The priest turned and spoke quietly to the men, who gathered close.

Their voices grew louder, first one and then the other. "No! You!" "No, not me."

"Come on!" said the farmer, who broke away and pulled one of the men with him.

They grabbed Eugene by his jerkin and yanked him into the yard where the sun shone as if God smiled on this affair. They threw him to the ground and tied a rope around his torso. Eugene cried out, "I am but a minstrel! With Augusto Troupe!" Horses in the courtyard, frightened by the scuffle and shouts, stamped the ground. "I am a harmless jongleur. I play the lute!" His shrill voice echoed on the surrounding stone walls.

Fleury snorted and yanked on the tether. The courtyard horses churned against their harnesses and neighed. Dogs darted and growled.

"Get up!" said several men.

"I purge evil spirits with my music," Eugene shouted.

When an aggressive dog nipped a horse's fetlocks, the animal raised both hind legs off the ground and kicked the yapping dog, sending it in flight across the yard.

Eugene struggled as the men towed him across the back yard. "I am a musician! Prithee! A mere musician!"

They dragged him toward the building with loose stones, a caving roof, and the smell of rodent nests. One man threw a rope with a noose over a branch of the nearby oak tree. It swung back and forth as a sharp breeze blew in from the field.

Eugene rolled on the ground, kicking and shouting, "I beseech you! Patience."

It took several men to haul him up on an old unused wine press barrel under the tree.

"I have no magic. If I was a sorcerer, I would turn you into bats!" he screamed. "I implore you!" He wiggled and squirmed.

From inside the dilapidated building arose ear-splitting squeals that grew louder. Through a crack in the roof flew a torrent of mayhem. The sky clouded with shadowy twitches. At once the men cowered, some dropped to the ground and crouched at the barrel, others flattened themselves against the stone wall. Some scurried toward the safety of the house. Above their heads, bat wings surged like a cyclone of cinders. Their ticks and pips swelled and burst in screeches.

Eugene sprang from the barrel and ran toward the barn. Dogs chased him, leaping and yelping. He escaped them by jumping into the caravan with Argon, who tried to sit. "Aargh!" Argon yelled at the dogs charging the caravan gate. Vomit burst from his mouth, which he aimed at the dogs.

Eugene freed himself by cutting the rope with the ax he had filched. He grabbed a pitchfork from a hay pile and fought off the hysterical dogs. "Away with you!" With a powerful "Arrrgh!" he stabbed and stuck until they retreated.

He pulled Fleury and the caravan outside, climbed into the seat and, with Argon lying in the back, called out, "Hoy, Fleury! Hoy!" The wheels bumped over the stony courtyard past the tethered horses, some of which reared, others pawed or stomped, wrenching their bridles.

The dogs chased them, yapping and jumping. "Onward!" Eugene flayed Fleury. The dogs rammed into one another, growled, and yelped and started a dog brawl.

The pitch and tumble of the caravan rattled Argon and, despite his trembling, he managed to hold on to the side rail. "Begone!" he bawled to a specter that confused him. His breath came in whooshes.

"Hold on, mon ami." Eugene glanced rearward and saw that dust obscured the farm. "Hoy, Fleury! Hurry! Hurry!" The lines flared in his hands.

Argon tumbled backward. Eugene slowed long enough for Argon to secure a hold. "Grab on to the seat," said Eugene as he slapped the lines on Fleury. "Go, Fleury!"

Fleury fled at a rattling pace past a fresh turned field and approached a woods. From the opposite direction came a cart filled with manure and drawn by an unwary ox. The driver was preoccupied with a silver snuff box he had pilfered from his wife's mistress.

"Move aside," yelled Eugene as Fleury, terrified by his voice, galloped full force forward. "Move aside!"

Instead of colliding, the drivers swerved to opposite sides of the two-rut road. They passed so closely that the caravan scrubbed a beech tree, wavered, almost tipped over, and bumped back on the ground uprighting itself. The ox cart tumbled over and spilled manure across the road and ditch.

Argon hugged the seat rail. Eugene yanked on the lines. "Ho! Calme-toi … calme … calme." The wheels shuddered. Fleury slowed and gave forth a high-pitched neigh that frightened birds into flight.

Eugene swallowed and breathed. "Good Fleury! Now I must calm myself." He dropped the lines and wiped his face with a handkerchief. Behind them, the wreck of the cart and manure spanned the road.

Eugene stepped down and called loudly, "Good sir, are you injured?"

The driver of the cart pulled himself to his feet and stood with a limp. He propped on the wheel of the overturned cart. He was about a furlong from the farm where he was to deliver the dung. And now this. "What kind of fool are you?" His eyes burned from specks of dust or manure. He rubbed them with his dirty hand, causing more irritation. "Who are you if not a logger-headed froth?"

Eugene heard no more. "Alak, kind sir, but your trouble is less than mine." With that he scrambled to the seat, slapped the lines on Fleury's rump, clucked, and called, "Hoy! Good horse! Make way!" Fleury gave a start and jolted forward.

"Milk-livered knave!" The driver cried to the departing wagon. "The devil scratch you."

ꙮ Scene 45 ꙮ
God be buggered

Those words will land all of us in gaol, or worse," said Leon, his back propped against a wagon. He whittled on a piece of wood that was becoming a cross.

"If there be dire consequences, it will fall to me." Béjart had directed the Augusto Troupe in staging Scene One of the mummy's play he had been writing. He was describing Scene Two.

"I agree with Leon," said Hubert, sitting on a three-legged stool.

"By cock! I have heard worse from other actors." Béjart spat out peppered words. The sun rested on the horizon. Singular birds tweaked the stillness.

"And they likely be moldering away in some gaol as we speak," said Leon.

"Let us consider it exact." Béjart grabbed the script from Hubert. "This be Sir Knight's lines: 'God be buggered! He is all powerful but cannot manage the coins in his purse.'" Béjart looked at them.

"If you say 'God be buggered' in a courtyard of Catholics, your head will be on a pole before dark," said Leon.

Béjart scoffed and slapped the script against his thigh. "The speaker is ill. He is raving with fever when he says that line."

Leon did not look from the wood trinket he was carving. "Some nosey sexton will shit in his drawers."

"Damnation! Alors I will strike it out. Begone 'God be buggered!'" Béjart said, though he believed his play had spiritual protection from the mummy.

"Read on." Hubert pinched snuff into his cheek.

Béjart said, "The knight's attendant speaks now, says, 'Hear ye! Sir Latour utters heresy.' Another attendant agrees."

"Read the part about holy merde." Leon rubbed the wood grain with a wax cloth.

Béjart raised up the script and searched the lines before reading, "'God takes in thousands of écus but always needs more. Holy Merde!'" He lowered the script and explained. "There can be no question but that the knight blasphemes the church. It is crucial to the plot."

Hubert coughed and cleared his throat. "The knight in the play is feverish and sick, but the Church will notice that the actor playing the part is sober."

"We are rarely sober," said Louise.

"And we will wail 'Holy Merde' as we are driven off the stage," said Leon.

Béjart shook his head. "The point of this scene is that the knight curses the Church while in a raging fever. And because of his blasphemy, his attendants desert him and leave him for dead."

"And we will suffer the knight's consequences," said Hubert.

"It is a divertissement!" said Béjart.

"Where is the comedie? Paysans pay for a laugh." Leon trenched lines in the wood with the point of his knife.

"This is a diversion from our burlesque," said Béjart.

"We will suffer a tragedy along with the play," said Hubert.

During the months of writing "King Claudius' Knight," Béjart had tried and failed to control the plot, only to find himself writing what he did not want to write. The scribbled grievances of the mummy's diary had flowed into the ink of his quill.

He came to believe the mummy had been a knight who had been sent by his lord to capture a thief but had become delirious with fever and mumbled blasphemies frightening his attendants who abandoned him. A blind witch healed him to resume his lord's command and pursue the thief. The plot that poured forth from Béjart's pen hewed to the mummy's story.

"Not to mention foul tomatoes … if not boiled oil," said Leon.

The small pear he whittled in the center of the cross was becoming a carved vagina.

"We will perform at night, with torches. A witch will crawl onstage and curse the knight just before he says 'Holy Merde!'" We will give him a beak and the head of a crow. Hubert, can you fashion a black cape with a cross on the back?" said Béjart.

The diary's troubling themes—the darkness in the Church, the absurdity of the aristocracy, the oppression of laborers—concerned Béjart. "It is not my fight!" he had roared when he had read what his quill had written. "Leave me!" But he could not sleep. Sir Latour's story possessed him.

"This will be a play like none ever acted before," Béjart said triumphantly.

"Of that you can be certain," said Leon.

"And no play like it will be acted again," said Hubert.

Three nights hence, the Augusto Troupe announced a play that was "A Voice from the Past." In the afternoon, Etienne gallivanted along the village streets and flaunted a placard shouting, "Come and see 'A Voice From the Past.'" Béjart had convinced the village elders that the torch-light show would burnish their reputations as well as set a standard for entertainment.

With the moon on the rise and stars appearing, Hubert secured wood staves in each corner of the stage and set the torches afire. In the absence of Argon and Eugene, Béjart hopped to the stage with his lute and opened the entertainment, singing with Georgette who played the psaltery. Leon followed playing the pipe.

The singers lowered their voices to whispers. Samuel tumbled on stage. The acrobatics lasted long enough for Béjart and Leon to exit and, sequestered behind the canvas screen, put on semblances of knights—metal helmets, breastplates, gauntlets.

Georgette, standing center stage, said, "My good dames and sires, gather near and you will sense apparitions. Enter the darkness parts. The story starts." She backed offstage.

Because Béjart's sight was impaired by the helmet's visor he walked clumsily. Leon and Hubert, as attendants, plodded behind him. By the time the knight, charged with retrieving a thief, fell into a fever on stage, the peasants shuffled restlessly.

A man and woman scuffled in the darkened distance, a slap rang out. Somebody yelled, "Bring on some bouncy orbs."

Béjart writhed on the floor, playing a fever but airing anger.

Leon spoke. "My lord, what ails thee?"

Béjart mumbled, "God be all powerful, but cannot manage the coins in his purse."

Hubert recited, "Our master suffers a most vicious malady."

Somebody yelled, "God save us from his misery!" Another, "Bring back the minstrels!"

"God be buggered!" Béjart spit out the line before he realized it. He bit his tongue. He had been convinced it was inflammatory, if not dangerous, and had not intended to say it. He mumbled quickly. "He takes in thousands of écus from us, but always needs more." He thrashed vigorously. The front of his breastplate popped free from the back piece. "Holy Merde!" He spoke more to himself than the audience.

The audience was stricken silent. A rock bounced on the stage, another, a hickory nut. Somebody yelled, "Did he say buggered?"

Leon lost his line. A rotten turnip thumped into his back.

A cry of "Nenni, myrrh." "Myrrh?" "It was buggered!" "He said it, buggered!"

The crowd gasped en masse. A burst of laughter. "You think that comical?" A fracas erupted and the laughter was throttled. "God, have mercy!" More fighting.

Hubert went off script, grabbed Béjart, and roared with a line meant to amend Béjart's. "God strike us dead if we do not execute this blasphemer." A dried horse turd flew in his face.

Behind the screen, Georgette scurried into an alley with the other actors.

Leon whirled around and shouted, "Leave him to the wolves." Somebody threw a dead frog that bounced on the stage. Leon took leave. Béjart shouted, "I am but a churlish varlet," but it was not heard above the tumult. He and Hubert hastened off the platform.

The audience booed and jostled one another. "Execute him!" "A pox upon him!" Men stepped on one another. "Get a rope!" "What ho!" A burly yeoman, inspired by "Stretch his neck!" "Pluck out his eyes!" climbed on the stage. The crowd followed him on to the platform. "All hail for Christ sake!" The advance charge went after Hubert and Béjart, who ran into the darkness. Leon, who had a head start, took cover in a hayloft. Hubert and Béjart hid behind a dung cart parked in a stable. Georgette and the others gained entry at the usurer's shop by claiming to be Jewish.

As the more hostile paysans searched for the actors in the dark alleys and back doors, combing disreputable haunts, others took over the stage, raised their voices, and tearfully prayed: "*Gloria Patri, et Filio, et Spiritui Sancto…*"

The parish priest came to the cathedral steps, surrounded by boys with torches. He nodded at an older boy and the church bell rang, producing a sharp and prolonged clanging that overtook the peasants' uproar. The tense rabble circled closer to the steps.

When only the bell could be heard, the priest held up his hand. The clanging stopped. The impartial stars shone on the crowd. Though a breeze brushed the faces, few of the men felt its purity.

The priest swallowed and cleared his throat. He knew that he must speak with God's authority. He had smelled the burning flesh of men and women convicted of heresy. Their cries disturbed his sleep. With his face lifted and his voice unencumbered, he said, "You prove yourselves to be soldiers of the Cross, and God will bless you." He made a sign of the Cross. Men and the few women bowed their heads. "Irreverent and ungodly words cause pain to our God and Father." He glanced at the crowd and looked to first one and then another saying, "Let us not return evil for evil." Torches hissed and spit. "It is for the Church to seek justice in this matter. And it is through the Church that God's will is made known."

In the darker corners, rogues mumbled. Their blood raced with the will to kick, yank, jolt, and clobber the heathens. They nudged one another. One fell backward over a pig curled into a pot hole.

"Go to your homes and rest peacefully this night. It is not for you, my brothers and sisters, to take revenge for our Holy Father. Give you good night. *In nomine Patris et Filii et Spiritus Sancti.*"

From the bell tower, a clanging tolled the hour. The priest waited at the steps, his breath stuck in his belly. He stood motionless like an archangel until the crowd shuffled apart and disbanded.

The Augusto players sneaked from their hiding places and crept back to the caravans. With quiet haste, they retrieved the horses from the public stable, packed up, and paid the gatekeeper a night's earnings to allow them to leave.

☙ Scene 46 ❧
in this accursed darkness you cannot see your feet

In the darkness with no torch to light the way, the caravans rattled. The horses were as silent as the fields. Béjart led them slowly, his eyes boring into the dark for pits or stones that might cause a wheel to crack or a horse to stumble. Leon went before Béjart as lookout. As they plodded along, the actors gave ear to every sound. Hubert coughed violently as he drove Béjart's caravan.

Second in the train came Samuel with Louise, who sat on the bench with him. Samuel said, "Béjart is ruined. He will not be allowed in any village in France." In the darkness, he could not see the tears on her cheek.

"He has no fear." Louise said to calm herself.

"That is his folly," said Samuel.

"Mayhap he will take us to the Low Countries."

"Nay. He does not speak Dutch. Nor do we."

"He will apply to the Church for forgiveness. We will find a generous priest. One who will forgive him," she said.

"What? Béjart? Beg forgiveness?"

The night air was unusually cool on their faces. Wisps of clouds blurred the stars as if the heavens had befuddled thoughts. Louise was unable to imagine the next day, much less a week hence.

Samuel said, "There are other troupes. They employ acrobats."

Louise said, "Béjart will not forgive you."

"Forgive me? Do you not see? He has doomed the Augusto Troupe." He realized late that his voice, as the only sound in a plane of silence, might be heard far and wide.

"The Troupe is his life."

"His life is run through, as far as I can see."

"What can you see? In this accursed darkness you cannot see even your feet."

"Mayhap Béjart has departed already. Mayhap the caravan moves like a ship with no commander." Samuel leaned aside and peered, as well as he could, around Béjart's wagon in front of them. He saw only darkness. Behind them Georgette, who drove that wagon, dozed from time to time.

Louise twisted over the side of the wagon. "I cannot see Béjart either." This gave her pause, for she expected to be abandoned by people she loved.

"A blind man can see that the Augusto players will be hunted like wolves." Samuel sighed. "Do you own Augusto stock?"

Louise pulled her robe closer and said with some pride, "Yes. I was granted part of Isabelle's share after she left. And you?"

"It was long in coming, but I too got stock after Isabelle left. Not that it is worth anything now. You tell me—what is the value of the Augusto Troupe now?"

"Béjart will make amends for losses."

"With what, prithee? With what?"

Béjart's thoughts played in many fields while the caravans rolled through the dark countryside. Breezes whispered, "You are free. Leave the actors and become a troubadour while you finish writing King Claudius' Knight." The trees sighed and conveyed thoughts to him: "Nobody can write the play but you." The crunch of wagon wheels on the grainy earth had the sound of a voice accustomed to long nights of lost dreams: "The play must be finished. It is more important than its accusers."

Clouds came and went between the caravans and the stars. A moody darkness prevailed and protected them from sight, for the remarkable appearance of the caravans branded them. Metal cinches jangled. The horses nickered one to another.

A dim glow appeared beyond the shadow of trees, a harbinger to sunrise. Béjart whistled. The caravans, guided more by the horses than the drivers, turned from the high road on to a wagon path embraced by overhanging boughs. Low growing branches scraped the caravans and slapped the drivers. When well removed from the high road, the wagons came to a stop.

The actors climbed down and gathered at Béjart's caravan. Béjart said, "Somebody has to go back to the village and rendez-vous with Argon and Eugene when they return." From a cloth sack he pulled a baguette and broke off pieces he handed to the weary players. Leon opened wine, quaffed some, and handed the bottle to Samuel.

"Etienne, will you go back to Brancion and rendez-vous with Argon and Eugene?" Béjart had taken measure of the risk. Etienne was less experienced and inadequate to deal with the hostility of the Catholics. At the same time, he had appeared seldom on stage and had been laden with costumes, which made him least likely to be recognized.

"Leon or Hubert will know the way better," said Georgette. "Etienne is but a boy."

"I am not 'but a boy!'" said Etienne.

"The Catholics will remember Leon and Hubert. They were on the stage with me," said Béjart.

"The country throngs with highwaymen. Etienne has no defense," said Georgette.

Leon handed a dagger to Etienne. "Wear it in your boot." He shoved the blade back into the holster. "I want it back when you return."

Etienne stuck the holster in his boot. "No need to fear. My head is well-filled. I will bring Argon and Eugene back with me."

That settled, Béjart said, "We will take cover in these woods for the nonce. And every day will be a performance for all of us."

Louise gazed at him. "Have you some magic to escape the sheriff?"

"And the rabid Catholics? They are thirsty for blood," said Samuel.

Béjart removed his trunk from his caravan, opened it, and picked through items, a mask, a molded nose, fake teeth. "Mayhap a scar or eye patch. We will hide our identity, at least until civility returns."

"What overcame you?" said Georgette.

"It was the mummy that twisted my tongue. I swear by the teeth of God, I did not say it." Béjart had previously sensed the mummy's anger, anger followed by bursts of inspiration. He took a wig with more hair than a lion's mane and put it on. "We are professional dodgers. We live many lives. We are playing a new part."

"Are you possessed by a demon?" Etienne's dark eyes opened wider than soupspoons.

Georgette scowled at Béjart.

Samuel stood and shook a fist. "Zut! You gull us!"

"Better a demon than some bishop," said Leon.

"Will a demon get us out of this?" Louise said.

"See a sorcerer," said Georgette. "And rid yourself of the mummy spirit."

Béjart did not want to be rid of the mummy's spirit. "No need to trouble yourselves. Our comforts are uncertain for the moment but with our skills, we can make whores of nuns."

"Spoken like the last note of a ballad," said Samuel. He sucked drops from the wine bottle.

The players opened their caravan gates and brought out stools and sat as the sky paled with dawn. Béjart produced an inked map and said to Etienne, "We know not how long we will be here." He marked likely places to meet up on the map of their expected route.

Georgette pasted a fake ulcer on his arm. "If highwaymen try to capture you, act sickly and show this. They will retreat at the sight of a bubo." She rubbed gray paint around his eyes, all the more to suggest illness.

Leon gird a rosary about Etienne's neck. "Always say first and last, 'may it please the Lord,' and if anybody accosts you, pray loudly, 'Miserere mei, Deus.'"

Etienne repeated the Latin phrase and said, "What does it mean?"

"Have mercy on me, oh God," said Leon.

"Be excessively religious and you will win favor," said Béjart.

Etienne propelled himself into the saddle of his borrowed horse. "God be wi' you." "Fare-thee-well!" cheered his companions.

"Excel in sobriety," said Georgette, who watched until Etienne disappeared.

Béjart said to the actors, "We will abide the day at our caravans. Go. Rest."

As the morning sun came through the trees, Hubert fell asleep in his caravan. On the cobblestone high road, early farmers going to fields passed where the forest trail turned-off, the squeak of carts and clop-clop of hoofs within hearing distance of the caravans. The actors eventually curled up in their cots for, if not sleep, rest.

Béjart shaved his mustache, pasted warts on his face, blackened a tooth, wrapped his belly in padding, and set out to explore their environs for signs of a gamekeeper. Many a forest was patrolled for possible poachers. Should he encounter a sign such as "Poachers dispatched to Satan," the Troupe had to leave forthwith.

"We firebrand poachers" was posted by the high road at some distance. There was no certain way of knowing where the property line lay. However, a field and farmhouse separated the Troupe from the sign, and Béjart came to the view that they were not parked in a nobleman's hunting forest.

In the afternoon, Louise built a fire and put their pot on the iron grate Hubert brought from the wagon. Water that Béjart brought from a stream was the beginning of a pea potage spiced with black bryony Georgette found growing by the roadside.

"The farmer's geese did not stray far enough from the yard," said Leon, who had been unable to steal one when he returned to a farmhouse they had passed the previous night.

In due time each actor brought his bowl and filled it with potage.

"Louise must have cooked this," spouted Samuel, forcing down a bite.

"All hail! What are we to do? There was not enough salt," said Georgette.

They began to eat the potage but not with relish.

Béjart stood and picked his teeth with a splinter vying for their attention. "As long as we have bosoms and cocks to tempt the grandees, we will draw crowds. But we must start anew." He paced a trough in the grass. "Emerging from these woods, we will become the Ragotin Players."

"Ragotin?" said Hubert.

"So … we will get out of the woods …" said Leon.

Béjart swept his arms as if to a grand ovation. "Ragotin! Du sang frais. We are born anew! Free from dirt and dross."

"Dross be damned! What about charges of heresy?" said Samuel.

"Do you think new blood will protect us from the sheriff?" The ridicule in Hubert's tone was obvious.

"Blood … and wigs and beards," said Béjart.

"You got us into a hellbound predicament," said Hubert. Georgette muttered agreement.

"By cock! Things have gone to rot!" said Samuel.

Béjart flung a conical hat to Samuel who flung it back saying, "Do not think that when the Augusto Troupe vanishes, so does the return due its stockholders."

"Our share of the props is no less than 30 écus." Georgette spoke over others mumbling complaints.

Leon, who owned the largest share after Béjart, said, "Let us hear Béjart's defense of the Ragotin Players."

Béjart, with an appreciative nod toward Leon, said, "We will travel the nights and camp the days until we reach Grenoble. I am acquainted with a merchant there. A fellow with three footmen at his heels. A bawdy man, but a patron of troubadours. We will be safe under his protectorship until the ardor abates."

"What is the name of this merchant?" said Leon, who had knowledge of nobles and wealthy families.

"He claims the name of Bayard, though 'tis well known that he is no descendent of le bon chevalier."

"Alors he too is a poseur!" Leon's words erupted with amusement, which relaxed the actors. They listened to Béjart's scheme, especially after he promised that the stock of each one would transfer from the Augusto Troupe to the Ragotin Players.

Béjart's head was filled with fidgety indecision. Finishing the play was as important as remaining with the actors. Maintaining the Troupe left little time to write. The calamity they now faced presented a distraction of major proportion. He foresaw bringing the Troupe back to safety and profit as the possible death knell of King Claudius' Knight. The mummy would not approve.

☙ Scene 47 ❧
Argon's poor bodily condition

Eugene drove Fleury hard and kept watch behind them. The caravan jolted over a rough stone which threw the wheels athwart the ruts.

"God's fury!" moaned Argon. "My gut be torn asunder. For the rats to feast upon."

Eugene only slowed enough to properly return to the road. Where it led into an open area with fields on each side, he rein-slapped Fleury and said, "Hup! Hup!" until they reached the cover of woodlands. Argon's restless moans ceased, as though his stomach had calmed despite the pitch and tumble of the caravan. In the silence, Eugene heard a low hum, an awareness that vaguely reminded him to quickly seclude himself. "Whoa!" He pulled the horse to a stop, climbed off the seat, sat on the ground and waited, expecting to come to himself with a sore mouth and red eyes.

The hum thinned as if coming through the eye of a needle. It was not Fleury's digestion. "'Tis not Argon. Nor myself," Eugene said to himself. It seemed to be inside his head. As time passed, nothing happened.

He climbed back on the seat. "Git up, Fleury." He listened. So faint the sound. It was the wind. It was bugs in the grass. It was a drone inside his ear. Whatever explanation he credited, it left him dissatisfied until, "It is the skull," he whispered to Fleury. "We must be done with it."

They approached a creek, trickling with much-needed water. A stand of chestnut trees bordered the high road, and though there was no thruway as such, a parking place was accessible to the caravan. Eugene stood down and led the horse through the trees until they were concealed from the road. Thus situated, they settled down.

Fleury ate grass. Eugene drank wine and gave some to Argon. He refilled their firkin with water. The chirp and drum of creatures in the grass ushered in night. While Argon slept, Eugene buried the skull.

Getting into their hideaway had been easier than getting out. To turn the caravan around, Eugene unhitched Fleury and manually backed the wagon up. He pushed, pulled, and turned until the shafts fronted the high road.

With the horse hitched back up and Argon lying in the back, Eugene stood beside the caravan and billowed the lines on Fleury's flank. "Hoy! Forward!" A wheel rolled on to a rock, tipped, and tumbled Argon across the boards. "Augh!" said Argon.

"Heigh!" Eugene yelled. Fleury jolted and the caravan lurched forward.

"Au diable!" moaned Argon.

The caravan righted itself. "No mere stone will deter us."

Eugene patted Argon on his shoulder. At the road he climbed on to the seat. "Fleury, walk on!"

The sun beamed on them. Argon slept. They passed vineyards and fields. Where field workers spread manure, a stink of much force assaulted them. "'Tis as bad as Argon's gaseous stomach," said Eugene.

Argon raised on his elbow. "Where is the water?"

"Lo! You are awake," said Eugene.

"I am dried up and unfed." Argon twisted up and looked at the sky. "Where are we?"

"It is two days agone since the divergence for Troyes. Methinks Auxerre is the next village of any size."

Argon rolled to his knees, grabbed the bench, and dragged himself forward. In his weak state, he lost his grip and fell backward.

Eugene slowed Fleury to a walk. "It is good to see you are booted and spurred, but you are in no condition to go."

At a farmhouse where they stopped for water, they had paltry cheese and bread, not enough food to stop Eugene's stomach from churning. Despite Argon's protest, when twilight approached, Eugene stopped at a monastery. They needed water and food, not only for themselves but for Fleury. The monks lodged them without questions.

The room the monastery provided them contained two cots, two chairs, and a table. The food was a broth and bread with wine. Eugene ate and Argon drank broth and wine. Both of them lay down and fell into a deep sleep.

The following morning, knock-knock came at the door. So soft was the knock the door whispered. Knock-knock.

Eugene awoke from a dream of another person in bed with him. To his horror it was the dead body of somebody he knew, but he could not tell who. He wiped his eyes and rubbed his scratchy cheek and said a prayer of thanks that it was only a dream. He thought of Brother Nicolas Vallans. A deep breath did not dispel a dread that the dream was an omen.

"I have a restorative for your friend," said Brother Ebers, holding a chalice in his hand.

"He sleeps." Eugene leaned back, giving the monk a clear view of Argon in bed.

"The sooner he takes this, the sooner his recovery." Brother Ebers had added into a restorative potion extra mitridate, for it had proved effective for numerous ailments. Argon shook off enough sleep to drink the potion.

Brother Ebers took special interest in Argon's poor bodily condition. Because of his success in treating illnesses, he assumed the mantle of apothecary not only at the monastery but for farmers and merchants who called on him. Each morning and evening he said a prayer of thanksgiving to God for his talent, for indeed, his hands had curative effects.

In a spare room near the kitchen, perhaps intended for storage, shelves were stocked with roots, herbs, minerals, and small vials containing poisons that the monk had collected. He, with greater understanding than an apothecary, understood that poisons in minute amounts had restorative qualities.

The two travelers would have slept through supper, had Brother Ebers not arrived with food for them, dark bread, salted fish, an apple, and a hardy broth for Argon.

Brother Ebers's attention to Argon kept them at the monastery for another day and night. While Argon benefitted from rest, potions, and simple meals, Eugene stealthily explored the cavernous rooms. The one he searched for was at the back door near the tubs and water where the nuns did the laundry. The brown tunics of the monks were neatly folded and stacked on a shelf.

On the third day, Argon awoke to the clearest morning he had seen in days. He helped Eugene hitch Fleury to the caravan. Brother Ebers gave them a vial of potion, should the illness linger.

"You do us too much honor," said Argon in a voice clear and even.

Fleury, rested and well fed, trotted down the lane that led to the high road. When they were far removed from the monastery, Eugene said "Ho! Halt." From the trunk under the seat he brought out the monk's tunic he had taken and put it on.

"Thankless knave," said Argon. He laughed freely and with gusto, intoxicated by the sound of his voice, which surged from a throat that had been hobbled for months. For miles, he was loud and noisy and incapable of silence.

⋑ Scene 48 ⋐
betrayed and wronged in everything

His appearance carefully honed to commonality — rough woolen shirt, legs bound with strips of linen — Béjart headed to the nearby farmhouse to negotiate for food. He slowed his horse to a trot upon seeing activity far ahead beside the road, a horse hitched to a tree. A peasant stood in the edge of the wood, leaning over something. As Béjart approached, the man glanced at him and hurried into the forest. The body of a fawn, shot through the neck with an arrow, lay on the ground. Béjart stood down and inspected what would make a fine meal for the Troupe.

The peasant, hiding in the bushes, realized the traveler was not the gamekeeper and vaulted out saying, "It belongs to me!" He stood between Béjart and the quarry. "I killed it in the road." His skinny frame was less menacing than the sword he clutched at his side.

"False-hearted liar. A fool can concoct a story superior to that," said Béjart, for obviously no hunter would remove downed game from a road and drag it into a forest where the penalty for poaching was serious.

"Methought you were Lord Fregoso's gamekeeper." The peasant looked at him with hollow cheeks, more in need of a good meal than Béjart. "Withal, it belongs to me." He wrapped a rope around the fawn.

"Mayhap you will share it with me." Béjart was hungry and viande was lying there, almost on his boots.

"'Tis mine. I have young ones needful of meat." The yeoman dragged the carcass nearer his horse.

Pounding hoofs approached. The peasant dropped the ropes and scurried back into the trees. Béjart, left alone with the dead animal, flung himself into his saddle and clapped spurs to his horse. Though he lanced his steed at full tilt, the stranger, obviously a gamekeeper, gave chase and gained on him. Béjart's horse, though good enough for riding, was no rival for the courser the stranger rode.

The gamekeeper grabbed the halter of Béjart's horse and pulled them to a halt. "Sirrah, you will follow me."

Béjart jumped off the horse and ran into the woods. The gamekeeper pursued him. Dodging thick beeches and oaks, he kicked up lumps of decaying leaves as he twisted from tree trunk to tree trunk. When he stumbled over a fallen pine, the gamekeeper grabbed his ankle. "I am no poacher!" his breathless voice echoed in the trees.

"We shall see to that," the gamekeeper panted.

With a dagger to his back, Béjart returned to the horses where he was hand tied to the pommel of his saddle. The chase had dislodged his fake beard. A scrape on his cheek bled through a scar he had plastered there.

The gamekeeper pulled from his face the dangling beard. "A guise to hide your identity? Wherefore?"

Béjart could have said he was an actor, but Brancion's Catholics were too near at hand. "Sire, my misleading appearance is to escape a most arrogant damsel who falsely claims I plighted my troth."

"Mayhap she will come to your assistance." The gamekeeper turned both horses back and they rode until they reached the dead fawn. The peasant's horse had shied and bolted.

"Do you have permission from Lord Fregoso to hunt this forest?"

"I did not hunt hereabouts or anywhere else. The man who

killed the deer ran into the woods." Béjart said *woods* instead of *forest* deliberately, to imply ignorance about the noble's ownership.

"You were hunting with another yeoman?"

"Nay. I was not hunting." Béjart worked his wrists against the ropes restraining him.

"Wherefore is this fawn dead of an arrow to the neck?"

"The yeoman who owns the runaway horse shot the arrow. As you see, I do not have a bow." Béjart struggled to keep his voice even.

"'Tis easy to discard a bow." The gamekeeper dismounted and, pulling Béjart's horse behind him, searched several rods in the forest and found the yeoman's bow. He held it up to Béjart. "Sirrah, your bow."

"'Tis the bow of the poacher. I swear upon Saint Eustace's body. I am but a hapless passerby."

On their way to the nearby village, they came upon the yeoman's riderless horse wandering along the road. The gamekeeper tethered it to his saddle.

As they resumed the journey, Béjart petitioned the gamekeeper. "Will you not search for the rider of this horse?"

The gamekeeper ignored him.

"Two horses. Two horsemen. One deer dead of one arrow. One bow. Do you not see that you make an inaccurate estimate?"

With his heart in his throat, Béjart followed the gamekeeper into the village where he stayed the night bound and tied in the public stables. The following day, he was shackled and taken to the Town Hall, a wood building with a bell tower where he appeared before what served as a local court — two consuls, and the son of Lord Fregoso. The case against him gained merit because of his fake beard and makeup, which were perceived as a ploy worthy of a knave.

Béjart stood and faced the table where sat the three men who had authority to decide his fate. He spoke with eloquence in words that would convince a half-wit that he was unjustly accused of poaching. He chose to deny his story of a disenchanted lover and fall upon the truth and hope for the best.

"You speak with the voice of an actor, as you describe yourself," said Lord Fregoso's son, whose face was as smooth as a woman's. His wig, of long ringlets that fell over his cheeks and reached his shoulder, required the respect of every person in the room. "As we well know, actors are deceptive by trade."

"Prithee, may I bring to the court members of my acting troupe, now encamped but a short distance." These words emerged with strings attached to Béjart's conscience, for with them he lay bare evidence that might well convict himself as well as Leon and Hubert of heresy.

One consul sitting at the table looked nervously at the lord's son and cleared his throat. "Your grace, this man has lied about his pledge of troth."

The other said, "An actor has no less need of poaching than a poor yeoman."

Béjart could have been sentenced to be hanged or to a life as a galley slave, but he still found little comfort in being fined one hundred pistoles and placed under the charge of Lord Fregoso until it was paid.

"What of his horses?" said the consul whose sense of justice never deviated from that of Fregoso's son's.

"My horses are my property!" Béjart, given the circumstances, saw no reason why he should not claim the yeoman's steed.

"As a prisoner you lose your right to property," said the young lord, much to the satisfaction of the two consuls, who had taken an interest in them.

"My lord prithee, we, your loyal deputies and steadfast consuls, are poorly compensated for our trustworthy service to the village," said one of the consuls.

"Over compensated! For sitting a chair and nodding your head," said Béjart.

The young lord slammed his fist on the table where the three sat. "You will give us due respect, sirrah."

The horses were awarded to the consuls, one for each of them. The consul who received Béjart's horse took pity on him and allowed him to keep his pannier with writings—the pages of "King Claudius' Knight."

Restrained by iron handcuffs, Béjart sat in a cart as he was hauled like a sack of barley to Lord Fregoso's castle. Béjart said to the guard riding horseback beside them, "I am wrongfully assigned to prison. Prithee, take a message to my compatriots."

"Every hedge-born knave says the same," said the guard.

The choppy ride came to an end in the castle's courtyard. His confidence foundered. He could hardly face a future of utter insignificance. His legs weakened as he walked to a clammy room dug under a flanking tower.

The guard pushed him down several steps that descended to a somber chamber. Béjart crouched to enter through an opening hardly bigger than a knight's shield. The stone walls, green and slimy, chilled his marrow; paving stones abominated his feet; ceiling pavers weighed on his brain; mildew haunted his nares. A window, located high on the wall and out of reach, allowed air and light, which saved him from a burial vault.

He was allowed a bucket of water and a privy pot that was emptied every day. Potage arrived cold. Bread moldy. He paced the small space from corner to corner.

Béjart's situation was so dire that he put aside the danger of exposing the Troupe to heresy charges and tried to get a message to them in the hope that they might find a way to come up with the money to pay his fine. He called to any servant who opened the door, whether to throw in a morsel of bread or shove in a water bucket. "Prithee kind sir, take a message to my wife. God will reward you."

Carved into the stone walls in a color like dried blood were indecipherable markings. He studied them for days. The writ returned in dreams that conjured up the mummy. He interpreted one of the more legible markings to be the words *gaze inward.*

"It is the mummy's doings. All of this." He had taken to talking to himself.

He picked up his script and reviewed scenes he had written — the knight Sir Latour, who was sent to find a criminal, one Pompeo Uciglio, had fallen in a fever and was abandoned by his attendants.

Béjart asked the guard to sharpen his quill. He began to add a scene in which Latour was rescued by a witch who lived in a cave with a blind man. The mummy took hold of his spirit and he wrote with boldness. He believed his play had purpose. Béjart looked forward to the shafts of morning light that streamed through the small window. He scribbled in a frenzy.

"More ink prithee," Béjart called to the guard who emptied his privy pot. The guard, who had been given the vile duty because he had been caught swiving with a prostitute on a bishop's tomb, took pity on Béjart's pleas and provided ink and paper.

Béjart wrote from morning until night, put down his pen and slept peacefully.

✺ Scene 49 ✺
the Ragotin Players

After several days in Brancion waiting for Argon and Eugene, Etienne grew restless. His escape from Georgette's domination had not resulted in the excitement he had expected. The fleas in the hay where he slept put welts on him. He had fallen from the loft one night when a rat bit his leg. The horses, including his own, shat and the smell woke him.

He found makeshift jobs to keep him in food and ale — raked the street, shoveled dung, hauled water. More recently he had favored ale to food. Some days his horse went hungry except for the carrot or apple he managed to steal.

After finishing his task of mucking the stables for the ostler, Etienne smelled of ordure. At the tavern, he ordered ale to clear the taste that stuck to his throat. The only other customer was a gray-bearded man wearing a floppy hat, his eyes closed. The barmaid

Etienne adored brought his tankard. "Damoisele, prithee, sit with me and I will buy another," he said.

"Brassy you are, for a stink-fart." She whirled away.

He drank his ale and ordered another from the barmaid, who stretched her arm to place the tankard before Etienne.

He was considering what to do if Argon and Eugene never returned to Brancion from Paris. What was he to do if the Augusto Troupe moved from their camp in the woods, and he was unable to find them? He gazed into the tankard and saw beads floating on the ale, like spit. Even the ale offered little comfort. For days he had heard no kind word. He was alone in Brancion without prospects. Other than a future of sweeping the street. Or shoveling muck. With bits of shit on his boots. Bits in the folds of his breeches. In his hair. He gulped ale. The future crushed him with stink-fart, moldy hay, festering rats, she-devils, not to mention a lifetime of rags and insults. Worst of all, there he sat, doing nothing. He just sat. And sat. And hated it. Hated it.

He returned to the stables and fed his horse a carrot he stole from the garden behind the woodcutter's shed. He brushed the horse's mane and tail. "Even you will be missed when you are gone," he said. "You are more fortunate than me."

In a nearby stall stood a sleek black charger that had not been called for in days. Etienne stroked its flank, considering the sort of man who would own such an animal only to ignore it. The horse deserved the sort of care Etienne could give it. If God were real, there would be more justice.

Eugene and Argon drove around the village square at Brancion. Since they had spent a portion of the money owed the wine merchant, their course avoided the Market Hall. It was not surprising to discover that the Augusto Troupe had departed. They went out one town gate and in another, looking for their contact.

A burly man with a mouth too crowded with teeth charged from the sideway and grabbed the halter of their horse. "Ho! This wagon bears the likeness of ones the heathen jesters drove."

His comrade, liver wrung with anger, looked at Argon and said, "This man is an actor. Guilty before God of heresy!"

"Father, wherefore do you ride with this man?" another said to Eugene, dressed in the monk's robe.

Eugene leaned away from Argon and looked at him. Turned and looked at the ruffian. "Nay, my good man. He has been kind to me. Gave me a ride when my feet swelled."

Their caravan, though not a conspicuous color of blue, did not look conventional.

"Fore God, there escaped from here a company of jesters possessed of the devil."

"Actors! Do you take me for a louse-ridden buffoon?" said Argon. "I come to Brancion for my master Monsieur Floriant, a master cobbler. To see to the market."

"On my conscience, you may be sure he is but a cobbler's agent," said Eugene.

The rogue's grip on Fleury's halter loosened. Argon swished the lines on the horse's rump. Eugene made the sign of the cross and said, "Pax vobis." The caravan rolled forward. The rogues fell back, obviously dissatisfied that there would be no hanging.

They parked the caravan behind the tanner's vats where the smell kept most people at bay. "I will look in the tavern," Argon said with a clear voice.

While Eugene stayed with the caravan, Argon walked about the village. He thought he saw Samuel at the barber getting a tooth pulled, but it wasn't him. It wasn't him at the farrier, the greengrocer, the ironmonger. Many faces, but not the one he looked for.

At the public stables, he recognized a horse belonging to the Augusto Troupe. Etienne wandered from one of the stalls with a curry comb and they fell upon each other. "Lo!" "Where have you been?" "It is well you are back!"

At the tanner, Eugene likewise greeted Etienne warmly. "In truth! At last!"

"Ave and farewell to this village," said Etienne.

"Firstly we have the wine merchant to pay," said Argon. He looked at Eugene. The shortage in money for the wine merchant presented a dilemma.

"Let us keep all the money," said Etienne.

"The merchant has powerful friends," said Argon.

"We will be caught and hanged," said Eugene.

A dung carter arrived with a load for the nearby tanner, who came out of the shed. The three actors retreated to the caravan and spoke quietly.

"We can hide out. They will not catch us," said Etienne.

"How far away is the Troupe?" said Argon.

"A day's ride. But they are in hiding." Etienne described the incensed villagers who chased them from the stage, the threat to Béjart of blasphemy. Which explained to Argon and Eugene the incident in the street.

"Are you not in danger?" Argon said to Etienne.

"I was not on stage when Béjart said, 'God be buggered.' And I wore paint thick as pig skin."

"Béjart said that aloud? On stage?" said Eugene.

"He did."

Eugene said to Argon, "Does the wine merchant know you are an Augusto actor?"

"I think not. I only played the lute." Argon's voice, which had kept him from the stage, was now full bodied at ranges loud or soft, high or low.

"We do not want Catholics as well as wealthy merchants searching for us," said Eugene.

"I will repay the wine merchant what money I have and suffer the consequences," said Argon. "You go with Etienne and return to the Troupe."

"He will get his money, if it takes your blood," said Eugene.

Argon didn't like the sound of that. The three of them rested. Eugene lay on the floor. Argon leaned back and tilted his head to the canvas. "What do we have?" he said.

"What? We have our cloaks and boots," said Eugene.

"Yea, but we also have Fleury, the caravan, and Etienne's horse," said Argon.

Eugene, posing as a monk, gained the confidence of the hostler who owned the stable and they agreed on a bargain. In exchange for Etienne's horse and the caravan, the hostler gave them money and a two-wheeled cart.

They hitched Fleury to the cart and went to the Market Hall where Argon paid the merchant. Free of debt, the three of them set out for the Augusto Troupe.

There were strange caravans parked in the forest where Etienne had left the Troupe. The three actors approached one the shape of Béjart's, but instead of red and yellow, it was painted purple and orange. Where *Augusto* would have been was *Ragotin* painted in fanciful lettering.

Leon shouted, "All hail! Our troubadours have returned!"

"Hoy!" The players came forward and gleefully greeted their return. "By my faith!" "Ave!"

Argon and Eugene surveyed the changed colors of the caravans and the novel drawings. Leon's griffin had disappeared and in its place was a dragon bird. He had drawn the decorative figures on the various caravans — a flaming sun, a blue fish, a smiling moon. The other actors had filled in colors.

"A fine work of art," said Argon.

"Nobody will accuse us of being the Augusto Troupe," said Eugene.

A wine bottle passed from hand to hand, one bottle, then another. The actors made light of Eugene's story of the bats saving him from a hanging. "Bats! Hoy, mayhap your wine was soused with a bit of nightshade." Seeing Argon's hollow eyes and gaunt face, the actors did not doubt the account of his illness.

Etienne sat on a stool and stuck his boots near the fire and warmed his aching feet with a new appreciation for the conviviality.

Argon noticed the absence of his father. "Where is Béjart?" he said.

"He has abandoned us," said Georgette.

"Nay! Not Béjart," said Argon.

"Have you searched for him?" said Eugene, who was not the only actor to notice that Argon's voice had clarity and a lively depth.

"He is not in the village. Not in the gaol. I looked," said Louise.

Hubert was washing byrony that Georgette had gathered in the meadows, poor excuse for a meal but edible. Days ago, the players had eaten their fill of venison when Leon came upon a recently killed fawn not far from their camp.

Argon said, "Have you looked in the chateaux hereabouts?"

"Chateau de Feurs is owned by Lord Fregoso. I was not allowed inside the barbican, but the steward said no stranger had called," said Leon.

"The farmhouses?" said Argon.

"I stopped at all I passed, but it was the same everywhere," said Leon as he shuffled cards, perfecting a way to sort particular ones to his advantage.

"I will find him," said Argon.

"Our camp was discovered by a hunter." Georgette placed cleaned byrony shoots into hot water to soak.

"The constable has given us four days to depart," said Leon.

"Four days?" said Argon.

"That was two days ago," said Hubert.

"Two days, and we must leave," said Leon.

"We cannot leave without Béjart," said Argon.

Argon searched the country thereabouts but turned up not a clue to Béjart. As the sun went down on the second day he returned to the players downhearted. The actors were packing the caravans, for until they had more distance from Brancion, they had agreed to travel at night. Eugene and Leon sat by the campfire with Argon as the others retreated to their caravans.

"Béjart will not know how to find us," said Argon.

"He would have found us by now, if that was his intent." Leon had personal knowledge of the devil that coerced men to pursue dreams that lay beyond their grasp.

"What is your meaning?" said Argon.

"Béjart is either unable or unwilling to be here," Eugene reluctantly admitted. He drained their bottle of wine with a gloomy sense of loss.

"He is unable. We needs find him and help him return," said Argon.

"You have made that effort. So have I," said Leon.

Argon stared at the dwindling flames. "I cannot leave."

"The Troupe cannot stay," said Leon.

Argon leaned forward, his elbows on his knees, his hands brushing back his hair, now growing since it had not been sheared. "I cannot leave."

"We are out of money and out of time. We must leave now, while it is dark," said Leon.

Eugene saw the despair in Argon's eyes. "Perchance, you will stay and continue to search. Leon will lead the Troupe until you catch up with us later." He looked at Leon.

Leon's glance at Eugene was a wary approval. He spit in the fire. "Is that your wish?" he said to Argon.

Argon swallowed what would hardly go down. "I will join you when I find Béjart."

Leon pulled a paper from his doublet. "This is Béjart's list of villages on a route taking south from Brancion. The marked ones are where we will stop."

Eugene looked at the paper. "Macon?"

"Nay. Macon is too near Brancion. We'll travel another night but we won't risk appearing in daylight until we've passed Macon. Thereafter we will stop at small villages along the way where we can perform without permission papers," said Leon.

"I will make a copy for Argon." Eugene took the paper.

"We needs re-figure the stock without Béjart's share," said Leon.

"I will hold his share until he returns." Argon's dark eyes, which took on the semblance of Béjart's harsh gaze, challenged Leon to dispute him.

Leon did not want a majority share, but he wanted more than he had. Nor did he want to govern the Troupe. Anonymity kept him from his older brother and a duel.

Once Leon took leave of the fire, Argon sat with Eugene.

"Your only home is with the Troupe," said Eugene.

Argon swept his fingers through his hair.

"Whether we are here or on the road, Béjart will find us." Eugene said what he hoped would convince Argon to depart with the caravans. Without Béjart, Argon was Eugene's best hope of protection, for he could not well fend off suspicions his malady occasioned.

Argon sighed.

"To protect Béjart's stake in the ownership, you needs think of what best to do."

"Yes, my friend. I ..." Argon faltered. Tears rolled down his cheek. He wiped them off.

Eugene lowered his head and prayed. He wasn't comfortable with forwardness but he clasped his friend on the shoulder. "Let us prepare to go. The night spreads a hopeful spirit."

With their three-legged stools, sheepskins, cooking pot, and bucket of embers secured in the caravans, the players hitched up the horses.

Leon drove Béjart's caravan. Argon led the way on Leon's steed.

✳

With *Augusto* replaced by *Ragotin* and their caravans reborn with different colors, they rode the night and slept and rested the following day and night. Then came the day they traveled in sunlight for the first time since leaving Brancion. Despite the emptiness caused by Béjart's absence, the day warmed their spirits. They breathed bountiful sun-filled air. Trees grew dense and green. The actors were not anxious about hidden Catholics or bailiffs. Birds flickered from beech to maple with shrill tweets.

Argon bought a chicken from a farmer, poviding a potage for supper. A calm dusk turned to night. They closed their eyes and slept.

The following day, Argon arranged for their first performance as the Ragotin Players. He put around his neck a leather cord from which dangled a small pouch containing the bony tip of Molière's finger. On the wood platform before an audience of villagers, his words rang out over the bustle of vendors, shouts of children, and barking of dogs.

The show was burlesque from start to finish. Samuel bounced on stage juggling eggs. Leon and Louise bantered in a risqué skit. Argon roared and laughed in song. "There were three ravens sat on a tree, Down a down, hey down, hey down, They were as black as black might be."

In the final farce, including most of the actors playing star-crossed lovers, scheming servants, and crooked-nosed knaves, Argon turned to Georgette, playing the role of his willful mother. "Is it not clear that all the ills of mankind, all the failures of the great leaders of our history, have arisen merely from a lack of skill in dancing?" The tone of his voice was perfect. Hoots and unruly laughter arose from the audience.

The End

9 781944 453183